PROPHET OF BONES

PROPHET OF

BONES

A NOVEL

TED KOSMATKA

ST. MARTIN'S GRIFFIN
NEW YORK

www.stmartins.com

Designed by Kelly S. Too

The Library of Congress has cataloged the Henry Holt edition as follows:

Kosmatka, Ted, 1973–
    Prophet of bones: a novel / Ted Kosmatka.— 1st ed.
        p. cm.
    ISBN 978-0-8050-9617-0 (hardcover)
    ISBN 978-0-8050-9618-7 (e-book)
    1. Scientists—United States—Fiction. 2. Prehistoric peoples—Fiction. 3. Indonesia—Fiction. I. Title.
    PS3611.O74923P76 2013
    813'.6—dc23

                                                                                    2012018226

ISBN 978-1-250-04259-0 (trade paperback)

St. Martin's Griffin books may be purchased for educational, business, or promotional use. For information on bulk purchases, please contact Macmillan Corporate and Premium Sales Department at 1-800-221-7945, extension 5442, or write specialmarkets@macmillan.com.

First published in hardcover by Henry Holt and Company, LLC

First St. Martin's Griffin Edition: July 2014

10 9 8 7 6 5 4 3 2 1

For Christine

PART I

If this is the best of all possible worlds,
what are the others like?

—VOLTAIRE

— 1 —

The Prophet set his nine-millimeter on the kitchen counter.

He leaned forward, bleeding hard into the sink, the only sound a rhythmic tap of blood on stainless steel. The blood struck in little dime-sized drops, bright red, gathering into a pool on the metallic surface. He hit the knob with the back of his hand and cold water swirled down the drain.

Behind him, feet crunched on spent shell casings as two men entered the room.

"My disciples," the Prophet said. He did not turn. "I knew you'd find me here."

But his disciples, for their part, remained silent. They pulled chairs out from the table and sat. They cocked their weapons. First one, then the other, making a point of it.

Somewhere in the house a TV blared daytime talk, or something like it—intermittent applause, and a deep male voice saying, *She a damn lie, that baby don't look nothing like me,* and the crowd hooting and hollering its approval.

The Prophet splashed cold water on his face, trying to clear the blood from his eyes. Head wounds bled like a bitch. They always looked worse than they were. *Well, not always,* he thought. He remembered the guard at the lab and clenched his eyes shut, willing the image away. Sometimes head wounds were exactly as bad as they looked. Sometimes they fucking killed you.

The Prophet peeled loose his tattered white sweatshirt, revealing a torso lean, and dark, and scarred. Tattoos swarmed up both arms to his shoulders—gang symbols across his deltoids, a crucifix in the center of his chest. He wiped his face, and the shirt came away red. The Prophet was not a big man, but wiry muscle bunched and corded beneath his skin when he tossed his stained shirt across the room. He was twenty years old or a thousand, depending on who you asked. Who you believed.

The Prophet turned and regarded his faithful. A smile crept to his lips. "You look like you could use a beer."

He walked to where the dead woman lay against the refrigerator. He kicked her body out of the way enough to open the door. Glass bottles clinked. "All they have is Miller," he said, a kind of apology. Blood trailed across the yellow linoleum. Not his blood, he noted. Not this time. He carried three beers back to the table and collapsed into a chair.

His faithful did not smile. They did not reach for their beers. They sat in their dark suits and black sunglasses; they sat perfectly still and watched him. The first was young, blond, baby-faced. A white scar ran diagonally across his upper lip where a cleft lip had been surgically corrected in childhood. If anything, the scar made him more boyish. The one imperfection in an otherwise perfect face. He held his gun casually, arm resting on the table. His white shirt collar was open at the neck, black tie loosened. The second man was older, darker—all jaw, chin, and shoulders. The hired muscle of the pair. But Babyface was still the one to watch. The Prophet knew this at a glance.

"What's your name?" he asked the blond.

"Does it matter?" the blond answered.

The Prophet shook his head. "I guess not." Babyface was right after all. In heaven there would be no need for names, for all are known to the eyes of God.

"We've been looking for you for a long time, Manuel," Babyface said.

The Prophet leaned back in his chair and took a long swig of beer. He spread his hands. "My followers," he said. "You have found me."

"You've cost a lot of money," the blond continued. "Which is something our employer could forgive." He took off his sunglasses and rubbed the bridge of his nose. He looked up, and his eyes were a bright baby blue. "But you've also caused a lot of trouble, which is something he cannot."

"I never asked forgiveness."

"Then we're agreed on the issue. None asked. None given." The man's pale eyes bore into him. He leaned across the table, pitching his voice low. "Tell me something, Manuel, just out of curiosity, between you and me, before this thing goes the way it's gonna go—what the fuck were you thinking?"

The Prophet wiped a runnel of blood from his face. "I was called for this. You wouldn't understand."

"Oh, I suspect you got that right."

The Prophet sipped his beer.

"So then where is it?" Babyface snapped, seeming to lose patience.

The Prophet didn't answer.

"Come on, Manuel. We came such a long way. Don't give us the silent treatment now." He tapped the muzzle of the gun on table.

"Our most holy is resting."

"Most holy?" Babyface laughed and shook his head. "You know, I thought that bullshit was a joke when they told me." He turned to his partner. "You hear this shit?"

But the muscle only stared, jaw clenched tight. Babyface turned back around. "Or maybe this is all just some game you're playing. Some elaborate con that didn't work out the way you wanted. I heard you're one to play games."

"No game," the Prophet said.

"So you believe it?"

"I do."

"Then you're out of your mind after all."

The TV droned on, filling the silence, the deep male voice cohering again from out of the background noise—*I told you she was lying about it. I told you.*

"Where is it?"

The Prophet lowered his eyes. "I laid him upstairs on the bed. It's peaceful up there."

Babyface nodded to his partner. The second man stood. "You don't mind if we check, do you?" Babyface asked. The second man turned and disappeared up the stairs, taking them two at a time. His footfalls crossed heavily above them as he moved from room to room.

Babyface stared from across the table, his blue eyes deep and expressionless. The gun never wavered, held casually in a soft, pale hand.

The footfalls stopped.

The Prophet took another long pull from his beer. "I fed him every three hours, just like I was supposed to."

"And did it matter?"

The Prophet didn't respond. In the distance, the TV broke into applause again. Theme music, end of show. The footfalls crossed above them, slower this time, coming down the stairs. A moment later, the second man was back, carrying a dark form wrapped in a blanket. The bundle didn't move.

The blond man flashed his muscle a questioning look.

"It's dead," the big man said. "It's been dead."

The blond turned to him. "It's not your fault, Manuel," he said. "Most of them die in the first few weeks. Sometimes their mothers eat them."

The Prophet smiled. "He will rise again."

"Perhaps he will," Babyface said. "But I'd like to see that trick." He raised his gun.

The Prophet took a final, cool swallow, finishing his beer. Blood dripped from his forehead and fell to the stained Formica table. He glanced around the room and shook his head. He saw broken dishes, stained wooden cabinets, dirty yellow linoleum. He looked at the dead woman, resolute in her silence. "Nothing good will come of this," he prophesied.

"That's where you're wrong," the blond man said. He smiled, and the old surgical scar curled his lip slightly. "This part will make me feel a whole lot better."

"Though you strike me down, there will be other prophets after me. I won't be the last."

The muscle placed the body on the table, and the blanket opened at one end. A small, dark arm swung free of the blanket—a tiny distorted hand. A hand not quite human.

"I've got a secret for you," Babyface said. "God hates His prophets. Always has."

"God cannot hate."

"That's blasphemy," the blond man said. He lifted the gun to Manuel's face. "God is capable of all things."

He pulled the trigger.

2

Paul liked playing God in the attic above his family garage.

That's what his father called it, playing God, the day he found out. That's what he called it the day he smashed it all down.

Paul built the cages out of discarded two-by-fours he'd found under the deck and quarter-inch mesh he bought from the local hardware store. He gathered small scraps of carpet, odds and ends of plywood, a bent metal bracket that used to belong to his mother's old sewing machine table.

Paul drew the plans out carefully on graph paper during the last week of school.

Two weeks into summer break, his father left town to speak at a scientific conference. "Be good while I'm gone," his father warned him as they stood in the foyer. "Keep studying your verses."

"I will."

Paul watched from the window as the long black car backed down the driveway.

Because he wasn't old enough to use his father's power tools, he had to use a handsaw to cut the wood for the cages. He used his mother's sturdy black scissors to snip the wire mesh. He borrowed hinges from old cabinet doors, and nails from the rusty coffee can that hung over his father's unused workbench.

That evening his mother heard the hammering and came out to the garage.

"What are you doing up there?" She spoke in careful English, peering up at the rectangle of light that spilled down from the attic.

Paul stuck his head through the opening, all spiky black hair and sawdust. "Nothing."

"You're doing something; I can hear you."

"I'm just playing around with some tools," he said. Which was, in some sense, true. He couldn't lie to his mother. Not directly.

"Which tools?"

"Just a hammer and some nails."

She stared up at him, her delicate face a broken Chinese doll—pieces of porcelain reglued subtly out of alignment.

"Be careful," she said, and he understood that she was talking both about the tools and about his father.

The days turned into weeks as Paul worked on the cages. The summer wore on, Lake Michigan humidity cloaking the region like a veil. Because the wood was big, he built the cages big—less cutting that way. The cages were enormous, overengineered structures, ridiculously outsized for the animals they'd be holding. They weren't mouse cages so much as mouse cities—huge tabletop-sized enclosures that could have housed border collies. He spent most of his paper-route money on the project, buying odds and ends he needed: sheets of Plexiglas, plastic water bottles, and small dowels of wood he used for door latches. While the other children in the neighborhood played basketball or *wittedandu*, Paul worked on his project.

He bought tiny exercise wheels and cedar chip bedding. He pictured in his head how it would be once he finished: a mouse metropolis. Rodent utopia. The mice themselves he bought from a pet store near his paper route. Most were white feeder mice used for snakes, but a couple were of the more colorful, fancy variety. And there were even a few English mice—sleek, long-bodied show mice with big tulip ears and glossy coats that felt slick under his fingers. He wanted a diverse population, so he was careful to buy different kinds.

The woman at the pet store always smiled at him when he came in. She was in her sixties, with bright, bottle-red hair and a pleasant, chubby face. A bell above the door would ring as he stepped inside the shop, and then he'd walk to the back, bend low, and stare through the glass at all the mice for sale. He'd tap his finger on the glass. "That one," he'd say. "And that one over there—the brown one in the corner grooming itself."

"Those are good ones," she always said, no matter which mice he picked. "Those are good ones."

Then the woman would pop the lid and reach inside the cage while the mice ran in berserk little circles to avoid being caught. Catching the mice wasn't easy. Paul understood their fear. For most of them, when that hand came down, it meant death. It meant they were about to join the food chain. He wondered if they sensed this, if they sensed anything at all. He wondered if they thought the hand was the hand of God.

"It's okay," he whispered to them, willing them to be still. "Not this time."

The woman put the mice in little cardboard travel boxes so he could carry them home in his paper-route bag. Later in the evening, when no one was watching, he snuck them up to the attic.

While he worked on their permanent homes, he kept his mice in little glass aquariums stacked on a table in the middle of the room. He fed them scraps of food he stole from the dinner table—chunks of buttered bread, green beans, and Ritz crackers. During the last weeks of summer break, Paul stood back and surveyed all he'd created. It was good. The finished cages were huge, beautiful habitats. He'd heard that word, "habitats," when doing research about zoos. Paul understood that his cages weren't *natural* habitats; they didn't have plants and rocks inside them. But *Mus musculus* wasn't a natural animal, not really. Maybe for a mouse, a habitat didn't have to look like nature. Maybe it looked like this.

In the attic, Paul opened the lids on the aquariums and released his mice into their new enclosures one by one. The mice advanced cautiously, sniffing the air—the first explorers on a new continent.

That afternoon, to mark the occasion, he set out on his bike to the local grocery store, where he bought a head of lettuce as a treat for the mice. He brought along his pad of graph paper, stuffed into his paper-route bag, and on the way back stopped at a park a few blocks from his house. The late afternoon sun slanted through the trees. The park was mostly empty. A few older kids hung out on the bleachers near the tennis courts. Kids his own age played near the swings.

Paul looked down at his graph paper and studied his designs. Already he could see ways in which the habitats might be improved. He put pencil to paper, bent over his work, and so didn't hear the footsteps behind him.

"What you doing?" The voice came from directly behind him.

Paul turned. It was Josh, a kid from his school, two grades older.

"I said, what you got there?"

"Nothing," Paul said. He knew Josh well. Knew his tactics from the school yard, all smiles and friendly until it turned bad.

"Doesn't look like nothing to me. Let's see."

Josh grabbed for the notebook and Paul jerked it away.

"Leave me alone."

The older boy slammed the pad out of Paul's hand and then kicked it, scattering the pages across the ground. He laughed. "I didn't really want to see it anyway," he said, and walked off.

Paul bent to pick up his drawings. The pad had split apart, and the papers were drifting away in the wind. On the bleachers, one of the older kids cackled. Paul had nearly gathered the last of his drawings when a sudden gust carried the final sheet toward the swings.

A narrow, sandaled foot came down on the paper, catching it.

"That guy is *such* a jerk," came a female voice.

Paul looked up from the sandal. A girl from the neighborhood. He'd seen her around but had never spoken to her. She didn't go to his school. He could tell by her long hair and dress that she went to Nearhaven. You could almost always tell Nearhaven kids that way. Just as they could tell the pubbies. And there beside her, on the swing, was a small boy. She bent, picked up the paper, and handed it to Paul.

"Thanks," he told her.

"You're as big as him. Why'd you let him do that?"

Paul shrugged. "He's older."

"I'm Rebecca, and this is my cousin Brian."

"Paul."

Rebecca turned and looked toward the bleachers. "We should go," she said. Josh was talking to the bleacher group now, glancing meaningfully in their direction.

Paul followed Rebecca and her cousin out of the park, riding his bike slowly as they walked beside him. The cousin, it turned out, was a quiet, gap-toothed boy of seven who was staying with Rebecca's family for summer break. Paul had no cousins, and he felt a momentary pang of jealousy. He had no family other than his parents.

When they arrived at her house, he was shocked to find how close she lived. On the other side of the street, one block down.

"We're practically neighbors," he told her.

Paul rode his bike up her driveway. The screen door squeaked as she opened it, but she didn't step inside.

"Those papers," she said. "What were you drawing?"

For a moment, Paul wasn't sure how to answer. She must have sensed the hesitation. "You don't have to say if you don't want to," she added.

Her saying that made it possible. So he told her.

"What do you mean, 'cages'?" she asked. She let the screen door close and sat on the stoop.

He pulled the pad from his paper-route bag. "Here," he said.

Rebecca took the papers, and her cousin leaned close.

"Construction plans, I guess you'd call them," Paul said.

She flipped to the next sheet. This one showed his largest cage, drawn out in intricate detail.

"You built this?"

"Yeah. It wasn't that hard."

"It looks hard to me. Where is it?"

"In the attic over my garage."

"Can we see?"

Paul glanced in the direction of his house. "No, I better not."

Rebecca flipped the page and studied the final drawing carefully. "It must have taken you a long time to put all this together."

"Months."

"What are they for? I mean, if these are cages, what's supposed to go inside?"

"Mice."

She nodded to herself. "Mice," she repeated under her breath, as if it made perfect sense. "Where'd you get the stuff? All the wood and nails."

Paul shrugged. "Here and there. Just scraps, mostly. Other stuff I had to buy."

The little cousin finally spoke: "My parents don't let me have pets."

"Neither do mine," Paul said. "But anyway, the mice aren't pets."

"Then what are they?" the boy asked. He stared over his cousin's shoulder at the drawings.

"A project," Paul said.

"What kind of project?"

Paul looked at the graph paper. "I'm still working on that."

The bell rang at two thirty-five.

By two forty-nine, school bus No. 32 was freighted with its raucous cargo and pulling out of the parking lot, headed for the highway and points south and east.

Paul sat near the back and stared out the window, watching the Grand Kankakee Marsh scroll by. Around him, the other kids talked and laughed, but only Paul sat silently, fidgeting with the large blue textbook on his lap, waiting for the road to smooth out so that he could read. As they crossed the bridge, he finally opened his life sciences book.

Today Mr. Slocam had gone over the study guide for the test.

Figure 73 showed two ellipses graphed like a crooked half-smile between an x- and a y-axis. The caption explained that the first slope represented the number of daughter atoms. The second slope represented the parent atoms. The point of intersection of the two slopes was the element's half-life.

"You will need to know this for the test," the study guide declared in bold heading, followed by a series of bullet-pointed facts.

The study guides were always like this.

Need to know this for the test. The common refrain of the public schools, where academic bulimia was the order of the day—and tests simple exercises in regurgitation. Paul knew the drill.

The bus made several stops before finally pulling to rest in front of his house. Paul climbed out.

His father was out of town again, at another scientific conference, so dinner that evening was a quiet undertaking. Later that night he went up to his room and copied his study guide onto a series of flash cards. Just before bed, he found his mother in the kitchen. "Will you quiz me?"

"Of course." His mother's doll face shattered into a smile.

They sat at the dining room table, and his mother flipped the first card, on which was drawn two crooked lines on an x- and y-axis. "Describe the point of intersection," she said.

"It's an element's half-life."

"Good," she said, flipping to the next card. "When was radiometric dating invented?"

"In 1906, but the results were rejected for years."

"Rejected by whom?"

"By evolutionists."

"Good." She flipped to the next card. "In what year did Darwin write *On the Origin of Species*?"

"In 1859."

"When did Darwin's theory lose the confidence of the scientific community?"

"That was 1932." Anticipating the next question, Paul continued: "When Kohlhorster invented potassium-argon dating."

"Why was this important?"

"The new dating method proved the earth wasn't as old as the evolutionists thought."

"When was the theory of evolution finally debunked completely?"

"In 1954, when Willard F. Libby invented carbon-14 dating at the University of Chicago."

"Good," his mother said and flipped another card. "And why else was he known?"

"He won the Nobel Prize in 1960, when he used carbon dating to prove, once and for all, that the earth was fifty-eight hundred years old."

3

Paul wore a white lab coat when he entered the attic. It was one of his father's old coats, so he had to cut the sleeves to fit his arms. Paul's father was a doctor, the PhD kind. He was blond and big and successful. He'd met Paul's mother after grad school while consulting for a Chinese research firm in Nanjing. Paul's mother had been one of the scientists at the university there, and she sometimes told Paul stories about working in a lab, about her home in China, and about meeting his father. "He was so handsome," she said.

After they married, they'd continued to work on the same projects for a while, but there was never any doubt that Paul's father was the bright light of the family. The genius, the famous man. He was also crazy.

Paul's father liked breaking things. He broke telephones, and he broke walls, and he broke tables. He broke promises not to hit again. One time, he broke bones; and the police were called by the ER physicians who did not believe the story about Paul's mother falling down the stairs. They did not believe the weeping woman of porcelain who swore her husband had not touched her.

Paul's father was a force of nature, a cataclysm. As unpredictable as a comet strike or a volcanic eruption. Over the course of his childhood,

Paul became an expert on his father's moods. He learned to interpret the tone of a brooding silence, could read whole volumes of meaning into a single blue-eyed glance around the side of a clenched periodical. He had two fathers, he learned. One who smiled and charmed and made people laugh. And another, who stormed. The attic over the garage was a good place to retreat to when the dark clouds gathered.

Paul studied his mice like Goodall's chimps, watching them for hours. He documented their social interactions in a green spiral notebook. At first he gave them names, borrowed from characters from his favorite books. Names like Algernon and Nimh. Later, as the population grew, he started giving them numbered codes instead, saving names for only the most special.

Mice are social animals, and he found that within the large habitats, they formed packs like wolves, with a dominant male and a dominant female—a structured social hierarchy involving mating privileges, territory, and almost-ritualized displays of submission by males of lower rank. The dominant male bred most of the females, and mice, Paul learned, could kill each other. Mice could war.

Nature abhors a vacuum, and the mouse populations slowly expanded to fill the new territories he'd created for them. The habitats thronged. The babies were born pink and blind, and as their fur came in, Paul began documenting coat colors in his notebook. There were fawns, blacks, and grays. Occasional agoutis. There were Irish spotted, banded, and broken marked. In later generations, new colors appeared that he hadn't purchased, and he knew enough about genetics to realize these were recessive genes cropping up.

Paul was fascinated by the concept of genes, the stable elements through which God provided for the transport of heritable characteristics from one generation to the next.

Paul did research and found that the pigmentation loci of mice were well mapped and well understood. He categorized his population by phenotype and found one mouse, a pale, dark-eyed cream, that must have been a triple recessive: bb, dd, ee. Three gene pairs lining up in just the right way, each diluting the coat pigmentation by a certain quantum, until you were left with a mouse with almost no coat pigment at all. But not an albino, because albinos had red eyes.

In November the school sent home an announcement about the science fair, which would be held in the spring.

"Are you going to participate?" his mother asked him as she signed the parental notification.

Paul shrugged. "If I can think of something," he said. He knew instantly that his mice were the answer, though he wasn't sure how exactly.

It wasn't enough to just have them, to observe them, to run the Punnett squares. He'd need to do real science. He'd need to do something new. And because real scientists used microscopes and electronic scales, Paul asked for these things for Christmas. His parents were pleased with his sudden analytical interest and bought him what he asked for.

But mice, Paul quickly discovered, did not readily yield themselves to microscopy. They tended to climb down from the stand.

The electronic scale, however, proved useful. Paul weighed every mouse and kept meticulous records. He considered developing his own inbred strain—a line with some combination of distinctive characteristics—but he wasn't sure what characteristics to look for. He imagined that his special new strain would be useful to science someday, a genetic model destined to play a role in some far-future discovery, but he didn't know where to start.

He imagined winning the science fair. He imagined his father proud of him, clapping him on the shoulder with his big hand.

Paul was going over his notebook when he saw it. January-17. Not a date but a mouse, January-17. The seventeenth mouse born in January.

He went to the cage and opened the door. A flash of sandy fur, and he snatched it up by its tail—a brindle specimen with large ears. Over the previous several months he'd become good at handling the mice. It was a knack you picked up without realizing it—the ability to hold the mice softly, so that you didn't hurt them, and yet firmly, so they couldn't get away. This mouse was not particularly fast or hard to catch. There was nothing obviously special about it. It was rendered different from the other mice only by the mark in his notebook. Paul looked at the mark, looked at the number he'd written there.

Of the more than ninety mice in his notebook, January-17 was, by two full grams, the largest mouse he'd ever weighed.

———

In school they taught him that through science you could decipher the truest meaning of God's word. God wrote the language of life in four letters: A, T, C, and G. A family of proteins called AAA+ initiated DNA replication, genetic structures conserved across all forms of life, from men to archaebacteria—the very calling card of the great designer.

That's not why Paul did it, though: to get closer to God. He did it because he was curious.

It was late winter before his father asked him what he spent all his time doing in the attic.

"Just messing around," Paul answered.

They were in his father's car, on the way home from piano lessons. "Your mother said you built something up there."

Paul fought back a surge of panic. The lie came quickly, unbidden. "I built a fort a while ago."

Paul's father glanced down at him. "What kind of fort?"

"Just a few pieces of plywood and a couple blankets. Just a little fort."

"You're almost twelve now. Aren't you getting a little old for forts?"

"Yeah, I guess I am."

"I don't want you spending all your time up there."

"All right."

"I don't want your grades slipping."

"All right."

"Your grades are what you should be focusing on right now, not screwing around with kids' games in an attic."

Paul, who hadn't gotten a B in two years, said, a third time, "All right."

The car slowed to a stop at a red light. "Oh," Paul's father added, almost as an afterthought. "There's something else. I don't want you hanging out with that girl from up the street."

"What?" Paul said. "Who?"

"The Nearhaven girl."

Paul blinked. He hadn't realized his father knew.

His father added, "You're getting too old for that, too."

The light turned green.

They rode the rest of the way in silence, and Paul explored the walls of his newly shaped reality. Because he knew foreshocks when he felt them.

He watched his father's hands on the steering wheel.

Though large for his age, like his father, Paul's features favored his Asian mother; he sometimes wondered if that was part of it, this thing between his father and him, this gulf he could not cross. Would his father have treated a freckled, blond son any differently? No, he decided. His father would have been the same. The same force of nature; the same cataclysm. He couldn't help being what he was.

Paul watched his father's hand on the steering wheel, and years later, when he thought of his father, even after everything that happened, that's how he thought of him. That moment frozen. Driving in the car, big hands on the steering wheel, a quiet moment of foreboding that wasn't false but was merely what it was, the best it would ever be between them.

4

Winter stayed late that year in the land of marshes and highways. A mid-March storm came howling down across Lake Michigan, laying waste to an early spring thaw. Murdered stalks of corn jutted from the snow, turning roadside farms into fields of brown stubble.

On most days, Paul lingered inside after school. But on some afternoons when his father wasn't around, Rebecca would meet him, and on those days the two of them ventured into the woods. They explored the frozen marshes that sprawled behind the back fence of the subdivision—a wild place beyond the reach of roads and sidewalks and parents.

Instead there were cattails, and sway-grass, and old-growth oaks. Dark water hidden under whole plains of snow. And the marshes extended for miles.

On that cold Saturday afternoon, Paul and Rebecca walked the trail down to the river. The morning had dawned cold and windy—northern gusts raking through the trees, a twenty-degree temperature drop from the day before. Their breath made smoke on the frigid air. They didn't speak as they walked; it was too cold to speak. They rounded a final bend in the trail, and the river lay before them: the Little Cal—a blank white ribbon that cut a swath through the heart of the wetland snowscape. Stubborn patches of dogwood and black oak clung to the riverside floodplain. In the spring, Paul knew, whole acres of lowland marsh would be transformed, submerged, become river itself. But in the cold months, the river retreated to its banks, dug deep, and capped itself over in ice.

It was a crazy thing to do, to play on the river ice. They knew this.

"Come on," Rebecca said.

"I'm coming. Hold your horses."

They walked the ice like a winding roadway.

Even in winter, the wetlands teamed with life; you could read the signs all around—animal tracks like lines of grammar on the snow. Sometimes deer came bounding through, graceful as dancers—just another shape in the woods until a white flash of tail drew your attention. Where one ran, the others followed, by some instinct staying clear of the ice.

Months from now this place would be unrecognizable. A burst of foliage, and the low shrubs would hide their bones in green. Everywhere he looked, Paul saw it—the endless cycle of birth, growth, and senescence. A cycle old as the first day. Old as God saying, Let it be.

The children's feet crunched on snow. They hunted lures that day, knives in hand, serrated edges making short work of twenty-pound-test line.

For three seasons of the year, the river belonged to fishermen—casting their lines into coffee-colored water through a web of low-hanging branches. Inevitably, some lures got hung up, and the fishermen would curse and pull on their lines, until those lines snapped; the lures would dangle over the river like unreachable, low-hanging fruit. The anglers fished three seasons of the year, but winter belonged to the children.

So they walked the ice like a roadway, serrated edges parting twenty-pound-test like strands of spider silk. They gathered red-and-white bobbers, and colorful spinners, and desiccated egg sacks wrapped in white nylon mesh.

The first to see the lure earned the right to claim it. There was no running on the ice. No rush to grab. They moved slowly, six feet apart to disperse their weight. They respected the ice and worked hard to learn its rules.

Paul was larger and heavier than Rebecca, so some lures only Rebecca could dare.

That Saturday, they walked the river south.

Here are some of the rules of ice. The ice is thinner near the shore-line, so getting on and off can be difficult. The ice is thinner near bends in the river, where the water moves quickest. In places where the snow cover is darker, slushier, the ice beneath is sure to be rotten and soft.

Last year, when walking alone on the ice, in that last leap to shore, Paul had broken through, his leg plunging into frigid water up to his knee. He'd been close to home, but by the time he'd been able to peel off his boot, his foot had been blue. A warm bath had brought it excruciatingly back to life.

But today he wasn't close to home. Today they were miles out to the south, and the day was colder. Today they walked in the middle of the river, like it was a roadway, knives drawn, tempting fate.

"Do you have science fairs at your school?" Paul asked as they rounded a curve.

"Yeah, every year," Rebecca said.

"Have you entered?"

"No, never. Why are you asking?"

"Because I'm going to enter this year. And I'm going to win."

"You sound sure."

"Sure enough," he said. His steps slowed. "Be careful, the ice is weak here."

Their feet made crunching sounds on the snow.

Rebecca touched his arm. "I see one."

Paul stopped. He looked to where his friend was pointing, up the river, near the bend. "Yeah, I see it. Green spinner bait."

They walked slowly. Rebecca moved ahead.

"Getting thin," Paul warned.

"I know."

"Slow down."

"Come on, Grandma. Don't be a wuss."

They inched forward. Paul stopped again. He studied the ice with his feet. Like Eskimos, they had a dozen names for ice, their own private language—the jargon of ice walkers. There was slick ice, and new ice, and chalk ice. There was rotten ice. There was ice-you-did-not-walk-on. You could feel the give, the gentle flex, a kind of sag. Ice on the river didn't break without warning. It wasn't like the movies: one minute you're standing there, then a loud crack—and splash, you're under. In reality, the ice had *flex*. And the sound . . . the sound was more of a creaking, like old leather, or the sound a tree makes in the two seconds between when it starts to fall and when it hits the ground—the low cry of rending fiber, of nature bending, failing. Of that which had been structured becoming unstructured.

In truth, you only heard a loud crack when the ice was good and strong. That's when you hear the cracks like gunfire, invisible beneath a layer of snow—a shotgun sound that propagates forward so fast that you hear it beneath you and up ahead at the same time.

They advanced.

Near the bend, the snow was darker, revealing a cycle of freeze and melt.

Paul walked until the ice creaked like old leather. Rebecca looked back at him. The wind blew through the trees, clacking branches against branches.

"You should stop," Paul said.

"It's not much farther."

"No, you should stop."

Paul spread his feet. He watched his friend; he listened.

Rebecca inched ahead. The ice groaned. She turned and made eye contact with him, her cheeks rosy with the cold. Long brown hair spilled out from beneath her knitted hat. She smiled at him, and something fluttered in his stomach, and it occurred to him at that moment that she was pretty. Her smile shifted into a look of determination, and she turned back toward the lure.

The lure dangled just ahead of her, ten feet forward at chest level.

Ten more feet and she'd have it.

Rebecca shifted her weight and took another step as the ice creaked like an oak in a storm. She paused, as if unsure of herself, before stepping again—a slow, gentle sag forming beneath her feet, barely perceptible. She stopped. You'd only see it if you knew what to look for, but Paul *did* see it—the way the whole area beneath her seemed to *give*, just a little, as she stood balanced in perfect equipoise. A bare centimeter at first, then more, a slow downward flex of the ice. There would be no warning beyond this. Rebecca shot Paul another look, then shifted her weight again—

—and took a long step back.

And another, and another. Backing away, accepting defeat.

The lure would stay where it was for another season.

"Next time," he told her when she was back on the thick ice again.

She shook her head. "It was this time or nothing."

Paul clapped her on the shoulder, and together they turned and headed for home.

As they walked, the sky darkened, evening coming on. Paul looked at his friend and imagined what it would be like to die that way, to drown in the cold and dark, carried forward beneath the ice by the force of the current.

He imagined crawling out on the ice on his stomach and reaching for her through the hole, because he couldn't have left her there to drown, not without trying—and he imagined the ice breaking and both of them going under.

The dark and numbing cold. An end to everything.

It wouldn't be so bad.

An hour later they were at her door, shivering from the cold.

"Shut your eyes," she said. It was dark now. The only light came from the streetlamp on the corner. Her face was a shape in the shadows.

Paul closed his eyes.

Her lips touched his. A gentle kiss. The first of his life.

She pulled away. "After today, I'm not allowed to spend time with you anymore."

Paul opened his eyes. "Why not?"

"Your father visited my parents."

"He *what*?" Paul stared at her, horror-stricken.

"He came and told them he didn't want me over there."

"But why?"

She shrugged. "He said we're getting too old to be playing together. We should play with kids from our own schools."

Paul looked at her. In their town, Catholics went to the public schools;

Presbyterians, Baptists, and Lutherans all had their own private institutions. "But you came today," he said.

"One last time. To tell you."

"Your parents don't have to listen. We can still hang out when he's not around."

"We can't," she said. "My parents don't want me to."

"Why?"

"Your father." She lowered her eyes. "My parents think he's crazy."

Later that night, Paul stood in the dim attic light next to the cages.

"This is what I wanted you to see," he told his mother.

His mother stood in the half-light.

"What is this?" There was something in his mother's voice. Some mixture of emotions he couldn't identify. She stood facing the cages, a startled expression on her face.

Paul held Bertha up by her tail for his mother to see. The mouse was a beautiful golden brindle, long whiskers twitching.

"She's the most recent generation," Paul said. "An F4."

"An F4, you say?" She shook her head with wonder. "Where did you learn these terms?"

"Books." Paul smiled as he looked down at the mouse. "She's kin to herself."

"So this is your project for the fair?"

"Yeah. I've been working on it for a long time."

"That's a big mouse," his mother said.

"The biggest yet. Fifty-nine grams, weighed at a hundred days old. The average weight is around forty."

Paul stroked the mouse's tawny fur. The little nose twitched—long colorless whiskers that existed at the very edge of visibility. Paul gave the mouse a tiny sunflower seed, and it rose up on its haunches, gripping the seed in tiny front paws. Paul had always thought there was something strangely human about a mouse's stance when it fed that way.

"What have you been feeding it to get so big?" she asked.

Paul put the mouse on her hand. "It has nothing to do with food," he said. "I feed all the mice the same. Look at this." Paul showed her the charts he'd graphed on the white poster board, like the figure in his life sciences book, a gentle upward ellipse between the x- and y-axes—the slow upward climb in body weight from one generation to the next.

"One of my F2s tipped the scales at forty-five grams, so I bred him to several of the biggest females, and they made more than fifty babies. I weighed them all at a hundred days old and picked the biggest four. Then I bred *those* and did the same thing with the next generation, choosing the heaviest hundred-day weights. I got the same bell-curve distribution— only the bell was shifted slightly to the right. Bertha was the biggest of them all."

"You just bred the biggest ones?" his mother said.

"Yeah. I keep the big ones in the glass aquariums, apart from the others."

"It was easy as that?"

"It's the same thing people have been doing with domestic livestock for the last five thousand years. Cattle are bigger now than they used to be. Sheep give more wool. Our chickens lay more eggs."

"But this didn't take thousands of years."

"No, it kind of surprised me it worked so well. This isn't even subtle. I mean, look at her, and she's only an F4. Imagine what an F10 might look like. I think I can make them even bigger."

She laughed nervously. "It sounds like you want to turn them into rats."

"Rats are a different species, but I bet with enough time . . . hundreds of generations . . . I might be able to get them close to that size."

Her face grew serious. "You shouldn't talk like that."

"It's just directional selection. With a diverse enough population, it's amazing what a little push can do. I mean, when you think about it, I hacked off the bottom ninety-five percent of the bell curve for five generations in a row. Of course the mice got bigger. I probably could have gone the other way if I wanted, made them smaller."

"You father won't like this," she said. She handed the mouse back to Paul.

"I know. I'll tell him about it at the science fair. After I've won. He can't get mad at me then."

His mother's brow furrowed. "I don't know," she said. "What if he finds them before the fair?"

"He won't," Paul said. He put the brindle mouse back in the aquarium. It scampered across the cedar chips toward the food dish. "Besides," he said softly, so that his mother couldn't hear. "This is all I have now."

"Just be careful," she said.

"There's one thing that surprised me though, something I only noticed recently."

"What's that?"

"When I started, at least half of the mice were albino. Now it's down to about one in ten."

"Why does that matter?"

"I never consciously decided to select against that."

"So?"

"So, when I did culls . . . when I decided which ones to breed, sometimes the weights were about the same on two mice, so I'd just pick one. I thought I was picking randomly, but now I'm not so sure. I think I just happened to like one kind more than the other."

"Maybe you did."

"So what if it happens that way in nature?"

"What do you mean?"

"It's like the dinosaurs. Or woolly mammoths, or cavemen. They were here once; we know that because we keep finding their bones. But now they're gone, and we can only see them in museums." He paused. "God made all life about six thousand years ago, right?"

"Yes."

"But some of it isn't here anymore." Paul looked at his mice. "What if it's like that with God? It wouldn't have to be on purpose, just a few percentiles of difference, the slightest perturbation from random, this big hand reaching down, picking which ones stay and which ones go."

Paul put the lid back on the aquarium. "Some kinds die out along the way."

It happened on a weekend. Bertha was pregnant, obscenely, monstrously. Her distended abdomen spread around her as she squatted on her haunches and nibbled at a piece of lettuce.

Bertha sat alone in the smallest aquarium, an island unto herself isolated on a table in the middle of the room. A little tissue box sat in the corner of her glass enclosure, and Bertha had shredded bits of paper into a comfortable nest in which to give birth to the next generation of goliath mice.

Paul dropped another piece of lettuce into the cage and smiled.

Whiskers twitching, Bertha lumbered forward across the cedar chips and sniffed the new arrival.

Then Paul heard it: the sudden hum of the garage door. He froze.

His father was home early.

When the garage door finally stopped, Paul heard his father's car ease into the open parking bay below. The brakes squeaked as the car pulled to a stop, and then his father cut the engine. Paul considered turning off the attic light but knew it would only draw suspicion. Instead he waited, hoping.

The garage was strangely quiet, the only sound the ticking of the car's engine down below. Paul listened, waiting for the tread of his father's footsteps heading into the house. The sound didn't come.

Paul's stomach dropped when he heard the creak of his father's weight on the ladder.

There was a moment of panic then—a single hunted moment when Paul's eyes darted for a place to hide the cages. It was ridiculous; there was no place to go.

The creaking ladder grew louder as Paul's father ascended.

"What's that smell?" his father asked as his head cleared the attic floor. He stopped and looked around, a pale disembodied head jutting from the floorboards. "Oh."

And that was all he said at first.

That was all he said as he climbed the rest of the way. He rose to his height and stood like a giant, taking it in. The single bare bulb draped his eyes in shadow. The muscle in his jaw clenched and loosened. "What is this?" he said finally. His dead voice turned Paul's stomach to ice.

"What is this?" Louder now, and something changed in his shadow eyes. Paul's father stomped toward him, above him.

"Are you going to answer me? What is this!" The words more shriek than question, spit flying from his mouth.

"I, I thought—"

A big hand shot out and slammed into Paul's chest, balling his T-shirt into a fist, yanking him off his feet.

"What the fuck *is* this? Didn't I tell you no pets?" The bright light of the family, the famous man.

"They're not pets, they're—"

"God, it fucking stinks up here. You brought these things into the house?"

"I'm sorry, Dad, I—"

"You brought this *vermin* into the house? Into my house!"

"It's a projec—"

The arm flexed, sending Paul backward into the big cages, toppling one of the tables—a flash of pain, wood and mesh crashing to the floor, the squeak of mice and twisted hinges, months and months and months of work.

His father kicked at the wood, splintering the frame, crushing the cage in on itself, stomping it to twisted wreckage. "You brought these things into *my house!*"

Paul scrambled away, just out of reach.

His father followed, arm raised, and the big hand came down on Paul's shoulder, knocking him to the floor, where his chin split against the rough wood. And still his father came, stomping toward him, while Paul rolled away. His big leg lashed out and missed. And he came again, arm raised high—but then stopped, attention snagged. His head turned toward the glass box. He strode to the middle of the room. He grabbed Bertha's aquarium in his big hands.

"Dad, no!"

He lifted it high over his head—and there was a moment when Paul imagined he could almost see it, almost see Bertha inside, and the babies inside her, a final generation that would never be born.

Then his father's arms came down like a force of nature, like a cataclysm.

Paul closed his eyes against exploding glass, and all he could think was *This is how it happens. This is exactly how it happens.*

There is a place where the sky touches the ground. Martial Joseph Johansson knew that place. He stared out through the glass bubble of the helicopter as it tunneled through the downpour. Rain sheeted off the glass, transformed by the curvature of the windshield into writhing little rivers that streamed away, found edges, fell. Became rain again.

"Five minutes, sir!"

The horizon, Martial Johansson knew, was an illusion of perspective. Below a certain altitude, each point in the sky occupies the horizon when viewed from some specific corresponding vantage. A formula could be deduced involving the curvature of the earth, the altitude of the helicopter, and the distance from the observer. So from some theoretical miles-off viewpoint, the helicopter sat like a microscopic insect on the dark line of the horizon. A lightning bug in a storm.

Martial closed his eyes.

The helicopter bucked beneath him, a deep vibration felt in every cell of his body.

Beside him sat his assistant Guthrie, looking at his watch. His knuckles were white on the handle of his briefcase. Although he'd worked for Martial for six years, Guthrie still hadn't gotten used to the frequent flights. Running a corporation the size of Axiom required Martial to be on three coasts, often in the same day. Mostly, that meant jets, but every now and then the helicopter was required. Guthrie still seemed a bit nervous in the helicopter, even in the best of weather. This was not the best of weather.

Martial coughed phlegm into a dark handkerchief. It took a moment for the coughing to subside.

"You okay?" Guthrie shouted over the roar of the helicopter.

Martial nodded.

The noise discouraged conversation. But this was okay. Martial was a man with little use for small talk.

The helicopter banked against the wind, and the world swiveled. Martial's stomach went light and feathery as he looked out through the glass. They were almost there. He could see it. From this height, the facility looked like any nice hotel retreat. Or maybe a high school campus that Frank Lloyd Wright had designed—all hard angles and elegant symmetry. A structure built so perfectly into the landscape that you secretly suspected it had always been there. Huge and beautiful, a sprawling compound of laboratories and research buildings, interconnected by a series of covered walkways. This was Axiom's epicenter, his third home.

The helicopter swiveled again, changing the world's orientation. Lights and a red cross, a helipad—and standing there, against the rain, waiting for the helicopter to land, three men in suits.

Always three men. Martial liked it that way. His security detail. Though he'd learned a long time ago not to trust anyone completely—even those closest to him.

All three had guns, but only two of the guns were loaded with live rounds. Nobody knew which two.

Not even the men.

The helicopter touched down with a gentle thump. The door swung open and cold, wet air blasted Martial's face.

He followed Guthrie out into the storm.

"Two transplants, and this fucking rain will be the death of me!" Martial shouted into the roar of the machine. The tropical storm had been born in the Gulf, two hundred miles to the south, and now it lashed the Gulf States, shedding its moisture as it moved inland.

Guthrie made some response, but the sound was yanked away. Guthrie ducked as he ran beneath the spinning blades. A common, involuntary reflex. Though Martial was a few inches taller, he stood upright and walked slowly, reaching up to hold his hat onto his head.

He'd done the math when he'd first bought the helicopter. He was six foot one. The blades, at their center, were eight feet off the ground. Therefore, he didn't need to duck. Later he read of a man who'd died in a windstorm, his head taken off by the overhead prop. For though the blades were eight feet high at the center, they drooped while the helicopter idled down; and during gusty weather an idling helicopter could be rocked ever so slightly by the force of the wind, producing a slight pitch. Blades that were eight feet off the ground in the center might be suddenly, on one side of the helicopter, only five or six feet at their spinning tips. Martial took the news as a lesson: When God wants you, he will take you.

The three men in suits walked forward to greet them.

"Sir," the first man said. This was Scholler. As big as he was dedicated, and one of Martial's longest-serving personal guards.

They shook hands. "I trust you had a good flight, sir."

"We're here, aren't we?"

"And glad to see it, sir."

Behind Scholler was Ekman. Blond, serious, unsmiling. He looked younger than his actual age, as much boy as man, but he was the one Martial trusted to handle the more difficult operations. A diagonal scar split his upper lip. To Ekman's left was Phillips, who really was as young as he looked. A newer asset. Ex-military and kept the crew cut.

They crossed the helipad to the waiting doorway. Once inside, they took the stairs down. "How were the latest trials?" Martial asked.

"Negative," Scholler said.

Martial nodded, accepting the news. "And how is he?"

"The same, sir."

"The others?"

"Another numbers reduction, sir."

"Cause of?"

"We haven't finished the autopsy yet but we'll—"

Martial cut him off with a raised hand. "What do you *think*?"

"Probably the same as the others. Methylation imprint. Unbalanced base-pair alignment."

"Which is another way of saying you have no idea."

"Yes, sir. You could say that."

There were men in Martial's shoes who did not sweat the details, who ran their companies like drivers raced cars, foot on the gas, aware only of the output of their machine rather than the intricacies of its inner workings. Martial prided himself on looking under the hood. To be any other way made no sense, considering the circumstances.

"I was hoping for good news," he said.

"Sorry, sir. The new trials are scheduled to begin next month."

Martial shook his head dismissively. "The price of progress. There's an old saying, If you want to achieve the impossible, you must first accept that you may fail."

They took the stairs down to the third floor. At the doorway, Martial paused and turned toward the smallest man. "Ekman, I'd like a word." The others continued down the stairs. Only Ekman followed Martial into the hall.

"The problem I tasked you with," Martial said. "I'm told you took care of it."

"Yes, sir."

"And the mess?"

"Cleaned up as best we could."

"Did you talk to him first?"

"Yes. We sat in the kitchen and had a chat."

"And your opinion?"

"My opinion, sir?"

"Of Manuel. His state of mind. His motive. Why did he do it?"

"I think he was crazy."

Martial nodded. "It seems to be an occupational risk." He stopped at the door of his private quarters. "And our property was recovered?"

"Yes. Deceased. The autopsy will take place at the same time as the others."

"Excellent work. I appreciate the efficiency with which you handled the situation."

Ekman dipped his chin slightly in response.

"Is there anything else I need to know?"

Ekman gestured toward the door. "She's waiting for you, sir," he said.

"Wait outside."

"Yes, sir."

Martial stepped through, and Ekman closed the door after him.

Martial kept apartments at several of his facilities. It made the travel more bearable. They were small and functional and clean. Everything his life wasn't. He wandered into the kitchen and mixed a drink. A tall one.

In his office, he found Sacha. She was standing at the window. She'd lost weight. They kissed awkward hellos on the cheek. "Joseph," she said, using his middle name. His Christian name. She wrapped her arms tightly around herself and pulled away.

"How have you been?" he asked.

She smiled. "As you see."

"You're looking healthy."

"Ah, the glow of docetaxel. They should market it to all the girls. Also, it keeps you thin. A wonderful purgative. And if you're lucky, the burst capillaries in your eyes give you that perfect come-hither look."

"You're particularly sarcastic tonight."

"Particularly?"

"What's wrong?" he asked.

"Nothing that a few months won't cure." She stared out the window for a moment before continuing. "I saw it again."

"Why do that to yourself?"

She stayed silent.

"I told you not to go down there again."

"But still I went, didn't I? Imagine that. A world where not everyone does what you say. The thought of it must keep you awake at night."

"Why did you go?"

"I heard it was sick."

"It was. It got better. And how about you?"

"I'm fine," she said. Though of course she wasn't. "That thing," she whispered, "it's not natural."

Martial took a sip of his drink. "Are any of us anymore?"

The words were out before he could stop them. Sacha had tried to kill herself three times already. Three times in seven years, each attempt more serious than the last. So when cancer had struck, it came to her as both a shock and a relief. The medical team told him before they told her. A thin medical report on his desk that explained exactly how she would die. Later, she'd found him in the cell lab, and he'd given her the news.

"If I'd only known," she'd said. And he'd understood that she was talking about the three wasted attempts. That last one a nightmare of blood and razors. When all she'd had to do was wait.

And then, with genuine surprise in her voice, she'd said, "But I thought only the good died young."

Now Martial took a seat on his couch.

"It's been a while since you've visited the lab," she said.

"Three months. Not so long."

"Time isn't the same here. I think you're avoiding me."

"Don't be silly."

She sat next to him on the couch. She laid her head in his lap, and he touched her hair.

"I worry about what will become of you when I'm gone," she said.

It was sarcasm again, he thought at first. But when she stayed silent, he was no longer sure.

Sacha had been a call girl once. Then something more. Then something less.

She had two months.

"You collect things," she said. "These fascinations. And then you never let them go."

"I let things go."

She shook her head. "One day you will be solely comprised of what you hoard."

"You can go anytime you wish."

"Is that what you tell yourself? You have always been a great liar. Even to yourself."

She was the only person who could speak to him like this. She was the only person with nothing left to lose. Soon, she would be gone. Perhaps this is what she'd meant when she'd said she worried what would become of him. That there would be no one left to tell him what he didn't want to hear.

"We're doing our best to keep you comfortable."

"The drugs are good, Joseph, if that's what you're asking. It's my memories that aren't comfortable. Can you do something for those?"

She stared at him, ice coming off.

He knew that she hated him. She'd hated him for a long time—for at least as long as she'd felt anything else toward him. This felt fitting to him. It felt deserved.

"Have you seen it yet?" she asked.

"Not yet, no. I just landed."

"It's changing."

"What do you mean?"

She was about to say something but stopped. He studied her. An oval face, pretty but too thin. She might have been a model once, if things had gone differently. She had the bones for it. There was a look in her eyes now that he'd never seen.

"I don't think you have any idea what you've done," she said.

"I know better than anyone."

"Better than me?"

Martial took another sip of his drink.

"You can't quite bring yourself to claim that, can you?" she asked.

"Everything happens for a reason."

"If you really think that, you're a fool."

There was a time when hearing those words, spoken in that tone, would have driven him into a rage, but now it elicited only the beginnings of a tired irritation. Still, she'd pushed him far enough.

"Your mouth is not the ocean," he said. "But still it can drown you."

The phone on his desk rang. He didn't move. He tried to remember if he'd ever heard that phone ring before. He hadn't realized the apartment even had a phone. After five rings, it stopped.

A moment later, an alarm began to sound. It came from somewhere in the distance. It wasn't a fire alarm. The phone rang again.

"I better get that," he said.

He stood and crossed the room.

He picked up the phone. "Yes?"

"There is a problem." It was Scholler.

"What kind of problem?"

"You better get down here."

"On my way." Martial hung up and turned to Sacha.

Just then, a new alarm sounded. Louder, closer.

Sacha's smile made Martial think of bitter almonds. "It's changed," she said again. "You'll see."

Martial walked out of his quarters. In the hall, a strobe light flashed red. He broke into a run, thousand-dollar shoes on tile floors. He panted as he ran. Within a hundred feet, his lungs spasmed, breaths coming in a series of high-pitched whistles. He slowed but didn't stop. *When God wants you, he will take you.*

Ekman found him in the hall. They ran together. They rounded the bend. It was a nightmare he'd once had. Down two flights of stairs. Lab lights flickering. A dream he woke sweating from. Only in the dream his feet were swollen and sticky, mired to the floor. In the dream, he couldn't move at all. They pushed through a double set of doors and entered the lab.

An Asian man stood swaying in the hall, holding an obviously dislocated shoulder. He was in shock, his white lab coat red with gore. From the other side of the wall came the sound of screams.

"Where are you cut?" Martial asked, catching his breath.

"I'm not," the man said.

Martial's other two guards burst into the room. Phillips, the youngest, didn't hesitate. He ran ahead, toward the screams.

Martial and his remaining guards followed.

The researcher shouted after them, "Don't go in there!"

They pushed through another set of double doors, the word ANTHRO-POGENY stenciled across the white surface.

Inside, a woman clutched at the mangled gore of her wrist. Her hand dangled at an obscene angle. "It bit me . . . it bit me" was all she could say.

Farther in were more researchers. He knew some of their names. Others he couldn't be sure of.

Behind him, the woman continued, "It bit . . ."

Another researcher stood at the shattered glass doors. He didn't seem hurt, but he looked dazed.

"What happened?" Martial snapped.

"A routine examination," he said. "There was the sound of the helicopter outside. We tried to get it back inside . . . but it . . . it didn't want to go."

Martial stepped through the broken glass doors and moved farther into the room. Somewhere, the screaming man went silent. Scholler pulled out his gun.

Up ahead, Phillips, the new asset, crouched low and kept moving.

"Stay back!" Martial called.

"There are people still alive in there!" Phillips shouted. On the opposite side of the room was another set of doors, bright red, leading to a secured area. Phillips pushed through and disappeared. From inside came a loud clang. Metal on metal.

Martial turned to Scholler. "Give me your gun."

"Sir?"

"Your gun. Now."

The guard handed it over. "The safety's off."

Martial strode forward and looked through the safety glass, into the next room.

"You should stay back, sir."

"Get the tranquilizers."

Scholler hesitated.

"Now!"

The big man crossed the room to the metal shelves.

"No live ammo, tranqs only!" Martial shouted after him.

Scholler opened the metal cabinets, fumbling with the tranq gun. He turned. "Sir, wait!"

Martial hit the button and the doors opened.

"Wait!"

Martial stepped through.

Blood everywhere, a severed arm.

A dead researcher lay spun at an odd angle, neck arched, face a mask of surprise. Scattered around him on the floor were blood and broken glass. Pieces of swivel chair, smashed lights. Broken ceiling tiles. And in the dark shadows farther into the room, a shape. The sound of weeping. This was the behavior lab.

Martial couldn't see Phillips.

Behind him, Scholler entered the lab, tranquilizer gun raised. Ekman was close behind him, his pale hair standing out in the shadows. Martial held up his hand. "Stop."

"Sir?" Ekman said.

Lights swung free of their cases, dangling on swaying chords. The sound of moaning. Then a flash of movement near an overturned table. Martial saw Phillips, up ahead, standing near the wall, saw his gun come up, tracking the flash of movement in the shadows.

"Phillips, stand down!" Martial shouted.

"There are people still alive."

"Phillips!"

The shape moved in the shadows.

"My God." There was panic in the young guard's voice, and disbelief. It was the first time Phillips had seen it. The gun came up.

"Stand the fuck down!" Martial screamed.

Phillips fired. The gun went off, lighting the darkness with a muzzle flash.

Martial raised his own gun at Phillips and pulled the trigger.

The gun clicked.

Phillips turned toward Martial, eyes going wide.

Martial pulled the trigger again and again, the barrel pointed at Phillips's chest—but the gun carried only blanks. Only two guards had loaded guns. Nobody knew which two, not even guards.

Phillips stared at Martial in disbelief—at the gun, the pulled trigger.

"I told you not to shoot," Martial said, gun still raised.

Phillips raised his own gun toward Martial, a reflex.

There were two pops, in quick succession. Red flowers bloomed on Phillips's shirt, center of mass.

Behind Martial, Ekman reholstered his weapon.

Phillips crumpled. He was dead before he hit the floor.

"He was raising his weapon toward you, sir," Ekman said.

Martial nodded.

A flash of movement crossed the room. The dark shape slid behind a desk that had been flipped onto its side.

Martial moved into the center of the room and sank to his knees. He dropped the gun, which clacked loudly on the tile floor. Around him, the room was a disaster. He saw strange prints in the blood. Something not quite a hand. Not quite a foot.

From the shadows came the sound of sobbing. The scrape of movement, the slap of bare skin on the floor.

"Come out," Martial said.

The sobbing grew louder. Then a strange voice, almost unintelligible: "I'm sorry. I'm so sorry."

"It's okay," Martial said softly. "Just come out. Come to me."

The dark shape moved into the light.

PART II

FOURTEEN YEARS LATER

There has existed, since the beginning, a finite number of unique creations—a finite number of species, which has, over time, decreased dramatically through extinction. Speciation is a special event outside the realm of natural processes, a phenomenon relegated to the moment of creation, and to the mysteries of Allah.

—EXPERT WITNESS, HERESY TRIALS,
ANKARA, TURKEY

Gavin McMaster stepped into the bright room.

"So this is where the actual testing is done?" he asked. The accent was urban Australian.

"Yes," Mr. Lyons answered.

Gavin shifted his weight and glanced around the room. His hair was long, more salt than pepper, worn in a thick ponytail that hung down over the back of his shirt collar. Behind him, the door swung shut with the telltale hiss of positive air pressure—a hedge against contamination.

It never ceased to amaze him how alike laboratories are across the world. Cultures that could not agree on anything agreed on this: how to design a centrifuge, where to put the test tube rack, what color to paint the walls—white, always. The bench tops, black. Gavin had been in a dozen similar labs over the years. Only the people made them different.

"Please wait here; I'll see if he's available."

Gavin nodded. "Of course."

He watched the small man scamper toward the research team working at the lab bench.

One of the team members, a broad, dark-haired man, sat hunched over a test tray of PCR tubes, pipette in hand. The young man straightened when Mr. Lyons whispered in his ear. He was big and young—Asian cheekbones, blocky shoulders. *His father's shoulders,* Gavin thought. Gavin knew it was Paul without being told.

Paul stood, pulled off his latex gloves, and followed Mr. Lyons across the room for an introduction.

"Gavin McMaster." Gavin stuck out his hand. "Pleased to make your acquaintance, Mr. Carlsson."

They shook.

"Paul," the young man said. "You can call me Paul."

"I apologize for interrupting your work."

"It's time I took a break anyway. I'd been sitting at that stool all morning."

"I'll leave you two to your discussion," Mr. Lyons said, excusing himself.

"Please," Paul gestured to a nearby worktable. "Take a seat."

Gavin sank onto the stool and set his briefcase on the table. "I promise I won't take much of your time," he said. "But I did need to talk to you. We've been leaving messages for the last few days and—"

"Oh." Paul's face changed. "You're from—"

"Yes."

"This is highly unusual."

"I can assure you, these are unusual circumstances."

"Still, I'm not sure I like being solicited for one job while working at another."

"I can see there's been a misunderstanding."

"What misunderstanding?"

"You called it a job," Gavin said. "We just want to borrow you, not hire you away. Consider it a temporary change of pace—a transfer position."

"Mr. McMaster, I currently have more than a full workload. I'm in the middle of a project, and to be honest, considering the backlog we're dealing with, I'm surprised Westing let you through the door."

"Is that what you're worried about?" Gavin smiled. "Your company is already on board. They've granted you a . . . let's call it a sabbatical of sorts. I took the liberty of speaking to management before contacting you. They were very accommodating."

"How did you . . ." Paul looked at him, and Gavin raised an eyebrow.

With corporations, the question of "how" was usually rhetorical. The answer was always the same. And it always involved dollar signs. Pay a company enough money, and they'll subcontract you any employee you want.

Gavin saw understanding dawn in Paul's eyes. "Of course, we'll match that bonus to you, mate." Gavin unfolded a check from his suit pocket and slid it across the counter.

Paul barely glanced at it. Instead he looked around for Mr. Lyons, who was nowhere to be seen.

"Is this how you usually staff a project?" Paul said.

"We'd prefer not to take on reluctant third-party participants, if that's what you're asking. On the other hand, we're on a tight schedule, and, as I mentioned, this is an unusual circumstance. We need to be wheels-up in twenty-four hours, so I'm afraid we really must insist."

"Insist? What if I refuse?" Paul's face was unreadable.

Gavin smiled. "Normally I'd take that as a negotiating tactic, angling for a bigger check. But that's not the case here, is it?"

"No."

Gavin studied the young man in front of him. "I was like you once. Hell, maybe I still am."

"Then you understand." Paul smiled tightly.

"I understand you better than you think. It makes it easier, sometimes, when you come from money. Sometimes I think that only people who come from it realize how worthless it really is."

"That hasn't been my experience," Paul said curtly. "Now, if you'll excuse me."

Gavin had seen this before, politeness like a wall. He understood it. *Did you learn that politeness from your mother, Paul? What did you learn from your father?*

"If you want to refuse, you can take it up with your management." Gavin stood.

"I will."

"But you might find they're a little more reluctant to part with their check. Until I hear otherwise, I'm going to assume your cooperation, as your employer assured."

"You can assume whatever you'd like."

"We leave tomorrow afternoon. You haven't asked what you'll be working on."

"Does it matter?" Paul said, the slightest irritation seeping into his voice. He was on the edge of walking away—but that same politeness held him there for the vital split second.

"Perhaps it doesn't," Gavin said. "Before you turn your back, I have something for you. Something perhaps more interesting than a check."

Gavin opened the latches on his briefcase and pulled out a stack of glossy eight-by-ten photographs. He held them out for Paul to take.

For a moment Paul just stood there, and Gavin was afraid the young man wouldn't accept them. If he walked away without looking, then tomorrow could be tricky.

Paul reached out and took the photographs from Gavin's extended hand.

Paul looked at the photos.

He looked at them for a long time.

"Give us two weeks," Gavin said. "If, after two weeks, you don't want to stay, we'll have you transferred back, no questions asked. And you can keep the check."

"Where were these taken?"

Gavin said, "These fossils were found last year on the island of Flores, in Indonesia."

"Flores," Paul whispered, still studying the photos. He leafed through them slowly, one after another. "I heard they found strange bones there. I didn't know anybody had published."

"That's because we haven't. Not yet, anyway."

Paul came to one photograph and stopped. He was silent for a long time, then said, "I'm not sure what I'm looking at here."

"Neither are we. Not one hundred percent sure, anyway."

"It looks adult, by the wear on the teeth."

"It is."

"These dimensions can't be right."

"They're right."

"A six-inch ulna?"

Gavin nodded.

"Then these are unique." Paul looked at him. "You must have people clamoring to work on this."

"We're holding these close to the vest at the moment."

"You could take your pick of samplers."

"We did," Gavin said. "Why else would I be here?"

Paul's brow furrowed. "I don't understand."

"You don't need to."

"No," Paul said. "Maybe I do." And just like that, the wall was gone. Politeness replaced by something different.

"You have the education and training we're looking for."

It was Paul's turn to raise an eyebrow. "So do other samplers."

"We need someone who works fast."

"I'm hardly the fastest."

Gavin sighed. "I don't know if archaeology was ever meant to be as important as it has become. Will that do?"

Paul only stared and said nothing.

"We live in a world where zealots become scientists. Tell me, boy, are you a zealot?"

"No."

"Then that's your reason. Or close enough."

— 8 —

Paul's father had died of a heart attack in the summer after his freshman year of college. It happened suddenly, leaving a thousand things unsaid.

The funeral procession followed the hearse from the church to the graveyard where four generations of his father's family lay buried. A green hill where Paul suspected that he, too, would someday find his final repose. His mother cried.

"I could take a semester off," he told her. "I could stay."

"No," she said. "Go back to school."

"You shouldn't be alone."

"I'm not alone; I have the church."

And it was true. For the last several years, as his father's behavior had grown more erratic, his mother had retreated into her Bible study. She spent five days a week up at the church. Sometimes she didn't come home.

"Your father's things are yours now," she told him.

"What things?"

"The things fathers give their sons."

On the last night he was in town, he went up to his father's room. His mother was downstairs. She'd fallen asleep on the couch.

Paul opened his father's closet. Shirts and ties. Books. In the back, near the wall, a loaded gun, silver black. He'd seen it before, years earlier.

He found a coin collection. Susan B. Anthonys, and a dozen Liberty Bells. There was a stack of scientific periodicals. Inside each one, a scrap of paper bookmarked a page. Paul realized these were his father's publications. All his published papers. Studies on antagonistic pleiotropy, heterosis, and the mitochondrial haplotype distribution of the Przewalski's horse.

Behind the stack of journals, against the wall, something caught his eye. He reached in and grabbed the green spiral notebook. He opened it, recognizing his own childish hand. His father had kept it, all these years.

He flipped the pages until he found it. Not a date, but a mouse. January-17.

He closed the notebook and threw it back into the closet.

The next day he headed back to school.

At Stanford, Paul double-majored in genetics and anthropology, taking eighteen credit hours a semester. He sat in classrooms while men in tweed jackets spun theories about Kibra and T variants, about microcephalin 1 and haplogroup D. He plowed into 300-level biology, where from the lectern his professor singled him out from the other students, responding to his question by saying, "You have the gift of insight, my boy." And then, to Paul's startled expression, he added, "You know which questions to ask."

There were classes in comparative interpretation and biblical philosophy. He experimented with fruit flies and amphioxi and, while still an undergraduate, won a prestigious summer internship working under renowned geneticist Mathew Poole.

He also scrutinized the fringe theories. He contemplated balancing equilibriums and Hardy-Weinberg. But alone at night, walking the dark halls of his own head, it was the trade-offs that fascinated him most. Paul was a young man who understood trade-offs.

In the medical library, he came across research on the recently discovered Alzheimer's gene APOE4—a gene common throughout much of the world—and he wondered how deleterious genes grew to such high frequencies. Paul discovered that although APOE4 often produced Alzheimer's, it also protected against the cognitive consequences of early childhood malnutrition. The gene that destroys the mind at seventy saves it at seven months. He read that people with sickle-cell trait are resistant to malaria; and heterozygotes for cystic fibrosis are less susceptible to cholera; and people with type A blood survived the plague at higher frequencies than other blood types, altering forever, in a single generation, the frequency of blood types in Europe. A process, some said, now being slow-motion mimicked by Delta 32 and HIV.

In his anthropology courses, Paul was taught that all humans alive today can trace their ancestry back to Africa, to a time almost six thousand years ago when the whole of human diversity existed within a single small population. And there had been at least two dispersions out of Africa, his professors said, if not more—a genetic bottleneck that supported the Flood Theory. But each culture had its own beliefs. Muslims called it Allah. Jews, Yahweh. The science journals were careful not to specify, but they spoke of an intelligent designer—an architect, lowercase *a*. Though in his heart of hearts, Paul figured it all amounted to the same thing.

Paul read that they'd scanned the brains of nuns, looking for the God spot, and couldn't find it. He examined, too, the theory of evolutionism. Although long debunked by legitimate science, adherents of evolutionism still existed, their beliefs enjoying near immortality among the fallow fields of pseudoscience, cohabitating the fringe with older belief systems like astrology, phrenology, and acupuncture. Modern evolutionists believed the various dating systems were all incorrect, and they offered an assortment of ridiculous and unscientific explanations for how the isotope tests could all be wrong.

The evolutionists ignored the geological record. They ignored the ice cores, the hermeneutics, and the wealth of biological evidence. They ignored the miracle of the placenta and the irreducible complexity of the eye.

"After all, the eye," his anatomy professor lectured, "is biologically useful only in the sum of its parts. It can't be reduced to functional precursor components."

During his sophomore year, Paul got a job cleaning cages in the biology department. There were snakes and rabbits and owls, and a lonely alligator with a broken jaw—a veritable mini-zoo on the campus grounds, all of it housed in state-of-the-art facilities and cared for by a small army of lab-coated undergrads.

That first day of employment, his trainer met him in the lobby, and he followed her around as she explained his duties. He watched her slender form as they walked the cement corridor. She was young, another student. Brown skin, beautiful dark hair.

"This job isn't what you think" was the second thing she said to him. The first was: "I hate to break your heart."

They took the stairs up to the second floor. "You come highly recommended, let's get that out of the way" she said.

"I do?"

She shrugged. "Let's assume. And you have stellar grades, too. You must, or you wouldn't be here." Her accent was subtle, hard to place at first. "But still, there are no strings you can pull to get a different set of duties, so don't bother asking. The new hires all want the monkeys, but that's not what you'll be working with mostly."

"Okay," he said. He followed her deeper into the facility. The research building was huge. It was a maze of rooms upon rooms. White walls and white tile. The top two floors were dedicated to the research library, but the rest belonged to the animals. She wore her dark hair in a ponytail that exposed the delicate curve of her neck.

"Besides that," she said. "You only *think* you want the monkeys. Monkeys are dangerous. They're fast and insanely strong for their size. Seven times stronger than humans, pound for pound. Plus, they bite."

She paused before a set of double doors and withdrew a pair of green foam earplugs from the breast pocket of her lab coat. Paul could already hear the barking from the other side, so he knew what to expect. As they entered the kennel, the sound became deafening. "And these are the dogs," she shouted, in case there was any doubt. "Another popular aspiration for new hires. But you won't be working with these either, unless one of the regular workers calls in sick for the day, in which case you'll probably be responsible for the bigger dogs." She gestured toward the row of German shepherds at the end. "They poop more," she added by way of explanation.

They took another flight of stairs.

"We house all kinds of animals in the facility. A few for the veterinary program and the psychology department, but most are for the genetics program, the medical school, and the experimental sciences."

"Which animals do you take care of?"

"Me?" She smiled, revealing neat white teeth and a dimple. "The monkeys, of course."

"I had a feeling."

She went on: "The monkeys and dogs are the positions that everyone seems to want, and that you probably won't stay long enough to get. So as the new guy, you'll get what's left over."

They came to a door at the end of the hall. The trainer swiped a badge and opened the door. She hit the lights.

Paul's mouth dropped open.

"And this is where you'll be working," she said, sweeping an arm out in front of her. "Welcome to the mouse room."

During his junior and senior years, Paul dove into archaeology. He examined the ancient remains of *Homo erectus* and *Homo neanderthalensis*. He examined the un-men: *afarensis,* and *Australopithecus,* and *Pan.*

He examined the shape and skin and touch of a girl named Lillivati.

They took a class together: ancient skeletal anatomy.

She also trained him for his job in the biology department. Her specialty: monkeys. Together they studied for tests, and they found reasons not to study, stealing moments between classes and work shifts.

Lillivati's long fingers clasped the small of his back, pulling him into her, dark hair an inky pool around her head while she whispered to him in Gujarati. Though he asked, she'd never reveal what she said to him in these moments. She'd only smile, her dark eyes half-lidded, and say, "It's dirtier than you think."

Students at most Ivy-caliber schools could be divided into three categories. First (of course) were those who were rich. Second were those who might or might not be rich but had, more significantly, gotten scholarships. Third were those who were going to graduate with a debt approximating the national deficit.

This third category could be subdivided. Some of these debt-indentured students would, after graduation, go on to make an amount of money even more obscene than the world-crushing debt they'd labor under. They'd work their asses off. Money would rain from the sky and sluice into the overflowing gutters of their bank accounts. They would, in fact, pay off their obscene debt without too much trouble and later wonder what all the fuss was about. Anybody could do it, right? They'd succeed largely because they were computer savants or good-looking, charismatic lawyers with the attention surfeit of competitive Chinese rice farmers and eidetic recall of corporate tax law, or because they'd invent Google or something. In short, they'd be able to pay off their obscene debt because they came out of the box preoptimized for dollar acquisition. The rest of the students in that third category were screwed, though.

Lillivati was in the first category; Paul, the second.

They used her room for sex, because her parents could afford for her not to have a roommate.

She was a year older than him and graduated early.

And true to her first words to him: she left. Or had to leave.

I hate to break your heart.

First, home to India. Then graduate school in Seattle.

Paul threw himself into his schoolwork, taking independent study in the osteochronology of ancient anthropoid remains.

In the world of archaeology, the line between man and un-man could be fuzzy, but it was never unimportant. To some scientists, *Homo erectus* was a race of man long dead, a withered branch on the tree of humanity. To those more conservative, he wasn't man at all; he was other, a hiccup of the creator, an independent creation made from the same toolbox. But that was an extreme viewpoint.

Mainstream science, of course, accepted the use of stone tools as the litmus test. Men made stone tools. Soulless beasts didn't. Of course there were still arguments, even in the mainstream. The fossil KNM-ER 1470, found in Kenya, appeared so perfectly balanced between man and un-man that an additional category had to be invented: near man. The arguments could get quite heated, with both sides claiming anthropometric statistics to prove their case.

Like a benevolent teacher swooping in to stop a playground fight, the science of genetics arrived on the scene. Occupying the exact point of intersection between the slopes of Paul's two passions in life—genetics and anthropology—the field of paleometagenomics was born.

And here he found his calling.

He received a bachelor's degree in May and started a graduate program in September. A year later, there came a letter and an airline ticket, and a company called Westing flew him to the East Coast for a job interview.

They sat in a conference room. The company logo was a DNA double helix.

"I won't finish my master's for another six months," he told them, confused by the offer.

"We're more interested in ability than academic credentials," the chief interviewer said. "The schools can't keep up. Field techniques are obsolete by the time the textbooks are printed. If you want to see the curriculum three years early, sign our employment contract."

"This is all moving so fast."

The interviewer smiled. "Like the field itself."

They shook hands over a glossy table.

Three weeks after that, he was in the field in Tanzania, sweating under an equatorial sun, collecting samples for later laboratory analysis. He drank quinine water by the gallon and dodged malaria.

They flew him back and forth between labs and dig sites.

All the while, he worked closely with his team, learning the proprietary techniques for extracting DNA from bones that were fifty-eight hundred years old.

Bones from the very dawn of the world.

The flight to Bali was seventeen hours, and another two to Flores by chartered plane—then four hours by jeep over the steep mountains and into the heart of the jungle. To Paul, it might have been another world. Rain fell, then stopped, then fell again, turning the road into a thing which had to be reasoned with.

"Is it always like this?" Paul asked.

"No," Gavin said. "In the rainy season, it's much worse."

The jeep slalomed along the rutted track, throwing rooster tails of black mud as it negotiated the pitched landscape.

Paul gripped the jeep's roll bar to steady himself and stared out into the thick growth that slid past on both sides of the road.

Flores, isle of flowers. From the air it had looked like a green ribbon of jungle thrust out of blue water, a single bead in the rosary of islands that stretched between Australia and Java. Sulawesi lay to the north, New Guinea to the northeast. The Wallace line—a line more real than any border scrawled across a map—lay miles to the west, toward Asia and the empire of placental mammals. But here a stranger emperor ruled.

Paul was exhausted by the time they pulled into Ruteng. He rubbed his eyes. Children ran alongside the jeep, their faces some compromise between Malay and Papuan: brown skin, strong white teeth like a dentist's dream. The town crouched with one foot in the jungle, one on the mountain. A valley flung itself from the edge of the settlement, a drop of kilometers.

The jeep wound its way through the crowded streets, past shops, and houses, and thronging tent bazaars, past smaller clapboard structures whose function Paul could only guess at. Small vans and motorbikes shouldered each other for space at intersections, horns blaring. If there were driving laws, Paul couldn't deduce them from the available data.

Rail-thin pariah dogs lurked in the gaps between buildings. Paul noted their colors with a geneticist's eye, reading their genes as they picked through the garbage, tails curved upward over their bony hips. The yellow one was Ay; the black-and-tan, at/at. And others: E/m, bb, s/i. He saw no solid blacks. That color variety hadn't been among the first dogs carried across the Wallace line in bamboo rafts. That kind didn't exist here.

The jeep pulled to a stop in front of a small two-story structure.

The men checked into their hotel, handing over 170,000 rupiah apiece. Paul had no idea if that was expensive or not, but he found his room basic and clean. He slept like the dead.

The next morning he woke, showered, and shaved. Gavin met him in the lobby.

"It's a bit rustic, I admit," Gavin said. His hair was pulled back into a tight ponytail, keeping it clear of his face.

"No, it's fine," Paul said. "There was a bed and a shower. That's all I needed."

"We use Ruteng as a kind of base camp for the dig. Our future accommodations won't be quite so luxurious."

Back at the jeep, Paul checked his gear. It wasn't until he climbed into the passenger seat that he noticed the gun, its black leather holster ducttaped to the driver's door. It hadn't been there the day before.

Gavin caught him staring. "These are crazy times we live in, mate."

"And the times require researchers to carry guns?"

"This is a place history has forgotten. Recent events have made it remember."

"Which recent events are those?"

"Religious events, to some folks' view. Political to others'." Gavin waved his hand. "More than just scientific egos are at stake with this find."

They drove north, descending into the valley and sloughing off the last pretense of civilization. "You're afraid somebody will kidnap the bones?" Paul asked.

"That's one of the things I'm afraid of."

"One?"

"It's easy to pretend that it's just theories we're playing with—ideas dreamed up in some ivory tower between warring factions of scientists like it's all some intellectual exercise." Gavin looked at him, his dark eyes grave. "But then you see the actual bones; you feel their weight in your hands, the sheer factual irrefutability of their existence . . ." Gavin stared at the road ahead. Finally, he said, "Sometimes theories die between your fingers."

The track down to the valley floor was all broken zigzags and occasional rounding turns. Gavin leaned into the horn as they approached blind curves, though they never came across another vehicle. The temperature rose as they descended. For long stretches, overhanging branches made a tunnel of the roadway, the jungle a damp cloth slapping at the windshield. But here and there that damp cloth was yanked aside, and out over the edge of the drop you could see a valley Hollywood would love, an archetype to represent all valleys, jungle floor visible through jungle haze. On those stretches of muddy road, a sharp left pull on the steering wheel would have gotten them there quicker, deader.

"Liang Bua," Gavin called their destination. "The Cold Cave." And Gavin explained that this was how they thought it happened, the scenario: this steamy jungle all around, so two or three of them went inside to get cool, to sleep. Or maybe it was raining, and they went into the cave to get dry—only the rain didn't stop, and the river flooded, as the local rivers often did, and they were trapped inside the cave by the rising waters, their drowned bodies settling to the bottom to be buried by mud, and sediment, and millennia.

The men rode in silence for a while before Gavin said it, a third option, Paul felt coming: "Or they were eaten there."

"Eaten by what?"

"*Homo homini lupus est,*" Gavin said. "Man is wolf to man."

They forded a swollen river, water rising to the bottom of the doors. Paul felt the current grab the jeep, pull, and it was a close thing, Gavin cursing and white-knuckled on the wheel, trying to keep them to the shallows while the water seeped onto the floorboards. When they were past it he said, "You've got to stay to the north when you cross; if you slide a few feet off straight, the whole bugger'll go tumbling downriver."

Paul didn't ask him how he knew.

Beyond the river was the camp. Researchers in wide-brimmed hats or bandannas. Young and old. Two or three shirtless. Men with buckets, trowels, and bamboo stakes. A dark-haired woman in a white shirt sat on a log outside her tent. The sole commonality between them all: a kind of war weariness in their eyes. They'd been here long enough to have been worn down by the place.

That was when it occurred to Paul that some of these people had probably been digging here, in this same camp, for years.

Every face followed the jeep, and when it pulled to a stop, a small crowd gathered to help them unpack. Gavin introduced Paul around. Eight researchers, plus two laborers still in the cave and another two still working the sieves. Australian mostly. Indonesian. One American.

"Herpetology, mate," one of them said when he shook Paul's hand. Small, stocky, red-headed; he couldn't have been more than twenty-two. He wore a shaggy, coppery beard. Paul forgot his name the moment he heard it, but the introduction, "Herpetology, mate," stuck with him. "That's my specialty," the small man continued. "I got mixed up in this because of Professor McMaster here. University of New England—the Australian one." His smile was two feet wide under a sharp nose that pointed at his own chin. Paul liked him instantly.

When they'd finished unpacking the jeep, Gavin turned to Paul. "So are you ready for the tour?"

Paul nodded.

The operation was larger than he'd expected. There were two different sieving setups, one dry, one wet, and a dozen tables and tents and benches, all spread out in a small clearing just beyond the mouth of the cave. A generator rumbled in the background, providing all the electricity for their lights and equipment. Construction-helmeted laborers shuffled to and from the cave, bent under their work, local villagers who spoke a language Paul couldn't understand.

"We used to sleep in the village of Terus during the dig season,"

Gavin said. "It's just up the road. But you'll be staying here." Gavin gestured toward a white canvass tent.

Paul lifted the heavy tent flap and stuck his head inside. The space was clean and functional, like the room in Ruteng.

"Why don't you stay in Terus anymore?"

"Safety issues."

"So Terus isn't a friendly place, I take it?"

"No, Terus is wonderful. It's their safety we're worried about."

Gavin's face produced a smile. "Now I think it's time we made the most important introductions."

It was a short walk to the cave. Jag-toothed limestone jutted from the jungle, an overhang of vine, and, beneath that, a dark mouth. The stone was the brown-white of old ivory. Cool air enveloped Paul, and entering Liang Bua was a distinct process of stepping down. Inside, it took Paul's eyes a moment to adjust. The chamber was thirty yards wide, open to the jungle in a wide crescent—mud floor, high-domed ceiling. The overall impression was one of expanse, like the interior of an ancient church. He followed Gavin deeper. There was not much to see at first. In the far corner, two sticks angled from the mud, and when he looked closer Paul saw the hole.

"Is that it?"

"That's it."

Paul took off his backpack and stripped the white paper suit out of its plastic wrapper. He peered down into the dig. "Who else has touched it?"

"Talford, Margaret, me."

Paul pulled a light from his backpack and shined it into the hole. It was then that he realized just how deep it went. A system of bamboo ladders led down to the bottom, thirty feet below. He was staring into a pit. "I'll need blood samples from everybody for comparison assays."

"DNA contamination?"

"Yeah."

"We stopped the dig when we realized the significance."

"Still. I'll need blood samples from anybody who's dug here, anybody who came anywhere near the bones. I'll take the samples myself tomorrow."

"I understand. Is there anything else you require?"

"Solitude." Paul smiled. "I don't want anybody in the cave for this part."

Gavin nodded and left. Paul broke out his tarps and hooks. It was best if the sampler was the person who dug the fossils out of the ground— or, better yet, if the DNA samples were taken when the bones were still *in* the ground. Less contamination that way. And there was sure to be contamination. Always. No matter what precautions were taken, no matter how many tarps or how few people worked at the site, there was still always contamination.

Paul staked the tarps down at one end and slid into the hole, a flashlight strapped to his forehead, his white paper suit slick on the moist earth. He gripped the ladder as he descended into the dark cold, the bamboo rungs flexing under his weight like thin ice. He wondered how much heavier he was than the average worker on the site. When his feet finally touched down on damp clay, he turned and squatted. The working floor was two meters by two meters.

From his perspective, he couldn't tell what the bones were—only that they were bones, in situ, half-buried in earth. But that was all that mattered. The material was soft, unfossilized; he'd have to be careful. It was commonly accepted that bones needed at least a few thousand years to fossilize. These were younger than a lot of archaeological finds.

The procedure took nearly seven hours. He coated the bone surface with sodium hyperchlorate, then used a Dremel tool to access the unexposed interior matrix. He snapped two dozen photographs, careful to record the stratigraphic context. Later it would be important to keep track of which samples came from which specimens. Whoever these things were, they were small. He sealed the DNA samples into small, sterile lozenges for transport.

It was night when he climbed from under the tarp.

Outside the cave, Gavin was the first to find him in the firelight. "Are you finished?"

"For tonight. I have six different samples from at least two different individuals."

"Yeah, that's what we thought, two individuals. So far."

"So far?"

"We're not sure how far down the cache goes. When we remove those bones, there could be more underneath."

"Is that common here?"

Gavin shrugged. "It's unpredictable. The deposits will go shy on you sometimes. You'll have a dozen feet of nothing, just sterile soil, and then you'll brush away the next centimeter and the dig will go active for another dozen feet: rat bones, and bird, and charcoal, and stone tools. Even *Stegodon*, a kind of pygmy elephant. Sometimes more interesting things."

"I'd say those bones were interesting," Paul said.

"So that means you'll stay on with us?"

"Yeah," Paul said. "I'll stay."

Gavin handed him a bottle of whiskey.

"Isn't it a little early to celebrate?"

"Celebrate? You've been working in a grave all day. Don't they drink at wakes in America?"

That night, around the campfire, Paul listened to the jungle sounds and to the voices of scientists, feeling history congeal around him.

"Suppose it isn't," Jack was saying. Jack was thin and American and very drunk. "Suppose it isn't in the same lineage with us, then what would that mean?"

The red-bearded herpetologist groaned. His name was James. "Not more of that dogma-of-descent bullshit," he said.

"Then what is it?" someone asked.

They passed the bottle around, eyes occasionally drifting to Paul like he was a priest come to grant absolution, his sample kit just an artifact of priestcraft. Paul swigged from the bottle when it came his way. They'd finished off the whiskey long ago; this was some local brew distilled from rice. Paul swallowed fire.

Yellow-haired man saying, "It's the truth," but Paul had missed part of the conversation, and for the first time he realized how drunk they all were; James laughed at something, and the woman with the white shirt turned and said, "Some people have nicknamed it the hobbit."

"What?"

"Flores man—the hobbit. You know, little people three feet tall."

"Tolkien would be proud," a voice contributed.

"A mandible, a complete cranium, segments of a radius, and left inominate."

"But what is it?"

"It is what it is."

"Exactly."

"Hey, are you staying on?"

The question was out there for three seconds before Paul realized it was aimed at him. The woman's brown eyes were searching across the fire. "Yeah," he said. "I'm staying."

Then the voice again, "But what is it?"

"That *is* the question, isn't it?"

Paul took another swallow—thinking of the bones and trying to cool the voice of disquiet in his head.

Paul learned about her during the next couple of days, the woman with the white shirt. Her name was Margaret. She was twenty-eight. Australian. Some fraction aborigine on her mother's side, but you could only see it for sure in her mouth. The rest of her could have been Dutch, English, whatever. But that full mouth: teeth like Ruteng children's, teeth like dentists might dream.

She tied her brown hair back from her face, so it didn't hang in her eyes while she worked in the hole. This was her sixth dig, she told him. "This is the one." She sat on the stool while Paul took her blood, a delicate index finger extended, red pearl rising to spill her secrets.

"Most archaeologists go a whole lifetime without a big find," she said. "Maybe you get one. Probably none. But this is the one I get to be a part of."

"What about the Leakeys?" Paul asked, dabbing her finger with cotton.

"Bah." She waved at him in mock disgust. "They get extra. Bloody Kennedys of archaeology."

Despite himself, Paul laughed.

— **10** —

This latest evidence brings us to the so-called dogma of common descent, whereby each species is seen as a unique and individual creation, discrete from all others. Therefore all men, living and dead, are descended from a common one-time creational event. To be outside of this lineage, no matter how similar in appearance, is to be other than man.

—Journal of Heredity

Bone is a text. It writes its history for those able to read it.

When Paul first started at Westing, he often worked late into the evenings. Many nights in the bone room, he would lay the skeletal remains out carefully on the clean blue felt, articulating the pieces, forming an assemblage. He matched the bones in front of him to the perfect image he held in his head.

But now, as he sat alone at the bottom of Gavin's pit, he found that no perfect image rose up in his mind. He looked at the bones, and his imagination failed him. The lights cast strange shadows across the phalanx of chalky gray-white material. Heat from the lamp made steam in the damp air. The pit smelled of earth and muck.

Somewhere above him, it was almost morning, just before dawn. In a few minutes, the rest of the camp would wake and the day would start. The team would congregate and climb down into the pit to continue the dig. Paul had woken early, needing one last look at what couldn't possibly exist.

"What are you?" he whispered into the silence of the pit. He gently blew dust away from the surface of the bone.

Anatomy textbooks say there are 206 bones in the human body, but this is not strictly true. There exists a range of variation. The number of vertebrae in the coccyx, for example, is not fixed in the human species.

Some people have more, some less. Also, there exists in some individuals of Mesoamerican ancestry an extra cranial suture. By virtue of its presence, this additional suture creates an additional bone: the Inca bone, which lies at the base of the skull in direct conjugation with the lambdoid suture and the sagittal suture.

In spite of what the Bible says, men and women possess the same number of ribs.

Bone is what remains of us after we're gone. It's as close as you can get to a permanent record of our lives.

It was in the silence and austerity of the bone room that Paul first learned that bones can answer you. They can whisper their secrets across a distance of millennia.

Now he adjusted the light. With a latexed hand, he brushed the dirt away. Here was the radius, impossibly small. Like a child's arm, though beside it rested a portion of tiny jaw—the adult molars already worn smooth.

Bone is made primarily of soft collagen and crystalline calcium phosphate. Although resistant to change and to decay, it is rarely featureless. Bone is the scaffolding on which our lives are slung, and it shows the marks of this interface. The stronger a person is, the more they mark their skeleton. There are foramina, tubercles, grooves, and tuberosities, the raised marks of muscle and ligament attachments. There are signs of trauma and healing, the stresses and strains of our lives, written in bone. And other secrets.

Bone is recycled by the living body. Calcium is laid down and picked up in a repeating pattern of formation and resorption. A never-ending cycle of birth, growth, and senescence. Like nature itself.

From above came a sound, the rattle of the tarp, pulling Paul from his reverie. Then a voice called down, "Paul?"

"Yeah," Paul answered.

"You're up early today." It was Gavin. "Didn't expect to see you down there."

"I was checking on one last thing."

"Everything okay?"

"Yeah. I'm good."

"You need anything?"

"No, I'm done here." Paul stood and gripped the ladder. He clicked off his light and climbed back up to the land of the living.

Days passed.

The dig continued. The rain continued. Jungle heat and jungle sounds. The hack of machetes on firewood. The chatter of men.

Flores.

In the distance, the Wae Racang River hissed white static against the rocks, an ever-present roar that played background music to the clamor of the busy camp.

By the fourth day, Paul had grown tired of watching everyone work. He had his samples carefully sealed in their protective lozenges. Until more bones were discovered, he technically had nothing to do, so he gave himself a job. He joined the local labor force and helped carry buckets of soil between the sieves.

At first the Manggarai workers eyed him suspiciously, this strange, big American with the Asian face, but as the hours wore on they gradually warmed to him. *Cebong Lewe* they called him, and later, sitting around the campfire, one of the researchers explained that this meant "bathe long," referring to Paul's habit of taking a dip in the river at the end of the workday. He lumbered among them, toting buckets of soil in each hand. He could carry more than they could, but he couldn't squat, couldn't kneel in the dirt, hunched for hours over the sieves. The workers rotated in their duties, first carrying buckets, then taking turns working at the fine-mesh grates. After only minutes at the sieves, Paul's knees were screaming. His calves burned like fire. He was too big, too heavy to fold himself up like that. He traded jobs with one of the bucket carriers, who seemed confused by the offer of trade. Paul realized the Manggarai viewed the bucket carrying as the work and the sieving as a break.

Back in the United States, Paul's principal form of exercise had been kayaking. He paddled the cold waters of the Chesapeake for three seasons of the year, pulling himself along with the strength of his arms.

Now Paul trudged the buckets back and forth—his body, he discovered, being particularly well suited to the role of pack animal.

The native population of Flores divided itself into a half dozen tribes:

the Lio, the Sikka, the Bajawa, the Endenese, the Ngadha, and the Nagekeo. Some of the tribes were related, others not at all. Paul had studied a book on the island's history on the long flight over. Flores sat in an intertidal zone between converging waves of Asians to the east and the older, endemic Australoid groups to the west. The men he worked with represented a complex mixture of both. Uniformly dark-skinned, many looked almost Filipino or Cambodian, with straight black hair and delicate frames; others were more Austronesian in appearance, with curly hair and strong noses. All chewed betel nuts as they worked, drooling blood-red spit into the dirt. They spoke two or three dialects apiece, and understood more.

For lunch, they ate simple meals of rice and fish, gulped small spotted eggs straight from the shell. They sipped rice wine while they ate—an extended hand, an offered jug. "Safer than the water," one of them said in perfect English.

Paul drank deep.

That evening when the dig shut down, Paul helped Gavin pack the jeep for a trek back up to Ruteng. "I'm driving two of our laborers back to town," Gavin told him. "They work one week on, one off. You want to come with me?"

"Sure," Paul said.

The trip up the valley was just as perilous as the trip down. If anything, the track had grown muddier.

Gavin rented Paul a hotel room for the night and gave him some money—three ten-thousand-rupiah notes. To Paul's questioning look, he answered, "About sixty dollars, American."

Paul showered properly and shaved his four-day stubble. He threw himself onto the bed. After the previous few nights in the camp, sleeping in a bag in a tent, this bed felt like the under-down of baby angels.

In the morning, he woke early and walked the streets, past the already thronging masses, into the bazaar. The sun angled down from a clear blue sky. A cool breeze blew up from the ocean several miles away, thick with the smells of jungle. Large black lizards, skinned and cooked, hung like ghoulish bunches of bananas from vendors' tent posts.

"Hello mister, hello mister!"

He walked on, ignoring the calls, losing himself in the crowds. Bright fabrics draped the small shops in color. The smells of spices and fresh fruit permeated the air—a multitude of vendors cooking their products in tiny, smoky stands wedged strategically into the flow of foot traffic. Music skirled from radios hung at the backs of shops, marking territory by aural display, outlining each vendor's sphere of influence.

He saw Chinese noodles and blue sarongs, and coconuts, and fish, and western T-shirts, and cigarette lighters, and shoes that would not fit him. People on bicycles and motorbikes.

He saw a trinket hanging from a post, a beaded necklace with a shark's tooth dangling from the bottom. He paused for only a millisecond, the slightest hint of hesitation, and a voice came out of the booth: "Hello, mister."

Paul turned. "How much?"

The shop owner came forward. He was old and gray and bent. His rheumy, bloodshot eyes did a quick appraisal. "With respect, sir," he said in good English, pointing to a pair of small signs that seemed to give two different prices for the same necklace. One sign read 25,000 RP and the other 15,000. "Very nice necklace. Grandson caught shark with own hands."

"Which price is it?"

"That depend," the old man said.

"On what?"

"On if you want haggle. You want haggle, we start this price here," he said, gesturing to the sign with the higher price. His knuckles were knobby with arthritis.

"I'd rather start there," Paul said, pointing to the other sign.

The man shook his head. "No, that the no-haggle price. If you want haggle, we start at twenty-five thousand rupiah. But don't worry, we talk price down."

"How far down?"

"Almost to here," he said, pointing to the lower price.

"Almost?"

"Can't haggle all the way to the no-haggle price. You understand, sir. I must earn something for my time, yes? Now I start. Mister, this is price of necklace." The old man pointed to the higher price. "Very nice necklace.

Grandson caught shark with own hands. I can go no lower. What you offer?"

Paul grinned and shook his head. "I'll take the no-haggle price." He opened his wallet and pulled out two ten-thousand-rupiah notes. He knew when he'd met his match. "Keep the change."

Paul found Gavin back at the hotel a few hours later.

"You had me worried," Gavin said. He was sitting at a table near the front steps, sipping coffee. The sun was higher now, but the building's awning provided shade.

"About what?"

"About where you'd gotten to."

Paul gestured around. "There's not a lot of places to wander off. This town isn't that big."

"Call it a healthy paranoia. To be honest, bringing you here has created some attention we didn't want yet. I had several meetings this morning—some of them unexpected. So far, we've shuffled under the radar, but now . . ." Gavin let the sentence die.

"Now what?"

"We've flown in an outside tech, and people want to know why."

"What people?"

"Official people. Unpleasant people. Indonesia is suddenly very interested."

"And I'm the outside tech in question?"

"The very same."

"I take it this interest is a bad thing."

"Interest from officials always is."

"Is it a question of permission?"

"We have all the right permits, of course, from the Ministry of Culture and Social Politics. And more permits from ARKENAS and the Department of Education—a mountain of permits, let me tell you, and half of them redundant. In Flores, bureaucracy is raised to the level of a martial art. Even our permits have permits, and all of it costs money. And worse than that, it costs *time*. Our visas come straight from the Indonesian Academy of Sciences. But maybe none of that will matter now."

"Why?"

"Because certain people might decide it doesn't matter. That's all it takes."

"Are you worried they'll shut down the dig?"

Gavin smiled. He remained silent for a while and sipped his coffee. Paul thought he wasn't going to answer, but then Gavin asked, "Have you studied theology?"

"Why?"

"I've long been fascinated by the figure of Abraham. You're familiar with Abraham?"

"Of course," Paul said, unsure where this was going.

"From this one otherwise ordinary sheepherder stems the entire natural history of monotheism. He's at the foundation of all three Abrahamic faiths—Judaism, Christianity, and Islam. When Jews, Christians, and Muslims get on their knees for their one true God, it is to Abraham's God they pray." Gavin closed his eyes. "And still there is such fighting over steeples."

Around them, Flores bustled on. A small gray van blared its horn at a swerving motorbike.

"What does this have to do with the dig?"

"The word 'prophet' traces back to the original Greek word *prophetes*. In Hebrew, though, the word is *nabi*. I think Abraham Heschel said it best when he wrote, 'The prophet is the man who feels fiercely.' What do you think, Paul? Do you think prophets feel fiercely?"

"Why are you asking me this?"

"Never mind." Gavin smiled again and shook his head. "It's just me rambling again."

"You never said if you think they'll shut down the dig."

"We come onto their land, their territory; we come into this place and we find bones that contradict their beliefs; what do you think might happen? Anything."

"Contradict their beliefs?" Paul said. "What do you believe about these bones? You still haven't said."

"I don't know. Strange bones like this, they could just be pathological."

"That's what they said about the first Neanderthal bones. Except they kept finding them."

"It could be microcephaly."

"What kind of microcephaly makes you three feet tall?"

"The odd skull shape and small body size could be unrelated. Pygmies aren't unknown to these islands."

"There are no pygmies this small."

"But perhaps the two things together . . . perhaps the bones are just a microcephalic variant on the local pygmy phenotype."

"So both pygmy *and* microcephalic?"

Gavin sighed. He looked suddenly defeated.

"That's not what you believe, is it?" Paul said.

"These are the smallest bones discovered that look anything like us. Could they just be pathological humans? I don't know. Maybe. Pathology can happen anywhere, so you can't rule it out when you've only got a few specimens to work with. But what my mind keeps coming back to is that these bones weren't found just anywhere."

"What do you mean?"

"These bones weren't found in Africa, or Asia, or Europe. They weren't found on the big landmasses. These tiny bones were found on a tiny island. Near the bones of dwarf elephants. And that's a coincidence? They hunted dwarf elephants, for God's sake."

"So if not pathological, what do you believe they were?"

"That's the powerful thing about genetics, my friend. You take your samples, do your tests. One does not have to believe. One can *know*. And that's precisely what is so dangerous."

"Strange things happen on islands." Margaret's white long-sleeved shirt was gone. She sat slick-armed in overalls. Skin like a fine coat of gloss. The firelight beat the night back, lighting candles in their eyes. It was nearly midnight, and Paul sat in the circle of researchers, listening to the crackle of the fire. Listening to the jungle. Gavin had already retired to his tent for the night.

"Like the Galápagos," Margaret said. "The finches."

"Oh, come on," James said. "The skulls we found are small, with brains the size of chimps'. Island dwarfing of genus *Homo*—is that what you're proposing? Some sort of local adaptation over the last five thousand years?"

"It's the best we have."

"But in five thousand years?"

"It's possible."

"Those bones are too different. They're not of our line."

"But they're from younger strata than the other archaics. It's not like *erectus*, some branch cut down at the dawn of time. These things *survived* here. The bones aren't even fossilized."

"It doesn't matter, they're still not us. Either they share common descent from man or they were a separate creation at the beginning. There is no in-between. And they're only a meter tall, don't forget."

"That's just an estimate."

"A good estimate."

"Achondroplasia—"

"Those skulls are as achondroplastic as I am. I'd say the sloped frontal bone is *anti*-achondroplastic."

"Some kind of growth hormone deficiency would—"

"No," Paul said, speaking for the first time. Every face turned toward him.

"No, what?"

"Pygmies have normal growth hormone levels," Paul said. "Every population studied—the Negritos, the Andamanese, the Mbuti. All normal."

The faces stared. Pale ovals in firelight. "It's the domain of their receptors that are different," Paul continued. "Pygmies are pygmies because of their GH receptors, not the growth hormone itself. If you inject a pygmy child with growth hormone, you still get a pygmy. It's a completely different etiology."

"Well, still," Margaret said. "I don't see how that impacts whether these bones share common descent or not."

The firelight crackled. James turned to the circle of faces. "So are they on our line? Are they us or other?" He looked around at the circle of faces in the firelight.

"Other," came a voice.

"Other."

"Other."

Softly, the woman whispered in disbelief, "But they had stone tools."

The faces turned to Paul, but he only watched the fire and said nothing.

———

They drank deep into the night. The wine put a nice buzz in Paul's head. One by one the researchers wandered back to their tents. Paul stood, enjoying the slight wobble to his legs.

Margaret stood, too. She grabbed his hand. "I want to show you something."

He let himself be pulled along, away from the tents, away from the cave, toward the river, to a place with tall grass and an overhang of trees. Crickets chirped loudly in the brush.

"What did you want to show me?" he asked.

"This, of course," she said, and then she kissed him.

He kissed her back, feeling her body move against him.

"Can you keep a secret?" she asked.

"Yeah."

"Are you sure?" She kissed him again.

"Absolutely," he said.

"Because people talk."

"What people?"

"All people."

"Not all people."

"Well, most people," she said, then kissed him again. "So this is our secret, just between us?"

He nodded. "Top secret."

"A girl could get a reputation," she said.

"Not from me."

"You're very convincing."

"My lips are sealed."

"Then just this once, okay?" She unhooked her overalls and let them fall to the grass. "Just this one time." Her bare breasts swayed in the moonlight, full and heavy. He touched her. She moved against him, skin on skin, and then her mouth found his, and they sank onto the grass.

Paul skipped the manual labor the next day. The sun blazed down and his head throbbed a dull hangover, reminding him that last night hadn't all been a dream. He kept an eye out for Margaret, but she hadn't emerged from her tent yet. Instead of heading to the sieves, he made his way up to the cave and stepped into the shadows. The sudden coolness was almost analgesic. He moved to the back, to the place where a bamboo ladder jutted from the ground.

He looked down at the men working thirty feet below. There were three of them. They'd excavated most of the bones that Paul had samples for and would soon be digging deeper, looking for more. The men at the bottom of the pit wore hard hats. Flashlights lit the base of the hole. The sound of the generator rumbled in the distance.

Paul tried to imagine the weight of all that dirt pressing down. He tried to imagine the processes that could have painted the bones with soil, layer after layer, year after year, until thirty feet of the world stood atop them. The floods, and the mud, and thousands of years.

James found him standing there. "A Catholic priest was first to dig here," he said, leaning over to glance down into the hole.

"When was that?"

"Oh, it was a long time ago—middle of the last century, after the Dutch first started trying to convert the island's heathen population into good, God-fearing folk."

"A priest archaeologist in the 1800s?"

James scratched his copper-wire beard. "Well, he wasn't *called* an archaeologist, mind, but he did do a wholly inordinate amount of digging for a fella with eyes turned skyward."

"Did he find anything interesting?"

"Stone tools, charcoal, a few bones. Father Theodor Verhoeven. He's been dead now a long time, and his work has been mostly ignored."

"He found bones? Like these?"

"Not like these. He didn't go that deep. The bones he found were more normal. His work probably would have been completely forgotten if not for the attention the cave is getting now."

"What about his other work?" Paul asked. "Did that go better than his digs?"

"Converting the heathens, you mean? Marginally better, I suppose."

Paul watched the men dig. Flashlights wavered at the bottom of darkness.

"Indonesia is one big mosaic now," James said. "Part Muslim, part Christian. All of it layered over the older ancestor worship and various other animist traditions. In some remote villages, they sacrifice pigs on Christian holidays."

"One religion absorbs the traditions of another."

"That's one way to put it," James said.

"And how would you put it?"

"I'd say one religion eats another. Means about the same thing but has a slightly different inflection. It's like one of the origin stories you still hear in the highlands—the first man having come from the ashes of burned bamboo. They still tell that story, though after the missionaries, they were kind enough to change his name to Adam. Flores is one of the religious borders. Always has been. There's been fighting in the Moluccas and Sulawesi. Bloody business. Maybe Gavin told you."

"He told me there was some trouble."

"And more coming, likely. And that was all happening before they even dug here," James said. "Lately it's been worse."

"It's just a research dig," Paul said.

"No such thing, these days. Between you and me, the sooner we're done, the better."

"Do digs like this end?" Paul asked.

"There's bedrock down there somewhere."

"I suppose that's true."

"So these samples," James said, gesturing toward the pit. "You're sure you can make 'em talk?"

"They'll sing. And it's more than just the DNA. There's also stable isotope analysis of bone matrix collagen."

"And this tells you what?"

Paul shrugged. "Lots of things. Ancient diet, trophic level, variation by latitude."

James nodded, taking this in. After a long pause, he asked, "Did Gavin ever tell you what this place was before?"

"Before it was a cave, you mean?"

James smiled indulgently. "After it was a cave, before it was a dig."

"No."

"They used it as a school."

"This place?"

James nodded. "Father Theodor, before he starting digging, taught school here for the local village children."

Paul looked down into the pit. "A place of learning, still."

The next morning started with a downpour. The dig team huddled in tents or under the tarped lean-to near the fire pit. Only James braved the rain, stomping off into the jungle. Paul watched him disappear into the undergrowth.

Gray clouds obscured the mountainside. The sieving crew made strong coffee and chewed betel nuts.

Gavin found Paul in his tent. He stuck his shaggy head under the tent flap. "I have to go back up to Ruteng."

"Again?"

"There's been an issue," Gavin said. "I've received some troubling news. You want me to take the samples with me?"

Paul shook his head. "Can't. There are stringent protocols for chain of possession."

"Where are they now?"

Paul patted the cargo pocket of his pant leg.

Gavin seemed to consider this for a moment. "So when you get those samples back, what happens next?"

"I'll hand them over to an evaluation team."

"You don't test them yourself?"

Paul shook his head. "I'm the sampler. I can assist in actual testing, but there are rules. I test animal DNA all the time, and the equipment is the same, but genus *Homo* requires a license and oversight."

"All right, mate, then I'll be back tomorrow." Paul followed Gavin to the jeep. There, Gavin surprised him by handing him the satellite phone. "In case anything happens while I'm gone."

"Do you think something will?"

"No," Gavin said. Then: "I don't know."

Paul fingered the sat phone, a dark block of plastic the size of a shoe. Something had changed. He could see it in the older man's face. He considered asking more but didn't.

Gavin climbed into the jeep and pulled away. Paul watched the vehicle struggle up the muddy track heading to town.

An hour later the rain had stopped and James was back from his excursion in the dripping jungle, smiling ear to ear. He returned to camp covered in mud but otherwise none the worse for the wear.

"Well, will you look at that," James said, holding something out for Paul to see.

"What is it?"

"Partially eaten monitor." His face practically beamed. "A species only found here."

"Partially eaten? You know, I would have shared my lunch."

The smile grew wider. "I'd have to be pretty hungry to take a chomp of this bit of jerky. A few bites, and it would likely be my last meal. Lots of nasty bacteria in these things, starting with their mouths. That's how they kill their prey, you know. They bite and then follow. For days, sometimes. Eventually, the bacteria does the job, and they move in for the kill."

Paul saw now that it was a clawed foot that James held in his freckled hand. It was the size of a St. Bernard's paw.

"That's one big lizard."

"Oh, no." He shook his head emphatically. "This was just a juvenile. They get a lot bigger."

"How big?"

"Big enough to worry about. Mother Nature is odd this side of the Wallace line."

"So it would appear."

"Not only are most of the species this side of the line not found anywhere else, a lot of them aren't even vaguely related to anything else. It's like God started from scratch to fill all the niches."

James reared his arm back and flung the rotting paw into the jungle. "I'd save it for my collection, but I don't have a way to preserve the tissue until we leave. Shame, really."

"This a big collection of rotting lizard parts you have?"

"Oh, you have no idea."

"How'd you get started in herpetology?"

"The bush, when I was a kid, was right out the back door. I was never any good at sports, so I used to play out there with my older brother, collecting lizards. It turned into a thing." He shrugged. "That thing turned into this thing, and here I am."

"Ah, so you have your brother to blame."

"To thank, you mean. I have him to *thank* for this lucrative and highly fulfilling career path. Also, it's a magnet for the ladies, in case you couldn't guess."

"A few days ago, McMaster mentioned a dwarf elephant."

"Yeah, stegodons."

"What happened to them?"

"They've been extinct for a long time now. This island was one of their last strongholds."

"What killed them off?"

"Same thing that killed off a lot of the ancient fauna on the island. The classic case, a volcanic eruption. We found the ash layer just above the youngest bones."

"Cataclysm," Paul whispered.

Once, lying in bed with a woman, Paul had watched the moon through the window. The woman had traced his scars with her finger.

"Your father was brutal."

"No," Paul had said. "He was broken, that's all."

"There's a difference?"

"Yeah."

"What?"

"He was always sorry afterward."

"That mattered?"

"Every single time."

— **11** —

A: *Incidences of local adaptation have occurred, sure. Populations adapt to changing conditions all the time.*
Q: *Through what process?*
A: *Differential reproductive success. Given genetic variability, it almost has to happen. It's just math and genes. Fifty-eight hundred years is a long time.*
Q: *Can you give an example?*
A: *Most dogs would fall into this category, having been bred by man to suit his needs. While physically different from each other, when you study their genes, they're all one species—though, admittedly, divided into several distinct clades.*
Q: *So you're saying God created the original dog but man bred the different varieties?*
A: *You called it God, not me. And for the record, honey, God created the gray wolf. Man created dogs.*

—Excerpted from the trial of the geneticist Mathew Poole

It came the next morning in the guise of police action. It came in shiny new Daihatsus with roll bars and off-road tires. It came with guns. Mostly, it came with guns.

Paul heard them before he saw them, men shouting in a language he couldn't understand. He was with James at the cave's entrance. When Paul saw the first assault rifle, he sprinted for the tents. He slid the DNA lozenges into a pouch in his belt and punched numbers on the sat phone. Gavin picked up on the second ring. "The police are here," Paul said.

There was a pause on the other end of the line. "I just spoke to the officials today," Gavin said. Outside the tents there were shouts—angry shouts. "They assured me that nothing like this would happen."

"They lied."

Behind him, James said, "This is bad."

"Where are you?" Paul spoke into the phone.

"I'm still in Ruteng," Gavin said.

"Then this will be over by the time you can get here."

"Paul, it's not safe for you th—"

Paul hung up. *Tell me something I don't know.*

He took his knife from his sample kit and slit the back of the tent open. He slid through, James following close behind. They crouched in the mud. Paul saw Margaret standing uncertain at the edge of the jungle. She was frozen in place, watching the men with guns, caught somewhere between running into the camp and running away from it. Paul moved his hand, a subtle gesture to catch her attention. Their eyes met, and Paul motioned toward the jeeps.

She nodded.

They all ran for it.

A dozen yards across the mud, moving quickly. They climbed into a jeep and shut the doors. The soldiers—for that's what Paul knew they were now—the soldiers didn't notice them until Paul started the engine. Malay faces swung around, mouths open in shouts of outrage. A gun came up, more shouting, and the message was clear.

Here was the choice, to comply or not. It always came down to a choice.

"You'll probably want your seat belts for this," Paul said. Then he gunned it, spitting dirt.

"Don't shoot, don't shoot, don't shoot," James whispered softly in the backseat, eyes closed in prayer.

"What?" Paul said.

"If they shoot, they're not police."

A round smashed through the rear window and blew out a chunk of the front windshield, spidering the safety glass.

"Shit!" Margaret screamed.

A quick glance in the rearview, and Paul saw soldiers climbing into one of the Daihatsus. He yanked the wheel to the right.

"Not that way!" Margaret shouted. Paul ignored her and floored the accelerator.

Jungle whipped past, close enough to touch. Ruts threatened to buck them from the cratered roadway. The Daihatsu whipped into view behind them. Shots rang out, a sound like Chinese firecrackers, the ding of metal. The land sloped downward, and for a moment the road dropped away from jeep's wheels, maxing out the suspension. The jeep landed and slid and bounced through the mud. Paul fought for control, spinning the wheel in the direction of the slide. The jeep fishtailed, and Paul spun the wheel in the other direction, gunning the engine. Mud sprayed the windows, and they accelerated through another deep rut, going airborne again.

James braced his hand against the roof of the jeep to keep from slamming his head. Margaret screamed in the passenger seat.

More shots rang out, but none struck the jeep. Their pursuers were having the same problem with the road. Still, Paul knew it was only a matter of time. There was no way they'd outrun them.

They rounded the bend, and the river came into view—wide and dumb as the sky itself. The road sloped down to the water's edge. Paul hit the accelerator.

"We're not going to make it across!" James shouted.

"We only need to get halfway."

Another shot slammed into the back of the jeep—a loud crack, the sound of hammer on metal.

They hit the river in a slow-speed crash, water roaring up and over and through the broken windshield, pouring inside in a single muddy glut, soaking the interior of the jeep, the smell of muck overpowering.

Paul stomped his foot to the floor.

The jeep chugged, drifted, caught gravel. The wheels churned across stone. They got about halfway across before Paul yanked the steering wheel to the left. The world came unstuck and started to shift. The right front fender rose up, rocking with the current. The engine died. Sudden silence.

They were floating.

Paul looked back. The pursuing vehicle skidded to a halt at the shoreline and men jumped out. The jeep heaved, one wheel pivoting around a submerged rock.

"Can you swim?" Paul asked.

"Now you ask us?"

"I'd unbuckle if I were you."

The jeep hit another rock, metal grinding on stone. Then the sky traded places with water and everything went dark.

Water surged through shattered windows. Paul caught half a breath before the river knocked him into the backseat.

His head slammed into something jagged, and he was suddenly upside down, underwater, face crushed into the jeep's roof. The river was a cold fist on his back, holding him down. The sound was deafening—rending metal and breaking glass, the scrape of stone on steel just beneath his cheek as the vehicle dredged the stony river bottom. Then the jeep rolled again, a violent movement, and the rear door flew open, twisted from its hinges—and he was suddenly out, flailing in the water.

He sucked in a lungful of air, trying to stay at the surface.

Gunshots came from behind them, bullets zinging across the water, and Paul ducked beneath the surface. He went deep, letting the cold river carry him. His shoulder slammed into a submerged boulder, knocking the air from his lungs. He surfaced again, gasping. More shots, farther away this time. Somewhere behind him, he heard the jeep slam into a rock. The cold fist of the river carried him forward.

Paul saw James paddling a dozen feet ahead of him.

"James!"

"Here!" came the answer. James coughed and splashed.

Then a moment later, from somewhere behind him: "Paul!" It was Margaret. The jeep loomed close behind, rolling in the frothing water. A battering ram ready to crush anything in its path.

"Stay to the side!" Paul shouted. "Let the current take you."

But behind Margaret the jeep hit a boulder, turned, wedged itself sideways. Water roared up and over the top, pinning it in place. Margaret kicked away.

Paul kept his feet out in front of him to fend off the rocks. Up ahead, a sound Paul knew. The roar of water, and the river dropped away.

"Jesus," James said.

There was no time for anything else. James was swept into a narrowing and then was gone, over some hidden edge. Five feet or a hundred.

"Look out!" Paul called behind him to Margaret. He sucked a deep lungful of air, and the river swept him over the falls.

There was no sense of falling, only of being in the grip of the river.

He hit and was pulled deep, spinning upside down. Kicking his way to the surface, he broke free and took a gasp of air. The current pulled him forward.

The river flattened over the next few hundred meters. Trees hung low over the water in a broad green drape, and the rapids slowly died away.

They dragged themselves out of the dark flow several miles downriver, where a bridge crossed the water. It was the first sign of civilization they'd seen since leaving the camp. For a long while, they lay on the rocky shore, just breathing. When they could stand, they followed the winding dirt road to a place called Rea. From there they took a bus. Margaret had money.

They didn't speak about it until they arrived at Bajawa.

"Do you think they're okay?" Margaret asked. Her voice wavered.

"I think it wouldn't serve their purpose to hurt the dig team. They only wanted the bones."

"They shot at us."

"Because they assumed we had something they wanted. They were shooting at the tires."

"No," she said. "They weren't."

Three nights in a rented hotel room, and James couldn't leave—that hair like a great big handle anybody could pick up and carry, anybody with eyes and a voice. Some of the locals hadn't seen red hair in their lives, and James's description was prepackaged for easy transport. Paul, however, blended—just another vaguely Asian set of cheekbones in the crowd, even if he was half a foot taller than most of the locals.

That night, staring at the ceiling from one of the double beds, James said, "If those bones aren't us . . . then I wonder what they were like."

"They had fire and stone tools," Paul said. "They were probably a lot like us."

"We act like we're the chosen ones, you know? But what if it wasn't like that?"

"Don't think about it," Margaret said.

"What if God had all these different varieties . . . all these different walks, these different options at the beginning, and we're just the ones who killed the others off?"

"Shut up," she said.

"What if there wasn't just one Adam but a hundred Adams?"

"Shut the fuck up, James," Margaret said.

There was a long quiet, the sound of the street filtering through the thin walls. "Us or other," James said softly, not a question but something else, the listing of two equal alternatives. After another long quiet he said, "Paul, if you get your samples back to your lab, you'll be able to tell, won't you?"

Paul thought of the evaluation team and wondered. He said nothing.

"The winners write the history books," James said. "Maybe the winners write the bibles, too. I wonder what religion died with them."

The next day, Paul left to buy food. There was no choice. When he returned, Margaret was gone.

"Where is she?"

"She left. She said she'd be right back."

"Why didn't you stop her?"

"How was I supposed to do that, hold her down? She said she wouldn't be gone long, and then she left."

They ate in silence. Noodles and fish.

Day turned into evening. By darkness, they both knew she wasn't coming back.

"How are we going to get home from here?" James asked.

"I don't know."

"And your samples. How are you going to get them off the island? Even if we got to an airport, they'd never let you on the plane with them. You'll be searched. They'll find the samples and they'll be confiscated."

"We'll figure out a way once things have settled down."

"Things are never going to settle down."

"They will."

"You still don't understand, even after everything that happened."

"Understand what?"

"What these bones could mean," James said. "When your entire culture is predicated on an idea, you can't afford to be proven wrong."

Out of dead sleep, Paul heard it. Something. At the edge of perception.

He'd known this was coming, though he hadn't been aware that he'd known until that moment. The creak of wood, the gentle breeze of an open door.

Shock and awe would have been better—an inrush of soldiers, an arrest of some kind, expulsion, deportation, a legal system, however corrupt. A silent man in the dark meant many things. None of them good.

Paul breathed. There was a cold in him—a part of him that was dead, a part of him that could never be afraid. A part of him his father had put there.

Paul's eyes searched the darkness and found it: the place where shadow moved, a dark breeze that eased across the room. If there was only one of them, then there was a chance.

He thought of making a run for it, sprinting for the door, leaving the samples and this place behind, but James, still sleeping, stopped him. He made up his mind.

Paul exploded from the bed, flinging the blanket ahead of him, wrapping that part of the room, and a shape moved, a theoretical darkness like a puma's spots, black on black—there even though you can't see it. And Paul knew he'd surprised him, that darkness, and he knew, instantly, that it wouldn't be enough. A blow rocked Paul off his feet, forward momentum carrying him into the wall. The mirror shattered, glass crashing to the floor.

"What the fuck?" James hit the light, and suddenly the world snapped into existence, a flashbulb stillness—and the intruder was Indonesian, crouched in a stance, preternatural silence coming off him like a heat shimmer. He carried endings with him, nothingness in a long blade. The insult of it hit home. The shocking fucking insult, standing there, knees bent, bright blade in one hand: blood on reflective steel. That's when Paul felt the pain. It was only then he realized he'd already been opened.

And the Indonesian moved fast. He moved so fast. He moved faster than Paul's eyes could follow, covering distance like thought, across the room to James, who had time only to flinch before the knife parted him. Such a professional, and James's eyes went wide in surprise.

Paul reacted using the only things he had, size, strength, momentum. He hit the intruder like a linebacker, sweeping him into his arms, crushing him against the wall. Paul felt something snap—a twig, a branch, something in the man's chest—and they rolled apart, the intruder doing something with his hands; the rasp of blade on bone, a new blackness, and Paul flinched from the blow, feeling the steel leave his eye socket.

There was no anger. It was the strangest thing. To be in a fight for his life and not be angry.

The man came at him again, and it was only Paul's size that saved him. He grabbed one arm and twisted, bringing the fight to the floor. They rolled, knocking over the table, and Paul came up on top. A pushing down of his will into three square inches of the man's throat—a caving in like a crumpling aluminum can, but Paul still held on, still pushed until the lights went out of those black eyes.

"I'm sorry," he said to the empty eyes. "I'm sorry."

Paul rolled off the dead man and collapsed to the floor. He crawled over to James. It wasn't a pool of blood. It was a swamp, the mattress soggy with it. James lay on the bed, still conscious, the neck wound a surgical gash at the carotid.

The blood from Paul's eye spattered the red beard, mixing with the blood that ran onto the bed.

"Don't bleed on me, man," James said. "I know all about you promiscuous Americans. No telling what you might carry, and I don't want to have to explain it to my girlfriend."

Paul smiled at the dying man, crying and bleeding on him, wiping the blood from his beard with a pillowcase. He held James's hand until he stopped breathing.

12

Paul's eye opened to white. He blinked. A man in a suit sat in the chair next to the hospital bed. A man in a police uniform stood near the door. "Where am I?" Paul asked. He didn't recognize his own voice. It was an older man. Who'd eaten glass.

"Maumere," the suited man said. He was white, mid-thirties, lawyer written all over him.

"How long?"

"A day."

Paul touched the bandage over his face. "Is my eye . . ."

"I'm sorry."

Paul took the news with a nod. "How did I get here?"

"They found you naked in the street. Two dead men in your room."

It came back to him then, all of it, like a weight settling onto him.

"So what happens now?"

"Well, that depends on you." The man in the suit smiled. "I'm here at the behest of certain parties interested in bringing this to a quiet close."

"Quiet?"

"Yes."

"Where is Margaret? Gavin McMaster?"

"They were put on flights back to Australia this morning."

"I don't believe you."

"Whether you believe or not is of no consequence to me. I'm just answering your questions."

"What about the bones?"

"Confiscated for safekeeping, of course. The Indonesians have closed down the dig."

"On what grounds?"

"It is their cave, after all."

"What about my DNA samples in the hotel room, the lozenges?"

"They've been confiscated and destroyed."

Paul sat quietly. He looked at the man, imagining his skull beneath the thin layer of epidermis. He knew all his bones would be smooth and fine, with hardly a mark of muscle attachment, the perfect gracile skeleton.

"How did you end up in the street?" the man asked.

"I walked."

"How did you end up naked?"

"I figured it would increase my odds."

"Explain."

"I knew what they wanted," Paul said. "And I was bleeding out. Being naked was the fastest way to prove I wasn't armed and didn't have the samples. I knew they'd still be coming."

"You are a smart man, Mr. Carlsson, leaving those in the hotel room." The suited man stood, apparently satisfied with Paul's answers. "So you figured you'd just let them have the samples?"

"Yeah," Paul said.

The man nodded his good-bye, then turned to leave. He closed the door behind himself.

"Mostly," Paul said.

On the way to the airport, Paul told the driver to pull over. He paid the fare and climbed out. He took a bus to Bengali, and from there took a cab to Rea.

He climbed on a bus in Rea, and as it bore down the road Paul yelled, "Stop!"

The driver hit the brake. "I'm sorry," Paul said. "I've forgotten something." He climbed off the bus and walked back to town, checking for a tail. No car followed.

Once in town, down one of the small side streets, he found it: the flowerpot with the odd pink plant. The flowerpot whose appearance and location he'd memorized the week before, when he'd first left the hotel room covered in blood. He scooped dirt out of the base.

An old woman shouted something at him, coming out of her house. He held out money. "For the plant," he said. "I'm a flower lover." She might not have understood English, but she understood money.

He walked with the plant under his arm. James had been right about some things. Wrong about others. Not a hundred Adams, no.

Just two.

All of Australoid creation like some parallel world.

But why would God create two Adams? That's what Paul had wondered. The answer was that He wouldn't.

Two Adams.

Two gods. One on each side of the Wallace line.

Paul imagined that it began as a competition. A line drawn in the sand, to see whose creations would dominate.

Paul understood the burden Abraham had carried, to witness the birth of a religion.

As Paul walked through the streets he dug his fingers through the dirt of the flowerpot. His fingers touched it, and he pulled the lozenge free. The lozenge no evaluation team would ever lay eyes on. He would make sure of that.

He slid the last remaining DNA sample into his pocket.

He passed a woman in a doorway, an old woman with beautiful teeth like dentists might dream. She reminded him of someone. He thought of the bones in the cave, and of the strange people who had once crouched on this island, fashioning tools from bits of stone.

He handed her the flower. "For you," he said.

He hailed a cab and climbed inside. "Take me to the airport."

As the old cab bounced along the dusty roads, Paul took off his eye patch. He saw the driver glance into his rearview and then look away, repulsed.

"They lied, you see," Paul told the driver. "About the irreducible complexity of the eye. Oh, there are ways."

The driver turned his radio up, keeping his face forward. Paul pulled off the bandage. He grimaced as he unpacked his eye, pulling white gauze out in long strips, pain exploding in his skull. It was more pain than he'd ever experienced in his life, a white-hot nova in his head. The gauze made a small, bloody pile on the seat next to him.

"A prophet is one who feels fiercely," he said, and then he slid the lozenge into his empty eye socket.

PART III

Nature does nothing in vain.

—ARISTOTLE

13

Gavin stepped out into daylight and spit blood onto the sun-bleached concrete. New South Wales, the sound of jets.

He scanned the faces at the airport entrance, looking for the familiar, the unfamiliar, the out of place. He saw people coming and going. Taxis and buses and cars. People in a hurry, people laughing or frustrated, people towing suitcases or duffel bags or children. He stood, and he watched, and he saw no one he recognized. He saw not a single thing to arouse his suspicions.

Gavin nodded to himself, accepting finally what he had before only suspected. They hadn't even bothered to have him followed.

He understood that for what it was: a parting insult.

He started walking, for the first time feeling like the nightmare of the last four days might really be over. The reality of being in Australia gradually sank in. He was home.

Unconsciously, he rubbed his swollen jaw.

It was his fault, of course. The beating. Everything.

He opened his cell phone and punched in the numbers.

"It's Gavin," he said. "I'm here." Then, after a silence: "It's bad."

He spoke for another minute, explaining what needed to be done. He snapped his phone closed and slid it back into his pocket. There were other calls he needed to make. Calls to the university, and to the embassy, but he didn't have the energy right now. There would be time for that soon enough. There would be official inquiries, investigations, an official response to everything that had happened. It would be out of his hands. For now, though, he just wanted to get to his office. Prepare himself for what was to come.

The soldiers had taken his briefcase and his papers. Of his various forms of ID, only his passport remained, and they'd let him keep that only because he'd needed it to board the plane. The soldiers had stood with him in the Jakarta airport terminal. They hadn't taken off his handcuffs until he'd stepped onto the aircraft.

A bus horn sounded. Gavin tasted blood in his mouth and spit again. Bright red. Like betel nut juice.

The beating hadn't been planned, because it hadn't been necessary. An overzealous guard said, "Move," and Gavin had been shoved hard down the hall to the interrogation room. Gavin hadn't liked that, being manhandled, and he'd glared over his shoulder at the guard. The guard only smiled. He was short and fat, maybe five-six, flat Malaysian nose, face like a fist.

Gavin slowed his walk and prepared for the next shove, rolling his shoulder away when it came—and the guard had lost his balance, embarrassed in front of the others. Then came the guard's roundhouse, splitting Gavin's lip against his teeth and sending him careening against the wall.

It's hard to fight back when you're in handcuffs.

He should have known better. Indonesia was not a place to confront authority. And the short cops, anywhere, were always the biggest assholes.

Gavin waved down a taxi. He collapsed inside and slammed the door.

"No luggage?" the driver asked.

"No."

"Where to?"

Gavin gave the address.

The driver looked skeptical. "A long drive," he said.

"And a big tip."

The taxi pulled away from the curb. The miles rolled by, and the shadows lengthened outside the window. By the time the taxi pulled up to the university offices it was evening, and the campus was in the process of emptying itself. Most of the faculty had already left for the night. He was grateful for that.

Gavin paid the driver and crossed the street to the building's entrance. He took the stairs up to the second floor and continued on to his office door, fidgeting the key into the lock. He stepped inside and hit the lights. He closed the door, being careful to lock it again behind him. He turned.

The envelope looked wrong on his desk. The stark white alienness of it.

Gavin sank into his leather swivel chair and pulled a bottle of good whiskey from his bottom desk drawer. He had the only key to this office. He wondered what would happen next. There were several different ways this could go. The envelope hadn't been there when he'd left.

He closed his eyes and thought of Margaret and his dig team.

During his interrogation, the Indonesian officials had done their best to impress upon him his good fortune. They'd done their best to communicate their extreme leniency, their kindness for not having him charged with the many crimes for which he was so obviously guilty, for not having him imprisoned, or tortured, or confined in close quarters with sodomites. The lead interrogator had sat across the table from him and said, "We are a forgiving people, a forgiving country, we Indonesians." He spoke in a thick Bahasa accent, his hands folded in front of himself on the table as if in prayer to a merciful and forgiving god. "We are tolerant to the point of indulgence. Tolerant beyond the point of our own best self-interest. This tolerance is taken for weakness by some. Tell me, do you think we are weak?"

Gavin said nothing.

"We are a kind people, and this kindness is often taken advantage of by foreigners. Tell me, do you think we are kind?"

Silence. A drop of blood dripped from Gavin's lip to his shirt.

The interrogator seemed to take this as a response. "You are a lucky man, Professor, and you shall just be deported for your crimes. If it was my choice, it would be different." He stood. "You are hereby expelled and your research visa revoked."

"What crimes?" Gavin asked.

"Attempted theft of national heritage materials," the interrogator said. "A very serious offense."

"I had the permits."

"That is strange," he said. "We have no permits on file."

Hours later, when Gavin was sitting in a dark cell, they told him, too, about James. An unfortunate "incident," they called it. His body found in a hotel room. A robbery gone wrong. A young life cut short. "We will, of course, be searching for the perpetrator."

Gavin wondered about Paul but did not ask. Wherever he was, Gavin couldn't help him. He hoped the boy wasn't hurt. He felt responsible for Paul, as he'd once felt responsible, in some ways, for Paul's father.

Gavin took another long pull of whiskey.

He looked down at the envelope that should not have been there. He saw his name written in a familiar hand. A hand he hadn't read in a long time. He tore open the envelope and pulled out a single sheet of paper. A ticket fell out. Gavin looked at it. It was a plane ticket.

He turned the paper over; on it was written a single word: *Come*. Gavin took another long pull of whiskey, concentrating on the burn.

14

Hospital white. The distant beep of an alarm.

Paul hauled himself to a sitting position when the nurse entered the room.

She was young and blond and might have been pretty on other nights, in other situations.

"You received quite an injury," she said while going over his chart.

Hospital small talk, Paul decided. That was one difference between the hospitals in the United States and those back in Indonesia.

Paul said nothing. There was nothing to say.

She glanced up from the clipboard. "It says here the enucleation procedure was performed out of country?"

"Yes."

"Where?"

"Maumere."

"They did a decent job, but you have some recent infection in the orbit. We have you on two hundred and fifty milligrams of penicillin via the IV, every six hours. It's working, so you got lucky. You're also on four milligrams of morphine, as needed. You have to ask for that, but we also give it through the IV, so it works fast. Do you have much pain?"

"Yes."

She injected morphine into the tubing of his IV. "This should help."

He felt the change by the time she walked out the door. A spreading warmth in his veins.

He slept. And saw James walking on the ice—the sky above scrawled black with branches.

Snow fell. The wind blew through the trees, while a lure dangled, swaying in the wind. James smiled, teeth bright red with betel nut.

A new sound woke him, and this time it was a man looking over the chart at the end of his bed. A man in a white doctor's coat. Over his shoulder, the windows had gone dark. Night had fallen.

The man caught his stare. He smiled. "I'm Dr. Harcoff. How are you feeling?"

"I don't know." It was an honest answer. What Paul felt was disconnected.

The doctor nodded like he understood. His stethoscope was silver. He wore a silver watch. "Your body has suffered a major insult," Dr. Harcoff said. "But in addition to the physical trauma, the loss of an eye can be an enormous psychological blow. We have counselors who can help if you feel you need it."

"No," Paul said. "I'm fine." He was alive, after all. James wasn't.

The doctor's brow furrowed. He scribbled something on the chart.

"An ocularist will fit you with a more permanent prosthetic in six to eight weeks. Right now you have something temporary."

"Why do I have to wait so long?"

"There's a window of best opportunity. If we tried to fit you with an artificial eye before that, there won't be enough healing. If we wait too long after that, then the socket can atrophy and it's hard to get a good functional result."

"Functional?"

"Your existing eye muscles will be attached to a new motility implant and you should get near-normal eye movement. That's important from an aesthetic perspective. Right now you have a silicone conformer in place to retain orbit volume."

"It's in there now?"

"Yes."

Paul nodded. The doctor moved closer. He placed the clipboard on the bed and opened the bandages around the wound. He studied it for a moment, then closed the bandages again.

"It looks like there will be some exterior scarring from the initial traumatic injury, but the wound has clean edges, and the stitches are good. Eye shape differs widely among individuals and you're fortunate; to be perfectly blunt with you, ocular prosthetics often seem less noticeable in people with epicanthic folds. For patients with prominent eyes, it's sometimes a challenge to reproduce a natural appearance." He paused and regarded Paul closely. "You'll have a diagonal scar across your eyelid, but the artificial eye itself shouldn't be noticeable at all. We'll be able to match your eye color exactly, and by the time we're done, the only difference between your new eye and your old one is that you won't be able to see out of it. Do you wear glasses?"

"No."

"How is the vision in your good eye?"

"Good."

The doctor nodded. "As for the silicone conformer currently in place, you just need to be careful when you wipe your eyes for the next few weeks. Most people opt to wear dark glasses or an eye patch until the conformer is replaced by a full prosthetic. The conformer doesn't simulate a natural appearance."

"When can I leave?"

"We're going to keep you a little longer for observation and to watch for infection. I should be able to let you know tomorrow. Do you have any other questions?"

Paul shook his head.

"Good. I can recommend a plastic surgeon later to deal with soft-tissue scarring."

"No, no plastic surgery. Scars don't bother me."

The doctor nodded and left. When he was gone, Paul stood and walked into the bathroom, pulling the IV pole behind him. He stood in front of the mirror. Being careful to keep his injured eye closed, he lifted the bandage to survey the damage.

He stared at himself.

His eye was fucked, he decided.

The scar neatly bisected his closed eyelid, crossing at a slight angle to the vertical and extending up to put a notch in the bottom of his eyebrow. It occurred to him how close he'd come to dying. If the knife had just gone a little deeper . . .

Then he opened the ruined eye. He stared at himself.

One eye was dark and piercing—like his mother's eyes. The other was a smoky white, the eye of a ghost.

The eye of the dead.

They kept him in the hospital for two more days. Time enough to hit bottom. Time enough to think about where things went wrong.

Mr. Lyons came to visit him on the second day. "We're so sorry about what happened, Paul. This was a tragedy."

And then other people from the lab.

"You gave us quite a scare."

"We're glad to have you back."

"The doctors are gonna have you up in no time."

And Hongbin, his coworker from the lab, ever the clown. "Someday they'll come up with a bionic eye," he said. He leaned close and whispered, "Then *you'll* have the advantage."

Later that evening, Mr. Lyons returned, a lawyer with him this time. Another suit. Hands were shaken, introductions made. "You don't need to worry about the bills," the man said. "The company is going to pick up everything."

Paul sensed that they expected a response. "Thank you," he said.

Mr. Lyons looked different.

Paul noticed it right away.

His face was different, all business this time. So this was it, then. The debriefing. Paul had been waiting for it. The two men sat. It was very formal. They asked their questions.

"Could you describe what happened, in your own words?"

So Paul told the story. Told it just how it was, just how it went down. Talked about the dig, and the bones, and the soldiers, and the river. He talked about the hotel room and the darkness. He talked about the throat like a crushed aluminum can, and only then did Mr. Lyons's face change again. A new look in his eyes, business falling away.

And then the corporate lawyer said it. The thing he shouldn't have. The thing that jangled, that told its own story.

"Did you get the samples?"

Paul stared at him. Bore into him with his one good eye.

The question had something pressing in from behind it, and Paul knew suddenly that their whole conversation had merely been foreplay. It had just been a prelude to this moment.

"No," he said. "No, they took everything."

The men nodded, as if pleased with his answer. They shook his hand again.

"I look forward to seeing you back at work," Mr. Lyons said. "And again, we're very sorry about what happened. Nobody should have to go through that." The men left.

Later that night, the doctor came in to check on him one last time. He made a short examination, then signed the discharge papers. An hour later, two nurses were wheeling him to the front of the building— "standard procedure," they insisted when he said he could walk. A cab sat idling for him at the hospital's entrance. He gave his apartment address to the man in the front seat.

And then the hospital rolled past.

Paul rested his face against the cool glass.

A bridge. Water. Baltimore, and a brick apartment block. The car came to a stop in front of his building. He paid the cabbie and took the stairs, two flights.

As he climbed, his eye started throbbing. No, not his eye, he told himself. The place where his eye had been. Like this, the place where his life had been.

The conformer felt heavy, alien, not a part of him. His head felt light, and he stopped at the top of the stairs, willing himself not to faint. He wondered about phantom limb syndrome; soldiers who'd lost an arm or a leg would sometimes swear they could still feel it, swear they could wiggle their toes. He wondered if that applied to eyes, too. Would he swear he could see something that wasn't really there? What would he see with his ghost eye?

Paul opened his front door and stepped inside. He put his keys on the hook near the door. Next he went to the kitchen and filled a big cup of water, and then he watered his plants, which were quite obviously dead. He hadn't had time to water them the first night he'd been back. That first night, when he still hadn't gone to the hospital yet.

When he'd come home first, after the airport.

His neighbor had seen the eye patch that night, and she'd been horrified. "What happened?" she'd asked.

Paul said, "You should see the other guy."

Now he went to his medicine cabinet. He steadied himself against the sink for a moment, waiting for the world to stop swaying. He opened the pill bottle, and there, at the bottom, just where he'd hidden it four days earlier, he found the lozenge.

15

Baltimore is a place half in and half out of the water.

It sits at the western edge of the Chesapeake, at the confluence of the Patapsco River and the Middle Branch of the great bay. Although it is more than fifty miles from the open ocean, the region's highways cross saltwater channels on two sides. There are tides and mudflats and seagulls. Shipwrecks jut from the shallows like the bones of leviathans. Here, the ocean has made an effort to move inland. It has made a point of it.

Baltimore is a place of bridges. The enormous Francis Scott Key Bridge stretches four lanes wide, shore to shore, a hundred feet above the waves. To the east of Baltimore, at Sparrows Point, the land divides itself into a series of lobed peninsulas that thrust for miles out into the open water of the bay. On a map, here, the line drawn between water and land forms a jagged male signature—jutting spines of rock and soil and marsh, the ins and outs of countless tiny waterways. It is a place of ancient, rusting mills, and dusty slag piles, and wildlife. It is a place at the very edge.

In the distance, along one of the farthest spines of land, at the edge of the edge, is Westing.

It is an old industrial park. A property that used to produce iron and steel and good pensions. A place backed against the water.

The gates are rusted chain link. Barbed wire spirals itself along the top of a sagging fence that disappears into secondary growth along the side of the road. Small shrubs sprawl from choked ditches.

The guard shanty sits just beyond the open fence gates. To the uninitiated, the property looks for all the world like what it used to be: some industrial relic, a dying entity, a place from the past. There is no street sign to tell you where you are. Weeds grasp for toeholds in every gathering of accumulated soil. To the local flora, this is postapocalypse. Life fighting its way back from concrete oblivion.

But beyond the single unsmiling guard, up the road and around the curve, the deepest nature of the place reveals itself, and it becomes part of another age.

The first time Paul saw the facility, he knew.

It was a place of glass and black magic.

Westing, hiding in broad daylight.

Paul pulled to a stop in his assigned parking space and turned off the ignition. He took a deep breath, listening to the silence in his car. His head hurt. Everything hurt. He blinked. He stepped out of the car and walked up the cement stairs to the building's entrance. From the gates, it looked like nothing at all, an abandoned property, but here, on the other side of the bend, it was state-of-the-art. Glass and sprawling, six stories of it, a building from a future that might never happen.

He flashed his badge to the desk guard and hit the elevator button. The guard seemed taken aback by Paul's black leather eye patch but said nothing.

The elevator dinged.

Paul got off on the third floor and made his way down the hall.

One of the secretaries—Julie, he thought her name was—smiled at him as he walked by. "Welcome back," she said.

"Thanks," he said. "Good to be back."

He was almost past her when she called after him, "We put your mail on your desk."

He arrived at his office. He paused at the threshold before pushing the door open and stepping inside. It seemed like months since he'd been here, years maybe. *Could it really have been only weeks?* That didn't seem possible. So much had changed since the last time. He was a different person now.

The lights in his office came on automatically, triggered by motion detectors Paul had never been able to locate. The only way to turn the lights off was to sit perfectly still for a long period of time. On some days, Paul was certain this period was ten minutes; on other days, an hour. The other researchers complained of it often; it was a common topic of conversation in the lab. "To keep the lights on, you have to wave your arms in the air," one might say, then add, "Like a rooster."

But Paul liked the dark. He sometimes found himself engaged in his work, typing on his computer, and there would come a loud click, and the lights would go out, and he'd find himself sitting in the shadows, facing a glowing computer screen. He'd look around the room in wonder. Darkness was a gift.

He put his briefcase down and considered the formidable stack of papers on his desk. He picked up the pile and leafed through his mail—magazines, mostly. *Principia Biologica, Theist-informatics, Materials and Method, Design Interpretation, Precept Monthly.* Trade magazines he'd never ordered but which had begun to show up, by some mysterious process, when he'd first gotten an office with his name on the door.

He tossed the whole pile in the trash and sat.

It was warm in his office. He loosened his tie and opened his white shirt, glancing around. His office was the caricature of an office, he decided. The furniture was office furniture, too small for him, bought from a catalog. The walls were painted office color. He imagined the can of paint had said "office" right on its side, as a signal to those in corporate purchasing. Have an office that needs painting? Here, use this.

There were no windows, and for that he was grateful. It made it different from the hospital room.

The books, too, made it different—shelves and shelves of books. Books stacked neatly in the corners; books on anatomy and archaeology and genetics; books about Peking man and Jane Goodall and the subatomic structure of the atom. Books on *Mus musculus*.

Other than the books, the room's principal ornamentation was a single dog skull, coated in paraffin wax, that sat on the corner of his desk.

"I'm home," he said, and then he put his face in his hands.

Bone is heavy. It is substantial. All bone at Westing had this in common: it had once been alive, but by the time Paul got to see it it was not.

It was late afternoon and Paul sat at his computer, staring at the images on the screen.

He clicked the mouse and new images appeared. He studied them for a moment, comparing them to the image in his head. He clicked again. He'd been at it for hours now.

New images appeared. He scrolled on.

When he was in college, he'd developed a fascination for skulls. He'd spent hours staring at the pictures: *Homo habilis, Homo ergaster,* the numerous and varied australopithecines. Each variety had its own museum holotype—the remains of a single diagnostic individual meant to perfectly represent the species. All additional specimens existed, by definition, at variance from these holotypes and were in some sense defined by them. Paul finally reached a point where he could recognize not just the species but the individual specimens themselves. The Taung child, Sangiran17, and Atapuerca 5. He knew them at a glance. There was the enigmatic Lusaka specimen—the holotype for a rare anthropoid species whose existence in the scientific literature depended solely on the interpretation of a single mandible. Sometimes the holotype and the complete record were the same.

In class once, a professor had asked if someone could name the kind of skull shown on the projector. Paul had raised his hand. "That's Amud 1," he'd said. The professor had blinked. "Neanderthal" had been the answer he was looking for. Neanderthals were an ancient population of man that had spread across Europe, western Asia, and the Middle East. They were an ethnic group. "Distinct," the professor said. "But no longer extant."

Whether their kind had been killed off or subsumed was hardly a matter of much debate anymore. Their genes made fractional contributions to most peoples north of the Red Sea—a small but measurable admixture variously interpreted in context with the great flood or the earliest sojourn beyond the garden.

In the summer between his sophomore and junior years, Paul had gone on a road trip, hitting half a dozen museums, because he'd wanted to see the bones in person. He'd already read what other scientists thought of them. He'd digested their theories, which he knew had changed over time, and would likely change again. Only the bones themselves were immutable.

In second-year anatomy, that same professor had placed five skulls on a table at the beginning of the class.

"Each of these skulls was dug out of the ground on a different continent," the professor said. "I want you to tell me which continent each skull comes from."

"How old are they?" someone asked, looking for a hint.

"They're all relatively modern; the oldest is from the eighteen hundreds. And this one here," the professor said, touching the top of one of the skulls, "is only a few decades old."

He looked out at his audience of students. In front of each skull, he placed a small paper sign facedown, so the students couldn't read them.

"This isn't a trick question. Each of these skulls belongs to one of the five major racial types," he said. "Write down the name of a continent for each skull. You have five minutes."

The students stared. They got up from their desks and approached the skulls. They picked them up and weighed them with their hands. The skulls looked similar to one another in a broad sense, though there were differences. The shape of the jaws varied, as did the shapes of the teeth, the mastoid, and cheekbones. It was difficult to tell how those differences in bone might translate into the soft-tissue appearance.

Each of the students wrote their answers on a small white card.

At the end of the class, the professor flipped the signs over, showing where the skulls were from. One was from Europe, another from Africa, the others from Asia, Australia, and the Americas.

Only Paul had gotten them all right.

"How did you know?" the professor asked him.

"I'm not sure," Paul said. And it was the truth. Maybe he'd gotten lucky.

"There are computer programs you can use," the professor said. "You take a dozen craniographic measurements at various points around the skull, and then you plug the numbers into the program. The software takes it from there and spits out an ethnicity, usually with a high degree of accuracy. But it's hard to tell sometimes with just the naked eye unless you have a knack for it. For some, the eye can do the same complex math that computers can." He gave Paul an appraising look. "Sometimes the eye is even better."

Paul nodded. The professor turned, addressing the entire class again. "There is a simple rule of thumb, though it doesn't always work. If you're ever in a situation where you need to make a quick educated guess, that rule of thumb is this. When you look at a skull for the first time, ask yourself what the first thing you notice is. The very first thing. What jumps out at you? If the first thing you notice is the nose, the midfacial region here"—he tapped one of the skulls with a ruler—"then the skull is likely Caucasoid. If the cheekbones are the first thing you notice, then the skull is likely of East Asian origin. And if it's the mouth—a marked sub-nasal prognathism—then the skull is likely African. So remember: Caucasians, nose; Asians, cheekbones; Africans, mouth. And keep in mind that when using this method, you'll be wrong about forty percent of the time."

Paul sat at his desk in his office and stared at his computer monitor. He scrolled down through the images. Saved on his computer hard drive were photographs of all the major anthropological specimens that had been found in the last sixty years. He was searching for one that looked like what he'd seen in Liang Bua. He continued scrolling until he got to the bottom and there were no more skulls to look at. The screen was blank. There was nothing small enough.

Nothing like Liang Bua.

He stared at the screen, and his mind drifted.

There were many skulls in the Westing bone room. Some of them were fantastically old. Others had been wrapped in life as recently as a few hundred years ago. Paul couldn't look at the skulls without hearing his professor's rule of thumb: *What jumps out at you?* And as with nearly all such rules, it was from the exceptions that the most interesting data could be drawn.

There was a loud click and the room went black. The only light came from the glowing computer screen.

Darkness like a gift.

16

Y ou're gonna clog your arteries eating that shit."

Paul followed Hongbin into the lunchroom, paper bag in hand. He sat with the group. Five researchers hailing from all points of the globe, eating wildly different meals. The lunch table took up one corner of the small glass room. The room was too bright and smelled of industrial cleanser. One wall lined with vending machines, the other with posters. A large sign entreated them to WASH HANDS THOROUGHLY BEFORE EATING. Below that, a smaller sign reminded them that WESTING IS A SECULAR FACILITY. This was both a reminder not to discuss religion in the break room and a mark of distinction, parochial labs having become more common throughout the world in recent years. Paul ate his usual burger and fries.

"Better than that crap you eat," Paul offered.

"It's called a balanced diet," Hongbin said. "You should try it sometime."

"Balanced? All you eat is Chinese."

"A billion brunettes can't be wrong," Hongbin said.

In days past, the joking might have escalated. Mothers might have been invoked. But they were still going light on him. Paul's experiences had made him different, like a man returned from the wilderness, or from war—a man who had seen things he would never explain.

"You eating real food," Paul said around a mouthful of fries. "Now, *that* would give me a heart attack." He took a swig of his Coke.

"You see, yet another reason to stick to my usual. I wouldn't want to be held responsible for your inevitable cardiovascular collapse." Hongbin tipped his white foam cup toward Paul. "To your health," he said, then sipped noisily from the straw.

"To my health."

"Speaking of health, have you talked to anyone in sequencing yet?"

"About what?"

"About anything."

"Haven't been up there yet," Paul said. In the two weeks he'd been back, he'd mostly stayed on his floor.

"So you haven't heard about Charles?"

"What about him?"

"He's not coming back."

Paul's brow furrowed. "I didn't know he'd left."

Hongbin took a bite of his noodles. "Some kind of extended leave," he said.

"Not what I heard," Makato chimed in.

"What did you hear?"

"Something different," Makato said. "A breakdown."

Strange Charles. Paul took another bite of his burger, considering the news.

Odd things happened in the long tail of the bell curve.

Like Charles.

"How long has he been out?" Paul asked.

"Since just before you got back."

They finished their meals. Paul crumpled up his bag and tossed it into the trash on the way out the door. "I'll catch up," he told them, then stooped and pretended to tie his shoe.

For Paul, the last couple of weeks had been about pretending. He'd driven to work each morning, pretending life was normal, carding himself through security doors like nothing was different. He nodded to people in the halls, simulating his old life.

Waiting.

Waiting for the Hallmark cards to stop, sent in pastel envelopes.

Waiting for an end to the phone calls. To the well-wishers, and drop-ins, and long-time-no-sees.

They'd come to his office to shake his hand, saying how happy they were to have him back. Makato had brought him a gift, a small bamboo plant grown in a tight spiral. They said how sorry they were to hear about his injury. That's what they called it, most of them: his injury. Only Hongbin had called it his eye, saying, "Seriously, chicks dig pirates."

Paul had smiled at that one. Hongbin.

Hongbin, square and muscular, raised outside San Diego by doctor parents. He was so thoroughly American that he didn't feel the need to Johnny up his name. Perhaps when he was younger he'd done it. Perhaps he'd gone by Henry, or Harry, or Benny. But not now. He was just Hongbin.

Paul accepted the cards and gifts. He waited to blend in again, to become part of the wallpaper.

News of what happened had preceded him—a story as communicable as any virus, passed by casual contact. He learned that people had heard there'd been a robbery in Indonesia, a break-in at the hotel, and things had gone badly somehow. He learned that people thought there'd been a struggle and a researcher had died. He learned that people thought the police had killed the assailant. Perhaps Westing had come up with the story, or perhaps the story had written itself, precipitated itself from the soluble facts—and become what it was, a thing so logical and reasonable that of course it must have happened that way. Of course.

And Paul said nothing to contradict the accepted version. It was easier to let it pass. Perhaps there need be no grand conspiracies in the world. Perhaps in this simple way are the world's secrets hidden.

Paul nodded and said all the right things.

"I'm fine," he told them when they came in to see him. "I'll be fine. Thank you."

And he waited for his chance.

Brandon from the second floor had stopped by his office one afternoon, and they'd talked about sports, because talking about sports felt normal and familiar. It was a comforting script, and they both had their lines.

"The Patriots," Brandon said. "I've got a feeling."

Paul nodded. "Could be."

"Yeah, this is the year," Brandon said. "I'm telling you. They're due."

And they could both pretend for a minute that maybe it worked that way.

Paul finished rearranging his shoelaces and stood. He headed for the stairs, glancing behind himself to see if anyone had noticed.

Most of the third floor belonged to the osteo lab. On the second floor were the tech offices and the storage vaults, along with the secretaries, the conference rooms, and the computer specialists.

But the fourth floor belonged to DNA. It was its own fiefdom.

Paul took the stairs up and pushed through to the fourth floor. He nodded to a researcher whose name he didn't know. The woman gave him an odd look but said nothing.

He walked the halls, refamiliarizing himself with the layout, counting the doors and exits, noting the badge swipes. The fourth floor had a ring-in-ring configuration, and his current badge got him only to the outer circle. The inner sanctum was out of reach.

He took the stairs back down.

Paul passed his days in a blur of busy, solitary work. He categorized the incoming bones and readied samples for the DNA analysis that would be performed on the fourth floor. He took photographs and made up specialized mulches.

Preparing a sample for testing required destruction of existing material, a small portion of bone. It was a solemn event. What was destroyed could never be brought back, so you had to be sure that what you'd learn was worth the cost. All knowledge requires some sacrifice.

Paul pulverized bone into a fine powder, to which a special solvent was applied over low heat, and then this slurry was injected into the sterile lozenges for preservation. The lozenges were then taken to the fourth floor, where the DNA samples were extracted and tests performed.

He did his job the way he'd always done it. It came easy to him.

If you stare at bone long enough, you come to appreciate its solidity. Its material constancy. For most aspects of living organisms, phenotype is a maddening blur—things like hair color, skin color, weight, muscle mass.

All difficult to quantify and subject to change. Subject to health and age, and season, and nutrition. Subject to being alive. Not so with bone.

Bone is resistant to the world's exigencies.

People less so.

In the evenings, Paul drove home in the dying light, fighting traffic on the Francis Scott Key Bridge. When he arrived at his apartment, he watered his plants, which, except for the spiral bamboo, were all well and truly dead. But he watered them anyway.

Each night he looked at himself in the bathroom mirror. He would take off his eye patch and study the scar. He'd look into the smoky ghost eye. "I am less," he said once, and this gave him pause. That he'd said it.

Each night he'd open his medicine cabinet. He would unscrew the top of the plastic bottle and look at the sample.

He arrived at the lab early one morning, before the rush of the other researchers and techs. In his office, he leaned back in his leather swivel chair, fingers laced behind his head.

He looked up and saw a face hidden in the grooves and notches of the acoustical ceiling tiles. He saw it clear as day: a nose here, the curve of a lip—and there, two shadowy eyes looking down. Depending on how he interpreted the lower lip, the face could almost seem to be smiling.

He looked at it for a long while, wondering how he could have been in this office for nearly three years and never noticed it, never sensed that face gazing down at him.

He shut his eye for a moment, willing the image away. When he opened his eye again, the face was gone. The grooves were still there. The textures. But they were just textures now and nothing more. A swirl without pattern.

He concentrated. He tried to see the face again but couldn't. No matter how hard he tried, he could assemble nothing from it.

That was happiness. Something you see for a moment.

The next afternoon, a new shipment of bones arrived, packed in green foam. Hongbin wheeled the samples in on a small metal cart. The label read XTN-2421. They could have been from anywhere, a series of small bone dissections completely lacking in morphological detail.

Paul crossed the room and grabbed his safety glasses, preparing for the procedure ahead. He adjusted the straps so that the glasses fit his face. Behind him, Hongbin started dividing the samples into two equal sets. Paul approached the counter and picked up the pestle. Working with bone meant working with your hands. He placed one small bone dissection into the mortar. In the early days of DNA extraction, they'd used drills for this kind of work. Most bones, the scientists had found, were barren of DNA. At speeds above 260 revolutions per minute, heat from the drill bit denatures protein structure. In trying to extract DNA, they'd destroyed it.

Paul applied the pestle, grinding the sample to a fine powder.

If you worked in bones long enough, you could be promoted to the fourth floor. But Paul had never wanted that. He'd never craved advancement.

Paul was a bone man. A field man. A necessary evil. The gene freaks knew him by his nucleotide base-pair sequence.

"Pestle," Hongbin said.

Paul passed Hongbin the pestle and started prep on the next sample. They took turns.

Everybody who set foot above the second floor had to be genotyped. It was the only way to publish in the hypercompetitive world of human genomics. You had to be able to prove you'd eliminated all sources of contamination, and having a walking, talking unmapped DNA factory wandering around your clean room was not acceptable. Until you genotyped everyone, it was like taking water samples in the rain. You couldn't be sure what you were testing.

The gene freaks lived and breathed DNA. They liked Paul because his sequence was rare. Paul had mitochondrial haplogroup D, a lineage common in East Asia. On his Y chromosome, he was R1a—a type common in Norway, Germany, Scotland, and Ukraine. It was a rare haplogroup combination, Far East meets far West, and it was almost never found in bones you dug from the ground. It made Paul's DNA easy to identify, which, in turn, made him invaluable as a sampler.

Other bone techs weren't so lucky. Jason had the western Atlantic modal haplotype (WAMH), a subset of R1b and the most common haplogroup in the Western world. Two others had the Cohen modal haplotype, and several Asian researchers possessed haplogroup C3, the famous twenty-five-marker Y-DNA profile thought to have descended from Genghis Khan and now found in nearly 8 percent of men across huge swaths of Asia and the Middle East. That was Hongbin's haplotype, a distinction of which he was inordinately proud.

"Pestle," Paul said.

"All yours."

But Greg Davis was the worst.

Greg Davis made the gene freaks cringe.

He had CRS itself, the Cambridge reference sequence. The sequence that all others were defined by their comparison to—the veritable mitochondrial holotype for the entire human species.

And there were other things, too, other pieces of history found in the lab.

Like MacAlister, one of the older lab techs.

"Pestle," Hongbin said.

Because Y chromosomes are passed from father to son, certain haplogroups associate with certain surnames. It was discovered several years ago by a researcher named Sykes that whole sprawling clans from Ireland and Scotland carried the same type of Y chromosome—a version of which could be traced back through the centuries to the historical figure named Somerset; the father of the clan Donald and the paternal ancestor of most of the MacDonalds, MacDougals, and Mac-Alisters in the world.

Somerset was the one who beat the Vikings back, who drove them out of Scotland after centuries of Viking raids. He united the clans against the invaders and became the greatest of the Gaelic kings. And it was only later, centuries later, after his descendants had grown and spread to the corners of the earth, after DNA technology had matured and advanced, that it was learned that this great Gaelic leader, who'd finally defeated the Nordic horde after generations of Viking rape and pillage, had himself carried Icelandic blood down his paternal line—the product of some ancient raid. And, therefore, it had been a man with a Viking Y chromosome who'd finally driven the Vikings from Scotland.

"Pestle," Paul said.

Thus does it work in the world. The wrong you do comes back to destroy you.

17

Gavin woke from a nightmare somewhere over the Pacific. He'd sweated through his shirt despite the airplane's chill. He blinked and rubbed his eyes. There was no relief upon waking, because once his eyes were open, he remembered where he was and where he was going. There was no waking from that.

He sat up straighter in his seat, trying to shake the dream from his head. Something about the jungle, a shape pursuing him in the darkness. The woman sitting two seats over from him hadn't stirred, which meant he hadn't shouted. So there was that, at least. She was reclined in her seat, blond hair falling across a peaceful face. He felt a momentary pang of envy. It had been a long time since he'd slept without bad dreams. He checked his watch: four A.M.

There would be no more sleep for him.

It started to get light a little after five-thirty, a gradual whitening of the clouds beyond the windows. He flagged down the flight attendant as she passed.

"Could I have something to drink?"

"Sure," she said. "What can I get you?"

"Water."

It came with ice. He drank it down and stared out past the wing at the brightening sky. He liked looking out the windows of airplanes. It was a view he never grew tired of. Down below, an ocean materialized from the gloom. The sun rose quickly over the next ten minutes; they were flying east, toward the dawn. A ridge of low white, wispy clouds ran in a line beneath the airplane, throwing dark patches of shadow on the glittering water. From this altitude, the surface of the ocean was rough and pebbly—not like waves but like the skin of an orange.

Gavin hadn't been sure he would use the airline ticket until he used it. Even standing in line, he hadn't been sure. A few times, he'd almost turned around and walked the other way. Gotten back in his car. Pulled out of the parking garage. *And what?*

That was the question that walked him through airport security and put him in this seat. Because it was a question with no answer.

Come.

And here he was.

Pretending there'd ever been a choice.

The plane began its descent to LAX a little before eight. One moment they were out over flat water, and then he saw white breakers, a beach, and America rose up to grab them. A gentle thump, the sound of the wheels. The longest leg was over. Once off the plane, he found that his connecting flight had been delayed until almost eleven. This left him with nothing to do and several hours in which to do it. For such circumstances had alcohol been invented.

He found his way to the airport bar and ordered a White Russian. Drank it down.

Then another.

Here self-destruction could kick in, if he let it. If he drank too much, they might not let him on the next flight. He'd heard of that happening. It wouldn't be his fault. Gavin supposed that in such ways people often killed themselves, if they lacked the will to do it directly. Taking too many pills, all the while telling themselves they'd be fine. Taking that next drink. Doing it by half measures—ceding control, not their fault. Rolling the dice.

"You want another?" the bartender asked.

"No," Gavin said. "Two will do me."

He stood and stretched. He found his way to Terminal 6.

Forty minutes later, he boarded his connecting flight.

He'd packed light for the trip. Three shirts, three pairs of pants, three changes of underwear. It had seemed the reasonable thing to do. Three days' worth of clothes. He tried not to think about the ticket being one-way.

The plane took off, and this time they flew inland. An hour later, gazing out the window, it became obvious how empty the land was of people, if not of their works. From this altitude, you might see roads scratched across the desert like Nazca lines. And farther east, occasional farms, spread like checkerboards—and in the corner of one farm he imagined a house, and in the house a room, and in the room a bed, and on the bed a man. The only one for miles.

Hours later, the plane landed and they were in a new city, and passengers again filed out, into the airport terminal.

Ten minutes after that, on the other side of security, stood a man with a sign: GAVIN MCMASTER.

The man was young and black, dressed in a dark suit and tie. He held the sign with casual boredom, as if he might have been there for quite some time.

Gavin walked up to him. "I'm your guy."

The man nodded. "Right this way, sir." He took Gavin's bag. "Your car is waiting."

Gavin had time to wonder if he was just a regular car-service employee or something more. He didn't have long to wonder.

The noise of the street hit him when the glass doors slid open. Buses and taxis, honking horns, the sound of tires. The smell of exhaust.

The vehicle was a limo, long and sleek and dark blue. The car-service man popped the trunk and placed his bag inside. Then he opened the rear curbside door for him. "If you will, sir."

Gavin climbed in and sank into soft leather.

The door slammed shut.

A blond man sat facing him in the near darkness.

"Hello," the man said. "You came, after all."

"So it would appear."

"Looks like I lost my wager," the man said. "I was betting against you."

"Sorry to disappoint."

"No, it's quite all right." The man smiled. His eyes were very blue, even in the darkness. "I'm happy to lose the bet," Ekman said. "It saved me the trouble of coming to get you."

The limo pulled away from the curb and merged into traffic. There was a momentary glimpse of sun—just a flash between clouds—and then the overcast came down again like a hammer. The traffic here was a nightmare. Gavin wondered how people lived with it, constantly tripping over one another, their lives literally clogged with the presence of their fellow man. In Australia, he'd experienced traffic, of course, but nothing like this.

The blond man stayed quiet, though his eyes never left Gavin. He had a youngish, almost pretty face, the beginnings of a beard stubbling his jawline. Although his hair was blond, the beard coming in showed a distinct shade of red. A scar bisected his lip, only partially hidden by the facial hair he wore to conceal it. He had on an expensive suit and shiny black shoes. Gavin knew that you were supposed to be able to tell a lot about a man by his shoes, but he'd never picked up the knack. He considered this for a moment and decided he was glad for it. Because as soon as you learn something like that, a simple pair of shoes can become a disguise.

The limo found its way to the highway. The next two hours passed in a haze of terrain so mind-numbingly flat and bland that it seemed they'd never left the runway. Such was Florida, apparently. Then finally, an exit to the right, and they pulled onto an interior access road that led deep into the coastal wetlands.

Here the land was still flat but punctuated by occasional ditches of brackish water, all of it hemmed in on the sides by thick vegetation. This was the jungle dream, he realized, or close enough.

They followed this road for ten minutes before the land opened up again as they rounded a bend. They passed through a gate going fifty miles an hour. A subtle, hidden border in the overgrowth. Gavin turned and saw the gate closing smoothly behind them, the limo having obviously triggered some kind of automatic-pass system. When he turned back around to face forward, they were rounding another, final bend in the road, and the facility loomed before them.

Then all at once, they were there. Axiom. If it wasn't in the middle of nowhere, it was in that postal code. This was no doubt not an accident of circumstance. Isolation had its benefits. The limo pulled to a stop. A moment later, the door opened.

"After you," the blond man said.

Gavin stepped out into the muggy afternoon air, his feet crunching on the white gravel.

Two men stood at the base of the steps to greet them. Behind them sprawled an imposing three-story building, a single monolithic facade of dark gray stone divided by modern tracts of windows. Except for the windows, it could have been from any age. The gravel drive formed a wide circle with a large flagpole in the middle. At the top of the pole, an Axiom corporate banner drooped in the humid air.

"Mr. McMaster, I presume," the first man said. He was taller than his partner, younger, darker. The other man simply stared. Both wore the exact same dark suit as his escort.

Gavin nodded.

"If you'll follow me."

Gavin followed the men up the stairs and through a wide set of double doors. The blond trailed behind. The doors led not into the interior of the building, as he'd expected, but, instead, through a short hall that flowed into a wide open space bounded by the two opposing wings of the facility. The building was roughly U-shaped, and in its center was a broad courtyard. It might have once been beautiful. Plush, overstuffed couches sat moldering along the wall. As he moved farther in, his puzzlement grew. Crates marked BIOLOGICAL HAZARD sat stacked in the hall alongside five-foot cylinders of hydrogen gas. It was like an Eastern European university campus in the extremis of some bizarre post-Communist decay. It was a place that defied comprehension. Part laboratory, part compound, part palatial estate. Gavin wondered what it had been before it became what he was looking at, but then he chided himself. It had, of course, been nothing. This place had been built to suit. The old man wouldn't have had it any other way. But the old man's vision of the place, whatever that vision might once have been, was now long deranged. What might have once been picturesque was overgrown and thronged with weeds. A path wound its way through the neglected territory at the center of the courtyard. Gavin followed the men across the lawn and around the side of the building, through a patch of woods and into a clearing. The first hint of a breeze stirred the air.

In all his years of association with Martial Johansson, he'd never been called to this place, though he'd heard the stories. The stories, it turned out, hadn't done it justice. Numerous outbuildings were spread over several acres of wooded landscape with winding roads and paved footpaths running between them. Each outbuilding looked as if designed by a different hand for a different purpose. One was gleaming and modern, another almost rustic and quaint. A third could have been a prison, dark gray walls rising twelve feet high. It was like some bizarre chess set designed by a very rich madman. Here and there were places where buildings had once stood and now only charred timbers remained, left to blacken and rot in the humid air. At one point, they crossed a small footbridge that arched over a narrow stream.

They came upon the old man in the garden.

Gavin hesitated when he saw him, his feet slowing on the muddy track.

The old man was turned away from them, his bald head shining in the glare of the sun—still tall and straight and severe. He'd grown into his years like an oak. His true age startled people. He was staring up the trail at something, as if distracted by a sound only he could hear.

Then the old man turned, and there was a momentary flash of expression across the broad, weathered face. Something that in other men might have been pain.

"Gavin," the old man said.

And here he was, stripped of legend. There were so many competing stories about him. He was incongruous, a phalanx of illogical contradictions. Here was a man who donated millions of dollars to medical research, yet kept his own discoveries to himself. He was petty and paranoid and utterly fearless. He'd saved lives and killed people. To some, he was an icon. To others, insane. But there was no denying the power he wielded. The truth was, the old man scared the shit out of Gavin.

"Sir," Gavin said.

"It's been a long time. How many years?"

"Too many."

"You're tan," the old man said. "That Indonesian sun has browned you up. Walk with me." He turned without waiting for a response.

Gavin followed. They walked down a path of stones. The three men trailed behind at a respectful distance, sweating in their dark suits.

The old man handed Gavin a pair of binoculars, and when Gavin took them the grip was slick with sweat.

Gavin had first met the old man twenty years earlier.

It had come down to money, though he'd let himself call it something else. The old man—and he was already old, even then—had let him keep the pretense of his ideals, at least for a little while. At least until Carlsson had come along.

How do you turn down everything you've ever wanted?

And the old man had known somehow. The divorce, the money problems, the barriers to advancement in the university system. Looking back, he saw that he'd been groomed from the start, though he hadn't perceived that at the time. Gavin had just been another piece in the old man's chess set.

They met that first time in Oakland, at an anthropology convention. The old man, already a force behind the scenes, had contacted Gavin for a meeting. "Martial Johansson would like to meet you" was what the invitation had said, and Gavin had gone to the conference room listed on the card and found Martial sitting behind a long table. They'd talked about genetics and the future of molecular biology.

A month later, he'd gotten a call. And then a plane ticket to a symposium in California.

Another boardroom. Another talk. And this time, a check. With zeros to spare. And he'd made the deal. It was only later that he'd realized it was a deal with the devil. Gavin wondered how many other deals the old man had made over the years. How many other checks he'd passed out.

"Thank you for coming," the old man said. "It was short notice, but considering the circumstances, I thought it best we speak in person." They rounded a bend in the trail, and here the ground was muddy and well trodden.

"It's good to see the States again," Gavin said. "And this place . . ." His voice faded.

"Is it what you imagined?"

"I wasn't sure what to imagine."

"It is strange times we live in," the old man said. His voice was cracked and failing, though his expression was as confident as Gavin remembered.

"Indeed, sir."

"Dark times," Martial wheezed.

The old man walked more slowly than the last time Gavin had seen him. His breath came in shallow gasps. If the rumors were true, he was on his third pair of lungs, and the anti-rejection drugs had compromised his immune system, rendering him susceptible to infections. Consequently, he didn't get out much. Instead, he brought the world to him.

They followed the trail down to an opening in the dense brush. Huge cages loomed before them, and in them, big cats.

"I come down here every day to watch them feed," Martial said. "Of all the animals at the facility, the cats are the ones I respect the most."

An enormous feline paced in the nearest enclosure, huge feet padding across packed dirt. The cage was a dozen feet high, a hundred feet long.

They moved closer, and Gavin could see that it wasn't a lion. Not really. Something close, but not a lion. It was four feet tall at the shoulder. A freight train of fur and bone and muscle.

The old man stood facing away from him, but Gavin noted his posture—the rigid shoulders had slumped a bit in the intervening years. The old man coughed, and it was a deep, hacking sound that didn't speak well of his health.

Gavin was startled to realize that in the decade since last he'd seen Martial, a chink had formed in his shell of seeming immortality. He was a sick man who'd grown used to being sick. Maybe the old oak was finally dying. Or maybe that was the thing about oaks. They can die for a long, long time.

The old man turned, and his eyes were red and rheumy. "It's a liger," he said, gesturing toward the enclosure. "You've heard of them, no doubt."

"Of course."

"The odd thing about ligers, they're always bigger than either of their parents. Ask why and you'll get some blather about imprinting, differential growth controls, the privileging of plus over minus alleles, et cetera. But the fact is that we really don't know why they get bigger. Most chalk it up to heterosis. Hybrid vigor. But that's a description, not an explanation."

Gavin nodded.

"This one's a cross of a lion father and a tiger mother. Nine feet long and still growing, as far as we can tell. Like a tiger, it swims. There's also a lesser-utilized cross—the tiger father and lion mother. This makes a completely different animal, did you know that?"

"No."

"The tigon isn't as large. They tend to have darker fur and smaller manes. They're also less social and behave more like tigers, but they do something true tigers don't. Do you know what that is?"

"No."

"They roar."

The old man stared through the bars. His face made an expression that might have been a smile. "We house a lot of animals here at the facility." He swept his arm wide. "I've been called a collector, but that isn't true. Collectors wish only to possess, but there's work being done here. Important work. We *do* things here, you understand."

"Yes."

At that moment, a cry rose up from the distance—a strange sound that Gavin couldn't place. It came from somewhere around the next bend of the trail, from a different series of cages no doubt, nestled somewhere farther out on the grounds. At first the sound seemed to be the howl of a wounded dog, or perhaps a monkey. But it changed as it rose in pitch, transforming into a screech of anguish.

Gavin looked to the old man for an explanation, but the old man offered only, "There are places here where the work is lost. Places I don't visit anymore."

It was then that Gavin noticed the bucket. It sat in the trampled grass by the old man's feet, white plastic, a five-gallon bucket coated in gore, dried blood and fat accreted along the lip and sides. The old man followed Gavin's gaze and bent toward the bucket, reaching inside. He pulled out a thick slab of dripping red meat. He held the meat in his gnarled hands for a moment, its bulk sagging in the middle like one of those novelty steaks served as marketing ploys in certain kinds of restaurants: five or six pounds, finish it in an hour and your meal is free.

With a grunt of effort, the old man tossed it through the bars, into the cage.

The giant cat lumbered forward and sank its teeth into the flesh. Its mouth jerked twice, movements too quick to follow, and the meat was gone. The old man continued, "Years ago, when I first started my work, I didn't truly understand the scope of what I'd undertaken. It was after graduate school, before the genetics boom, back before cytology caught my interest. I was unsure of the direction I wanted to take. I had only questions, and no clear path before me by which I might someday arrive at the answers."

Gavin tried to picture Martial Johansson unsure of anything. His imagination failed him.

"Working with animals reveals many things about nature," the old man continued. "Animals, you see, will develop a compromise with captivity." And here Martial paused; he bent and pulled from the bucket another dripping slab of meat. His hands were coated in blood. "With enough time, they come to understand it. They need to eat, after all."

Martial tossed the second slab of meat through the bars, and the big cat snatched it out of the air with paws the size of dinner plates. It gulped the meat down in a single swallow. The big cat's head came up, and its eyes locked on them through the bars. Huge tan eyes—a liquid predator stare that raised the hair on Gavin's arms. The big cat began to pace.

"But not so with the lion," Martial continued. He gestured through the bars. "The lion is different from other animals. The lion is an animal with whom no compromise is possible."

The old man kicked the white bucket over and blood poured out, draining into the grass. A clutch of black flies sprang from the bucket and circled angrily as the old man bent and picked up a last chunk of meat. "I came to realize that for the lion, its hatred outweighed its need for food." Martial gestured toward the cage again. "Like this big beast's father here."

The big cat followed the old man's gestures with its eyes.

"Every day I'd go down to the cages, and I'd watch the lion watching us. And when I fed it, those eyes would turn toward me, three feet away, and my insides would go all soft, because my body knew that stare. Even the first time it happened, my body knew—some feedback mechanism in my brain recognizing what death looks like, that big beast staring at me. And I knew something else. I knew what none of the other researchers knew. I knew, absolutely, that if anyone ever left the cage door open, that lion wouldn't just escape. It would kill as many people as it could before it was shot."

The old man threw the last chunk of meat through the bars. The cat was on it in a flash of movement. A moment later, the meat was gone. "Now this one, this half lion, I'm not sure of. Is it like its father, I wonder?" The old man stared at the big cat. "If so, I don't see it. Or maybe it's too sly to let me see."

The big cat resumed its pacing.

"That lion," Gavin asked, "where is it now?"

"I killed it," the old man said. "That was a long time ago."

They watched the big cat in silence.

"There is an ancient proverb," the old man said at last. "Begrudge not the lion's existence. Be thankful God didn't give it wings."

The old man started coughing. He reached into the back pocket of his pants and pulled out a blue handkerchief. He coughed into the blue cloth for a moment and then wiped his hands meticulously with it before putting it back in his pocket.

Seconds more passed in silence as they watched the big cat pacing, and Gavin realized that the old man was waiting for something.

"Flores, sir?" It was the only way to encapsulate the question, the only way to phrase it in its entirety.

"Things went badly in Flores," Martial said.

"They did."

"People died."

"Yes," said Gavin.

"The reports I read made me very unhappy. It was a mess. Come, there's something else I want you to see," the old man said. He turned and headed farther up the trail.

Gavin followed. Here the trail was well marked, a short path through a stand of trees to another ring of cages.

There was a paddock and, inside it, a small group of horses. Looking closer, Gavin noticed a small zebra mixed in with the herd.

"The horses are a special treat," Martial said. "The meat is delicious, by the way. Zebras hybridize very easily with horses, did you know that?"

"No, I didn't."

"The offspring are sterile, of course, but they're strong and healthy. They grow large. The stripes are codominant, extending up the legs but usually without spreading over the torso."

Gavin watched the herd graze.

"Do you know what you get if you shave a zebra?" the old man asked.

"No."

"A zebra, still. The stripes are on the skin as well."

Gavin nodded.

"Horses, zebras, and donkeys all hybridize easily. All you have to do is put them in the same enclosure. Lock them up together, and they take care of it. No cloning required. Nothing fancy. Put sperm in contact with egg, and Mother Nature handles all the heavy lifting. As species, they aren't particularly closely related to each other, separated by nearly eight percent of their genomes. A donkey is as different from a zebra as an orangutan is from a gorilla."

The old man led Gavin past the paddock, toward a row of large cages attached to a small building. The cages were obviously runs of some sort. Whatever animals they housed were hidden in the building.

These cages were taller. The bars closer together.

The old man gestured toward them. "I wouldn't get any closer to the bars. They're very fast when they want to be, and they have access to their run; I see the door is open." Ignoring his own advice, he took another step forward. "Chimps," he said. "Have you ever worked with them?"

"No."

"They are fucking bastard animals." Spittle flew from the old man's mouth when he spoke.

The sound of his voice drew them.

They entered the runs through a small steel door in the side of the building. Four of them, one after another, knuckle-walking the packed earth, moving in single file. They stopped a few feet from the bars, staring out at their visitors. Then the largest chimp sat, seeming to lose interest.

"No closer," the old man muttered. "If we went just a few feet closer . . ." His hand reached out, trembling slightly. A sheen of sweat covered his scalp. "A few feet closer, and it could reach us through the bars."

Martial dropped his hand to his side. "The chimp is a strange creature. Very like the lion in some respects." He chuckled, with a bitter, humorless sound. "It has the ability to be offended. It can hold a grudge. But it is in some ways more dangerous."

"More dangerous than a lion?"

"It has one major difference from the lion. It can *feign* docility, you see." He waved a hand in the direction of largest of the chimps—a thick-limbed, muscular form squatting in the dirt. "This one here . . . is the worst of our pets. It bit off the face of one of our keepers. It bit off his fingers and his toes. It broke his arms. But it left him alive. Why would it do that?"

"I don't know," Gavin said, resisting the urge to step back from the man who sweated and shook before the cage.

The beast looked dumbly on. Gavin watched it, its dark eyes following the old man's face.

"I am not so good at feigning, Gavin. I never have been."

"Sir?"

"And there are certain things coming. Things I will need help with. Can I count on you?"

"Of course."

"No, I mean it. I am not the man I once was. I have become impatient in my increasing years. I have no patience for fools. I am not a politician, and yet I am forced to deal with politicians."

"I understand, sir."

"I will need you here from now on."

Gavin stared at him, uncomprehending.

"An executive position, you might call it," the old man continued. "There are difficult things coming, and I can use a man like you. I will need you here full-time from this day forward." There was finality in his tone. Gavin realized this wasn't a suggestion.

"But my . . . my work," Gavin stammered.

"Will continue. Will expand. You'll find opportunities here that you never knew existed."

There came a howling again from the distance. The same strange, twisted cry.

"Things you never dreamed of," the old man said. "But I need two things from you."

"What?"

"Loyalty. Commitment."

"You—"

The old man held up one hand to stop him. "Do not say it unless you're prepared to back it up."

"You've *always* had that, was what I was going to say. But this is a different kind of arrangement than what we had before. I have my career, after all."

"You do," the old man said flatly. "You still have it."

Gavin stared at the old man. The grizzled old visage.

"And if I don't come?"

"Then who can say."

Martial turned back toward the chimps. "But that's the stick, Gavin. You haven't seen the carrot. There are things happening that you couldn't possibly guess at. Important things. Things that you'll now be a part of. Things that will change the world."

Gavin was silent.

The largest chimp rose and moved closer to the bars.

"You've been on my payroll, in some capacity or other, for the last twenty years, but only in a part-time, as-needed capacity; it's time you received a promotion. Do I have your commitment?"

In the end, there wasn't a choice. When working with Martial, there was never a choice. Gavin wondered, vaguely, what he was losing. What was he giving up? "You have it," he said.

"Good," the old man replied. His tone was matter-of-fact. "Then that is settled. Now, about the subject of Flores, which you mentioned. The reports I've read are serious. Very serious indeed."

Gavin said nothing.

"It couldn't be helped," the old man said. "Everything that happened. I want you to know that."

"I don't understand," Gavin said.

"Who controls the bones controls their interpretation. You understand that, do you not?"

"Yes."

"We got word that the Indonesians were going to shut down the dig, so we had to act. Still, death wasn't part of the plan."

Gavin stared at him. "The plan? What do you mean you . . ." But Gavin couldn't finish, a suspicion freezing the words on his tongue.

"I mean nothing but exactly what I said," Martial responded. "More than that, you'll understand in good time." The old man looked directly at him. "But for now, there is something *I* don't understand."

"What is that?"

"Paul."

Gavin studied Martial's face, but it gave away nothing. Behind him, up the trail, Gavin again noticed the three men in suits.

"You told me to pick the best team, so that's what I did," Gavin said. "You said I could pick whoever I wanted."

"And you picked him, of all the samplers?"

"I did."

"Why?"

"He came highly recommended. He had the right credentials."

"Do you think I'm a fool?"

Gavin thought of the pacing cat. "Because I was curious," he said. "And I felt he was owed something."

"Owed something." The cracked and failing voice became steel. "What was owed?"

Gavin met the old man's eye and said nothing.

Martial nodded. "Do you feel the debt is paid?"

"I wish I'd never involved him. I regret it. If I'd known it would happen like that, I never would have brought him to the island."

In the distance, the strange sound came a third time. The distorted cry. The skin tightened at the back of Gavin's neck.

He looked into the old man's face and found the usual confidence had vanished, replaced by the expression of a man who didn't have all the answers. The cry continued, rising higher, a strange mewling like nothing Gavin had ever heard before.

"I was told that he crushed a man's throat," the old man said.

"I don't know anything about that."

"If true, it was an unusual response to the circumstances. An unexpected response."

"What would have been the expected response?"

"To those circumstances? To die, of course." The old man rubbed his palm over his sweating head. "You brought him into this." The old man's eyes burned. "You are responsible for what happens."

"I understand."

Martial nodded to himself. "You've put me in a very difficult situation."

"No more difficult than if it had been somebody else on the team."

"Again, you call me a fool."

"If not him, it would have been somebody."

"But it wasn't."

"No."

The old man turned to look at the crouching chimps.

After a moment, he spoke: "So then tell me this. Is he his father's son?"

"In some ways."

"Is he going to let this go? The deaths. The things he's seen."

"He might."

The old man shielded his eyes from the sun, still blazing even as it set. He wiped his cracked lips with the back of his hand and coughed into his handkerchief again. Then he asked the question that had drawn

Gavin across thousands of miles of ocean, inexorable and inevitable from the first moment: "Can we trust him?"

Gavin watched the big chimp in its cage. He considered lying for a moment, but he knew the old man would see it on his face.

"No, we cannot."

18

The glass wall formed a single, seamless barrier unless you knew where to look.

The doors had no handles, no smudges, glass on glass, and it all unfolded on invisible hinges, swinging inward as Paul approached. Behind him, across the short stretch of marble flooring, the elevator doors closed with a soft ding.

The fifth floor.

Heaven.

Paul stepped from the elevator entryway and onto the soft carpet of the administration level. He'd been here only once before, on the day he'd been hired. He remembered being very impressed with the lighting. The ceilings were beveled at complicated angles, hidden lights reflecting off recessed ceiling panels. The effect produced a well-lit room that nonetheless lacked windows or any visible means of illumination. That first day, waiting for his interview, he'd sat in the comfortable reception area and looked for a shadow, any shadow. There were none. The light was just everywhere, all at once. Like the inside of a video game.

Across the room, a beautiful woman sat behind a large, curved structure that was intermediate between a desk and a high, elegant countertop. This was the receptionist. She was not just beautiful, Paul decided as he approached. She was stunning. Her blond hair was cut in a short bob that framed the perfect oval of her face.

Soft music played in the background. A soothing jazz. The carpet was plush, deep red; it yielded underfoot. The room smelled of flowers.

It was the kind of room you'd choose to die in, if you had to choose a room.

"Can I help you?" The woman parted her lips. Her eyes were liquid blue pools.

"I'm here for Mr. Belshaw."

"Certainly. He's expecting you, Mr. Carlsson." Her hands moved behind the counter, hidden from view. Like the lights. "You can go right in."

There was a click, and across the room a door opened—the first in a series of doors that extended down a long hall. This door was heavy and wooden.

Paul crossed a league of carpet. Belshaw was sitting when Paul entered his office. "Please," Belshaw said, gesturing to one of the leather chairs near his desk.

The office had the same lighting as the reception area, the same recessed ceilings. The floor, though, was polished hardwood. Near the door Paul noticed a light switch and felt a pang of jealousy.

"You requested this meeting, Paul. What can I do for you?" Belshaw leaned back in his chair, his wide hands interlocked behind his head.

He was in his fifties, a large man, tan and fit. His broad face was relaxed and confident, the face of a man in charge. Farther down the hall, Paul knew, were other offices with light switches and hardwood floors, other administrators in five-thousand-dollar suits—men Paul would recognize on sight, though he'd never been introduced: the big bosses, their names and faces picked up over time the way employees always pick up that kind of information. By osmosis. And if you kept walking down that hall, passing door after door, you'd eventually reach the end, Paul knew, and there would be a final doorway and a final big boss, who was not there most of the time yet maintained an office still, and a private secretary even more beautiful, somehow, than the stunning receptionist.

"I'd like a transfer," Paul said.

The broad face changed. The brows furrowed. "You aren't happy in sampling anymore?"

"I'm happy, but I feel I need to move on."

"What did you have in mind?"

"The fourth floor," Paul said. "Testing."

Belshaw stared at him. He was trying to understand what Paul was really asking.

"You feel you deserve a raise," Belshaw said. "I think we can address that to your satisfaction."

"That's not it." Paul did not offer anything further.

"Paul," and here the man paused, gathering his objections. "You do good work. We usually keep field techs in sampling for several years before promoting—"

"It doesn't have to be a promotion. You can pay me the same—I don't care."

Again the brows furrowed. This new detail really seemed to confuse him.

"Are you not happy in bones?"

"I need a change, that's all."

Finally, leaning forward: "Perhaps there are other adjustments that can be made."

"No other adjustment would be adequate."

"If it is an issue with travel, I can assure you that we have no intention of sending you out on field assignment until you feel ready. We're not interested in rushing anything."

"I don't ever want to go into the field again."

"I understand that you've been through . . . an ordeal. But I think you're making a rash decision."

"I'm not."

"We'd be promoting you above several senior samplers."

"You keep calling it that."

"It would be a promotion," Belshaw snapped. Belshaw was used to getting his way. There was a brusqueness in him. Brusqueness was an asset whose value was not to be underestimated in an administrator's career. Paul had often thought that managers failed or succeeded more on the basis of their temperaments than due to any other factor. But here was a man both smart and brusque. The kind of man for whom "no-nonsense" would doubtless appear no fewer than three times in any quarterly evaluation. The highest possible praise.

"How much longer were you planning on keeping me in sampling?" Paul asked.

"How long have you been with the company?"

"Four years."

"Then another three at least."

"So your plan was to move me eventually. I'd simply like you to bump that date forward. Keep my pay where it is now."

Belshaw leaned back in his chair again, considering Paul across the broad surface of his desk. "Have you talked to your direct supervisor about this?"

"No."

"Why come to me?"

"Because you can make it happen."

"There is an established system in place. Why should we disregard the system and move you ahead of other samplers who've put in their time? Why move you to the front of the line?"

"Because I gave an eye."

Belshaw closed his mouth. He looked at Paul for a long time. Paul had said it: the thing, of course, that was always under the surface. Obvious as a black leather eye patch. It was a betrayal; Paul saw that clearly in Belshaw's eyes. It was a betrayal to mention his eye, to play that card. But Paul knew in that moment that he had won. He knew that Belshaw would give in. He could see it in the man's face. He would give in, but he would not forget. Men like Belshaw didn't appreciate being backed into corners. The silence drew out between them. "I will get back to you by the end of the week," Belshaw said. He rose to his feet and extended his hand. The meeting was over.

Paul shook the proferred hand. He didn't say thank you. He didn't say anything. He simply nodded and left.

Later, Hongbin sat in Paul's office. He leaned back, flinging his yo-yo. Down, up. Down, up. The string broke.

Hongbin was philosophical about it. "Now it is just a yo," he said.

Paul thought of telling him. He thought of explaining everything. He thought of telling him about what had really happened on Flores, and about the sample he'd hidden and what he planned to do. But he couldn't. It wouldn't be fair to Hongbin. It wouldn't be right to expose him to the risk.

"So you are leaving bones," Hongbin said.

"No," Paul said. "I'm never leaving bones."

19

Evidence of Expansive Introgression

[Translated from Russian.]

The geographical distribution of the 25-microsatellite Y-chromosome haplogroup C3c was educed from the analysis of 4,600 blood samples taken from phyletic populations across Eastern Europe, Asia, and the Indian subcontinent. Analysis shows that the highest frequency of the 25-microsatellite sequence is found in southern Mongolia, with significant recurrence presenting across most of China, as well as among the Altaian Kazakhs of Russia and the Hazara of the Bolan Pass area of Pakistan. The limited variation of the 25-microsatellite marker demonstrates an anomalously young age for this group relative to other local haplogroup distributions, suggesting that this distribution resulted not from normal population expansion but from a series of "introgression events" into a preexisting population matrix. The current geographic range of the 25-microsatellite sequence is proximally bounded by the expansive limit of the Mongol Empire in the thirteenth century. This unusual distribution can best be explained as the genetic artifact of a massive reproductive advantage conferred on a single paternal lineage of that time period. The origin of this lineage likely traces to southern steppe tribes of Mongolia, and to Genghis Khan.

Paul received word on a Friday. There was no fanfare. The news arrived in his in-box; he was being transferred to testing the following Monday. A 7 percent pay raise. The paperwork called it a promotion.

Mr. Lyons came by and congratulated him and shook his hand. "Sorry to see you go," he said. And Paul could tell that the man meant it. Paul's own emotions were more conflicted on the matter.

On Saturday, he got blindingly, stupefyingly drunk for the first time since Flores. He took Sunday to recuperate, puking only once, his face resting on the cool white porcelain.

On Monday he left for work early, taking the scenic route. He wanted to see the water from the road. He crossed the bridge as the sun came up along the far side of the bay.

He got to the parking lot early and carded himself inside. The guard nodded to him as he crossed the lobby. Paul took the elevator to the fourth floor, where he was supposed to meet Janus, his new supervisor. The fourth-floor lobby was similar to the fifth, only instead of an elegant folding wall of glass origami, here the wall was smooth steel, with a single steel door on which the words GENE FREQ LAB was stenciled in bold block letters.

Home of the gene freqs. Gene freaks.

There was no bone-freq lab, but the third-floor workers were still called bone freaks. Paul figured it was like rhinos. The first rhinos discovered were called white rhinos in anglicized bastardization of the local dialect. It had nothing to do with color. Still, when a second species was discovered, there was never much doubt about what to call them: black rhinos. Defined by opposition. And never mind that both species were gray.

Paul tried the door. It was locked. A card swipe glowed red from the wall.

Paul had been trained in school to test DNA, isolating base-pair sequences from bones and junk and contaminants. The index was what mattered, though. The comparison assays. Without the index, there was nothing to compare the sequences to. It was just noise, raw code. Meaningless pattern.

You had to have the index to know what you were looking at.

That was what they did on the fourth floor, on the other side of this door he couldn't open.

A little after nine o'clock, Janus finally arrived. He was lanky and ruddy, with florid, pockmarked skin and a down-turned mouth. His thick, strawberry hair paid for his face. Although he was well into his sixties, his hair was nothing short of luxuriant. The first time Paul had seen him walking the halls, he'd assumed it was a hairpiece, but it wasn't. Janus combed it straight back from his forehead, as if to accentuate the fact that his hairline hadn't crept back a millimeter since grade school. His eyes were small and sharp and hazel.

"I see you're here early?" Janus said. Janus, Paul knew, liked asking questions that were really statements. That way you couldn't disagree with him.

"Yeah," Paul said. "Early bird and all that."

Janus looked at him, wary condescension on his pitted face. Then the look changed to pity as his gaze lingered on Paul's eye patch. Somehow that was worse. Paul wondered what Janus had been told about the transfer. Did he know how hard Paul had pushed for it? Did he know he'd jumped his place in line?

"We'll start with you making the fixative," Janus said, then turned, swiped his card, and opened the door to the lab.

Janus led him down gleaming halls, past rows of windowless clean rooms, past men in white paper jumpsuits who carried steel trays crammed with samples in agarose gel. On the other side of glass doorways, men faced Pyrex isolation booths, arms extended through long latex gloves that stretched into the booths' interiors. Paul and Janus passed a small lounge area; a vending machine hummed in the corner while researchers stood talking and sipping their coffee.

"You'll eat in the lounge. There's no food or drink in the lab area," Janus noted. This rule, Paul discovered over the next week, was taken very seriously. This was different than the floor below, where techs sometimes ate at their desks or in their labs, if they didn't feel like facing the confines of the lunchroom.

That first week on the fourth floor, Paul learned little about actual testing that he didn't already know. He'd done fixative before; he'd done simple base-pair testing. But the fourth-floor subcultural information he gleaned was priceless. The fourth floor might have been a different world.

Janus showed him bits and pieces over the next several weeks. It wasn't training so much as a careful rationing of information—the slow, reluctant release of sacred knowledge to one who may or may not be worthy.

It began with the machines. Dark blue obelisks, designed from scratch by Westing engineers. The machines had no names but only generic markings nameplated to one side: FUNCTIONAL GENOMICS. They translated data into the Bioinformatic Markup Language that computers could use for polymorphism analysis. The sample arrays were interpreted by scanners that picked up the fluorescent tags activated in the sample matrix. The ratio of red-to-green fluorescence in the hybridization solution assembled a pattern; special recognition software then coded that pattern into a language the computers could archive.

There were rumors that certain gene freaks had long sequences memorized and could read genes like prose, ticking off amino acids like most people read words in a sentence. The other bone techs didn't believe these rumors, but Paul did. He understood the power of obsession.

Once, in college, he'd attended a lecture on axolotl salamanders. "A fascinating species from the perspective of intelligent design," the professor had said. "They are one of the rare species of salamander that don't have a terrestrial form. Unless, that is, you inject them with thyroxine." The professor paused to write "thyroxine" on the board.

"They live out their entire lives in the water, growing and reproducing—happily living out their aquatic existence." He turned back toward the classroom. "But if you inject them with thyroxine, it all changes. Their skulls broaden and flatten. They lose their gills. They go through all the metamorphic changes other amphibians go through." He paused, letting the implication sink in. It was like all the axolotl salamanders of the world were just waiting for humans to come along with their hypodermic needles full of thyroxine. "The species has genes for the entire biological infrastructure of metamorphosis already in place, passed silently and invisibly from generation to generation."

This had bothered Paul greatly at the time. It was a riddle, hidden in their genes. A message, some said. And strange biological cults rose up around it. He read about the experiments. He saw the aquariums filled with dozens of salamanders—all living out their placid, watery lives without ever once stepping foot on dry land. Unless you injected them with thyroxine. And that's all it took, that addition, that single ingredient, and they became another kind of creature entirely.

People could be like this, too.

One morning two months after Paul returned from Flores, he took his sample from the medicine cabinet and drove to work with the lozenge in his jacket.

He nodded to the gate guard as he pulled onto the property. The sample was in a Tylenol bottle in his pocket. The pills rattled as he walked.

As he pushed through the front doors of the lab, he considered all he was risking. His job, his career, his life. He wondered what would happen if they discovered that he'd lied to them. He felt a sudden urge to turn and walk out, to get into his car and drive to the nearest bridge, and throw the sample into the bay.

The elevator doors opened before him. He stared at them for a moment without moving. The doors began to close, and he stuck his arm in to stop them. They opened again. He stepped inside and took the elevator up.

Paul hid the lozenge in the testing lab. He shoved the Tylenol bottle into one of the forgotten drawers, behind several boxes of latex gloves and a snarl of old VWR tubing used for nitrogen tank assemblages.

The sample would be safe there, at least for now. As safe as it could be.

When Janus arrived, twenty minutes later, Paul was already working on the day's fixative solution, beginning the prep for all the samples that needed to be tested.

20

Cohanim: A Y-chromosome Analysis Using SNP and STR Markers

DNA samples extracted from the mucosal swabs of 645 men were referred for Y-chromosome analysis. The test subjects self-reported as being of either Sephardic, Kurdish, or Ashkenazi Jewish descent, and all were typed for Y-chromosome DNA sequence. The Y-chromosome profiles of each group were compared to each other, as well as to a fourth, existing control group of non-Semitic men of Middle Eastern descent. Analysis of genetic distance indicates close proximity between the Sephardic and Kurdish groups, with the Ashkenazim and non-Semitic Middle Eastern Y chromosomes demonstrating as distinct isolates. In addition to these divisions, deeper analysis suggests intrapopulation substructure within the Ashkenazim, revealed as an unusual haplogroup distribution among the subset of the Jewish priesthood (the Cohanim). Identity within the Cohanim is highly prescriptive, being passed only from father to son by rigid patrilineal descent. Further testing elucidated a phylogenetic division between Cohanim and non-Cohanim Semitic males. The demographic cohesion of the 6SNP-6STR genetic motif infers hereditary continuity between present-day designates of the Cohen surname and ancient biblical Hebrews. High-resolution Y-chromosome analysis establishes that this distinct paternal lineage among the Cohanim is in accordance with expansion from a single male progenitor and thus conforms to long-established rabbinic assertions of paternal descent from the biblical Aaron, brother of Moses. From these data, it can be inferred that Moses likely belonged to Y-chromosome haplogroup J1.

It was nearly seven and the sky was still brightening toward full morning. Paul drove with the windows down.

The air smelled clean and fresh. Like the ocean before a storm.

As he pulled into the parking lot, he took note of the number of vehicles in the lot. He opened his little green notebook and wrote down the time and the number of cars: "7:49—3 cars."

He climbed out and walked toward the building. He'd beaten the front-desk guard in and so had to use his card to swipe through the entrance doors.

Though the workforce of Westing was a cross section of the human species, most of the researchers were Asian; but then, Paul thought, most humans were Asian, so this was perhaps not altogether unexpected. The other researchers came from all over the world.

Paul sat in the lounge during his breaks, listening to conversations.

It was like a joke. Put an American, a Filipino, a Kenyan, and a Korean in a room. What will they talk about?

Women.

There were also run-of-the-mill complaints.

"That's what I keep telling him, but he doesn't listen."

"Why don't you go home and cry to your old lady?"

"I do, but she doesn't listen, either."

"John doesn't listen, your wife doesn't listen, Hongbin doesn't listen. Who else?"

"Tom doesn't listen, either."

"Not even Tom?"

"No."

"All these people don't listen, what's that tell you?"

"Tells me I'm the only smart one."

Paul did his best to learn the procedures. It was more than monotony and memorization. There were flashes of insight. Conversations with the other techs. Laboratory minutiae.

It wasn't just the disciplines—bones and genes—that were stratified at Westing. There were differences, too, within the gene freaks. A stratified hierarchy, with the assayers firmly at the top, information trickling down.

Paul got to know some of the other techs. He learned their stories.

Each tech's area of expertise was compartmentalized; each understood his or her given data sets. There was little cross-training. The different labs required different badges, and the person who prepped was never the person who tested.

The samples all came to Westing through the third floor—carried in the bones themselves, or in lozenges sampled from the dig sites. After that, the samples were typed and turned into data—and then relabeled, repackaged, and sent to the assayers, whose job it was to interpret the data and send the information upstairs.

Paul's own badge got him through the door of the testing lab, but the deeper assaying labs were still off-limits.

The way the system was designed, the typers knew the sample origin but couldn't translate the raw code into meaningful information. The assayers divined meaning from the nucleotide base-pair sequences but knew nothing of the origin of the samples, or from which bones they'd derived.

Of all the recent techs, only Charles had access to the master bank of data sets. He alone could cross-reference. But it turned out that even his access wasn't complete.

Only the fifth floor knew all the secrets.

Fifth-floor heaven, looking down.

The first time Paul had encountered Charles, he'd been confused by the man. It was Paul's first week at Westing, and a stranger walked into the break room. The man tried to strike up a conversation about bird-watching. Paul told him politely that he wasn't really into birds, but the man was undeterred. So began a half-hour soliloquy on the avian visual system.

Paul would learn over the course of the next few days that Charles could talk endlessly about two subjects: birds and quantitative reverse polymerase chain reaction assays.

Charles had worked in the gene frequency lab. He was tall and thin and pale. It was difficult to guess his age. He was balding, with wisps of curly, sandy-colored hair going gray at the top, but his face was smooth and young. He might have been thirty or forty-five. He tended to bounce when he walked—and he was always walking. Even when he spoke to you, he was walking, pacing back and forth, continually on the move.

Charles could do the autism trick; he'd show you if you asked.

It was almost diagnostic.

If you told him the date of your birth, he could tell you what day of the week you were born. He could do it instantly. When Paul learned this, his surprise shifted. He'd heard of people like this, of course. Many of them were in institutions.

Paul went from being surprised that Charles was so strange to being surprised that he was so normal. There were terms for what he was, after all. The fact that Charles could drive and hold a job meant that most of those terms would have the qualifier "high-functioning" in front of them.

Hongbin had his own term for him, though: "association savant." Charles worked in multiple variant analysis.

Among the gene freaks of the fourth floor, he was the chosen one.

"Can I help you?"

The secretary's name was Bratton. She was a formidable middle-aged woman partial to sweaters, black-rimmed glasses, and small mouse figurines. The figurines were glass mostly, of a cute anthropomorphic variety that seemed more than a little out of place in a research lab. She positioned them conspicuously around her workstation, as if to counteract the no-nonsense matter-of-factness that she exuded from every pore of her body. When Paul met her, she did not strike him as the kind of woman who would have a deep and abiding love for small glass mouse figurines. She was one of the two secretaries on the fourth floor and handled the various secretarial needs of the gene freaks. She did not get coffee.

"I'm running behind," Paul said. "I was hoping you could help me with something."

"If I can."

"I sent Charles some rush samples a few months back, and I need the results yesterday."

She stared at him over the tops of her glasses as if swatting away requests like this was a part of her job description that she particularly enjoyed. "You're the new tech transferred from the third floor, right?"

"Yeah."

"Well, I'm sorry to be the one who has to inform you of this, but Charles is on leave."

"Leave?" Paul said, hoping his surprise sounded genuine.

"Yes."

"I had no idea."

"Yes."

"Nothing serious, I hope."

"Let's hope not."

"Any idea when he'll return?"

"I haven't been informed of a return date."

"Well, these samples were a rush, and I still really need the results."

"Other teams are taking over Charles's workload. I'm surprised you hadn't heard. There shouldn't be much of a delay."

Paul did his best to scowl. "I'm already past deadline on these samples."

"What is the project number, and I'll get—"

He cut her off: "It's okay. I'm sure they'll get done. You wouldn't know what project Charles was working on just before he left?"

"I really wouldn't have any idea."

"Okay, thanks." He turned to leave, then stopped. "I don't mean to pry, but you wouldn't happen to know the circumstances of his departure?"

"I'm really not privy to that kind of information."

"I understand. But what I'm really asking is, do you think he's coming back?"

The secretary shrugged. "I couldn't say."

Which, of course, could be interpreted in one of two ways.

Paul studied her closely, pushing one last time. "I mean, he's not gone for good, is he?"

Ms. Bratton gave him a quizzical look, as if she were trying to decide how to answer—or perhaps how to tell him to mind his own business. "He's still technically an employee, if that's what you're asking. He's just on indefinite leave."

"Thank you."

Paul waited until after five o'clock, when the halls started to empty, and then slipped down the hall to Charles's office. After glancing around to make sure he wasn't being observed, he opened the door and stepped inside. The door closed silently behind him.

That was the thing about having badged checkpoints for each department. Once you were on the other side of security, it meant the offices didn't need locks.

Charles's office was the same size and shape as his own, a rectangular cell half as wide as it was deep. However, it had a window that received the afternoon sunlight, which now poured in through half-lidded blinds to bake a corrugated pattern across the white tile floor. Although nearly an architectural clone of Paul's own office, it was as different from his as two rooms could be.

A large steel desk faced the door. Behind it was a row of short, gray filing cabinets. Bookshelves lined the opposite wall, and in them were not books but endless rows of binders. There were no posters on the walls. No paperweights on the desk. The little pieces of personality that tended to salt people's work spaces were missing here. The computer, too, was different—a different creature entirely from the one that sat on Paul's desk. This was a machine meant for serious code crunching. Three flat-screen computer monitors of various sizes were arrayed around the broad desktop.

One whole wall of Charles's office was whiteboard. Nearly floor to ceiling. A small stool sat beneath it to allow Charles to reach any unscribbled corner of the white expanse. Currently the whiteboard was thoroughly graphitized with a massive accumulation of arcane chemical formulas and long strings of nucleotide base-pair sequences; lines connected different sequences. Paul realized why there were no bits of personality in the office. This, the whiteboard, was where Charles lived. It was the ultimate expression of his personality.

Paul opened the desk and sorted through the contents.

He had a plan in mind, if he was caught. He'd say he was looking for an old folder he'd given Charles. An old data set that he'd lost copies of. It wasn't a ridiculous possibility on its surface, but he doubted the excuse would hold.

Paul yanked open another drawer. Inside were pens and papers and paper clips. A lower drawer held stationery and user's manuals. Below that, a box of throat lozenges and ten issues of *Microscopy Monthly*. Deeper strata held papers and receipts, and even an old credit card bill in Charles's name.

Paul checked the filing cabinets next, leafing through the carefully ordered manila folders. He found template documents and data request forms dating back seven years—all neatly filed. He found copies of reports that went back even further: purchase orders, submission results, the entire record of everything Charles had ever done here. Or almost everything. He double-checked. The most recent file, the one dating to Charles's last month, was absent. There was no record of what Charles had been working on just before he'd left.

Paul closed the cabinet and looked around the room. He must be missing something. He tried to put himself in Charles's shoes but found he couldn't. Asking yourself, "What would I do if I were Charles?" was an exercise in futility.

No one was Charles.

Paul had never known him well, but there were stories you heard.

Probably half the guys in the lab were geniuses. You had to have an IQ above 136 to be a genius. Charles was the kind of genius that other geniuses called a genius when they weren't talking about something as definable as a score on a standardized test. His head didn't work the same. Charles was different.

Paul knew he had to hurry. The longer he was in the room, the greater his chances of being caught. He stared at the whiteboard again, looking closer this time. In one corner he noticed a cladogram—a broad tree of life with various branches spreading outward and upward. The tips of the branches each had a different label: *crow, owl, finch, penguin, ostrich,* and on and on. Dozens more. These names were attached to lines that swept down toward the trunk of the tree before converging just beneath a horizontal dotted line. Everything below that dotted line was labeled *God's imagination*. It was there that all the lines connected.

Paul stared at the whiteboard.

There were so many Charles stories.

They circulated around the lab.

Charles taking nine minutes to park his car, sliding into his spot again and again until he got it just right, each tire equidistant from the yellow lines.

Charles who always knew what time it was and never needed a watch.

Charles who startled.

Paul noticed the wastebasket then, overturned, wedged under the desk. He crossed the room, pulled it free, and looked down inside the small metal cylinder.

Inside the wastebasket was a jumble of tissues and wadded-up papers, but beneath the refuse, near the bottom, he saw the corner of a manila envelope peeking out. He bent and picked the envelope out of the trash. It was heavy. He opened the top and upended the contents onto Charles's desk.

Several sheets of eight-by-ten photographs spilled out in a long line, facedown, like the pile in a game of rummy. Along with the heavy photos was a single piece of white printer paper, folded neatly in half.

Paul unfolded the paper. On it was a list of words:

Grayson Group

The Smith Museum

Carner Laboratories

The Gernert Institute

The Field Museum of Natural History

Johnston Laboratories

Paul folded the paper in quarters and shoved it into his pocket for later consideration. *The Field Museum.* Some memory tickled. What was it about the Field Museum? Why did that ring a bell?

Paul looked down at the backs of the photos on the desk. He flipped them over.

They were photographs of bones.

Grayish white. In situ.

The Flores bones. Or something like them. These were different shots than the ones he'd seen before. The angle was different; they'd been taken from a few feet up, but there was no doubt what the pictures showed. Paul looked through the photos one by one. The last photograph stopped him. It was a skull. A different specimen than the one he'd seen. More complete. A full upper mandible, two eye sockets, a right temporal bone.

Paul slid the photos back into the manila folder and turned toward the whiteboard again.

God's imagination.

One early morning, when Charles had been parking, another researcher had beeped his horn. Charles startled and jammed his foot on the gas, jumping the curb and taking out a huge swath of fencing that bordered the parking lot. He then backed out and pulled away, tires squealing. He drove home and didn't come back to work for three days.

When he finally did return, he stayed in his office.

The management was aware of the situation and sent a memo to everyone (such memos were often sent to everyone, so that the person it was really intended for wouldn't feel singled out) that mentioned an accident in the parking lot and suggested that, while no one was in any kind of trouble, the party or parties responsible should come forward so that insurance information could be exchanged.

Charles didn't come forward. He drove his smashed car to work every day and parked at the far end of the lot. Black paint from the wrought iron had rubbed off on the side of his car. A six-year-old could have looked at the car and the fence and put two and two together. Charles drove his bashed-in car to work every day and stayed in his office.

The managers convened a meeting, and they ultimately decided that the company would simply fix the fence. They never went to Charles. They weren't sure how he'd handle it.

Charles didn't care about the money. He didn't need money or want money or pay attention to money. Paying for the fence would have been easy for him. He was just afraid of being in trouble. That's why he hid.

Paul glanced over at the filing cabinet, thinking about the empty spot where the last file had been removed. "Why did you leave, Charles?" he said aloud. "What forced you out in such a hurry?"

He stared at the formulas scrawled in Charles's indecipherable hand. "What was it that you found?"

21

Bone cannot lie.

Bone has no opinion, no cultural bias. It cannot be argued out of existence. If you stop believing in bone, bone does not notice, or care. It will still be there, in the ground or in a museum drawer—an answer to itself.

Paul stood in the doorway of the bone lab, watching Hongbin unpack the latest box of samples. He hadn't been down here since the transfer. He knocked on the door.

"Ah, so you're back already?"

"What can I say? I missed you."

"It was only a matter of time," Hongbin said. "How's it going?"

"Slow. It's a Monday."

"You've got to climb the peak of that activation energy demand, huh?"

"Something like that."

"How's the fourth floor treating you? Is it everything we always dreamed it would be?"

"And more."

"So champagne flows from the water fountains?"

"Of course not. We get our champagne in volumetric flasks, like civilized folk."

Hongbin shook his head sadly. "You're just like the rest of them. In it for the glamour."

Paul moved farther into the lab and laid a manila envelope on the lab bench. "But the osteo lab still gets all the action, I see. What do you have there?"

Hongbin shrugged. "The usual," he said. "Coded samples. No idea."

"They asking for the full prep?"

"The works."

Paul made himself useful, helping Hongbin unwrap the padding. In the end, there were two human femurs, a small part of a pelvis, most of the middle and distal phalanges. It felt good to be back in the bone room. The samples could have been from anywhere. Part of a Roman burial, or perhaps an unexpected find during a construction dig somewhere in the United States—with Westing being the next logical destination after a coroner deemed the remains of no evidentiary interest, i.e., likely both Native American and old.

"Female?" Hongbin asked.

"Or a gracile male." In some populations, it was notoriously hard to tell the difference.

Paul studied the femurs.

Bone does not change to fit your theories. If your theory does not fit the bone record, those bones will continue on, defying your theory forever. Like a thorn in your brain.

DNA is like this, too.

"How many cores do you need?" Paul asked.

"Two should do it. Any guesses on type?"

Paul looked carefully at the bones. "Adult. Other than that, I don't know."

"Ethnicity?"

"Not a clue," Paul said.

Paul touched the bone.

Each population is related to every other population. Science tells us we are all descended from a single people—the root of the tree of human diversity to which all populations must trace back.

Carbon dating established the age of the earth and provides a starting date for when this diversity must have begun. Since the age of the earth is known, and the present genetic diversity can be tested, it is a simple thing to calculate what the mutation rate must have been to yield that diversity. Simple, inescapable math. (Number of years since all human populations were one) x (base-pair substitution rate per million nucleotides) = (existing base-pair diversity per million nucleotides). This formula can be flipped to yield the mutation rate: divide the base-pair diversity per million nucleotides by the number of years, and you arrived at the base-pair substitution rate. Once you have the mutation rate nailed down, you can use the genetic differences between two populations to pin down the number of years for which they've been diverging.

The deepest clade division exists between the San Bushmen and the rest of the world. Here, humanity split first. West African Bantus are more closely related to Icelandic fishermen than they are to the San. After the San, the next to split were the central African Pygmies—and then after them, humanity floresced into a dozen families, a hundred peoples. Tribes carrying the mutations for M and N mitochondrial haplotypes left Africa shortly after creation, curling along the arc of the Indian Ocean, passing through India, Thailand, Malaysia, and Australia. Another branch spread north and west, into Europe; another went east, into China and Siberia, eventually crossing the Bering Strait into the New World, where they would one day build great cities, and temples to the sun, and there await their destruction by God-fearing men. (And, in the process, leave their bones to be found by strip-mall construction crews across the continent.)

But all traced back to Africa. All traced back to the original, deep clade division. All had human mitochondria. All were one people, diverging for as long, but no longer, than the world had been in existence.

Paul took a quick core sample from the femur in front of him.

"What do you think would have happened without carbon dating?"

"What do you mean?" Hongbin said.

"I mean, before carbon dating, there were all these different theories."

"Okay."

"But now we know."

Hongbin shrugged.

"What a moment that must have been," Paul said. "That first objective test of the age of the earth."

"Has to be a first for everything."

"It could have gone either way."

"No, it couldn't."

"Well, *now* we know that. But back then we didn't."

"Still."

"It could have," Paul said. "Do you think he was nervous?"

"Who?"

"The guy doing the first test."

"I don't know. Maybe."

"I mean, what if dating had shown an ancient age for the earth?"

"Millions of years, you mean?"

"Yeah, like the evolutionists used to say."

Hongbin considered this carefully. "It would have killed religion."

"You think?"

"Yeah, killed it dead. It would have put science at cross-purposes with religion."

"Maybe."

"So what does that look like, I wonder. A world without religion."

"Chaos, man," Hongbin said. "Riots in the streets."

"Or maybe it would have ended all the religious fighting. Maybe the world would have been a better place."

"That's crazy. A world without religions."

Hongbin took the last of the core samples, and together they wrapped the bones back in their padding.

Finally, Paul asked the thing that had brought him down there: "Do you know what Charles was working on just before he left?"

"Charles? No."

"Do you know anyone who might know?"

"Why?"

"Because I found something."

Hongbin gave Paul a sidelong glance as he finished packing the bones. "You gonna keep me in suspense, or what?"

Paul wouldn't risk telling him about the photographs. "A list of names," he said instead. "A bunch of different research labs and museums."

Paul took the folded piece of paper from his pocket and spread it out on the counter. "Do any of these places mean anything to you?"

Hongbin read the list.

"No," he said. "I can't say they do. Where'd you get this list?"

"From the garbage can in Charles's office."

"So now you're a cleaning lady?"

"In my spare time," Paul said.

"Why do you want to know about these names?"

"I'm trying to figure out what Charles was working on."

After a long time, Hongbin said, "I've worked here for six years now."

Paul watched Hongbin as he put aside the core samples and wrapped the bone back inside its protective plastic covering.

"I have a child and a career," Hongbin continued. "I have responsibilities. A mortgage. You asked if I knew what Charles was working on before he stopped coming to work. The answer is, I don't want to know."

"I hear you," Paul said. He folded the paper and put it back in his pocket.

"I'm not sure you do. I'm saying, maybe *you* don't want to know, either."

"That's the thing," Paul said. "I do."

"You should leave it alone."

"What if I can't?"

"Can't? There is no can't."

"What if I won't."

"Then you need to be careful."

"I will."

"More careful than this."

Back in his office, Paul considered the creased piece of paper. At his desk, he Googled the first few names on the list.

The first name: Grayson Group. A research lab in Germany. Two hundred employees.

The second name: the Smith Museum. Despite its moniker, a private repository for bone remains, closed to the public. The third name: Carner Laboratories, a research lab in Austria. Privately held, sixty employees. Did work on genetic-testing equipment.

After a little deeper Googling, the fourth name came back a pharmaceutical lab. Texas. Just a web address and a post office box, no employees listed. None of the companies seemed connected to each other.

Paul scanned farther down the list. The Field Museum.

The Field Museum.

He'd been there once, a long time ago. Hallowed ground for those interested in strange bones.

It was a small world, archaeology. Everything circling back on itself, the circles getting smaller the higher you went.

He typed the name into the search bar. He clicked, then clicked again; the next page took him to a website.

A blue whale served as a heading. Below that, dinosaurs, and the Chicago skyline set as a backdrop. Then came your standard museum menu: Recent Exhibitions, Coming Attractions. Halfway down the page were the Special Programs—and below that, something that promised Fun for Kids.

He browsed the Special Programs, but nothing jumped out at him as being particularly pertinent.

Down at the bottom of the screen, he clicked the About Us button. He picked "Our Staff," then scrolled down through the names. Eleven pages of names. Eleven pages of job descriptions. Biologists, zoologists, curators, a dozen other titles. An army of workers, page after page of smiling museum staff.

"Ah," he said when he saw it. And then he remembered.

That's why the name had stuck out.

"Of course."

There were only a limited number of places where talented, ambitious students ended up. He'd heard that after graduate studies she'd gone on to teaching. Then work in a museum.

In the middle of a page of little thumbnail photos was a small picture that caught his attention: a photo of a dark-haired woman and, below that, a name and job title. Lillivati Gajjar, research assistant, paleographic analysis.

That night, Paul took the long way home. He pulled a bottle of cheap red wine from the fridge and poured himself a glass. The glass emptied, so he refilled it. He refilled it again. Then again.

He saw James, standing in the sun. *Herpetology, mate.*

He felt the steel enter his eye, heard the sound it made inside his head. The rasp of blade on bone, a sound you heard with your entire skull, not just your eardrums.

His right hand wandered up to his eye patch.

He saw Lillivati standing in the cages, her right arm covered in blood. *The new hires all want the monkeys.*

Junior year, she'd snuck him into the medical research library after hours. She had keys to the entire research building, so she could get through any door. He'd tracked her half-naked between the canyons of books—stumbling first upon her blouse, then her socks and shoes, finally her pants, lying between the shelves of ancient tomes that dated back to Sophocles. He'd caught up to her on the top floor of the library—near the shelves at the very back, where the ancient boiler system (also from Sophocles's time) discarded its excess heat most efficiently, producing a beautiful pocket of warmth in the otherwise cold and drafty building. Her location of capture was no accident on her part, he suspected.

He'd come around the corner and found her lounging on the table, naked and waiting, panties shed like some molted skin. She was so beautiful in that moment that it hurt to breathe, streetlights distilled through the high windows, cutting strange shadows across rows of books. He moved forward and kissed her. He took her on the table in the middle of the room, while her sounds echoed in the empty library. Somehow, the table held them.

Afterward, they dressed, and she used her keys to let them behind the checkout desk. "Want to see the other rooms?"

"Why?"

"Because they're locked."

There were conference rooms and offices and a strange room that seemed to house every photocopier in the world.

"What about that room?" Paul asked, pointing to a door in the deepest, most forgotten part of the library.

"Off-limits," she said.

"Sounds interesting."

"Yes, but no," she said. "I could lose my privileges for showing you."

"What about what we just did up there?" he asked, gesturing with his head toward the top level and the warm place from which they'd just come. "You couldn't lose your privileges for that?"

She smiled. "Well, for that, too," she said. "But opening this door would be much more serious." She considered the possibility for a moment. "Also, less worth it."

A few weeks later, Lilli got out of classes early. She surprised him and joined him in the rodent room just before the end of his work shift.

He didn't see her enter.

The rodent room was enormous. The repository of thousands and thousands of mice, like a constantly churning engine into which food was teaspooned on one end and out of which baby mice were retrieved on the other—with waste products recycled, data archived, biological material processed and shipped. It was beyond Paul's wildest boyhood dreams. The engine churned and Paul met the lab's contractual obligations. He produced mice for the various scientific departments. He produced feeders, and research mice, and inbred strains. All carefully cataloged. All carefully controlled and accounted for.

But within this big churning engine, small irregularities sometimes arose and persisted.

Like energy lost from a system due to the heat of friction, barely noticeable, siphoned away—a small, private stock.

In the end, of course, he could not resist.

"It started with a piebald mouse," he told her. "I came across it in a mixed litter. He carried white spotting, like a lot of the mice here, but it was expressed to a degree that was unusual. The white patches covered more than half his body. I picked another mouse that had a lot of white spotting, and I bred him to her. I kept it up for several generations, retaining the mice with the least amount of color. I was a half dozen generations in when I noticed the drooping ears. The ears were small, deformed. The cartilage didn't develop right. I bred that mouse to other closely related mice, and I had a whole strain of mice with drooping ears."

"How long have you been doing it?"

"More than a year now. Seven generations."

He reached into the cage and pulled out a mouse. It was mostly white, with only a small patch of color on its rump.

"It's so calm," she said, eyeing the little rodent in his hand.

"That's the other thing," he said. "As a strain, they're very docile. They don't seem to have much of a fear reaction. They're also sort of slow."

"You bred for that?"

"No, I only bred for maximum expression of white spotting. The drooping ears and docility seemed to just happen."

Her expression grew serious. She was quiet for a moment; then she said, "There's something that you have to see." She took him by the hand.

"Now?"

"Now."

She led him back to the research library and slid her key into the forbidden lock.

"I thought you said you couldn't show me what's in here."

"You need to see this," she responded.

She led him down a narrow hall and opened a metal gate.

"These are the banned books," she said.

They stepped inside the tiny room. Every surface seemed lined with books. Floor to ceiling. On the floor, in stacks, books had been piled into tall columns. There were books by Charles Lyell, Friedrich Nietzsche, Asa Gray, Thomas Henry Huxley. Paul spied *Philosophie Zoologique*, *The Principles of Biology*, and even a battered old leather-bound edition of *Modern Synthesis*. And many other books, too, whose authors and titles were unfamiliar to him.

"Why do they keep them?"

"Well, they're books. You can't *burn* them. That's always a PR nightmare. But you can lock them away where nobody can read them."

Paul thought of the secret repositories of books that must be hidden away the world over. How many other books were piled behind locked doors?

She went to a particular shelf. She scanned the titles.

"Here it is," she said. She opened the book and riffled through the pages.

"What is it?"

"Scientific periodicals. Bound in book form. Ah, this is it!"

She flipped the book open and set it on the table in the middle of the room. "The foxes," she said.

Paul looked. Just as she'd said, it appeared to be a research paper on foxes.

"You've already read this, I take it?"

"I've read a lot of these books."

"I thought you said it wasn't worth the risk."

"I meant to you. The risk to you."

"Why show me now?"

"Because you're already at risk."

Paul looked closely at the document.

"The translation from Russian is banned," she said, "but not the actual study itself. Consequently, this article gets cited sometimes, but the original research isn't available. It's a strange gray area. This is one of the few English translations."

"I can take this home?"

"No. It can't leave. Read it here."

Paul sat down at the table to read. Lilli went to sleep in a chair, resting her head on a desk.

It took him an hour and a half to read through it. He understood why she'd wanted him to see it.

He woke her.

"So they bred tame foxes."

She sat up and rubbed her eyes.

"They bred for docility," he said, "and they got white patches on the coats and drooping ears."

She nodded. "Like a side effect."

"And in my mice, I bred for maximum expression of white spotting, and I got docility and drooping ears."

"Like a side effect."

"Like it's all connected. Domestication syndrome," he said. "What else can I read?"

"Whatever you want."

She let him read through the night.

He woke her a little before dawn.

"We'd better go," he said. "People will be coming in."

As they left the library, he asked her, "Do you believe in this stuff?"

"What?"

"All those banned papers."

"Of course not. Not most of it," she said. "Most of it is ridiculous. Just old crank writings that were disproved long ago. But I think we should have the right to read it."

"You don't think it pollutes the mind?"

"Only if you let it."

"They ban that stuff for a reason," Paul said. "A little knowledge can be dangerous."

She shook her head. "All knowledge is good. It's what we do with it that matters."

22

It was a full day's drive to the museum. Paul left first thing in the morning, getting out of town before rush hour struck. He caught breakfast a few hours up the road, a Sausage McMuffin. Coffee black. The hills of Pennsylvania like some beautiful green oil painting flush with full summer—a series of wide, shallow valleys, too picturesque to be true, that he passed through at sixty miles per hour. He hit the state line a little after noon, lost in a daydream, road-numb and hungry again.

He wondered what she'd say when she saw him.

It had been a long time. A lot could change in six years. Everything, in fact.

He tried to remember their last words and found that he couldn't recall them—not specifically.

Nothing too horrible, but she'd said it; he could remember that much—something about not wanting to see him again.

He'd considered phoning first, but he didn't want to risk the call. The part of his brain that whispered against paranoia had been getting quieter and quieter lately. And recent events had caused it to shut up entirely. The paranoid part of his brain said he needed to worry about tapped phones, and the nonparanoid part responded with "Yeah, what he said."

The truth was, Westing had him more than a little spooked. He wasn't sure what they were capable of.

From the east, Chicago was something you crept up on, passing through a series of sprawling little suburbs until you finally rounded a curve in the highway and saw skyscrapers in the distance. Paul double-checked his map. Once in the city, he found his exits and descended to the surface streets, winding his way to the museum. At some point, it began to rain. He pulled into the closest lot he could find and paid an exorbitant fee to park his car. He grabbed the manila envelope off the passenger seat and climbed out.

It was a museum of the old guard, back when they knew how to build them. Huge Parthenonian pillars—baroque stonework and intricate detail, all on a scale designed to awe. Like Greek ruins before they were ruins, and with none of this new postmodern simplicity that seemed to govern the design of public works today. It was stone, mostly. And what wasn't stone looked like stone. A structure in the form of a response, built after the turn of the last century; Chicago saying, Here is a building that will not burn.

Paul splashed through puddles and climbed the broad marble risers to the entranceway. He pushed through—a tiny glass man-door that seemed out of place on a building whose lobby could accommodate a battleship. Footsteps echoed in the expanse. A hundred people milled. Families with kids, tourists with cameras. Up ahead, in the central expanse, elephants shared space with dinosaur bones.

Paul stared for a moment at the enormous skeleton.

He'd always found articulated skeletons to be somewhat unsettling. Standing there, upright, an unnatural creature. It didn't bother him when the bones were lying flat, resting on felt, assembled in rough approximation to a natural formation. But the single extra step of having them standing upright was one step too far. It *implied* something that wasn't there. Bones connected by ghost tendons and ghost ligaments, held in place by ghost flesh. An artificial construction. In this case, it was a dinosaur, *Tyrannosaurus rex,* or something like it. A species drowned long ago and buried for thousands of years, now brought to light.

He approached the information desk. "I'd like to speak with someone from bones."

The woman behind the counter looked at him as if he'd spoken Chinese.

He changed tacks: "I'd like to speak with Lillivati Gajjar."

"She's an employee here?"

"Yes."

"What department?"

"Paleographic analysis."

Again, the look. Like he'd spoken Chinese.

"She works with bones," he said.

"I'll see what I can do."

She got on the phone and dialed a number. There was a pause, and then the woman spoke into the receiver: "A man is here to speak with a Lillivati Gajjar."

Then came another pause. "Okay, connect me." After a few moments, she said, "Hello, this is the information desk. There's a man here to see Ms. Gajjar. Uh-huh."

The woman turned to him. "What is this about?"

"I'm an old friend."

The woman repeated Paul's words into the phone. Another pause. "What did you say your name was?" the woman asked.

"Paul Carlsson."

Again she repeated his words. There was a longer pause this time.

Long enough for him to wonder what the other side of the conversation sounded like.

"I'm here from Westing," Paul said. "It's a laboratory. I'm here to talk about bone samples."

"He said he's here from a lab," the woman said. Another pause. Then: "Yes. Yes. Okay." She hung up.

"She's coming down. You can wait for her there." She gestured to the seats along the wall.

"Thank you."

Paul walked over to the benches and took a seat. Time seemed to slow. He laid the manila envelope across his legs and watched the reflection of people in the polished floor as they walked by. He listened to the clack of shoes, the slow rhythms of the visitors' conversations. The light was beautiful, he decided, coming in through the massive skylights in the ceiling.

Five minutes later, he caught sight of Lillivati crossing the wide anteroom. She was as beautiful as ever. Tall and slender. Her hair was short, cut in a pixie style around her oval face. She was wearing a white lab coat with the museum's name stenciled across the breast.

"You've gained weight" were her first words to him. She reached out to shake his hand. Her hand was delicate and cool to the touch. Then, tilting her head to the side, she smiled. "It suits you. You were always too thin before. Follow me."

She led him outside.

They found a quiet place at the edge of the building, under an alcove, and watched the rain begin.

"I only have a few minutes," she said, lighting a cigarette. "I'm in the middle of a hell day."

"Thanks for talking with me."

"It's been years, Paul. I always wondered if I'd see you again."

"I didn't think you'd want to hear from me."

She brushed his comment aside with the wave of a slender hand. "For a long time, I hoped to hear from you."

"Then what happened?"

"I stopped hoping. Life goes on."

"It certainly does."

"So you're here, Chicago," she said. It wasn't a question.

"Yeah, I drove in from Baltimore today."

"Drove? Jesus, what, you don't believe in airplanes?"

"I believe in them. But I wanted this trip to be a little more under the radar."

"What does that mean?"

"I'm just being cautious."

"Ah, married."

"Uh, no, that's not what I—the situation at work requires some delicacy."

"This isn't a social call then, is it?" she asked.

"No, not exactly." He glanced up at the big stone columns. "How did you end up here?"

She took a puff of her cigarette. "They were hiring."

"But still," he said. "This doesn't seem like the kind of thing you were interested in."

"It's work. I'm interested in working."

"What happened to digs and primatology?"

"Life happened. Positions aren't easy to come by. But this has me working in the field, at least. Before this, I was stuck teaching." She faux-shuddered. "Me in front of an endless stream of students, semester in, semester out, giving lectures, assigning course work. Can you imagine?"

"I can imagine it."

"It was hell."

"It couldn't have been that bad."

"It was an exercise in futility. I taught them, and then every semester they came back dumb again."

"Different students."

"Not to me. To me, they were the same, every year."

"Jesus, you really *weren't* cut out to teach."

"Told you. Now I'm working with primate bones. It's interesting. It's something." She took another drag of her cigarette.

"How much do you know about Westing?"

"I've heard of it. So you work there?"

"I do. At the moment."

She raised an eyebrow.

"It's complicated," he said.

"You always were."

"Does your museum archive bones from Westing?"

"We get a lot of bones from a lot of different places."

"Including us?"

"I really wouldn't know."

"The bones that come in, do you ever see them?"

"It's not my specialty."

"What does that mean?"

"It means I'm not involved with those projects. I deal with the primates. I handle the cleaning, the cataloging, the identification. I'm one of the most junior researchers here, and anything even vaguely worth publishing gets handled by others. I'm a glorified lab tech. Actually, come to think of it, I'm not even glorified. Just a lab tech. I do a lot of the basic cleaning and testing."

Paul nodded. "But you could get access to the other bones if you wanted?"

She looked at him closely. "Why do you want to know?"

"It's probably best that I don't tell you quite yet."

She crushed her cigarette out on the concrete paving and dropped it into the receptacle. "You've got to be kidding."

"You'll just have to trust me."

"You drive here unannounced after not speaking to me since college. 'Trust me' really isn't good enough."

Paul sighed. He leaned back against the cold stone. "I worked at a dig site a few months ago. We found some bones. There were some irregularities, and I'm checking up on something."

"You worked at a dig site for Westing."

"Yeah."

"And now you're checking up on something, only they don't know you're checking up."

"Something like that."

"So you drive all this way, and this is your pitch?"

"I realize that it must seem a little odd."

"Then you won't mind if I tell you to fuck off?"

Paul lowered his head. This wasn't going as he'd hoped.

"Do you have access to the bones?" he asked one last time.

"No, the bone room is under lock and key."

"You always had a way with keys."

For the first time, the briefest flash of a smile—despite herself. It faded quickly.

"Yeah," she said. "I did, didn't I?"

"But I guess a lot has changed since then."

"Not so much," she said. "The doors have gotten harder, though."

He made an impulsive decision. Until that moment, he hadn't been sure if he'd do it. "There's one more thing I can show you." He held up the manila envelope.

"Okay."

He slid the pictures out of the envelope. He handed them to her one by one, until she held all seven.

"What are they?"

"I was hoping you could tell me. They're dig pictures, but I'd like to know what you think of the bones."

"It's hard to tell from just photos."

"Have you ever seen anything like this come through here?"

"No, nothing like this. Not that I've seen. Even in books."

"What can you tell me about the bones, using your expertise?"

"Nothing, really. I don't see a scale. I don't have stratigraphic data. I don't have anything. These could be fake for all I know."

"Assuming they're not fake."

"Well, they're bizarre then. They don't look human," she said.

"You're sure?"

"Of course I'm not sure. If I had the actual bones, I'd know more."

"You said you do testing here. DNA?"

"No, of course not. Just simple stuff. Isotope analysis of bone matrix collagen."

"To determine migration patterns?"

"And other things. Diet and trophic level. If there's a reason to test it."

Paul nodded. "How much do you know about what goes on with the bones after they're delivered here?"

She stared at him, searching his face. "Where were those bones dug up?"

"You don't want to know more," he said.

"You know what? You're right. Maybe I don't want to know any of this."

"I wouldn't blame you."

"Break's over," she said. "I have to get back."

After a moment of awkward silence, he stuck out his hand. She shook it. "Thank you," he said.

She turned and walked toward the building's entrance, but she stopped after a few steps. "There is something odd, though," she said, turning back toward him.

"What?"

"Bones come in, and they stay. For the most part. But now and then, we'll get a shipment, and they're cleaned and then repacked and shipped out to somewhere else."

"Shipped out to where?"

"I don't know."

"It would be a huge help."

"I honestly don't know."

"Is there a way to find out?"

"Not my area. That's all I can tell you."

"Lilli—"

"I wish I could help." Her tone said the conversation was over.

"Of course." Paul tore off one corner flag of the manila envelope and wrote his cell phone number on it. He gave it to her. "If you see anything that might change that, give me a call. Any information would be greatly appreciated."

He shook her hand again. "Thank you for your time."

He turned his collar up against the damp and stepped out into the rain.

Paul got a hotel for the evening and stayed the night. He left the next morning, preparing for the long drive back.

Halfway between Indianapolis and Dayton his phone rang. Unknown caller.

He hit the button and it was her voice: "I was able to track down a location for you. Quick, got a pen?"

Paul pulled over on the side of the highway.

"Ready."

"It's 12467 Hallis, Toomey Hills, Florida. A company called Axiom. That's where the bones are shipped sometimes."

"Thanks, Lilli."

"Tell me I won't regret this."

"You won't," he said. He spent the rest of the drive home hoping that was true.

23

The congressman stood in the central courtyard, sweating in the shade. His personal security detail flanked him to the right and left—four men with active eyes and identical dark jackets. By the congressman's impatient expression, Gavin judged that they'd been standing there for some time.

"Peter," Martial exclaimed loudly, as he and Gavin stepped finally into the courtyard's muggy air. "Welcome to Axiom."

The congressman didn't smile. His eyes narrowed. Behind him, his security detail pivoted slightly in response to the approaching party. Gavin had the sense that some training was in play—just where to stand, just where to look, eyes scanning for potential threats while simultaneously locating possible exits. He wondered, idly, if the men had been trained to jump in front of a bullet, if necessary. Who among them would react first, if it came down to it? Who would rush most quickly to die for this man?

Martial and Gavin crossed the overgrown expanse of the central courtyard, their own security detail following at subtle remove. Gavin was careful to walk an important half step behind the old man as they approached. Even from a distance, Gavin could see the beads of sweat on the congressman's brow. He was a tall man, dark hair graying slightly at the temples. Large and ruggedly handsome, he seemed the perfect physical embodiment of a certain breed of modern politician. As if the physical appearance of elected officials were constrained by some selective process. If he'd been an actor, they would have cast him as president or CEO. Regardless of what his other qualifications might be, he *looked* the part, which was perhaps the most important qualification of all, when you came down to it. Now he stood in the ninety-degree shade, waiting for his tardy host to provide some excuse for keeping him waiting.

Martial offered none. Instead, he smiled and stuck out his hand. "I trust your flight went well?"

The congressman shook Martial's hand but ignored the question. "You never responded to my invitation." His voice was flat and hard.

"The summons, you mean? Washington. Yes, well, we're in the middle of something important. I'm afraid we've been very busy of late."

"Do you think I'm not?"

Martial gestured to Gavin. "Allow me to introduce my associate Gavin McMaster. He's one of our researchers here, until recently an outside asset but now brought more fully into the fold. Gavin, Congressman Peter Salinder, our friend in Washington."

Gavin extended his hand, but the congressman didn't even look at him.

"I don't like my invitations being ignored," the congressman said. His face was stone, but his eyes smoldered with barely controlled anger. More than just a rugged face after all, Gavin decided.

Gavin lowered his hand.

Martial didn't react immediately. He let the silence grow between them, meeting the congressman's stare with his own. Behind each of the two men, their guards eyed one another with wariness across the gap of undeclared hostility. It was the Korean Peninsula, the demilitarized zone.

"Anything you wanted so urgently, Mr. Congressman, we could have discussed over the phone."

The congressman glared at him. "You're joking, of course."

Martial smiled. "Or, if the phone is unacceptable, and you really needed to see me, well, here I am." He opened his arms. "I'm always amenable to meeting here, at our facility."

"Thus making me complicit."

"Congressman, now who's joking?" Martial asked. "You've been complicit all along. Come, let's get out of this heat."

Martial turned and led them back through the courtyard and into the building. Their respective security retinues followed a dozen steps behind.

"To what do I owe the honor of your distinguished company?" Martial asked. The air-conditioning stood like an invisible membrane as they crossed the threshold into the building. Martial veered them immediately left, toward the eastern wing of the complex. This was the part of the facility Gavin was least familiar with. The research staff mostly used the west side of the complex.

"There's been chatter," the congressman said.

"What kind of chatter?"

"The ugly kind. The kind that can get out of hand."

"There will always be whispers in the halls."

"But this talk has a body behind it. Where there is a body, the talk isn't so easily dismissed."

"A body?" They continued down the corridor, dress shoes making clicking noises on the tile.

"Skeletal remains, actually. Found in a shallow grave in a rural area a few hundred miles from here. Decomposed for more than a decade."

"I don't see what that has to do with us."

"Dental records match the body to an old missing person's report, and suddenly this body has a name. That name has a paper trail that leads him back here."

"Here?"

"An employee of Axiom, according to tax records dating to the time of his disappearance. Do I need to tell you his name?"

"Manuel."

"Yes."

"An unfortunate accident," Martial said. The old man led them toward a corridor that Gavin had never explored before, a hall down which Gavin had occasionally seen the old man disappear for hours at a time.

"A bullet in the face is an accident?" the congressman said.

"It can be."

"Who was he?"

"One of our workers here. A deranged lad. A tragedy, really, and a mess not cleaned up as well as I'd hoped, apparently."

"There are people asking questions."

"Then make them stop asking questions. That's what you do, right?"

"We give you latitude to do your work, but our indulgence isn't endless."

They came to a wide set of double doors at the end of the hall. Martial pushed through the doors, and Gavin paused in the entryway. He stuck his head through the open doorway and looked at what lay beyond.

Gavin blinked. It was a place of worship. A church. Here, in the middle of the research center. Like a chapel in a hospital.

A dozen pews lined up in neat rows before an altar that stood upon a raised dais. Behind that, a simple cross graced the far wall. The room was dark and silent. White walls and small, rectangular stained-glass windows.

"Come into my cathedral, gentlemen."

Gavin and the congressman followed the old man inside. An electronic scanner above the door flashed green as they entered. Martial got a few steps down the aisle before he turned. "A necessary precaution against unwanted ears," he said, gesturing toward the scanner. "Green means there are none." The old man smiled. "In here, none should hear us but God."

Martial cast a look at the guards, then at the congressman. The congressman hesitated, considering. He moved his head almost imperceptibly toward Martial's guards, a complex conversation without a single word. Martial nodded. "Please wait outside," he said to his security.

"Keep them company," the congressman told his own contingent.

The security teams backed away from the doorway, and the door closed with a loud click.

Martial walked down the aisle of the little church. He took a seat on the left side, third pew from the front.

Gavin and the congressman followed. Gavin sat in the row behind Martial, while the congressman took a seat directly beside the old man. Gavin knew his place. He was to remain silent until needed. Martial had made that very clear. "You're to watch and listen," the old man had told him earlier, when they'd discussed the congressman's impending meeting.

"Unless I lose my patience with the fool. Then feel free to jump in and try to defuse the situation."

But looking at him now, Gavin didn't see a fool. The congressman was right to be concerned.

Gavin watched the two men, sitting side by side in the bizarre little church. What made a church a church? It wasn't the size. It wasn't the pews, or the altar. It was the quiet, he decided. A special kind of quiet that happened only in churches. He thought of Liang Bua.

"The man who died, what did he do here?" the congressman asked, breaking the moment.

"It has been some years," Martial said.

"Then to the best of your recollection."

"He was a handler."

"Of what?"

"Of animals. He was a low-level worker, back when our hiring practice was less carefully tuned."

"He was killed in Miami."

"Yes."

"There was also a dead woman."

"He was deranged, as I said. We had no part in that."

The congressman sighed. "This is bad business."

"It's a hiccup. Nothing more."

The congressman's mouth became a line. "Congressman Lacefield is looking into it."

"Lacefield? Should I know that name?"

"You know it well enough."

Martial glanced up at the white cross hanging on the wall. "A simple, unfortunate death is a little beneath his pay grade, isn't it?"

"Normally, I'd expect you'd be right. But it seems that for you he will make an exception."

"Why is that?"

The congressman laughed—a sound without any mirth at all. "Perhaps you imagine yourself to be a man without enemies?"

"Truth always has enemies. Lacefield is just the latest."

"Is that what you tell yourself this place is? Some kind of truth?"

"One path to it."

Martial reached down between his legs and lowered the padded kneeler to the floor. He slid to his knees and folded his hands on the pew before him.

"Lacefield's supporters might see it differently," the congressman said. "And they are as numerous as our own."

"If not as influential."

"Yet. But remember that our supporters are not the only religious organizations to seek a voice in Washington. Lacefield has his hand in a different offering tray. There are those who predict a complete reshuffling in the next election."

"Then you'll have to make sure we don't give them a cause."

"We can't sweep this under the rug," the congressman said. "This is a tricky time right now. You are being watched."

"I have nothing to hide," Martial said.

The congressman's face flashed anger again. "There are times when I can't tell if you're mocking me or just insane. Your jokes won't go over so well back in Washington."

Martial said nothing, but instead closed his eyes in prayer.

The congressman leaned forward and knelt close to the old man. He leaned into him, whispering softly, so that Gavin could barely hear: "We've known about the shallow grave for years. We've even known about your little beasts. But the thing that has me out here are the rumors. Rumors you would not want your enemies to hear."

The old man's head stayed lowered in prayer.

"There are rumors about a place called Flores, Martial. There are rumors that something bad happened there. There are rumors that you got your hands on strange bones."

"Bad things happen all the time. As for the bones, they were stolen."

"Stolen."

"By the Indonesian authorities."

"That's not what the Indonesians say."

"Nonetheless."

"There are also rumors of new experiments."

"Would you like me to show you, Congressman?"

The congressman looked up at the cross hanging on the wall. He bowed his head briefly.

"Congressman?"

"No," he said. "You fucking bastard. You know I don't want to see."

Martial nodded.

"This *project* you have here," the congressman hissed, "it has grown over the years."

"Like a flower."

"It was never envisioned like this."

"It is like any flower: the perfect expression of God's will."

"With all due respect, there are those who say you have too much freedom here. There are those who feel we should leash you in."

"Then I say, with all due respect, Congressman, just fucking try it."

"That's a dangerous attitude."

The old man turned toward him, face reddening, on the edge of saying something. He opened his mouth to speak.

Gavin chose this moment to intervene. "There are dangers for all involved," he said. "Care should be taken."

The two men glanced at him briefly, then turned their attention back to each other.

The congressman smiled. "You're toying with the wrong man," he said to Martial.

"Toys are for children. I don't play games."

"Neither do I."

The congressman rose to his feet and stepped into the aisle. He faced the altar and crossed himself; then he turned and left without another word.

The door slammed behind him.

Gavin lowered the kneeler in his own row and dropped to his knees. He let the silence envelop him.

"You agree with him, don't you?" Martial asked Gavin without turning to look at him.

"I think it's dangerous to anger him."

"He came today. He was here. That means he can do nothing."

"He's a congressman."

"They are less powerful than gnats. No, that's not true," Martial said. "That's the wrong way to look at it." He considered for a moment before speaking. "You're right, they *are* powerful, but they are also fragile. It is a fragile power, so vulnerable to attack. It is in this way they are like gnats. They realize their vulnerability, and this is what makes them weak."

Gavin watched the back of the old man's head.

"What vulnerability?"

"To public opinion. To the withdrawal of support. To exposure." Martial turned to look at him. "You don't yet understand how it all works," he continued. "Running for office requires money. Lots and lots of money. Campaigns are expensive, after all."

Martial rose to his feet. "Come," he said.

They left the church room and took the corridor back toward the main part of the complex. The security detail fell in behind them again, until Martial waved them off. They melted away like butter. "To get the money to run for office, the politicians need the churches. The people in the pews. The special-interest groups. The churches fund the politicians, who use their votes to fund government programs—which outsource certain things to outside contractor groups like Axiom."

"I see."

"Not yet, you don't." They arrived at another set of doors. A-17 was stenciled on a nameplate on the wall. Martial pushed through, and they moved into a deeper, older part of the facility. They came to another room that Gavin had never seen before. As they crossed the room, Gavin glanced around in wonder. It was enormous. If the other room had held the silence of a church, this room had the size. Endless rows of cages climbed the walls, floor to ceiling. Chrome bars. Tiny, empty cubicles, six feet high, stacked one on top of another, cage upon cage, extending to the ceiling. As they passed the cages, Gavin tried to imagine what they might be expected to contain someday.

Martial continued: "We're funded by the votes of politicians, who are funded by the churches, who have a vested interest in the status quo. Knowledge is power, after all. We're the funnel here. We release too much information, or the wrong kind of information, and the politicians suddenly have a lot to answer for. They have screaming donors. Midnight phone calls."

"I still don't understand."

They pushed through another set of doors and took a flight of stairs down to a lower level. Here there were no windows. They entered another room—this one bristling with activity. For a moment, Gavin's mind couldn't take it all in. Lab-coated techs moved through the room like bees in a busy meadow. Some carried clipboards. Others pushed carts. Gavin saw one who held a baby bottle. She was pretty and serious, but his eye snagged on the bottle, so incongruous in the setting. He watched as this technician crossed the room to where an incubator sat near a wall beneath a halo of light, surrounded by beeping machines and digital readouts. Within the incubator, he saw a shape. A small bundle.

The tech moved against the incubator, sliding the bottle and her arm through a small aperture in the side. Inside the glass enclosure of the incubator, a tiny hand reached up to hold the bottle.

"Not everything is meant for prying eyes."

Gavin stared at the little hand curled around the bottle. He moved no closer. He didn't trust himself to speak.

"We never lie, here," the old man said. "We just control the truth."

When Gavin found his voice, he asked, "And get what in exchange?"

"Isn't it obvious?"

The old man gestured toward the incubator.

"We get freedom."

"Freedom to do what?"

"To play God."

24

Paul followed Janus down the hall, arms full of sample tray, being careful not to spill the gel.

It was Paul's sixth week of training, and he'd finally been assigned to a project. "The Endangered Species Project" Janus had called it, saying the words slowly so that Paul would understand the gravity of the task. For some kinds of scientists, conservation was ideology. Save an animal, and it was like saving the world, one unit at a time. Paul envied men who felt this way. It had been a long time since he'd believed the world could be saved as easily as that.

Paul watched Janus run the samples. They were working with bald eagle DNA, testing the degree of heterozygosity of an inbred population in Colorado. They loaded the assays into the machine and hit the button.

"Pay attention to this," Janus said. "This is the thing you watch for."

Janus was tall. Almost as tall as Paul, so they were looking nearly eye to eye as they stood there in front of the machine. Janus seemed to have gotten used to the eye patch now, that earlier flash of pity now replaced by a nearly constant look of irritation.

"You put in a sample, and the machine spits out data. Then you plug the data into a program. The rule of thumb is, heterozygosity good, homozygosity bad."

"Got it," Paul said. As if he'd needed to be told.

"Too much homozygosity leads to a paucity of immunity haplotypes. Like cheetahs. All practically twins, a bottleneck within a bottleneck. These eagles might not be much better."

Paul nodded. Despite appearances, the genes of men, he knew, like the genes of eagles, were less diverse than most species. A function of our creation, some said. Man, after all, had been made on the last day. Made in His perfect image.

Paul put the samples of eagle DNA in the tray and hit the button.

"I'm going to lunch," Janus said.

"Go ahead," Paul said, without looking up from his work. "I'll finish up this batch."

"You sure?"

"Yeah, I'd rather get it done."

"Okay." Janus left.

When Janus was out the door, Paul continued to work. He waited two minutes, counting to one hundred and twenty in his head. After a hundred and twenty seconds, he figured that Janus had made it to the elevator. If he'd gotten that far, there was a good chance that he wouldn't turn around and pop back into the lab for some reason. Paul put down his samples and rushed across the room to the forgotten drawer. He pulled out the old Tylenol bottle at the back.

He dumped the lozenge into his hand.

For a moment, his breath caught in his chest.

It had been a long time since he'd looked at the sample. For the last several weeks, he'd almost been able to pretend that none of it was happening, if he wanted to. But now, here it was.

Green and smooth to the touch. The lozenge was made of a special protein membrane, vacuum-sealed with a pocket in the middle. It was still hermetically sealed. Still protecting its secrets.

He inserted the applicator tip into the lozenge like a hypodermic needle and drew out a tiny sample of fluid.

The rest he knew by heart. Mass-production analysis, in two-million-letter sequences. But the key, he understood, wasn't in the sequences; it lay in finding the places where the sequences were different. That's where the software came in. He injected the sample into the agarose, adjusted the settings. He hit the button. The machine whirred to life.

From a genetic standpoint, most life on earth was quite similar. It was all just variation on a theme: adenine, guanine, cytosine, and thymine, repeated in a pattern and packaged in chromosomes. Even the sequences themselves didn't differ a whole lot between species. Humans and chimps were identical across the vast majority of their sequences. But tiny differences could result in big changes in the organism. The entire human genome was more than three billion letters.

He went to the keyboard and typed the restriction codes.

The prompt flashed on the screen: Sample Type?

Paul typed five letters: Human. He wondered if it was true.

"Now we find out," he whispered. Then he hit Enter.

Paul looked at the clock.

The read would take about fifteen minutes. Janus usually spent around twenty eating his lunch. It would be close.

Paul sat on his stool and waited to be found out or not.

Time dragged.

The machine hummed.

Paul stared at the machine as if watching it could hurry it.

Finally, an interminable time later, it beeped.

Paul checked his watch. Janus would be back any minute. He hit Print. He walked across the hall to retrieve the printout from the laser printer.

Gly – lle – Yal – Glu – Gln – Ala – Cys – Ser – Leu – Asp – Arg – Cys – Pro – Yal –Lys – Phe – Tyr – Thr – Leu – His – Lys – Asn - Gly - Met - Pro – Phe - Tyr - Ser - Cys – Yal - Leu - Glu –Yal - Asp - Gln -

Page after page of it, building into a thick stack. And this was only a small, representative sample—a compilation of hypervariant loci compressed into an amino acid chain. Hot spots, not the genome entire.

It might as well have been Morse code. Paul shoved the hard copy into his backpack and put the lozenge back into the Tylenol bottle. The lozenge contained enough sample for another analysis, if needed. He shoved the Tylenol bottle into his front pants pocket. Then he plugged his jump drive into the computer and saved the files to it. After that, he hit Delete. And it was like it had never happened.

Except for the jump drive.

Except for the printout.

Five minutes later, Janus returned. He came through the door and walked across to the lab bench.

He looked down over Paul's shoulder.

"You didn't get much done while I was gone," Janus said.

"It's slow work."

That night, Paul sat in the darkness of his apartment, reading the code. He read it for hours, tracing the letters with his mind.

He wasn't one of the gene freaks. He couldn't read the amino acid sequence like prose. But the answer was there, in the code.

Paul went to his desk and opened the top drawer. He rummaged through the detritus of past projects, odds and ends, looking for something.

There.

He found it. The card was white with a single black magnetic strip running along the back. A Westing security card.

All the Westing cards looked the same. The size of credit cards, they were utterly featureless, meant to be carried in a wallet. Paul had broken this one the previous winter, a day near zero, and the cheap plastic had cracked in his pocket, a fault line splitting the magnetic strip, rendering the card useless. He'd gotten a replacement card the same day but had forgotten to turn his old card in.

Paul looked at the printout again: an impenetrable sequence, a language he couldn't understand. What he needed was the Rosetta stone to tell him what it meant.

He knew just where to find one.

25

I'm good at Ping-Pong," Paul told him.

"Really?" said Makato in monotone.

"I'm the best player I know."

"You don't say."

"It's true," Paul said. "My reflexes are catlike. I may be the best player in this state."

"Good for you."

"Perhaps the world."

They sat at the lunch table, eyeing each other across their half-eaten meals. Paul had heard about Makato and Ping-Pong.

"I've played a little Ping-Pong in my day," Makato mentioned.

"Really?"

"Just a little," Makato said.

"Are you good?"

"Who, me? No, I wouldn't say I'm *good*. No. Below average. Far below average."

"Perhaps we should play."

"Oh, I wouldn't be any competition."

"Still, it would be fun," Paul said.

"I wouldn't want to bore you."

"You won't bore me. Maybe I could give you a few pointers."

"It's true I could use some instruction."

"So you'll play?" he asked.

Makato, who Paul knew well enough not to believe for a single nano-second, said, "Sure."

They met at the Omni Sports Center on Victoria Street after work the next night. The Ping-Pong tables were on the second floor. Paul wore a T-shirt and khaki cargo shorts. Makato arrived in a red track suit. Makato stretched before they started.

Paul knew he was in trouble from the very first serve.

They played for ninety minutes. Makato scored at will.

Paul discovered two things while he played Makato. First, that he could produce no volley that Makato could not return and, second, that Makato had the ability to make the ball dance in a way that Paul was certain defied all forms of physics other than quantum mechanics. Paul suspected the ball reverted to wave form during his various eye blinks when momentarily freed from the constraints of objective observation. In ninety minutes, Makato gave up seven points.

After Ping-Pong, they hit the steam room. Makato barely seemed to sweat. They sat on the hot wood while the steam opaqued the room around them. The steam worked its way into Paul's skin. "You played well," Makato told him.

"Hardly."

"No, for an American, very good."

After the steam room, they grabbed towels for the showers.

It was a simple thing to do. To lift Makato's wallet.

He allowed himself to undress more slowly, and then Makato was naked, heading for the showers, and Paul opened his locker. They had the change room to themselves, so there were no witnesses to the theft. Paul pulled the wallet from Makato's pants pocket. He noted the address on the driver's license and then slid out the Westing security card. He put Makato's card in his pocket and replaced it with the broken blank he'd retrieved from his drawer.

The cards were cheap plastic, and they often broke. It would not be a strange thing to open your wallet one day and find your card cracked and useless. It happened all the time. The guards would have your new card ready within an hour.

Makato would think nothing of it.

Paul closed the wallet and put it back in Makato's pants. Then he hit the showers.

Later that night, MapQuest found the address.

Paul waited for three A.M., then drove with the windows down. The air smelled like rain.

Thankfully, there were no dogs barking in Makato's neighborhood, and very few streetlamps.

There were several different ways this could go. Paul knew from Google Maps that Makato's house had a garage. If his car was inside the garage, this would be difficult. If the car was parked outside, it would be easier.

Paul parked two blocks from Makato's address. He turned his engine off. The Matrix's headlights stayed on for a full minute. Paul waited, hating this. Car manufacturers obviously didn't have stealth in mind when they designed their vehicles. In the old days, a criminal could turn his headlights off immediately. Heck, Paul was old enough to remember cars that you could actually *drive* without your headlights on. Now choice had been removed. Everything was automatic. Even the seat belts conspired against him. After a trip to the market, Paul usually had to buckle in his groceries just to get his car to stop beeping at him. Finally, the lights went off. Paul climbed out.

He moved silently up the street, walking quickly. He saw Makato's house, and he saw Makato's car parked in the driveway. A sensible Honda.

Paul moved through the dewy grass and pulled out his knife. He crouched against the back wheel of Makato's car. He slid the blade between the treads and into the tough rubber—exactly where a piece of road debris might be expected to pierce the tire. It was more difficult than he'd expected. He felt the tire give, and the blade slid in.

A quick hiss of escaping air.

"Sorry, Makato," he whispered. "I owe you a tire."

The wind blew from the west. Paul slid the kayak into the water, moving a few feet offshore. He put one foot in the bottom, then crouched low and sat, kicking with his other foot. He used the paddle to leverage himself off the bank, heaving with his shoulder as mud scraped along the bottom, until silence, and just like that he was away. The Chesapeake rocked gently around him.

He paddled slowly, keeping a rhythm, easing the kayak into deeper water.

The kayak was eight feet long, light and nimble. At 235 pounds, Paul was at the upper end of its capacity.

The lights from the opposite shore made trails on the water. Paul had never kayaked at night. To do so wasn't safe. To do so on a body of water like the Chesapeake, with its tides and freight traffic, was downright stupid.

He paddled. He put his back into it. His shoulders. Right-left-right-left-right, pushing the water behind him.

Out on the bay, the only sound was the dip of his paddles as they entered the waves. There was no way to silence them, but total silence wasn't required for what he needed to do.

Right-left-right-left-right-left.

The lights from shore slid by. He tried to mark the distance but soon gave up. He would know the spine of land when he came to it. It would be the last jut of rock before the bay opened up into a broad curve. If he saw the lights of Baltimore on the water, he'd have gone too far.

Water dripped onto his head as he paddled—flung from the upper paddle as he brought it forward in a high, quick arc. Moving on the water required muscles Paul didn't often use. It had been months since he'd taken the boat out for a swim. After ten minutes, his shoulders started aching. Then his back. Then the thick trapezius muscles tightened across the tops of his shoulders and up his neck. He paused, letting the kayak coast. The silence of the bay was suddenly astounding. He was thirty yards from shore in one of the most densely populated places in the country, but in that moment the solitude was complete.

He started paddling again.

Right-left-right-left.

Paddling was digging, was the forceful displacement of water.

Up ahead, the curl of rock revealed itself as blackness. Flat black against the dark shine of the water. He pulled harder with his right arm, easing gradually closer to shore.

In ten minutes he was there, the black shore looming above him now—reeds and mud and rising gravel. He sensed the water shallowing beneath him and gave a last powerful thrust, then coasted.

The boat scraped bottom, its nose easing upward onto the muddy bank. Paul climbed out and slid the paddle into the hollow of the kayak. He dragged the boat into the bushes.

He crouched, breathing hard—the enormity of what he was doing sinking in. He was here. He was really going to do this.

He stood and checked his backpack, then made his way upward away from the water. He wore dark clothes: black sweatpants and a black hooded sweatshirt.

He moved quickly up the slope, out of the reeds and brush, and there was suddenly grass under his feet. He ran. The darkness was not absolute. There was a quarter moon out, and it lit the way toward the building, across an expanse of manicured landscape.

Breaking into an unfamiliar building was difficult. Breaking into a building you'd worked in for four years was substantially easier. Particularly if you'd made the right preparations.

He ran toward the building and didn't stop until he was against it. He stood, breathing, listening, his back pressed against the cold steel structure. The building rose above him. There was no sound.

He made his way around to the far corner and then slid toward the lower window. He sat. He leaned forward and pressed on the window. It swung inward. A hundred-thousand-dollar security system won't help if somebody purposely disconnects the alarm on one window.

Paul dropped his backpack through the open window. The point of no return.

"Well, this is it," he whispered to himself. He began to lower himself through the window and into the building. It was a tight fit; he squeezed through one shoulder at a time and dropped to the floor. He was in a storage room that contained paper towels, gloves, cleaning supplies, and a sink.

Standing upright, he took the flashlight from his backpack and slung the pack over one shoulder. He moved through the darkness. Here, like no time since the hospital, he felt the loss of his vision. He stopped. He calmed himself and started walking again. Once he was out of the storage room and away from the window, he dared the flashlight. White light made a circle on the floor.

He'd done some checking, and as far as he knew there were no motion detectors inside the main hallways. If there were, then he was fucked, and there was nothing he could do about it.

He didn't trust the elevators, so he climbed the stairs.

Buildings seemed to have a different life at night. A secret life. Things are transformed by context. Like himself. During the day, he was a researcher. A respected scientist. But here, now, he was a criminal. A man in a hood who was trespassing on private property. If he was caught, then all the years of school—all the education, and the money, and his status as a scientist—it was all over.

He thought of James. He knew it could be worse. There were worse things to lose than your career.

He pushed out of the stairwell and onto the fourth floor. At the door, he pulled out Makato's card. The door said GENE FREQ LAB in bold block letters.

Paul glanced at his watch. It was five forty-five A.M.—earlier than Makato usually arrived, but not unheard of. Makato was often the first person to arrive at the lab. If somebody looked at the entry logs several weeks from now, this five forty-five swipe might not jump out of the data set. It might not raise interest, might not present itself as a mystery that required an answer. Makato himself, if later asked, might not remember what time he'd come in on this particular day. He might not remember which day he'd gotten a flat tire and arrived late. He might not remember which day, exactly, his card had broken.

This five forty-five swipe was the kind of thing that might, just maybe, slide under the radar. But once Paul swiped through, there'd be no going back. He would have to hurry.

Paul took a deep breath, put the card into the reader, and swiped downward. The door beeped and opened.

He rushed inside, following the dark hall around the corner and sprinting past the door to the type lab where he and Janus worked. The lab he needed now was a little farther down the hall. Paul stopped at the door. ASSAYS was written on it in black letters. Paul placed the card in the reader and swiped downward. The light turned green and the door clicked open. He stepped inside and the lights came on automatically.

The room was large. Larger than the type lab by a dozen feet, with several broad desks and a stockpile of bulky equipment lining one wall. Gone was the wet lab setup—the sinks and the glassware and the centrifuge. Here the samples being studied were data. A pure data set. This was a math lab.

One wide window faced the parking lot. On the opposite wall were maps of chromosomes—large blowups of karyotypes and complex three-dimensional graphs that he didn't understand. There were computers and filing cabinets and a single oversized photocopy machine. In the corner sat a circular computer terminus with four big flat-screen monitors arrayed in surround to a black leather swivel chair. This was where Makato sat.

Paul stepped over to the desk and sank into the leather. He looked at the screens. It was like sitting at a drum set, everything within reach. He ran his hand along the central keyboard.

He turned on the machine and the screen flashed to life. Blue light.

After a moment, the screen prompt:

Username:
Password:

Passwords had to be changed weekly, and the last user had to pick the new word. Tradition in the lab required you to sticky note the password to the side of the monitor, so that the next user could find it. The username was always the name of the instrument.

Paul felt along the side. There. He pulled the sticky note off the monitor. He stared at it. He stared at it for a long, long time.

He typed "assay" for the username.

For the password, he keyed in what was written on the sticky note. He typed the word "Flores."

The screen flashed, went dark, and then an input screen popped up. The system had been designed by the same people who'd designed the type lab's system, so Paul knew what to do.

Paul took the flash drive from his pocket and uploaded the file.

The screen changed.

Run analysis?

Paul typed "Yes."

The screen flashed again, and a white box popped up. Paul hesitated. He wasn't sure what to type. Finally, he typed "all." Then he hit Enter.

The computer chirped, running the cross-reference.

Outside the window, dawn was breaking. There was a sudden wash of light. The first headlights came into the parking lot. Paul was out of time.

The computer continued to chirp for several seconds, and the screen changed.

No matches. Run bootstrap comparison?

Paul hit Yes.

The machine chirped.

Security pass required.

Paul's hands bunched into fists. Why was there another security code?

He typed "Flores" again and then hit Enter.

Password fail.

Another car pulled into the parking lot. And, with it, Paul knew, another employee, who would soon climb out of his vehicle and head up to the building. Paul imagined the men entering the building. Imagined them taking the elevator up to the fourth floor. He had two minutes, maybe three.

He typed "Flores" in again, being sure to hit every letter perfectly.

Password fail.

"Fuck," Paul muttered.

Three failures would lock the system down, triggering a series of security protocols that would lead directly into deep shit. This was not the time to be playing the password guessing game.

He stood and reached his arm around the side of the computer, feeling for more sticky notes. There were none. He opened the desk drawer. Again nothing.

"Fuck," he said again.

Paul hit No, then Exit, then Log off.

The machine groaned as the hard drive worked.

Paul pulled the black sweatshirt over his head and stuffed it into his backpack. Underneath he wore a white shirt and tie, his usual laboratory attire. He tugged his sweatpants down and pulled them off over his shoes, revealing gray slacks.

The computer chirped again.

Log off complete.

Paul yanked the flashdrive from the port and clicked Shut down. The machine chirped.

Shutting down.

Three seconds passed. Five seconds. "Jesus. Seriously?" Paul glanced at the doorway. "Come on."

Nothing was happening.

"Fuck it," Paul said and hit the power button. Cold shutdown.

He sprinted across the room and out the door. He crossed the hall in five long strides and was at his own door, card in hand. He swiped into the type lab just as the elevator doors dinged.

Janus stepped into the hall.

27

That night, Paul walked inside his apartment building with the flash drive in his pocket.

He took the stairs up and on the third floor passed two men in the short hall leading up to his apartment. This seemed strange to him, two large men he did not recognize. Men who didn't make eye contact as he passed. Paul turned and watched them disappear down the stairs. When they were gone, he continued to his apartment. There were only two doors at the end of the hall. There wasn't a lot of places they could have been coming from. Paranoia, he told himself.

Still, he knocked on his neighbor's door. The old woman, Mrs. Anderson, answered.

"Did you just get visited by two men?" he asked her.

"What two men?"

"Visitors. Did you just receive visitors?"

"I have visitors? She stuck her head out into the hall.

"No, I was asking if you'd just had visitors."

"No, no visitors in a while."

"Thank you," Paul said.

The old woman eyed him suspiciously and shut her door.

He opened his apartment door and stepped inside. Nothing looked different. The same random chaos. Papers on the table. A few dishes in the sink. A cup sitting out on the counter. If they'd been inside, they'd left no evidence.

The next day, Paul arrived early to work. He nodded to the guard and took the elevator up.

He smiled when he realized that he'd beaten the secretaries in. On impulse, as he reached Charles's empty office, Paul looked both ways, then slipped inside.

This time the room looked different.

The office had been ransacked. Gone were the stacks of papers and neatly ordered binders. The desk drawers were open, their contents gutted, scattered across the floor. Anything resembling a work in progress had been taken away. Paul stared at the whiteboard where the formulas had been. Everything had been erased.

There were so many Charles stories.

The time Paul had overheard him talking to Leonard, the two of them in the hall, arguing like an old married couple.

"Don't you remember?" Charles asked.

"No," Leonard said.

"You said it was slide two fifty-three."

"I don't remember," Leonard said.

"I said, 'Okay' and walked around to the other side of the bench."

"It was six months ago."

"Remember, you said slide number two fifty-three was showing signs of necrotization, and then I said we'll have to start using the two percent solution, and then Michelle walked in. Remember?"

"I remember something like that, but it was a while ago."

"And then she said, 'Do you have a—' "

"Jesus, Charles, was it cloudy that day? Do you remember that, too? Was there an airplane flying overhead? What was the weather like that day?"

"It was sunny."

"Really, are you sure? What time of day did this conversation happen? Was it nine-oh-five or nine-oh-six? Was it the second Tuesday of the month?"

Paul zeroed in on one of the messiest-looking piles. He searched through the chaos of papers, hoping to get lucky. After five minutes, he found it.

He held it up in front of his face. An envelope, a bill from an insurance office. In the center was Charles's home address.

28

Paul Google Mapped his way to Charles's home, which turned out to be an apartment.

A small, neat walk-up, not far from the water in a quiet, gentrified part of town. A simple fourplex with a dark shingle roof and blue siding. It wasn't at all what Paul had expected. Or maybe he wasn't sure what he'd expected. There were always stories circulating around the lab about other companies trying to hire Charles away. Each time it happened, he'd go to the bosses, who would match the offer. Somebody must have told Charles that this was the thing to do. If Charles made a lot of money, the apartment didn't show it. It was a humble, simple building, in a humble, simple neighborhood.

So that is what a company does when its star decides not to work anymore, Paul thought. It keeps paying him, so he won't work anywhere else.

Paul climbed out of his car and walked up the short sidewalk to the door.

He knocked.

There was a long silence, then the sound of rustling from inside. The curtain beside the window parted, though Paul couldn't see into the darkness of the interior. He could make out only a hand on the curtain. Long, pale fingers. For a moment, nothing happened. Then the hand withdrew, and the curtain settled again.

Paul waited for the door to open but it didn't happen.

He knocked again.

A few moments later, the door opened a crack.

Charles's face appeared. He looked like he'd lost weight.

"Hey, Charles."

"Paul," he said. "What do you want?"

From most people, such a salutation would be rude. From Charles, it was an honest question. Nothing more, nothing less.

"I want to talk to you."

Charles looked at him through the gap. They'd been acquaintances, but never friends. Charles had no friends, not really.

"Come in."

Charles retreated from the doorway, disappearing into the shadows. Paul pushed the door open and followed him inside. He closed the door behind him.

The interior was neat and clean. Almost sterile. A functional brown couch sat against one wall. There were books in a shelf. A TV sat in the corner. A reasonable love seat rounded out the room.

"Would you like something to drink?" Charles asked. Paul sensed that some protocol was being followed.

"That would be great. Water is fine."

Charles disappeared into the kitchen and returned a moment later with a glass.

They sat on the couches. Paul put his pack on the seat next to him.

"So, Charles," Paul began, "how have you been?"

"I've been well." Charles sat with his hands on his knees. He looked uncomfortable, unsure of how to navigate the social niceties of an unexpected visitor.

When it became apparent that he wasn't going to say anything else, Paul said, "I haven't seen you at work in a while."

"No, not in a while."

"What have you been up to?"

"I've just been here." Charles looked around the room. "Yeah, just here."

Paul saw no reason not to avoid the point. "Charles, why aren't you at the lab anymore?"

Charles nodded to himself. As if he had some private list in his head and he'd just checked off an item.

"I don't work anymore," he said.

"Did they force you out?"

"They didn't force me. I resigned."

"Ms. Bratton says that you're still on the payroll."

"It was their idea. A sign of respect for my service, they said."

"It sounds like they want to keep you happy."

"Yeah."

"Are you coming back?"

"No."

Paul pulled the envelope of photographs out of his backpack. "Charles, what are these pictures of?"

Charles's face showed surprise. "I thought I wouldn't see those again."

"What are they?"

"They came in with a project. I was never able to learn more."

"When did this happen?"

"Right before you left for Flores." Charles lowered his eyes. "I heard about what happened there."

"Do you know the password for the analysis computer on the fourth floor?"

"Yeah."

"Will you tell me?"

Again Charles nodded, but not to Paul. Another item checked off the list. He stood. "Would you like to see something?" he asked.

"Sure," Paul said. "If you want to show me." He followed Charles into the kitchen, where Charles sank into a chair at his kitchen table. Where other houses might have dinner plates or place settings, here the table was covered with drawings. Dramatic, bold illustrations of birds, scratched out in charcoal against a white background. The drawings were piled everywhere. Some of the birds were flying. Others were perched on twigs. Birds of various shapes and sizes, with a whole assortment of different beak shapes.

"You're an artist," Paul said.

"No, no."

"They're beautiful."

Charles shook his head. "I just draw what I see. I didn't make the birds, after all; they are what's beautiful." Charles caressed one drawing with his long fingers. "That's the true artistry. I just copy."

Paul picked up a stack of drawings. "May I?"

"Sure."

Paul leafed through the papers. "This must have taken you quite some time."

"I enjoy drawing them," Charles said. "It's relaxing. Why do you want to know the password?"

"Because I want to break into the lab and run a comparison on a sample I took."

Charles picked up his charcoal pencil and placed the point on one of the drawings. He traced along the outline of the bird's leg. He did not nod to himself. That response hadn't been on his internal list.

"What sample?"

Just like that, it was the moment to leap or not. To trust him or not. "A sample I smuggled out of Flores."

Charles didn't look up from the drawing. His face didn't change.

"A sample of something new," Paul said.

"I heard about your eye," Charles said. "I heard you were mugged, but that's not what really happened, is it?"

"No."

"Then what did?"

So Paul told him everything. He told him about the Tylenol bottle, and the samples, and the flash drive. It felt good to say it. To tell someone about it. To risk it all. Charles's face barely moved during the telling, though he did wince when Paul mentioned the knife attack. He only nodded, taking it all in. The perfect receptacle of knowledge.

When Paul finished, Charles nodded again, then said, "The password I last used was 'deep clade.'"

Paul smiled. His trust, at least, had not been misplaced. "The Post-it note on the side of the computer said, 'Flores.'"

"They must have changed the security pass since I left."

"Is there a way to find out what it's been changed to?"

"Were there any other Post-its?"

"I didn't see any."

Charles was silent for a moment. "Then no," he said.

Paul pulled out a chair at the table and sat. He leafed through the drawings again.

"I like drawing finches the best," Charles offered. "Darwin drew wonderful finches."

"You follow Darwin?"

"He was wrong about everything, but he drew beautiful birds. So that's something, at least."

Paul leafed through to a final picture. A finch on a rock, the beak a delicate, curved scimitar.

Charles said, "You need to be careful of Janus."

"He's my lab partner. He's the one training me."

"Don't trust him. You have to be careful."

"I try to be."

"You don't want them noticing you. You don't want them suspecting you."

"I think they already do."

"Then it's already too late."

Paul placed the drawing back on the table.

"Why do you want to test the Flores DNA?" Charles asked.

"To learn the truth."

"Why?"

"Because people died. And because I need to know. That's what science is supposed to do, isn't it? Track down the truth, wherever it takes you."

"What will you do with this knowledge, if you get it?"

"Expose it."

"What would you expose?"

"The murder, the corporation, the conspiracy. Everything." He searched Charles's face for a reaction, but there was nothing. "People have died," Paul said finally. "The truth is being hidden."

"What will you do if you find out more than you expected?"

"What do you mean?"

"You told me about your bones and Flores. There are also things I can tell you."

"I'll listen to anything you want to say."

"During my years at the company, I have seen many sequences. It is something few people come to appreciate, the subtle shape of the codes. During my work, I was doing a search of a database, and I mistyped the code I was searching for, a short nucleotide sequence. The search came up zero. This did not make sense. I found the mistake I'd made, a small typo, but still that did not solve the riddle. How could this simple mistyped code not exist in the database? In all the thousands of species on file, how could this sequence not be found in any of them? I searched every database we had, and I realized that this particular sequence of letterbases did not exist anywhere in the genome of any animal tested."

"Is that unexpected?"

"It was a short sequence, a few dozen base pairs. It should have been somewhere, but it wasn't. It was an outlaw code."

"Outlaw code?"

"Yes. It was verboten."

"I don't understand."

"Long sequences are unique because of statistical improbability. But certain short sequences—all short sequences, actually—should pop up again and again in the animal kingdom. Runs of twenty or thirty base pairs should occur by chance many thousands of times in thousands of species. But some are missing."

"How could they be missing?"

"I don't know."

"So you're saying that sometimes these short sequences . . . you can't find them."

"Yes. Because they're not there." Charles leaned back in his chair and glanced out the sliding glass door. His eyes got a faraway look. "And there are other things, too," he said. "Other irregularities that I found. Sometimes I would build cladograms, and it's possible to show how different sequences might be linked, simple mutations building on earlier mutations, and it's possible to build trees, not just for recently derived substructures—like breeds of dogs or human ethnic populations. But for everything. All life. All tracing back to a single beginning."

"How long ago?"

"Longer than the world has been in existence."

Paul went back to the living room to get his backpack and set it on the floor in the kitchen.

"I tested the DNA of the Flores sample," he said.

Charles's face lifted from his drawing. "You have the raw code?"

"Yes. I brought a partial copy."

"May I see it?"

Paul unzipped the pack and pulled out the stack of paper. He handed it to Charles.

Charles stared at the first page and something happened in his face. A change.

"Can you read it?" Paul asked.

Charles smiled. Actually smiled. "No. No, I can't. I just like the patterns. I get a feel for the patterns is all. Like music in my head."

"Does one sound different than another?"

"Oh, they all sound different. They're all beautiful."

Charles flipped the page, scanning down the sheet with his index finger. "A worm genome is no less beautiful or complex than a blue whale's, no less beautiful than any other kind of life. Life is life."

He flipped another page.

"But sometimes, I think I can almost tell the species apart. Like music, again. The really, really long pieces."

"If you can tell one kind from another, can you tell what species you're looking at?"

"No, no, I'd never say that. It's just a feeling I get. Like when you're listening to two different jazz tunes. You can sometimes tell they're the same artist, even if you can't name the song."

Charles closed his eyes, as if listening to some hidden music only he could hear.

"I've seen this before," he said. "Or a part of it. They went to great lengths not to give any one researcher the whole thing."

"What do you mean?"

"It came in while you were in the hospital. Shipped from Indonesia."

"That's not possible. The bones were confiscated, and I had the only DNA samples."

Charles shrugged. "It's what happened."

Paul nodded. "What species did they say the samples came from?"

"It was just a number code. No species designation."

"What did the results show?"

"I never saw the comparison assays. I just saw a few thousand lines of raw sequence."

"What did you think?"

"It's why I left."

Charles flipped through more pages. Outside the window, evening was beginning to fall.

"This is how it works," Charles said. He picked up a pencil and started drawing again, an absentminded doodle. His eyes lost their focus. "I can read the sequence—A, T, C, and G. Nucleotide base pairs all lined up in a row, one after another." The pencil traced the curve of a beak. "Every three letters corresponds to a certain amino acid, and you can picture it in your mind, see the shape, and the amino acids combine one after another to form proteins, following known rules of conformation, hydrogen and carbon, single and double valence bonds, all of it folding and bending according to stringent, merciless logic." He drew the arc of the bird's wing. Charcoal on paper, a dusting of feathers. "More amino acids are added as the sequences get longer, and you can see the proteins in your head assembling from just the code, hundreds of letters, and here is where it gets tricky, because at the level of the protein, it is not just the sequence that matters but the direction in which it is read, and I close my eyes." Charles closed his eyes, a look of rapture on his face. The hand continued to move across the page, continuing to draw. The bird's feet took shape. Perched on a branch. A finch, Paul realized.

Charles continued: "The conformation of the protein changes as you imagine the amino acids lining up, and the whole thing flips into a new configuration that affects the shape of what's come before, and it grows and becomes more complex, building on itself, each bond following the known rules, and you can almost reach out and touch it, until it gets to a certain size . . . and then I lose it." Charles opened his eyes. He stared at Paul. "It gets too big for me to hold in my head, a few thousand amino acids folding in just the right way . . . and it loses coherence. It slips through my fingers."

"You can see that?"

"For a little while."

"I've never heard of anybody being able to do that."

"It's nothing so special."

"Protein structure visualized from just a base-pair sequence? I disagree."

"No, I am a failure. I have tried and tried and I can get no further." Charles looked down at his drawing. The bird was complete. A finch, perched on a branch. Lifelike, caught in the act of living.

"It is a zebra finch," Charles said. "Have you heard of it?"

"It sounds familiar."

"They sing beautiful songs in the wild. Whether instinctual or based in culture, no one knew; so an experiment was performed. It turns out that if you raise a zebra finch in captivity, where it never hears another finch, those songs are lost, replaced by simpler calls."

"So they are learned."

"But a strange thing happens if you take these cultureless birds and raise them together over successive generations. The songs grow elaborate over time, each generation building upon what came before, until after a certain number of generations, the wild-type song culture is reestablished. Generated de novo. So in a sense, these cultural songs were there in the genome all along."

Charles handed Paul the drawing.

"Using a system of math called recursive equations, it's possible to model how this could happen. I wonder if it works like that with human cultures as well."

Paul gave the drawing back to Charles. "It's a beautiful picture."

Charles placed the drawing on the table with the others. "Imagine what God must see when He looks at us," he said. "Imagine the mind of God, able to visualize amino acids and all the conformational laws right down the physics of the nuclear bonds, up through protein structure and up into cellular structure. Imagine that. A visualization up through meiosis, and cell synthesis, and ATP, and up through multicellularity into organs and organ systems, and up into the whole living, breathing, functioning higher organism that has to then go out and hunt for its dinner, or photosynthesize—and then reproduce itself, generation after generation, subtle variations in behavior and instinct, social organization, territoriality, migration, song culture, down through millennia. Now *that* is amazing. To be able to hold all that in your mind at once. To be a figment in the mind of God."

Paul stared at Charles. He didn't know what to say.

Finally he asked, "What about the new code?"

"That's the thing," Charles said. "The reason I left."

"What?"

"To me . . ." Charles continued. "It was a strange music. I don't want to listen anymore."

He restacked the printed sheets and handed them back to Paul.

"So what do I do?" Paul asked.

"With the photos of the dig? I'd burn them and forget them."

"And if I can't?"

"You have the code. You have the assays. The rest is just math."

"What do you mean?"

"You don't need the lab equipment. You can do the comparison anywhere with a computer powerful enough."

"Will you help me?"

"No. I've said too much already."

"I can't do this by myself."

"Then don't do it."

Paul looked at the birds scattered across the table. Despite what Charles had said, the drawings held their own beauty, distinct from the birds themselves. They were their own work of art.

"Thank you for your time, Charles."

Paul stood. Charles walked him to the door.

"One last thing before I go," Paul said. "There was a list of names in your office. Museums and laboratories. What were you doing with that list?"

"Following the money."

"To those places?"

"Yes. Money has descent, just like any living thing. There are trophic levels."

"What do you mean?"

Charles shook his head. "I'm done with that now. I don't want to think about it anymore." Charles shifted his weight from foot to foot.

Paul could see that Charles was growing agitated. "Thank you," he said. "So you're sure that you're not coming back?"

"I'm sure."

"Then this is good-bye."

Paul stuck out his hand. Charles hesitated at first but shook it.

"What are you going to do with yourself?"

"I'm going to search for the recursive equation for human culture," Charles answered. "And I'm going to draw."

"Good luck to you," Paul said.

He turned and walked down the steps. He got as far as the sidewalk before Charles stopped him, calling, "Wait, there is one thing."

Charles disappeared back inside, leaving the door open. There were a few moments of silence, and then the sound of ripping paper. Paul walked back up the steps.

Charles returned and handed Paul one of the finch drawings. "On the back," he said.

Paul turned it over and saw a phone number and address.

"It's a computer guy," Charles said. "He costs money, but he's good at what he does."

"Which is what, exactly?"

"What you need."

"Thank you, Charles." Paul shook his hand again and walked back to his car.

29

Morning began with coffee, thick and black. Then toast and three eggs. On the way to work, Paul drove through the steady, desultory rain of Baltimore.

He found one of the third-floor secretaries at her desk.

Be careful of Janus, Charles had said.

"Where do the bones go when we're done with them?"

Ms. Bratton looked up from her computer monitor. The question had startled her out of her normal morning routine. "Several different facilities."

"Is there a way to get a list?"

"Not that I'm aware of."

"There must be a master list."

"Perhaps you should ask your immediate superior."

"Thanks."

Paul swung by his office and pulled a random stack of papers from his filing cabinet. He took the elevator down to first-floor shipping. It was at the back of the building. Samples came in and went out, a steady turnover from and to all points of the globe. If the fifth floor was the company's brain, shipping was its endocrine system.

The head shipping guy's name was Rob.

Paul had seen him around but had never talked to him.

Paul knocked on the door. The man looked up from his computer.

"Can I help you?"

Paul waved the stack of papers. "Yeah, I think there may have been a mix-up, and I just need to double-check."

"What seems to be the trouble?"

"I have some samples that apparently never got to where they were supposed to go. Is there any way you can track them down?"

"Sure." The man tapped out a quick pattern on the keyboard. "You got tracking ID numbers?"

Paul shuffled through the pages in his hand. "Somewhere . . ." He made a performance of scanning the papers, slowly sifting through the pile in his hands, until he was back at the beginning again. Eventually, Rob lost patience.

"Where were they going?" he asked.

"They were headed out for archiving. They came out of the fourth floor."

"Animal bones?"

"No, human mostly."

"Oh," Rob said. "That's easy. Most human remains get sent to the Field Museum, in Chicago."

"Oh, right, I remember now," Paul said. "That *is* where they were supposed to go."

"When did you ship them out?"

"Two or three days ago."

"Well, that explains it," Rob said, taking on a whole new demeanor. "They wouldn't even have arrived yet. It takes four or five days to get there sometimes."

"Oh, sorry about that. I didn't realize."

"If the samples still haven't showed up in a week, then drop back by."

"Okay, thanks." On a hunch, Paul asked Rob another question: "Do we have anything shipped from a place called Axiom?"

"Axiom, Axiom." Rob checked his screen.

"A Florida address," Paul said.

"No, nothing shipped in from Axiom."

"Thanks."

"But we do ship things *to* Axiom."

"We do?"

"In fact, we have a shipment going out now. Right in the next room."

"Thanks."

Paul entered the shipping room. Great stacks of crates and boxes were spread over the concrete floor. On a steel table in the back, he found a box labeled "Axiom."

He grabbed the X-Acto knife sitting on the table and cut the tape. The box opened, revealing a dozen neatly sliced bone samples wrapped in plastic.

Paul reached in and took one out. He slipped it into his pocket and then taped the box shut again.

Paul headed for the elevators. "Thanks," he called out to Rob as he passed his office. "You were a big help."

30

Paul pulled up to the curb and put his Matrix in park. He looked down at the address written on the back of the finch drawing, then back up at the old building. The numbers on the wall read 2213, in raised black letters. Paul glanced up and down the block. This wasn't the greatest of neighborhoods but, for better or worse, he was in the right place.

He climbed out and ascended the short riser of cement stairs. A car horn blared in the distance. From a window across the street wafted music, all bass.

This part of Baltimore was all two- and three-flats. Architecture dating to the turn of. Bricked like brick was free back then.

The place might have once been nice. Now graffiti marked the walls, drawn on top of old graffiti in layers like archaeological strata. They were a few city blocks from the water, on the wrong side of the bridge.

It seemed an unlikely place to find a computer specialist. Even an illicit one who worked for cash under the table.

Paul hit the buzzer twice before a voice came on: "Yeah?"

"I'm the guy who called earlier."

"Who?"

"We talked."

"That's a little vague."

"Charles sent me."

A few seconds of silence. "That's specific enough. Come on up. Third floor."

The door buzzed.

Paul took the stairs two at a time.

At the top and around the bend, a young face leaned out from a doorway.

"In here," the face said, then disappeared inside.

Paul followed through the open doorway.

"Close it behind you." The voice came from somewhere in the living room.

Paul closed the door and stepped farther into the apartment.

The guy was pale with shaggy black hair and dark eyes. He was thin to the point of undernourishment, mid-thirties, good-looking, with a sharp profile and a narrow, boyish face. He sat on a ratty couch, a box of pizza sprawled open in front of him. He wore a black leather jacket, even though it had to be close to eighty degrees in the room.

"Oh, and did you lock it?"

"Uh, no," Paul said.

"Go ahead and lock it."

Paul went back and slid the bolt.

"You never know around here. You want some pizza? Giordono's."

"No, I'm good."

"Well, here, take a seat." He gestured with a slice of pizza toward a chair next to the TV.

Paul sank into the chair.

"I don't mean to be rude," the guy said. "But I'm starving. Absolutely starving. First chance I've had to eat all day. You don't mind, do you? Giordono's got the best pepperoni in town." The words came in quick bursts, like machine-gun fire. He spoke twice as fast as a normal person.

"No, it's fine," Paul said. "Eat away."

"I was at the doctor today for, like, three hours—psoriasis, the bane of my life—and they had me filling out these forms, because it was my first time there." He took a bite of pizza, barely stopping for breath. "And you know those boxes you're supposed to check, the ones that list you had this and you had that?"

"Uh, not really."

"The paperwork when you first see a new doctor. There's a clipboard, and a sheet of paper with a list of every disease in the world."

"Oh, right."

"Well, there's this spot where you're supposed to list the causes of death for close relatives. You know, after all these boxes you have to tick off. Your grandfather died of x marks the box. All I could write was 'Germans.' They didn't have a box for it."

"I suppose they wouldn't."

"I mean, my parents are still alive, and as I'm filling it out, I'm thinking of my great-aunts and great-uncles and grandparents, all the ones who have actually died, and I've really got nothing to go on, you know?"

Paul nodded.

"I mean, that's what family history is for. Your grandfather drops dead of a coronary at sixty, then you shouldn't eat cheese, right?"

"Sounds logical."

"But I don't have anything like that. I mean, for all I know, I might come from a family of immortals. Our one Achilles' heel: fucking Germans."

"Plausible."

"If I get hit by a car and killed in the street, you watch, it'll be a German car. I'm Alan, by the way."

"Alan," Paul said, "about the analysis."

"Right." The computer guy held up a finger while he took a huge last bite of pizza. "The analysis," he muffled.

"Are you sure you can do this?"

"It's the apartment, right? A shit hole, I know. Doesn't exactly give off the vibe I'm the kind of guy you're looking for. I can understand that. People have expectations. But trust me, I'm the guy. I'm just a little short of apartment fundage right now. Besides, you're just flushing money when you rent, so the shit holes are always the smart places to stay until you can afford to buy." He paused, seeming to think about it. "Unless you get mugged or shot or something. That changes the cost-benefit analysis somewhat."

He cleared a space on the coffee table and plopped down an old, beat-up laptop, a *Half-Life 3* sticker pasted across the lid.

"Let's see it," he said.

Paul handed him the flash drive.

"This your only copy?"

"No, I made a duplicate."

"Good man. Never give out your only copy."

The guy plugged the drive into his computer. "What have we here? Let's see." He took another bite of pizza while he waited for the system to load. "Two files?" he asked.

"The first sample is the proband, the second is the reference."

"Doesn't matter which is which," Alan said. "The analysis will just provide a statistical correlation."

"You've worked with DNA before?"

"A sequence is a sequence," he said. "It's just data. So who do these belong to?"

"Better I don't tell you."

"Ah, some paternity blackmail case. I hear you."

"Nothing like that. The reference sequence is human. I'm not sure what the other one is. That's what I need you to tell me."

"I'm assuming the files are compressed."

"Yeah, is that a problem?"

"No, it's just a matter of finding the decompression algorithm."

"And how do you do that?"

"For biological systems, there are only six in common use. I'll just plug them in to see which one works. So you just want a comparison?"

"I need to know how divergent the two samples are. Are they the same species or different?"

"Divergence will be easy enough to test for, but where the species line falls isn't my area. After decompression, a simple comparison analysis will tell you the percentage difference. Will that work?"

Paul nodded. "That'll tell me what I need to know. If the samples are close enough, can you calculate time to most recent common ancestor?"

"The percentage difference is all I can promise, but there might be existing programs I can run to get you the other result. I'll have to do some research on it. This isn't something I do every day, you see, but it shouldn't be that complicated. The main problem will be the size of the data set being compared. Even with compression, these files are huge."

"That computer can handle it?"

"What, this one? Shit, no. This is just my gaming rig. I have access to a computer at work that'll have the balls for this, though."

"Work."

"Don't sweat it. It's at a private company, and I know how to delete project history. Nobody will know."

"How long will it take?"

"Ah, well, that depends. How long do you want it to take?"

"As soon as possible."

"Then maybe a week."

Paul opened his wallet and pulled out five crisp hundred-dollar bills.

The guy took the money. "Two days, maybe three."

"I need it faster."

Alan shook his head. "It'll be two days no matter how many hundreds you've got in that wallet. It'll take me a day to track down the right programs, then another day to run the analysis, double-check, and generate the report."

"Okay, then that will have to do." Paul stood.

"Pleasure doing business with you."

"I'll see you in a few days," Paul said and took the stairs back down to his car.

31

Paul was in the lab when they came for him.

A security guard knocked on the door.

"Paul Carlsson?"

Paul looked up from his work. "Yeah."

"If you'll come with me." It was a guard Paul hadn't ever seen before. And Paul had seen all the guards.

"Why do you want him?" Janus asked. Janus was standing on the other side of the lab counter, mixing fixative.

"We have some questions we need to ask," the guard said.

Paul looked at Janus. "I'll be back in a few minutes."

"Okay," Janus said, though the look on his face said that he wasn't particularly hopeful.

Paul followed the security guard down the hall to the elevator. A thick finger stabbed the button for the sixth floor. This explained why he hadn't seen the guard before. Paul had never been to the sixth floor. Except for the little round number in the elevator, he might not have known there *was* a sixth floor. What could be above heaven?

The door dinged open and they stepped onto matte black tile. There was no grand, beautiful entrance here. No glass wall. This floor had no pretenses to keep up. At a steel door, the guard swiped a security pass and led Paul down a narrow hall. At the end of the hall was another door.

"What's this about?" Paul asked.

"You'll have to take it up with them."

The guard opened the door and motioned Paul inside.

Three men sat at a table waiting for him. Two of them were strangers, but the third had a face he remembered well. A face etched in his memory. The guard closed the door and stood next to the wall.

"Please sit," the first man said.

He was middle-aged and bland, wearing a suit that probably cost as much as Paul made in a month. The man next to him was older, round-faced, unsmiling. At the other end sat the face he remembered. The lawyer from the island.

Paul pulled the chair out and took a seat.

He felt an involuntary response to the lawyer's presence. He resisted the urge to reach up and scratch at his eye patch. He made a point not to look at him and instead looked at the man sitting directly across from him. As if to prevent this, the lawyer spoke.

"Hello, Paul."

"Hello."

"It's nice to see you in circumstances better than when we last met."

"Yeah."

"Though, actually, when you think about it"—here the lawyer made a point to look at his two colleagues—"maybe these circumstances aren't any better, after all."

The other two men didn't so much as blink. They just stared across the table at Paul.

"In fact," the lawyer continued, "maybe it's worse."

On the table was a large file. The lawyer opened it.

"These are your log-in times for the duration of your employment at Westing."

Paul was careful not to let his face show anything.

"You're usually here by eight-thirty, though the time does fluctuate a little. Less than most; you're fairly consistent. Would you consider yourself a consistent person, Paul?"

"About normal, I suppose."

"No, I wouldn't say that."

The lawyer pulled out another sheet. "SAT scores in the ninety-ninth percentile. You're a smart guy, Paul."

Paul's mouth dropped open. "How did you get my SATs?"

"They're part of your school records. Your school records were made available to your employer upon conditions of your initial interview process. Don't you remember?"

"No, I don't."

"That's the thing about fine print. Nobody really reads it, do they? As I was saying, you're a smart guy."

"Smart enough."

"Before here, where did you work?"

"A college lab."

"Doing what, exactly?"

"Cleaning up shit, mostly."

The lawyer pulled out another sheet of paper. "Says here you were an animal tech."

"Like I said."

"Father deceased. Mother lives out of state. No sibs. No extended family."

"That's right."

"You see, Paul, I'm just trying to get a feel for who you are. I'm trying to understand you."

"That's flattering."

"Would you have any idea why I'm so interested in you?"

"I don't have a clue."

"There is a problem, Paul."

"What kind of problem?"

"A security problem."

"I'm sorry to hear that."

"We've had a breach, you see, which is why they called me. I'm the guy they call when a potentially complicated situation arises, and this is potentially very complicated."

"That's awful."

"We have reason to believe that someone broke into the lab during off-hours."

"I hope you catch him," Paul said, then added, "or her."

"Oh, I don't think there's any doubt we'll catch him."

"I like your confidence."

"You don't mind if we ask you a few questions, do you, Paul?"

"Is that a question?"

"Have you ever entered the lab at hours other than working hours?"

"No."

"Have you ever broken into the lab?"

"No."

"Have you ever knowingly or unknowingly unlocked any doors or windows that could allow another individual or yourself to access the facility during off-hours?"

"How could I tell you if it was unknowingly?"

"'Unknowingly' gives you an out. You could say, 'You know, I do think I left the door unlocked, but I had nothing to do with the three guys who broke in later.' That kind of thing. Have you ever unknowingly disabled the security of the lab?"

"No," Paul said. "Not that I know of."

"Have you ever worked on any unsanctioned projects?"

"What do you mean?"

"Have you ever preformed any testing without the express consent of a supervisor or persons in charge of testing protocols?"

"No."

"Done any testing that was not directly supervised?"

"No."

"How's your eye, Paul?"

Paul looked straight at him. "Fuck you."

The man in the expensive suit turned to the lawyer. "Are we done here?"

"We're done," the lawyer responded.

"No." It was the round-faced man, sitting in the middle. He folded his hands in front of him, his expression very serious. "You can help yourself here, Paul."

Good cop, bad cop. Paul knew the formula, as did any watcher of American television. They weren't cops, but the principle was the same. And it was actually a bit reassuring.

"We have reason to believe you're involved in this somehow," the man went on.

It was reassuring because it told Paul that he wasn't totally fucked yet. Power only bothered with good cop when they still had something they needed. But still, the noose was tightening. It was just a matter of time. He had a few days maybe, if he was lucky.

"You've been through a lot in the past months," the good cop went on. "That's something we understand, and we can work things out. We just need you to talk to us."

"I don't know what you're talking about."

"You're making a bad choice, Paul."

"No, he's not," the lawyer said. He smiled. He knew that Paul saw the charade for what it was. "It's not going to matter one way or the other."

"I wish I could help you," Paul said.

"Are we done here?" the third man said again.

"Yeah, we're done."

"We're done," the lawyer said.

The third man spoke again: "You'll need to turn over your laptop for security reasons, Paul."

"I understand," Paul said. "The sooner we get this done, the better."

The lawyer chimed in: "I'd agree with that, Paul. It's just to eliminate you from suspicion, of course."

"Of course."

"It's up in my office," Paul offered.

"What is?"

"My laptop."

"Oh, we know where it is," the lawyer said. "We already have it."

32

Paul never even went home.

The highway. The rolling dark.

For a long time, he wasn't sure where he was going.

When he knew, he placed a phone call.

"Sure," she said. "I know a place."

They talked for a minute, and he hung up the phone. The hours rolled by. He stopped for gas in Ohio.

He pulled into the lot on Dearborn ten minutes later than he'd expected to. The clock on his dash read 10:45.

"Shit," he said.

He slid into a parking spot, cut the engine, and checked the GPS on his phone one last time. The blue dot and the red dot were on top of each other, so he was in the right place. She'd said the place was dark and quiet, but from where he sat it looked anything but.

He checked his face in the rearview mirror. A bloodshot eye stared back at him. After an evening of driving, he'd made the mistake of grabbing a quick nap—twenty minutes' sleep at a rest stop on the side of Highway 94. Waking up had been harder than just going without sleep.

Paul ran a hand over his wild hair. He was exhausted. The rain was coming down again, a slow drizzle that puddled the streets. He pulled his hood over his head and ran out into the rain. The moisture felt good on his face; it made him feel more awake.

"Dining alone?" The maître d' asked. She was short and thin and pierced. From inside, music was thumping.

"I'm meeting someone," Paul said. "She's probably already here. Is it okay if . . ."

The maître d' waved him through.

Lilli, it turned out, had gotten the dark part right. The restaurant was so dimly lit that he had trouble seeing the faces of people more than a few tables in front of him. He did his best, scanning the room, looking for something familiar. The crowd was young and hip and moneyed. Mid- to late twenties, mostly. City people in city styles. Paul waded into the room, dodging an oncoming waiter with a steaming plate of Italian.

A raised hand caught his attention. He lifted his chin, and Lilli waved him over to her table in the corner.

"So you came after all," she said. Her pixie cut was gelled into a complication of short, flowing spikes. Like fire, if fire were black. Large hoop earrings accentuated the curve of her delicate neck.

Paul sank into the leather booth, squeezing his bulk behind the table. "Sorry I'm late."

"I was beginning to think you wouldn't show up."

"Traffic," he said, the start of some excuse. Then he simply told the truth: "I ended up catching a quick nap. It's been a bad day."

"So it would seem," she said, raising a glass of pink liquid to her lips.

"Thanks for meeting with me."

"I didn't think I'd hear from you again. You look like shit, by the way."

He smiled. "Thanks."

"It must be something pretty important that has you out here again. Something tells me it's not my good looks."

"Don't underestimate yourself."

"But?"

"But no," he said. "There have been some recent developments."

"More of your photographs?" she said, then sipped.

"A drink," Paul said. "A drink first." He waved down their waitress, who came to their table carrying a glass carafe of clear liquid.

"Sparkling water?" she asked.

"I'd like my water to sparkle, yes," Paul said. "And I'll have a Coors." He turned to Lilli. "You want another?"

"I'm good," she said, holding up her tall glass. "This is my second."

When the waitress had left, Paul pulled a small plastic bag from inside the pocket of his hoody. "I brought something for you."

"You shouldn't have."

He set the baggie on the table. "You might be more right than you know."

"Is that what I think it is?"

Paul nodded. "That depends. Do you think it's a bone sample?"

"The way to a girl's heart. Where did you get it?"

"The shipping department at Westing. It's a sample that was on its way to that address you gave me."

"Why bring it to me?"

"This is what you said you needed, right? Bone collagen, to tell more about the bones in the photo."

"There are certain tests, yes, in regard to ecological niche. So this is a sample from those bones?"

"Maybe not those bones exactly, but I suspect it's from the same dig."

"You suspect? Something tells me that you came by this sample by less than legitimate means."

"If you want to back out, I understand."

"Back out? Nobody ever said I was in."

"Is that a no?"

"It's a maybe."

Paul looked at her closely. "If you want to walk away from this, I wouldn't blame you at all. I'm probably crazy to bring it to you. You don't owe me anything."

"I know," she said. "Just tell me this: is it important?"

"Yeah," Paul said.

"How important?"

"I'll put it this way. I'm not going back to my job after this."

"I'll do it."

"You're sure?"

"I wouldn't say I was sure, but I'll still do it. I can get it done in an afternoon. Besides, this cloak-and-dagger stuff is way more interesting than my usual day-job bullshit."

"What's your usual day-job bullshit?"

"Working with specimens. Paperwork. Dealing with interoffice headaches."

"Sounds nice."

"It's not."

"Is that angst I detect?"

"Angst is psychological lupus," she said. "It's the mind's immune system turning on itself."

"You've thought that out."

She smiled. "Angst is what's wrong when there is nothing wrong."

"I thought that was depression?"

"No, most people who are depressed are depressed because their lives suck. Don't look at me like that—it's true. My sister was depressed. She was doing a job she hated, in a relationship with a guy she hated. Voilà, depression. She quit her job and now she's a broke, happy lesbian. Depression is the mind's way of telling you that you're not doing what you should be doing. Can I see the sample?" She held out her hand.

Paul gave her the baggie. It held a small disk of bone, wrapped in plastic. "So this is enough to test?"

She weighed the baggie in her hand and made a quick inspection of the contents. "Yeah, this should be enough."

The waitress came with Paul's beer. "Thanks," he said.

"Do they know you took it?" Lilli asked once the waitress had left.

"Not yet. How soon before you'll have your results?"

"Depends when I can get lab time. A few days, probably."

Paul took a long pull of his beer. Behind him, the restaurant noise rose in pitch, a rowdy group entering the room. Drunken college kids fresh from a bar and now looking for food before resuming their bar crawl. He'd never been them. That carefree. He lowered his eyes back to his beer, noting the bubbles rising in the amber liquid.

"You're not going to get in trouble for this at work?" Paul asked.

"No, it's a small thing," she said. "Nobody will notice. I practically run that part of the lab."

"I don't want to cause you any problems."

"I work in a lab where nothing happens. My life didn't turn out exactly how I'd wanted it to. This is as adventurous as I get."

"Your life turned out pretty well, I think."

"So what about you?"

"What about me?"

"How'd your life turn out? Other than theft, or illicit dealings in ancient remains, or whatever this is."

"Three-quarters of a master's degree, then on to Westing. Four years in the field, then back and forth to the lab."

"You like it?"

"I did."

"But not now?"

"No, not now. Now I wish I'd stuck with mice. Your turn."

"Ah, me." She sipped her drink. "Graduate studies, then Sri Lanka for a year. A disastrous marriage. A divorce. Teaching. Then lab work."

"Marriage?"

"We wanted different things."

"What did he want?"

"A virgin."

Paul choked on his beer.

"Well," she said, "among other things."

Despite himself, Paul smiled. Back in college, he'd made the mistake of asking if her name meant anything in particular in her native language. For the next year she'd given different answers according to her mood, warning him once, during a mock wrestling match, that her name meant "great vengeance." Another time, during a study session, she'd declared him the beneficiary of a study partner whose name derived from a word that meant "supernatural patience toward fools." And once, after a particularly coquettish display of feminine flexibility in her dorm room, she'd offered "virginal" as the literal translation of Lillivati.

"Ah," he'd told her. "Like when a bald guy is named Harry."

She'd tackled him for that one.

A few months after they'd broken up, he'd looked her name up on Google. It meant "free will of God."

"I'm sorry things didn't work out for you and your husband," he said. "I'm not."

"You said what he wanted. What was it that you wanted?"

"Never what I thought I wanted, it turned out."

Paul nodded softly. He understood the feeling.

"So what's next?" she asked.

"For me? Unemployment, probably. At best."

She raised her glass. "To unemployment."

"To discovery," Paul said. They clinked glasses and drank.

Paul finished his beer in three long gulps. "You never asked about my eye."

"I was waiting to see how important it was to you."

"I haven't decided."

She looked at him quizzically. "It suits you," she said finally. "Like the weight."

"What does that mean?"

"You were too Abercrombie before. Too pretty, back in college."

"You never told me that then."

"Well, of course not." She drained the last of her drink and slapped the glass down on the table perhaps a bit too hard. "Are you ready?"

Paul dug his keys out of his pants pocket. "Ready if you are."

He laid cash down on the table, and they stood and made their way out of the restaurant.

When they were outside in the chilly night air, she asked him, "Feel like sightseeing?"

"Sure."

"You drive," she said. She walked around to the other side of his car and climbed in. They pulled out of the lot.

"Take a left here," she said. She guided him to the museum.

They parked in the employee lot. They climbed out of the car and she led him around the side of the building.

"We're not going in?" Paul asked.

"Even better. I'm in the mood for a walk." They passed beneath a steel brachiosaur, and she took his hand in hers.

It was a ten-minute walk to Millennium Park. Skyscrapers served as backdrop, glass spires stretching upward into the darkness all around.

The sculpture, if you could call it that, was impossible not to like. You approached it from a distance, waiting to see yourself in it, a mirrored heaven.

"*Cloud Gate*," he said, reading the sign.

"Locals call it the Bean."

"Some bean."

The whole of the Chicago city skyline was reflected in its silvery curvature. A story and a half of oblong, polished steel.

They followed the shoreline back to the museum, and once there she didn't lead him to the car. She took him around to the side entrance near the parking lot and let them into the building. A girl of keys, still. They took the elevator to the third floor, to the maze of lab suites and research offices. A place that was off-limits.

Wood paneling lined the halls, a deep reddish brown.

He followed her down the narrow corridor. It was an old place of wood and books—and down one sleek, wooden hall, near the research library, behind a locked door, there was the bone room.

"Do you want to see?" she asked.

An hour later, at her apartment, they were careful about it. Touching slowly first, with their hands. Then the rest of themselves. They started in the front room, on the couch, knocking cushions to the floor.

Her apartment was tiny, colorful. The dining room table sat a few feet from the front door. Beyond that, the kitchen cubicle—and beyond that, the hall. She led him by the hand, pulling him toward the bedroom.

The bed angled out from the far corner—white blankets, neatly made, and, against the wall, shelves of books.

The sounds of the street below filtered through the windows. A distant car horn, sporadic traffic. She pulled his shirt over his head.

"Now you," he said, unbuttoning her blouse. She shrugged out from beneath it, her golden brown shoulders suddenly exposed.

She sat on the bed, fumbling with his belt.

His pants thumped to the floor, and then she stood, kissing him again, slipping out of her slacks.

When they were naked, she slid backward onto the pillows, pulling him toward her.

It was what he remembered, and a little more.

Afterward, in the darkness, she slipped her hand into his.

She reached up to touch his eye patch. "Does it ever hurt?"

"Sometimes. You're sure it doesn't bother you?"

"No." She smiled. "Honestly, you could be way less good-looking and I still would have dragged you into bed."

"You should write Hallmark cards."

"I should. I can see it now: Happy Valentine's Day. You could be twenty-five percent less sexy and I'd still want to sleep with you."

"Better than the alternative, I guess."

"What do you mean?"

"I could be barely hot enough. One wrinkle away."

She laughed. "Who are you?"

"Just me. The same."

"No, not the same. Everyone is always two people at the same time."

"What do you mean?"

"Who we are, and who we're becoming. People change."

"Do you always think this much?"

"It always happens the same way," she said.

"What?"

"What comes next."

"And what's that?"

"Not this week, or next week. But eventually."

"What?" he coaxed.

She touched his arm, sliding a finger along his bare skin. Her face grew sad in the half-light spilling in through the window. "I get bored," she said.

Paul was silent for a long time. "Is that what happened last time?"

"With you? No. I learn everything I can, like there's this hunger inside, but then something happens to it."

He squeezed her hand, running a finger along her narrow forearm.

"It happens every time," she continued. "Once I learn everything there is to learn."

"You lose interest."

"Yes. But you were always different."

"How?"

"I never thought I learned everything. Sometimes it felt like I barely knew you at all."

33

Paul stayed in Chicago over the weekend, sleeping at Lilli's apartment for another two nights.

She gave him a mug of coffee for his drive, and he left for home the same time she left for work.

When he got back to town, eleven hours later, he slowed at his apartment complex. Two men stood outside, smoking. They were the same two men he'd seen in the hall the previous week. Only this time they weren't coming or going. They were waiting. It didn't take a great leap of deductive reasoning to figure out who they were waiting for. Paul slunk down in his seat and drove past without slowing. The men didn't see him, but there was no question that something had changed. The noose around his neck was tightening.

The computer guy picked up on the third ring.

"Hello."

"Alan, it's Paul."

"Hey."

"Did you finish the analysis?"

"The report is almost done, but I wanted to double-check some of the fine-grain analysis."

"How fine-grain?"

"Just eliminating confounds."

"Do you have a result?"

"Yeah."

"That's good enough. Whatever is done, I need to pick it up."

"I can have the rest of the report done by morning."

"That's too late."

There was a pause. "I don't really like you changing the game plan on me."

"It can't be helped."

"You in some kind of trouble, man?"

"No, no trouble."

"Then what's the hurry?"

"I just need to square things away."

"Whatever the fuck *that* means."

"Yeah, whatever the fuck. I've got the money. Full price."

"Your money, man." There was silence. Then: "Come by and pick it up anytime."

"I'm on my way."

"You mean now?"

"Yeah."

"Okay, I'll save the report to the same drive you gave me, and you can have your data back."

"Sounds good to me."

"And after this . . . don't call me again. You make me nervous."

"That's a deal."

Paul hung up and sat considering his phone for a while. He texted Lilli: *When can you have the tests done?*

Her reply came a minute later: *Should be able to test in a few days.*

He texted back: *The sooner the better.*

A half hour later, Paul pulled onto Alan's block. He drove past the apartment twice.

He didn't see anyone waiting. No men in suits. Nothing suspicious. But still, things didn't feel right.

He opened his phone and punched the numbers.

"Hello."

"You need to meet me," Paul said.

There was a pause on Alan's end. "I thought you were coming here?"

"No, it's better we meet somewhere else. You bring the drive and I'll bring the money."

"You're acting real sketchy, man," he said.

"It'll be fine."

"I don't like this."

"You don't have to like it."

"Maybe I just smash this drive with a hammer and forget I ever met you."

"You'd be doing us both a favor."

"Then maybe I will."

"Do what you have to."

There was silence on the line. The crackle of static.

"Where do you want to meet?"

"The bridge two blocks over."

"My jacket is already on."

Paul watched the front steps. He was parked a block and a half away, but he had a clear line of sight to the front of Alan's building.

He opened the text feature on his phone and typed in Alan's number. Then he typed the words *STOP, GO BACK.*

His finger hovered over the Send button but did not press it. He waited.

Although Alan had said his jacket was on, it still took three minutes for a man to exit Alan's building—small and slight, wearing Alan's leather jacket, a baseball cap pulled down over a head of dark hair. If it wasn't Alan, it was a guy who looked just like him.

Paul scanned the street carefully. He saw nothing out of the ordinary. No one followed. No one stepped from the shadows. Alan looked both ways, then turned and moved up the sidewalk, disappearing around the corner. Paul waited a full minute before closing his phone. He climbed out of his car and walked one block over, heading for the bridge. The streets were quiet this time of the night. The traffic was light. Few pedestrians on the sidewalks. Around the corner, the bridge loomed into view. The structure itself was an old, iron monstrosity, about 150 yards long, an intermittently lit suspension of two-lane road. A pedestrian walkway crowded one edge of the traffic lanes. The bridge crossed a sloping landscape of trees and brush that dropped into a low, dark river in the center of the span. Up ahead, Alan stopped against the handrail under a streetlight, about a third of the way across. His collar was turned up, the cap still hiding his face.

Paul approached.

As he got closer, he waved.

Alan waved back.

There was something in his stance. Something off about it. Paul's pace slowed. Alan seemed to sense this, and he turned slightly, his face coming out of the shadows for a moment, and it was then that Paul saw it. The bruises. Two black eyes. A broken nose.

Paul stopped. He was thirty feet away.

"Alan?"

Alan refused to look him in the face. Paul noticed that his hand was bandaged. Soaked through in blood. Blood dripped to the pavement.

"What . . ." Paul began, but there was no need to finish the question.

From somewhere behind Paul came the sound of a gunning engine. Paul turned. A gray van surged up the street, its bright lights bearing down on them through the darkness.

"I'm sorry," Alan said. "They made me."

Paul ran.

He sprinted past Alan along the walkway, pumping his legs as fast as he could. The sound of the engine grew louder, until it was right beside him. He chanced a look and saw a blond man in the driver's seat, glaring at him. The squeal of brakes and doors opening—then shouts.

"Stop right fucking there!"

"You're only making it harder!"

"No, let him run." It was the last voice that brought Paul's gaze around again. A twisted voice from out of a nightmare.

A dark, hooded figure was stepping away from the van. A long coat flapped in the wind, and beneath the hood Paul caught the flash of something that his mind couldn't process. A face.

Paul bolted. Footfalls closed in on him. He ran as fast as he could, but it wasn't fast enough. The thing hit him like a locomotive. A dark man-shaped thing that bulged out from beneath a gray trench coat. Paul slammed into the railing, slipped, spun, fell. He staggered to his feet, turning to look at his attacker. It was a few inches shorter than him but wider. The darkness and a hooded sweatshirt hid its features.

"You're making this fun," the shape said.

Paul lunged away but it was faster. Much faster.

The blow knocked Paul off his feet. He hit the corrugated grating.

And now the others were there.

The blond man, grinning in the dark.

In the distance, a scream. "No!" Alan tried to fight them as he was shoved into the open van. One of the men jumped into the driver's seat and the van sped along the bridge, screeching to a halt right in front of Paul, blocking his view of the roadway.

Paul pulled himself to his feet and hooked an arm around the bridge railing. Here the bridge was still above land, not water. A tangle of branches spread below.

He angled away from them, moving along the walkway, but the hooded shape advanced, cutting him off.

"They don't get out much," the blond man said, gesturing toward his hooded partner. "They're a specialized set. Bad at some things, good at others. But this kind of work, hunting down men—it's like they were *born* for it."

Paul backed up against the rail.

"Another step, and I'll jump."

The blond man smiled. "Do us a fucking favor."

They came for him in a rush, the hooded figure moving faster than the others, and Paul leaned backward, the small of his back pressed against the railing. His legs came up . . . only instead of going over, he put everything he had into a two-legged kick at the hooded, incoming face. The thing's head snapped back with the force of the blow. Then fast—so fast—a huge arm came up like a piston and smashed Paul in the side of the head, sending him spinning over the rail, and then he was falling.

An iron grip caught him by the ankle.

He looked up in shock, and there was the dark shape glaring down at him. Impossibly fast, impossibly strong. Paul weighed north of two-thirty and this thing had him in one viselike hand.

Paul looked down and saw the tree branches a dozen feet below. It was impossible to tell how high he was. Where he'd land. What he'd land on.

Paul looked up at the leering face. For the first time, he got a good view of it, in the light from a passing car. Under the hooded sweatshirt, the face was impossible. Huge and prognathic, thin lips peeled back from teeth like no human ever had—enormous canines, clenched down with insane intensity. The eyes had no whites—just dark pools of rage.

And then that impossibly strong arm *pulled* and Paul's two-hundred-thirty-plus pounds were drawn inexorably upward.

Paul used his other foot to kick the demon in the face, and then he fell.

Free fall.

The sound of rushing wind. The soft, supple texture of the last few moments of his life.

Then branches clawed his face, and Paul spun, clutching—boughs coming apart in his hands, body twisting in the darkness, as he smashed through the leafy canopy—the crackle of rending wood getting louder as the thin outer branches bent under his weight, carrying him downward before snapping, and still he hung on, the taste of leaves, pinwheeling, taking on angular momentum as his body careened off the thicker branches.

Sounds like bones breaking, like gunshots; then a huge blow to the back of his legs, and his body swung beneath the branch, spinning—and then a moment of nothing, free fall again, and time slowed to an instant crack.

He hit the ground.

There were two things in the universe.

Darkness.

Pain.

Waking like sleeping. Half-conscious, aware only that he was alive. Shouts rained down from high above. From another world.

"Paul? You dead, Paul?"

PROPHET OF BONES   239

"I think he's dead."

"We need to check."

Paul was on his back. The entire world above him. He sat up, and the pain was excruciating. He collapsed into a heap. Blackness.

The men.

The thing.

Paul opened his eye again, slowly this time, trying to remember what he was supposed to do.

His head throbbed. His thoughts were jumbled. Where his spine had once been was now only white-hot screaming pain. His eye burned.

When he thought he could sit up, he did, and the pain laid him out again.

From somewhere above, the garbled shouting grew louder. Then silence. Instinctively, he knew the silence was worse.

They were coming for him.

They.

And that brought it back.

All of it.

He remembered the impossible face. The iron-strong hand.

Paul climbed to his feet and made them move.

His right leg was agony, but it supported his weight.

He limped up the hill for a few steps, then stopped. That hill, he realized, was what they'd be coming down to meet him. He changed course, moving down the hill, toward the water, scrambling through the underbrush. He made his way to the river.

The foliage opened up before him, and there was the sudden expanse of water. Paul crouched and scooped a handful onto his face. It was shockingly cold. He dumped another handful over his head.

Voices drifted down from somewhere above.

They were searching. He looked right and then left, trying to make a decision.

He went left, hugging the shoreline, trying to put distance between himself and the voices. This took him under the bridge and along the other side. He moved as fast as his damaged body could carry him. The limp was getting worse as his muscles tightened up.

The voices grew louder, so Paul moved a few yards up from the river-bank. This way, if they made it to the riverbank and looked downstream, they wouldn't see him.

Distance was the thing. The only thing. It was what mattered, putting distance between himself and them. When he'd gone another hundred yards, pushing twisted branches out of his way, he allowed himself to veer upward again, climbing the hill. He was on the other side of the bridge now. If they'd sent anyone down the hill on this side, he was finished. It was as simple as that.

He climbed, and the hill grew steeper, the underbrush less dense. The sound of traffic filtered through the bushes above. Soon a streetlight was throwing faint illumination through the foliage. Then, with a last upward surge, his thigh muscles burning, he was up and out.

He stepped onto a crumbling sidewalk. It was like being born.

He kept his head down and limped up the street, away from the bridge. Two blocks over, he circled back toward his car.

If they knew where he'd parked, if they'd left a guard, he was done.

He came around the corner of the building. He eyed his small black Matrix. He saw nobody nearby, but then again, he wouldn't. Sometimes, pretending you had a choice was a waste of time.

He limped to his car, opened the door, and climbed inside.

He hit the ignition, shifted into drive, and pulled away from the curb. Without putting his seat belt on. Never had that infernal beeping sounded so good.

There were only so many places he could go.

His apartment was out of the question.

Paul drove quickly through the city streets, heading for the highway. It started to rain again.

First he'd need money. That before anything else.

But then a thought occurred to him. Even before money, he had to warn Charles. If they'd followed him to the computer guy, then it was hard to tell what they knew. It wouldn't be much of a stretch for them to know he'd talked to Charles. Paul flipped open his phone but closed it again. His phone records might be compromised. If not now, then possi-

bly later. If he called Charles, it would show up on a spreadsheet somewhere, and later it might make trouble for Charles. Paul didn't want that.

Best to warn him in person. Tonight. Before things had a chance to
spiral any further out of control.

It was a thirty-minute drive across the city.

When Paul finally pulled onto Charles's street, he made a point not
to slow down. He drove past the building, searching every shadow, working up his nerve. Again, nothing suspicious. By now Paul had realized
that this didn't mean much. There'd been nothing suspicious at Alan's
place, either. He parked two blocks away and walked it.

The sidewalks were puddled, but at least the rain had stopped. Paul
kept his head down, walking with purpose. If he saw anything fishy, he'd
take off, he decided. He'd never been much of a runner, and now, with
his leg screwed up, he'd be even worse, but maybe with enough of a head
start, he figured, he could make it back to his car. These were the things
he was thinking about as he approached Charles's apartment.

The windows were dark. Nothing stirred. Up and down the block,
people slept in their beds, oblivious to the world outside their locked
doors.

At Charles's front door, Paul stopped. He listened. He put his ear to
the door. Nothing.

He knocked.

A few seconds passed with no sound.

No shuffle of feet.

The door didn't open.

Paul knocked again, louder this time.

Again, nothing.

He turned to leave, but in the dim glow cast from a streetlight he
noticed the bootprint planted in the lower middle of the door. He noticed
then, too, the jamb was slightly askew, as if somebody had closed the door,
and then somebody else had it kicked in.

Paul tried the knob.

The doorknob didn't turn, but the door swung inward, broken from
the jamb.

He pushed inside. The door made a soft thud as it coasted into the
doorstop.

Absolute darkness.

"Charles!" he called out, moving into the entranceway.

There was only silence.

"Charles, it's Paul. Your door wasn't locked."

His hand fumbled at the wall, searching for a light switch. He found one, and the living room burst into view. He moved deeper into the apartment but saw nothing out of place. Nothing out of the ordinary.

"Charles, are you okay? I'm just here to check on you."

Every book neatly in its shelf. The room neat and tidy.

Perhaps Charles was just out for the evening.

A late-night stroll. A trip to the movies.

But, of course, these suppositions all felt wrong. It was nine P.M. Paul would have bet his life savings that Charles hadn't seen a movie in ten years. And late-night strolls could be dangerous. Charles would never have done that.

Of course, talking to Paul had been the real danger.

In the kitchen were the drawings from earlier. The birds. Only here was the first indication of something strange. Most of the drawings were stacked on the table, like during his visit, but a few had fallen to the floor. In the middle of the linoleum was a large torn drawing. Paul bent and picked it up. Only half a bird—the missing piece cut a jagged wound across the bird's upper torso. The top half was missing. Paul looked around the kitchen but couldn't find the other half of the drawing.

He moved down the hall, toward the bedrooms. "Charles!" he called again, though he'd lost hope of hearing a response. Now he only prayed that Charles wasn't home. He pushed open the first door. The bedroom was clean and tidy, the bed neatly made.

Paul made a quick glance into the hall bathroom, which was empty, and then moved finally to the second bedroom. The last door. He turned the knob and pushed the door open. He flipped the light on.

He flipped it back off again.

He closed his eye. He breathed, trying to unsee.

The second bedroom had been used as a storeroom for art.

Charles was on the bed.

Paul took a deep breath and flipped the light switch again.

One arm was twisted beneath him. The other was draped downward, pointing at the floor.

His face was nearly unrecognizable. Only by his sweater, and his thin limbs, and his curly, sandy hair was Paul able to recognize him. Paul stepped farther into the room, moving closer. Charles's eyes were half-lidded, caked in a thick crust of blood. His skull had been crushed in on one side like a dropped pumpkin. His throat was a bloody ruin—flesh torn wide, bright and freshly red, the blood not yet even congealed. A thick wad of paper was balled up and shoved into his mouth as a gag. Without having to look, Paul knew. The missing half of the bird drawing. He'd choked to death on it.

Blood coated the blue wallpaper in a fine mist. A crushed filing cabinet lay on its side in the corner.

In that moment, Charles's throat convulsed, releasing a gout of blood. An outward burst of air guttered through the open wound.

Paul dropped to his knees as the throat worked again, sucking air this time, collapsing in on itself. A horrible gurgling as the lungs rattled with fluid.

At first Paul didn't understand what he was seeing. And then he realized: traumatic tracheotomy.

They thought they'd choked him to death on his own drawing, but the body still lived. Sucking air through the ruined throat.

Paul reached out but couldn't bring himself to touch the dented, crushed-in skull. Wherever Charles was, it wasn't here. There was no room for him in what remained.

The gasps came and went over the next few minutes, the space between them growing longer. The final breath happened in a slow rattle. Only then did Paul reach to touch his hand.

A rage built inside him, that such a thing could have been done to so gentle a man. That a mind such as his had been snuffed out. Paul felt a sudden crushing guilt, because he was not worth a Charles. His life did not balance the loss of the life taken. It was too much to bear. Better that he'd left it alone. Better that he'd died back on Flores.

For a moment, the rage outweighed the fear, and Paul did not turn away. He didn't run. He went to the dead man, who hadn't been his friend but had been a person he respected.

"I'm sorry, Charles," he whispered.

Charles's face was turned away. There was no forgiveness there.

"If I had known this could happen . . ."

But hadn't he? Hadn't he known?

"That was in Indonesia," he said out loud, talking to himself. "I didn't know it could happen here." A part of him, however, didn't believe that he'd ever believed that. That it would be different just because they were no longer in that wild place.

Maybe it was all the same. Everywhere. And you just told yourself stories so you could sleep at night.

Paul bent toward the man he'd known mostly through stories. He pulled the bird drawing from Charles's mouth. It came with a dark clot of congealed blood, leaving his broken mouth still slack and open. This was somehow worse, and Paul couldn't take it anymore.

This attack had happened hours ago. They'd come here first, before they went to Alan's. Charles must have given them Alan's name. Paul realized that Alan was probably dead, too, by now.

"I'm sorry," Paul said.

Then he turned and fled. He took the time to wipe his fingerprints from the doorknob, closed the door, and ran.

34

Gavin stood in Martial's office. The old man glared at him from across an expanse of polished mahogany desktop.

"There has been an unfortunate series of events," the old man said. His flat gray eyes bore into him.

Gavin had learned to keep his face blank around the old man. It was best to show no emotion. Martial had summoned him from bed in the middle of the night and now they stood in his office, watching the tail end of a tropical depression lash at the windows. For Gavin, the last several weeks at the compound had been anything but comforting. He'd become more and more convinced of the old man's mental instability. He'd seen evidence of it all around him—in the emotional outbursts, the irrational beliefs. Then there was the bizarre state of the facility itself. A thing no sane man would helm. But more disturbing than his craziness was the terrifying reach of the man's power, a thing he'd also borne witness to in his time at the old man's side.

"How unfortunate, exactly?" Gavin said, keeping his tone perfectly neutral.

"People have died," Martial said. "More people are going to die."

Gavin sat down in the red chair facing the desk.

"You brought Paul in on this," the old man continued.

"I know."

"I've tried to be . . . tolerant. Circumstances now force my hand."

"What do you mean?"

"Events have conspired to leave me no choice."

"There's always a choice."

"What would you have me do?"

"He could be of value to you," Gavin said.

The old man shook his head. "He's a liability."

Liability. That was a word you never wanted pointed at you. Not by Martial. Liabilities had a way of disappearing. Of being neutralized. Erased from the equation. It was how Martial conducted business. Gavin had worked for Martial for the last twenty years, but for most of that time he'd been at the periphery. Just another cog in the grand machine, doing his part at a safe remove from the more unpleasant aspects of the business. Here at the compound, however, he'd gotten a firsthand glimpse of how Martial ran his empire.

"That's only because you haven't tried to make him into an asset," Gavin said. He swallowed hard. Saying this was a risk. Saying anything contrary was a risk.

"We're beyond that now," the old man said.

"You don't know that for sure. Considering what happened with Paul's father, do you really want this on your head? The father *and* the son?"

"You yourself said we couldn't trust him."

"There are ways he can be *made* worthy of trust." This was a thing Gavin understood far too well. It could be done by a dozen different methods, over the course of several years. You don't sell your soul all at once. You do it in parts, so that when you wake up and look in the mirror one day it's gone, and you're not even sure where you lost it.

"It is a tricky business," the old man said, but there was hesitation in his voice.

"No trickier than the alternative."

"What's *your* alternative?"

"I can talk to him. I can reason with him."

"And what makes you think we can reason with him now?"

"We take away all his other options."

The old man sighed. "This thing that should be so very simple has grown so very complicated. And you want me to complicate it further?"

"Out of complexity comes nuance. Maybe he deserves a chance. Considering who he is."

The old man coughed into his handkerchief. The handkerchief was red. The old man used red handkerchiefs now so the blood wouldn't show.

"So be it."

Here Gavin's face betrayed him. Surprise.

"You won't regret it," he stammered.

"Don't speak to me of regret. I've a lifetime of regret."

"Thank you, sir."

"Don't thank me yet. It is a final chance. But I'm not sending you alone."

The old man hit the buzzer on his desk. "Send her in."

There was a moment's pause, and then the door opened.

Margaret walked in.

"Sir," she said, speaking to the old man. Then she turned to Gavin. "Hello, Mr. McMaster."

Gavin closed his mouth with a snap. "It's good to see you're well," he said. He hadn't laid eyes on her since Indonesia. He'd heard she'd made it out all right, but beyond that, nothing else. He wondered if she'd been working for the old man all along, or if she was a new convert to the cause.

"Margaret has already been briefed on the situation. She's agreed to accompany you."

Gavin realized then that their conversation had been theater. Martial had already made the decision before Gavin had stepped into the room. It had all been artifice—part of the old man's plan to get Gavin behind the objective.

"You'll have your chance to get him on board," the old man said. "But if he hesitates . . . if he shows the slightest inclination toward refusal. Then he's a problem that will be solved in the quickest, easiest way."

Gavin looked over at Margaret. She stared straight ahead, her face set in stone.

"Do you understand?"

"Yes," Gavin said. "I understand."

And he knew then that Margaret had been working for Martial for a very, very long time.

35

Paul drove north. Just the road for its own sake, the slow accumulation of mile markers ticking off the distance between himself and the disaster that his life had become. Each time he thought of a place he should go, he found a reason it wouldn't work. Wherever he went, they would find him. There was no place far enough to run.

And what they'd done to Charles . . .

He shook his head, trying to put the images out of his mind.

If they'd done that to Charles, there would be no mercy for him. Paul considered this while he drove. Perhaps it was fair. First James, now Charles. Two men who'd still be living right now if not for him. Perhaps it was only fair that Paul paid what was owed. He'd caused so much destruction already.

He pulled off the highway and stopped at a gas station.

He filled his tank.

Would they have access to his debit records, he wondered? Would they be able to track him? He imagined it turning up in the murder investigation, once his body was found. He imagined the detectives puzzling over his expenditures, noting the times and places where he'd spent his last days, trying to divine some hidden meaning in the chicken entrails of his credit card statement. Or perhaps it wouldn't be a murder investigation after all, but merely a missing persons report. He wasn't giving them enough credit. Perhaps his body would never be found.

Paul paid at the pump, then went inside and bought a six-pack of Coke and a hot dog. There was an ATM next to the bathroom, so he withdrew the maximum amount, four hundred dollars. That would get him a little distance, at least, though it would no doubt produce a paper trail that the police could follow later.

And maybe more than just the police.

A chill crept across Paul's neck.

Lillivati.

Had he used his debit card on the way out to see her?

Had he put her in danger, too? He tried to remember if he'd stopped for gas in Chicago. He'd paid cash to enter the museum; he recalled that much. He remembered the text then, and his stomach dropped. If they had access to his phone records, they'd be able to track her down.

And the bone. Jesus. She still had the disk of bone.

He grabbed his phone. He scrolled down through the texts, and there it was: *Should be able to test in a few days.*

"Jesus," Paul hissed.

He ran outside, dove into his car, and stomped on the gas. The tires chirped as he headed for the highway.

He drove through the night, careful to keep his speed under seventy-four. It was after dawn by the time he made Chicago, the Tuesday morning traffic already starting to build. He parked his car in the same lot as before, though at this hour there were a lot more empty spaces.

After parking, he sat and scrolled through his phone list again, looking for her number. He found it, and his finger hovered indecisively over the Call button. Eventually, he put his phone away. The less traceable contact he had with her, the safer she'd be.

He reached into the backseat and grabbed a book that had been sliding around the floorboard for the last few months. *Comparative Embryology.* He'd gotten it at a conference last spring and had been meaning to bring it up to his office to shelve with the rest of his collection. Now he was glad he hadn't. He needed the paper. He ripped a page out of the

back, blank on one side. After rummaging for a while in his center con-
sole, he located a pen. A few quick shakes brought the coagulated ink to
life, and he started writing, opting for short and blunt.

They know. I'm so sorry for bringing you into this. Meet me with the bone
in an hour down at the far end of the Lakefront Trail. After that, I'll be
out of your life. For your own safety, forget I ever contacted you. I'm so
sorry. Flush this note.

He folded the note in half and climbed out of the car. He popped the
hatch and pulled out a ratty baseball cap that had gotten wedged in one
corner, along with an old jacket. One of the benefits of driving an old car,
he realized, was that it had a long time to accumulate various forgotten
cargo that might come in handy for surreptitious activities. He pulled the
cap down over his eyes. It wasn't a disguise, really, but at least it made him
less recognizable at a distance. Or at least that's what he decided to tell
himself.

He left the parking garage and crossed the street, taking his time as
he strolled the walkway around to the far end of the block. The Field
Museum glowed bone white in the early morning sunshine, huge and
sprawling, contained on all sides by a border of cement walkway. A man
in a tattered jacket stood at the corner hawking newspapers. Paul bought
today's issue and found a park bench with a good view of the museum's
south entrance. It wasn't a great plan, but he was about as inconspicuous
as he could manage on short notice.

Then he waited.

He scanned the same headline over and over without really reading
it—VATICAN PEACE TALKS BREAK DOWN—flitting his eye toward the
entrance every ten seconds.

She arrived at eight-fifteen on the nose, pulling into the small west
parking lot in her sporty green Cooper.

Paul stood and shook out the paper.

He waited for her to exit her car, and then he moved quickly, closing
the distance and intercepting her at the bottom of the wide steps.

Her face revealed shock, but not fear, at seeing him. He knew then
that they hadn't gotten to her yet.

"Paul—"

"Don't speak," he told her. "Just smile."

The shock changed to confusion, then concern. A moment later it smoothed out to an even expression that might have been interpreted as a smile.

"We're going to shake hands like old acquaintances who just bumped into each other, and then we'll go our separate ways."

"*Okay . . .*" she said slowly. Her brow furrowed.

He held out his hand and she shook it. He palmed her the note.

"I can explain more soon," he said. "But for now, read the note."

He tipped his cap to her. "Good day."

"Bye, I guess," she answered.

And with that he continued walking. She turned and climbed the steps.

He took the sidewalk all the way around the museum and eventually made his way back to the parking lot, occasionally glancing behind himself to see if anyone was following. No one was.

Once in his car, he pulled out of the lot and eased into traffic, continually checking his rearview.

It was a five-minute drive to the parking lot.

He waited for her at the far end of the Lakefront Trail, the broad cement walkway that hugged the shoreline between the museum and the yacht club. He watched the boats rock and sway on the undulating waves. Out over the water, the sun rose higher in the sky. Behind him, seagulls pinwheeled against the backdrop of skyscrapers.

It was almost ten when she joined him. By then he was sitting on the cement ledge, his feet dangling over the water. She sat. Her elbow touched his.

"As far as kiss-offs go," she said, "this was pretty creative."

"That's what you think?"

"No." She looked at him. "I see your face . . . and no, I don't think that."

"Did you bring the bone?"

"I brought it." She shifted her hand, showing him the small plastic bag. "What happened?" she asked.

"I wouldn't know where to begin."

"You're in some kind of trouble?"

"Some kind, yeah."

"I don't understand this," she said.

"That's probably good. The less you know, the better. I've told you way too much already."

"So that whole 'forget I ever contacted you' thing?"

"For your safety."

"So you meant it."

"Not because it's what I want."

"This is bullshit."

He shook his head. "I'm not worth the risk. I'm really not."

"This is ridiculous. So you stole bone samples. What are you worried about, making me an accessory or something? Fine, I get that, but let's not be overdramatic about the whole thing."

"I wish that were all this was."

Her brow furrowed again. "If that's not it, then what is it?"

"Much worse."

"Maybe not as bad as you think. What are the chances that this just blows over?"

Paul smiled. He watched the boats. "Zero."

"There must be something that I can do. My uncle's a lawyer."

"No, it's not like that. You don't understand how much danger I've put you in."

"I'm a big girl."

"The last guy who helped me is dead."

For a moment there was no change in her expression; she looked at him as if trying to decide if he was serious. Finally, she said, "What?"

He nodded.

"What do you mean, *dead*?"

"Does it have another meaning?"

"Because of this?" She handed him the bone.

He took it and slid it into his pocket. "Not specifically this, no." He pulled the Tylenol bottle from his pocket and dumped the lozenge into his hand. "This, too. It's a DNA sample from bones found on Flores. I did an analysis, and there are people who don't want the results exposed."

He scanned the passersby, the walkers along the shoreline, looking for anyone who might be watching too closely. He slipped the lozenge back into the Tylenol bottle and put the bottle back into his pocket.

Up ahead, along the walkway, two men stepped into view. They were dressed in khakis and polo shirts. There was nothing unusual about them. Nothing to catch the eye. Other than the fact that they were there.

"I don't want you involved," Paul said.

"It seems like I already am."

"Not if I can help it."

She shook her head. "I already tested it."

"What?"

"The bone, just now, today. It's why I'm late. I tested the bone collagen in the lab at work before I came here."

Paul glanced at the khakied men. They were closer now, moving quietly. They weren't talking, weren't looking out over the water. "Walk with me," he told her.

He put his arm around her, and they walked in the direction of his car. He looked over his shoulder; the two men had picked up their pace and were thirty yards away now.

"I never would have involved you if I'd known this would happen. You believe me, don't you?"

"Yes."

"Good," he said. "Because now there's no other choice. It's time to run."

"What?"

"Run," he said. "Now."

He grabbed her hand and took off toward his car.

She ran. "What the hell?"

"Come on!"

He glanced over his shoulder; the two men were sprinting toward them.

She turned and looked. "Shit," she said.

Paul fished his car keys out of his pocket as they ran, crossing the small parking lot. He hit the unlock button as he approached his faded old Matrix. The car beeped. From behind another vehicle, a man stepped into his path. He'd been waiting there, hidden between the cars. Paul lowered his shoulder into him.

Lillivati screamed.

The man flew backward, clutching at Paul's arm, jerking him off balance.

"Get in the car!" Paul shouted. Paul was taller and outweighed the guy by forty pounds, but still it was a close thing. Paul spun the guy over the hood of the car, managing to yank himself free. A moment later, Lilli was in the passenger seat, opening the driver's door from the inside. Paul jumped in. He slammed the door and hit the locks just as the other two men showed up. They pulled on the door handles on both sides of the car as Paul started the engine.

"Get out of the car," the first one said. He was mid-thirties and built like a marine.

Paul shifted the car into gear and backed out of the parking space.

"You're just making this harder," the marine said.

On the opposite side of the car, the other guy screamed at Lilli, "Open the door!"

Paul put the transmission in drive just as the passenger window smashed in, glass exploding everywhere. Lilli screamed and punched at the hand that reached through. The hand found the inside door handle and pulled. The door came open. Paul gunned the engine, and the man hung on.

"Get out!" Lilli screamed, punching at the hand.

Up ahead a black sport ute backed out of its parking spot, trying to block their way. Paul had to slow, and the man reaching in grabbed Lilli's shoulder, trying to pull her from the moving car.

"No!" Lilli screamed, clutching now at Paul's arm.

The car's seat-belt warning beeped wildly.

Instead of stopping, Paul jerked the wheel to the right—but only a little. He sideswiped the reversing vehicle. There came a loud thud as the open passenger door slammed against the SUV's rear quarter panel, and the man at the door was suddenly gone. The door was closed again.

Paul gunned the engine, taking the curve at the parking lot entrance at twenty miles per hour. The Matrix burst out onto the city streets, crossing the intersection at Lakeshore Drive. Horns blared.

Beside him, Lilli sat shaking, saying nothing. She gripped the door handle hard enough to whiten her knuckles.

A quick glance in the rearview told him they weren't out of the woods yet. The black sport ute he'd sideswiped in the parking lot was now following.

Paul pushed the little Matrix as fast as it would go, swerving in and out of traffic. On a straightaway, he'd be no match for the V-8. But in this kind of congestion, the tiny Matrix actually had the advantage.

Paul took the turn onto Michigan Avenue at ten miles per hour, earning more blaring horns.

"Those guys were sent by your lab?"

"No."

"Then who?"

"It goes a lot higher up than that."

Paul took a left, then a right. They were downtown, skyscrapers looming above them, deep in a canyon of buildings. He checked the rearview every five seconds. For a minute, he thought he'd lost them, but then he saw the black SUV behind them again, half a block back. Up ahead, a red light. Traffic stopped.

"This isn't good," he said. They were in the right-hand lane, but the street ahead was a one-way, no right turn.

From somewhere behind them in traffic, the sound of screeching tires. Car doors. Shouting voices.

Paul saw them in his side mirror then. Two suited men running between the stopped lanes of traffic. The men closed the distance. A moment later, they were there. The left rear window exploded inward as the butt of a gun connected. Paul hit the gas, cutting the wheel to the right.

Tires squealed again, more blaring horns, and he was suddenly going the wrong way down Randolph. Into a wall of oncoming vehicles.

A truck swerved out of the way—and then the car behind it, with no time to react. Paul clipped mirrors with an oncoming BMW.

Paul laid on his horn, hoping to catch the attention of oncoming traffic. He took the first right, driving under the L train, and merged back into the flow of traffic. The city shadows deepened. An urban canyon.

"That was too close," Paul said.

Beside him, Lilli was still silent. Still gripping the door handle. Broken glass glittered in her hair.

"Are you okay?"

She nodded stiffly but didn't look at him.

Paul took Wabash through the stoplight and continued on.

"What are we doing?" Lilli asked finally.

"We're hoping to get lucky," Paul said, checking his mirror again.

At that moment, they came to a green light, and Paul saw a black SUV stopped at the intersection. It was a different truck: no sideswipe damage to the rear, but the same make and model.

"I should have known that wasn't gonna happen," Paul said.

He yanked the wheel to the left, turning against another one-way—this one less crowded. The truck gunned its way across the intersection behind them, giving chase. Paul floored the accelerator again.

"If you've got any ideas," Paul said. "Now is the time."

"Ideas for what?"

"On how to get out of here."

In the rearview, the black truck was gaining on them.

"Turn here," she said.

"Up there?"

"No, right here. *Here!*"

Paul jerked the wheel and stomped on the accelerator again, hurtling down a narrow access road. Here the buildings were closed in; no traffic, but parked box trucks crowded along the walls of the buildings.

"There's an underground station up ahead," Lilli said.

"Where?"

They bounced across an intersection without slowing, going momentarily airborne as the car's suspension lifted the tires from the roadway. They struck with a loud scrape, and Paul fought with the wheel as they flew down the access road. Ahead, the roadway became even narrower, reduced to little more than an alley between buildings. Dumpsters bulged out from either side, and Paul had to swerve to avoid striking them. The speedometer climbed to forty. Behind them, the larger vehicle lost ground, half a block back now as it slowed to avoid a dumpster.

"Look out!"

Paul jerked his gaze forward again and dodged another trash container.

Ahead, the road ended in a T. Cross-traffic sat in gridlock. Paul skidded to a stop.

They sat breathing for a moment.

They looked at each other.

Paul glanced in the rearview mirror again. They were out of time.

"Out," Paul said. "Now."

They flung the car doors open and sprinted up the street, abandoning the car where it sat. Lilli ran to the right, and Paul followed. Somewhere behind them, a car horn started blaring, but Paul didn't look back. He followed Lilli up the block, weaving through the foot traffic toward the tunnel entrance. They were near Millennium Park—the Bean, he knew, would be shining in the sun up ahead. He looked toward the stairwell. The sign above the opening read MILLENNIUM STATION. Lilli never hesitated.

He followed her down the stairs and into the underground station, the great maw of the city swallowing them whole.

They kept moving, that was the important thing, following the stripes on the floor as they tunneled deeper into the station. Shops molded themselves to the walkway perimeter, becoming part of the circulinear passageway that wound its way forward.

A minute later, Paul and Lilli were at the commuter trains. Paul saw that the far train was boarding, so he and Lilli wormed themselves into the shuffling crowd. They stepped onto the train, among the last to board. The doors closed behind them.

Paul was drenched in sweat, his heart pulsing in his ears. He tried to control his breathing, imagining that every eye was on them. He moved forward through the train, trying to pick the most crowded car.

"Here," he said finally.

They sat, taking the last open seats.

A moment later the South Shore announcer spoke: "Now leaving. Next stop Van Buren."

Out on the platform, Paul saw a suited man walk by. The man was craning his neck, looking into the train cars. He continued on, disappearing from sight, moving toward the front of the train. Just then, the train lurched forward.

A few moments later, the man came into view again. He was standing in place, staring into the train cars as they slowly lumbered past.

Paul sank as low into the seat as he could go. There was no place to hide.

The car rolled slowly forward and the man's eyes found Paul. Recognition. The man's expression went angry.

Paul saw that it was the guy he'd scraped off against the sport ute. The side of his face was red and raw.

The man lunged for the doors, running alongside, trying to open them, but the train quickly pulled ahead.

The man continued to follow, sliding farther and farther back as he ran, his eyes finding Paul again, until he ran out of platform and stopped. Paul put his face to the glass and watched him disappear.

The train rocked beneath them, a gentle lull. The sound of the tracks.

The train emerged into open air. Buildings flew by.

"They won't have enough men to check every stop," Paul said. "The farther we go, the wider the net they'd have to cast in order to catch us."

"So you think we got away?"

"We'll know at the first stop. If one of them boards the train, then no."

Lilli put her head on his shoulder. They passed beneath a broad overpass, the world going dark for a moment before they came out the other side.

The conductor worked his way up the line.

"Tickets?"

"We don't have any. Can we buy them now?"

"Sure, where to?"

"Where's the train going?"

"After Van Buren, the next stop is Fifty-seventh Street."

"No, farther up."

"Hegewisch, Hammond, East Chicago, Ogden Dunes, Michigan City."

"Two tickets to Ogden Dunes."

"Sixteen dollars."

Paul paid in cash. The conductor handed over the change and the stubs and moved on.

"What about your car back there?" she asked.

"It's the least of my worries."

"Van Buren," announced a catenated male voice.

The train slowed to a stop. Paul and Lilli stared out the windows. No black trucks. No athletic men in dark suits.

The train doors opened. People got on, but nobody suspicious. After a minute, the doors closed again.

Paul felt Lilli release a long breath. The train started moving again.

"They didn't get here in time," Paul said. "Now they won't know if we've gotten off already or not. After this, it gets harder for them."

They took the train through two more stops. .

They watched the buildings through the windows. Tall beige skyscrapers, fire escapes zigzagging up the side. Lake Michigan visible in stolen glimpses through the buildings, until the tracks veered and the neighborhood changed. The tall buildings gave way to smaller structures, brick apartment buildings and houses. The train rolled past a landfill, parklike, covered in green grass, but rising steeply as no park would.

Paul saw liquor stores and gas stations and, later, on the north side of the tracks, power lines and the rise of industrial buildings. The train passed a church, its twin steeples piercing the sky to the south—a huge dark structure with stained-glass windows, beautiful in the slant of the sun.

"Next stop Hegewisch," a voice called out over the intercom.

Paul and Lilli stayed in their seats.

Sometime after that, the train passed into Indiana, making stops in Hammond and Gary. Through the window, Paul saw enormous pipes and white smoke—huge metal structures that dwarfed all the buildings he'd seen outside of Chicago, like rusting metal skyscrapers laid on their sides. On the roof of one were the words USS GARY WORKS. The great sprawl of the mill rolled by for miles.

Paul looked around at the other travelers. The South Shore was a commuter train. People coming from and going to work. Men and women going about their daily lives.

"Who died?" Lilli asked.

Paul looked at her. Her face was somber. "What?"

"You said the last guy who helped you is dead." Her voice went low, almost a whisper, so the other passengers couldn't hear her. "Who was he?"

"His name was Charles. A coworker of mine."

"How did it happen?"

"Badly."

"How bad?"

"Bad enough you wouldn't want to hear about it."

Outside the window, the landscape was changing from urban to rural. Like a line had been drawn. Paul watched the brown cattails flash by, a small wetland hugging the tracks. On the other side of the wetlands, woods spread away in the distance.

"You said you tested the bone," Paul said.

"Yeah," Lilli said.

"What did you find?"

"They had a ten percent fish diet. Twenty percent small rodents. Thirty percent large mammal."

"They were hunters?"

"Hunter-gatherers. Same profile you see everywhere. Their remaining percentages were plants. Nothing out of the ordinary for ancient bones. Just the typical human pattern."

"Just like us," Paul whispered. He rested his face against the cool glass.

They got off the train in Ogden Dunes. The station was a narrow parking lot that looked out across the road at a long white picket fence bordering a newer upscale housing development. A short walk to a nearby Marathon gas station produced the phone number for a local cab company. The cab dropped them at the nearest hotel, a Days Inn, where Paul paid in cash.

They showered together, and Paul picked glass from her hair. Afterward they made love on the sheets, and for a while Paul could lose himself in that. He could pretend none of the rest of it was happening.

Paul got dressed and scouted the neighborhood. He bought chicken dinners from the local Denny's and brought them back to the hotel. A strange déjà vu overcame him as he returned. It was the second time he'd been holed up, hiding. Waiting out the worst of it. The last time hadn't ended so well. There was nothing like running for your life to put things in perspective.

Lying in bed the next morning, coming out of an anxiety dream, he ran through their choices in his mind.

She must have guessed his thoughts, because she said, "We should go to the police."

"What?" He hadn't known she was awake yet.

"The cops. We could go to the cops and tell them what we know."

"What do we know?"

"Your coworker is dead. We know that. And we know we're being hunted."

He nodded. He wondered if Charles's body had been found yet. He wondered about the computer guy, if he was still alive. Most of all, he wondered how Axiom planned to cover up what had happened. They weren't stupid. Some plan must be in place. But the plan, whatever it was, had included Paul being dead. So maybe there was a chance.

"And then what?" Paul asked. "After we go to the police."

"And then what, what?" Lilli responded.

"We go down, we make our report at a police station. And then what? We go home while they investigate? We live our regular lives?"

"Why not?"

"Because they'll kill us."

"Then there's witness protection."

"Something tells me it wouldn't be as simple as that."

"What other choice do we have?"

The complete and utter hopelessness of the situation came crashing down on him.

At that moment, his phone rang, the sound coming from his pants on the floor. It startled him; he'd completely forgotten about it. He slipped out of bed and fished it from his pocket. He looked at the display: a number he didn't recognize. He considered answering but let it go to voice mail. Twenty seconds later, the phone chirped, letting him know a message had been saved to his box.

He logged into voice mail.

"You have one new message. First message."

The voice that spoke next was familiar. Deep and gravelly, with a faint Australian accent.

"We need to talk, Paul. I know what's happening to you, and I can help. You can trust me. I'm here in the U.S.; we need to meet, alone."

Paul listened to the message three times.

He switched the phone off and flipped it onto the other bed. He pulled his shirt on and told Lilli he was going to go snag them breakfast. It was only a short walk, so he kept walking, going where his feet took him, exploring the local restaurant scene. Scouting locations again. He gave himself a few minutes to think. By eight o'clock, he'd given up on that. He knew he'd meet Gavin. What else could he do?

He'd trusted Gavin once. Maybe he could trust him still.

Paul walked back to the motel, a bag of doughnuts in hand.

He dialed the number.

"Hello." It was Gavin's voice.

"There's a town outside Chicago called Portage," Paul said. "Can you be here by tomorrow?"

"Consider me on the next flight."

"Write this down."

There was a pause. Then: "Go ahead."

"A restaurant called the Lure, not far from the South Shore train line in Portage, Indiana."

"All right."

"Tomorrow night around six?"

"I'll be there. Paul—"

Paul hit End and turned his phone off.

36

The Lure was busy with the Wednesday dinner rush. Waitresses glided past, arms full of drinks. Paul knew this kind of place. During the day, it would tend toward business lunches. In the evening, it would be more of a mixed crowd—part bring-a-date-to-dinner, part college hangout, part family diner. Usually, Paul liked restaurants like this one for their burger specials. Tonight he liked it for this: it was crowded, which meant it provided a lot of witnesses.

He got a table in the corner. A booth of dark brown wood under a moose head. It felt good to be back in a real restaurant with a real menu you could hold in your hand, instead of picking combo meals from an overhead display. He hadn't been at a sit-down restaurant since before Flores. It felt like it had happened in a different life.

The waitress came by and Paul ordered a Corona. A beer would help calm his nerves. She returned with his drink a few minutes later.

"You ready to order?"

Paul tried to imagine eating, but his stomach was tied in knots. "Cheeseburger," he said out of force of habit.

"We'll fix you right up," she said.

Paul sipped his drink and eyed the front door. A few minutes later, at six on the nose, Gavin walked in.

He stood near the entrance, scanning the room. For a moment, Paul sat perfectly still, hidden among the crowd. Gavin looked thinner. Older somehow, as if the intervening months had aged him as many years. Paul waved his arm.

Gavin caught the motion and crossed the room.

"Paul," Gavin said. He extended his hand. Paul shook it.

Gavin sat.

The older man was silent for a moment, as if gathering his thoughts for what he was about to say.

Paul sipped his drink.

"I work for the people who are looking for you," Gavin said. "I want to be clear about that right from the beginning."

Paul nodded, accepting this. It had always been a possibility. The fact that Gavin had told him was a good sign.

"How bad is it?" Paul asked. He wasn't even sure what he meant by that. It just felt like a true question.

"This?" Gavin asked, spreading his hands as if to encompass the entire situation that hung between them. "It's the end of the world."

Paul nodded again. Because of course it was. "Well, you don't sugarcoat things, do you," he said.

"All out of sugar," Gavin continued. "This is going to go badly."

"For me?"

"For both of us."

"Did they send you here to talk to me?" The important question.

"Yes."

"You should know that I don't have the DNA or bone samples on me. They're someplace safe. If something happens to me, you'll never find them."

"I'm not here for that. I'm just here to talk to you. To reason with you."

"What do they plan to do?"

"That's up to you."

"I get to decide? Okay, then I vote they leave me alone."

"Well, it's not that simple."

"It never is. What do they want from me?"

"Cooperation," Gavin said. "Just cooperation."

"What kind?"

"You know too much about things nobody is supposed to know about. That makes you a liability. People like Martial don't like liabilities."

"Martial?"

"The owner of Axiom."

"I've never heard of him."

"You wouldn't have."

"You work for him?"

"We all do. You included. Half of certain universities. Various politicians. Though the politicians might think it's the other way around."

"I don't understand."

"You're not supposed to. Who do you think owns Westing?"

"What? Axiom?"

"Through an umbrella corporation. How do you think I got your employer to cooperate so easily to release you to go to Flores?"

"If you work for him, and you're here, then this is a trap." Paul studied Gavin's face for a reaction.

"What I said on the phone was real. I can help you."

It wasn't a denial, exactly. "How?"

"By bringing you in."

Paul laughed. "You must be joking."

"No."

"In where, exactly?"

"*In* in. Inside. Into the fold. The things you've seen are nothing compared to what's on the other side of the pay wall. Things beyond your wildest dreams. Things not exactly ethical. Things that can't be risked."

"You sound like a true believer."

"No," Gavin said. "Never confuse me with that."

"Then what are you?"

"The Inquisition created many a convert, make no mistake."

"And if I say no?"

"You can't say no."

"That's not much of an offer then."

"It's the best you'll get from the old man. I had to argue your case to make it happen. This could have gone the other way. You have no idea how lucky you are."

"It did go the other way. You know about Charles?"

"I've never heard that name. I don't know anything about him. Regardless of what's happened, there's still a chance to take this in another direction. For you, at least."

At that moment, the food came. It seemed obscene to eat. Paul's stomach was clenched into a tight ball. He pushed his fries around the plate but couldn't bring himself to take a bite. Gavin pulled out his wallet and put a fifty on the table.

"Not hungry?"

"No."

"Come on then," Gavin said, tapping the cash on the table. "There's someone you have to meet."

Paul followed him out the door.

Gavin drove them to a river. A place behind chain-link gates. They'd ridden in silence, Paul's apprehension growing as they left the main road. Dusk had stripped away the colors, rendering everything in charcoal— the trees, the winding asphalt path, the rusting metal railing. The place might have been a boat launch once, but now it was just a crumbling concrete ramp, overgrown with weeds. Even the river seemed used up and old. A dark flow of brown water maybe thirty feet wide, winding its way inexorably toward Lake Michigan, still some miles distant. Gavin pulled the car to the side of the ramp and stepped out.

A woman stood facing out at the water.

Paul and Gavin approached, and the woman turned around.

"Hello, Paul." It was Margaret.

Paul was careful to control his emotions. He didn't let his face change.

"Margaret," he said. "So you made it out of Flores after all."

"It's good to see you, too." She smiled. Her hair was tied back tightly. Dark business suit. She looked like a different person.

Paul looked her in the face and said the only word he had to say to her: "James."

Her smile faltered for the slightest millisecond before rising up again. "It wasn't an easy choice I made, Paul."

"When you left the hotel room, where did you go?"

"To the people in charge."

"Why?"

"It was the smart thing to do."

"Is that what you tell yourself?"

"It's just a simple fact."

"So you made the decision for all of us."

"Somebody had to. And don't get high and mighty with me. You didn't even know who we were working for."

"But you knew, didn't you?"

"Of course I knew." She laughed. "You misjudge me, Paul. You think I'm an archaeology student who became an Axiom asset? You've got it backward."

"They killed him, you know. James."

"He killed himself by staying."

"Didn't look like suicide to me. I was there."

"It was unfortunate."

"Unfortunate?"

"It's what happens when you fight the system. You lose."

"He was our friend. You worked side by side with him for months. How do you sleep at night?"

"I sleep just fine."

"I can't believe I fucked you."

This time her smile grew. She pulled out a gun and pointed it at Paul's face. "Careful now. That's no way to talk to a lady."

Paul looked around at the trees and the empty river, and he realized this had all been planned. The isolated location. Margaret and her gun. The whole thing had been a trap after all.

"Margaret," Gavin said. He spoke softly, almost in a whisper. During the course of the conversation, Gavin had stepped away from Paul, so that he was standing off to the side.

When Paul glanced over, he saw that Gavin had a gun, a small silver pistol, pointed directly at Margaret's head.

Margaret didn't move. "What are you doing?" Her voice was flat and emotionless.

"It's not supposed to happen like this," Gavin said.

"This is the way it happens," Margaret said. "You're not going to shoot me."

"We're supposed to give him a choice."

"You're right. What do you choose, Paul?"

"With a gun to my head?"

"Yeah," she said.

"I *still* can't believe I fucked you."

"Wrong answer. Sorry, Paul."

Her finger began to flex on the trigger, and two shots rang out. She slumped to the ground, dead. A pool of blood spread out from her body while Gavin's gun smoked in the dim light.

"Fuck," Gavin said.

Gavin kicked her body into the river, and they watched it drift away, bobbing in the current. They climbed back up the ramp to the car and drove off. Paul guided Gavin to the hotel where Lillivati waited. There was no reason not to.

Gavin shifted into park and turned the car off. The yellow sign from the Days Inn shone through the windshield. They sat for a moment in the semidarkness, neither of them moving.

"Why'd you do that?" Paul asked.

"It had to be done. She would have killed you."

"Why stop her?"

"It was the right thing to do."

Behind them, semi trucks rolled by on the highway. The car windows vibrated with the rattle of their air brakes.

Eventually, softly, Gavin spoke again: "I knew your father. I should have told you."

Paul turned to look at him but his face was hidden in the shadows. "It was a long time ago," Gavin continued. "Just after you were born, in fact."

"How did you know him?"

"We worked on related projects. We were colleagues, of a sort. We were friends."

"Friends."

"Yeah."

"I don't remember you from the funeral."

"No, by then your father had gone his own way. I hadn't seen him for years by that point, though I heard about what happened. He deserved better than that."

"Is that why you brought me on the dig to Flores?"

Gavin nodded. "I wish to hell I hadn't."

"Me, too."

Gavin climbed out of the car.

Paul led him up to the motel room.

Lilli opened the door.

"This is Gavin," Paul said. "He's here to help us."

Gavin shook her hand.

She looked at Paul. "How do you know we can trust him?"

Gavin looked at her but said nothing.

They stepped inside the motel room.

"We know," Paul said.

37

Paul had lost the rain.

They drove south for days, sticking to side roads whenever they could, winding their way through small towns and mountain passes. They bit off their days in three-hundred-mile increments, crashing at cheap hotels for the night, paying in cash. They ate in diners and truck stops. They passed white clapboard chapels and parking-lot-ensconced mega-churches—the biggest of which rivaled shopping malls in size and football stadiums in attendance. Billboards for the churches occasionally flanked the highways on both sides. One sign in particular jumped out at Paul, horrifying in its simplicity: a jet-black background on which three words were written in letters ten feet high: HELL IS REAL.

As if there were any doubt.

Gavin talked as Paul drove. Lilli slept in the back while Gavin's rental car ate up the miles.

Gavin had a plan. He doled it out in small chunks, a nightmare that kept getting worse.

"You think that will work?"

"I think it *can* work."

Paul nodded. That was good enough. It was better than hopelessness.

Lillivati made a noise in the backseat, nursing her own nightmares as the car rolled on through the darkness.

On the fourth day, in the mountains, it began to rain. The rain came down hard, a midsummer monsoon, and the windshield wipers struggled to keep up.

Paul leaned forward, trying to see through the pouring rain. The water came down in buckets. Here and there, cars pulled to the side of the road or parked beneath overpasses. The mountain passes were narrow, and there wasn't much room for error. Paul hadn't seen rain like this since Flores.

Eventually, he gave in to the storm and took the next exit.

"Time for gas," he said, though the tank was still half full. "Maybe grab some coffee." He got no complaints.

He pulled into the station, climbed out, and started pumping gas. The overhead canopy kept him dry. Thirty-one dollars later the nozzle clicked.

He checked his wallet for cash—always cash—then eyed the rain for a moment, hesitating. It was cold in the mountain passes, and between him and the gas station door were a dozen yards of downpour. He turned his collar up against the chill, then sprinted across the wet pavement—and that's when he noticed it.

He stopped. Halfway across.

The rain fell all around him, drenching him immediately.

He looked around. He reached out to touch the water falling from the sky.

The rain was a curtain. He touched it, reached his hand through it.

With one eye, he had no sense of depth. No sense of being *in* the rain. Even with the rain pouring down on him, there was no sense that he was a part of it.

He realized that he'd lost the rain all those months ago in Flores and hadn't even known it until now.

Paul walked into the gas station and paid the bill in cash.

When they were on the road again, Gavin said, "You okay?"

"I'm fine."

———

They arrived in Atlanta and got two hotel rooms by the airport. Planes descended in a steady, staggered formation, coming down over the five-story hotel where Paul had paid for a whole week—a dashed line of tin and aluminum slanting its way down from the sky to land with a distant squawk of rubber.

They got an early start the next morning, pulling out of the parking lot by ten A.M.

Paul rolled the window down and stuck his hand out into the muggy air. It was already hot. As different from the raining mountain passes as a place could be. Heat was its own thing here, in Atlanta. Something you were made aware of as you stepped outside, a force that enveloped you. You opened the car door and it hit you like an oven blast. Sweat sprang to your brow.

They found a pay phone at a run-down convenience store a few blocks from the hotel. It might have been the last one in existence.

Gavin stepped out to make the call.

"You said we can trust him," Lillivati said after Gavin had stepped away from the car. "Why is that, exactly?"

Paul watched Gavin squinting in the sun, punching the buttons on the ancient pay phone that jutted from the edge of the parking lot. Traffic rolled by behind him. Jets up above. People milled in and out of the convenience store's parking lot. Atlanta was like this. On the move. Paul turned his head to glance at Lilli. They were like this, too.

"He was supposed to bring me in," Paul said.

"Maybe that's what he's doing?"

Paul shook his head. "There were two of them when he came to get me."

"So maybe this is part of the plan. A way to trick you into going where they want you. Maybe he's only pretending."

"He's not pretending."

"How can you be sure?"

"There were two of them when he came to get me, and the other one's not alive anymore."

She stared at Paul.

"Him," Paul said to the question she didn't ask. "He pulled the trigger."

She glanced toward the pay phone.

A moment later, the car door opened and Gavin sank into the driver's seat. He slammed the door closed and gunned the engine to life.

"I made the call," he said, then shifted the car into reverse.

"What did he say?" Paul asked.

"Don't get ahead of yourself. I got through to someone. The message should find its way to him. Now we wait for the phone to ring."

"That's our strategy?" Lilli asked.

"Calling it a 'strategy' is perhaps too kind," Gavin said. "But a man in Martial's position has enemies."

"And the enemy of my enemy . . ." Paul said.

"Not a friend, no. Don't ever confuse him with that. But he has a vested interest in helping us."

That night they ate at an IHOP just outside the city. Lilli was on her second coffee before she brought up the call.

"So who is it, exactly, that we're waiting to hear back from?"

"A congressman they mentioned by name. Lacefield."

"You met him?"

"No. But his name came up. They said he was investigating Axiom, so I figured he was a good man to reach out to. I reached out. Now we wait for him to reach back."

"What's the endgame?"

"Exposure," Gavin said. "Total exposure. It's the only way we get out of this. We give Lacefield everything. The bone. Everything I've learned. All the secret experiments. That's what I'm offering him."

"Experiments?"

Gavin nodded.

"How does that help us?"

"We shine a bright enough light on this, and maybe we become too noticeable to disappear."

"So we go to the authorities," Lilli said.

"There are authorities, and there are authorities. You have to choose wisely."

"And this Lacefield guy is going to help us?" Lilli asked.

"If he wants Martial bad enough," Gavin said. He took a sip of his coffee. "It's the only way out of this that I can see."

The waitress came with their food.

"You mentioned experiments," Paul said. "What kind of experiments are we talking about?"

Gavin toyed with his food. "I haven't seen everything. I . . . don't think I even scratched the surface, really. There are places I didn't go. Whole parts of the facility that were off-limits. The things I did see made me not want to know more."

"What kinds of things?"

"Things I wouldn't have thought possible."

"I've seen the impossible," Paul said.

"Ah, Trieste, you mean," Gavin said.

"Who?" Lilli asked.

"They take him along sometimes, I heard. On manhunts after dark."

"So it has a name."

Gavin nodded. "A name. It has that."

Lilli pushed her plate away. Her meal half-eaten. "It?" she asked. "What do you mean, 'it'?"

"It's not the strangest thing I've seen there," Gavin said.

"Then what is?"

Gavin moved his food around but wouldn't look up from his plate.

"What is Trieste?" Lilli asked.

"I think he knows," Gavin said, gesturing toward Paul with his fork.

"Let's say I don't." Paul understood Gavin's reluctance. To say it out loud seemed profane somehow. But Paul wouldn't make it easier for him.

"What?" Lilli repeated.

"There are strange things on the compound. Some things part human." Gavin's face was grim. "Part not."

Paul nodded. Lilli, for her part, looked at them like they were crazy. "You can't be serious."

"The old man has a thing for hybrids," Gavin said. "Of all kinds."

Lilli stared at Paul in disbelief. "How is that even possible?"

"I've seen it," Paul assured her. He held out his arm, still covered in bruises. "There was a bridge. I barely got away. It could have been a lot worse."

"He crosses different species?" Lilli said.

"It's not so hard," Gavin said. "It happens in captivity all the time. Horses and donkeys, lions and tigers."

"But why do it?" Lilli said.

Gavin shrugged. "Why does that man do anything? I don't know. Maybe because there's no one to tell him not to. Maybe because he's crazy."

There was a long silence at the table. "What is it like?" Lillivati asked softly.

"Trieste, you mean?"

"Yeah."

Gavin's eyes took on a faraway look, but he didn't answer.

Paul answered for him: "It's a monster."

38

It took two days for the phone to ring.

Two days in the hotel. Gavin lay awake at night, picturing all the ways his plan could go wrong. When he slept, he dreamed of the river. The sound of gunshots. Margaret's face.

It was a brief, anonymous call. Gavin's cell rang as they were eating lunch at a fast-food place. "Write this down," said the man on the line; then he spoke a number. "Call from a pay phone at two-thirty." The line went dead.

Gavin hung up. He looked at Paul, who was sitting across the table from him. "That was it," he said.

An hour later they turned into the convenience store's parking lot and pulled up next to the pay phone. Gavin climbed out. Paul and Lilli waited in the car.

Gavin poured quarters into the metal phone, then punched in the numbers he'd written on a scrap piece of paper.

The phone rang. On the fifth ring, somebody picked it up.

"Hello."

"I was told to call."

"So this is Gavin," the voice said. "I've heard so much about you."

"Then you have me at a disadvantage."

"Come now, you must have heard something about me or you wouldn't have tried to reach me."

"This is Mr. Lacefield?"

"It is."

"I heard you're no friend of Martial Johansson's."

The man on the line chuckled. "If that's all you've heard, then you've heard the most important thing, considering your current situation. I understand that you have some information for me."

"More than just information."

There was a long pause on the line. Gavin filled it. "In addition to information, we also have—"

Lacefield interrupted. "Not on the phone. We need to talk in person."

Another pause.

"Where?" Gavin asked.

"There's a pier on a lake. A place called Alcove Beach. You can find it on local maps."

Gavin held the phone to his cheek but didn't speak.

"It's wide open there. A public place. We'll talk."

"When?"

"Tomorrow. Two o'clock. Is Paul with you?"

Gavin stiffened. "How do you know about Paul?"

"It's part of my business to know. As you said, I'm no friend to Martial Johansson. So is Paul with you?"

"Yeah, he's with me."

Another long pause.

"Bring him."

"Okay, I'll bring him along."

"Good. Then I'll see you soon." The line went dead. Gavin hung up. Gavin climbed into the car and shut the door.

"Well?" Paul asked.

"He'll meet with us," Gavin said.

"You don't sound happy." Paul waited for him to explain.

"He knew about you. Somebody already has feelers out."

"Is that good or bad?" Lilli asked.

"I don't know. But at least he knows we're serious. This is risky for him, too. If he didn't have a lot on the line, he never would have gotten back to us."

39

The next day, Paul was up before the sun. He stood at the curtains of the hotel room, looking out at the early morning traffic. The sky was just beginning to lighten in the east; red taillights glowed bright in the semi-dark. He turned away and walked to the bathroom, where he shaved a five-day stubble. Not quite a beard, but well on its way to it. A trait from his father's side of the family, hairy as Vikings. As a child he'd seen pictures of uncles he'd never met, pale men with full, thick beards. His own father had shaved nearly every day of his life. Now, holding the razor in his hand, Paul had the impulse to shave his head, too, some instinct rising up inside him. In the end, he didn't, but only because he'd have to explain to Lilli why he'd done it, and he wouldn't have an answer. He'd read once that gladiators had often cut their hair in preparation for battle. It was also a sign of mourning.

A Bible verse rose unbidden: *And Job arose, tore at his clothes, shaved his head, and worshipped.*

He put the razor by the sink.

His morning routine woke Lilli, who joined him in the steaming shower. Water rained down on her, plastering her spiky black hair to her head. She closed her eyes and moved against him.

"You're up early," she said.

"I'm sorry I dragged you into this." He wrapped his arms around her.

"It's not your fault. You gave me a choice, remember? I chose."

"You didn't choose this."

"And neither did you. You didn't know all this was going to happen."

"It's still my fault. If I hadn't contacted you . . ."

"I'd still be at my job. So what? I don't blame you."

"I blame me."

"Well, stop," she said. She wrapped her arms around him and kissed him. Water cascaded over them, but not between.

After, they dressed and met Gavin in the lobby. They found him sipping a hot cup of coffee and reading the newspaper in a plush green chair of the sort that seemed built exclusively for use in hotel lobbies.

Gavin glanced at his watch when he saw them. "You ready?"

Paul nodded.

They walked out to the car and drove to Alcove Beach in silence. No one spoke, save Paul calling out the directions he'd printed from the hotel computer the night before. "Turn here," he said as they approached their destination.

They paid four dollars at the booth, then followed a narrow roadway that led up to an immense parking lot. Gavin drove to the very front, where beach sand had begun to drift up onto the pavement. He put the car in park and they climbed out. The sun beat down on them. "You stay here," Gavin said.

"I'm coming," Lilli said.

"No." Gavin's voice was firm.

"That's bullshit," she snapped. "You think because—"

"Your gender has nothing to do with it, I assure you," Gavin said. "You have the bone. It's as simple as that."

Lilli looked skeptical.

"It's our leverage here. Someone has to stay back."

"What about him?" Lilli asked, gesturing to Paul.

"They already know about him. Mentioned him by name, in fact— remember?"

Paul raised his hand to shield his gaze from the sun and looked out toward the pier. "This congressman of yours seems particularly well informed," he said.

"And what if things go badly?" Lilli asked.

"Then you coming along certainly wouldn't help. In fact, it would be even worse, because then the bone would be compromised. You're our insurance policy."

Gavin tossed Lilli the keys. "If there's a problem, don't hesitate. Just go."

Paul and Gavin climbed up onto the sand. Just over the rise, people played volleyball and lounged in the sun. Two teenagers tossed a football back and forth, while children seemed to run everywhere. Lifeguards sat on huge white chairs, surveying it all with an air of casual disinterest. Paul saw the water—children splashing in the shallows, toddlers sitting at the waterline with their mothers.

Paul and Gavin veered to the left as they trudged through the loose sand, walking until they eventually came to the edge of a low cement walkway. The long sidewalk ran parallel to the beach, extending for a hundred yards before ending at a short stairway that led up to the pier. The pier was weathered old concrete, ten feet wide, jutting a quarter mile out into the lake.

"Do you see them?" Gavin asked as they walked.

Paul nodded.

There were already men in position. It was easy to pick them out once you knew they were there. A man in a sport jacket and a baseball hat, sitting on the low cement wall. Another man leaned with his back against a pavilion, casually reading a newspaper. A third man, standing on the beach, gazed out at the water. His hand rose to his ear for a moment, and his lips moved. That one wasn't even trying to be inconspicuous. He was the one they were *supposed* to see.

Halfway to the pier, they passed another man. This one was sitting with his legs draped off the side of the walkway, flip-flops dangling from his feet. Paul wasn't sure about him.

And past them all, up ahead, standing alone on the pier, casting a line out into the water, was a lone fisherman.

Paul and Gavin climbed the six steps up to the pier.

Even from a distance, Paul knew it was him. He might have recognized the man from pictures, or maybe it was something in his stance. Like he was waiting. He was in his mid-fifties, tall, and stocky without being fat. He wore a fisherman's cap and a fisherman's vest. A bright orange tackle box sat next to him on the pier. He was halfway out on the pier, an eighth of a mile from the beach. Plenty of time to see people coming. Plenty of privacy from prying ears. It took them a full three minutes to walk out to him.

As Paul and Gavin approached, the fisherman glanced briefly in their direction, then threw a long cast out onto the water.

"Not so much as a nibble yet," the man said as Gavin and Paul closed the distance.

"Sorry to hear that," Gavin said.

"Well, what's the old saying? That's why they call it fishing, not catching."

"Congressman Lacefield, I presume?"

The man responded with the slightest nod while reeling in his line.

"This is Paul," Gavin said.

"I know who he is," the congressman said curtly. "Grab a pole, the both of you."

That's when Paul noticed two poles lying along the cement, wedged against the riser that ran the length of the pier. He picked up both and passed one to Gavin. The one Paul kept for himself was slightly larger, an open-face reel, cork handle. It gleamed. It was probably ten times more expensive than any fishing pole he'd ever held.

He checked the lure. Green spinner bait. He thought of lures dangling over ice but pushed the thought away.

"So this is some serious business you find yourselves in," the congressman said.

"Serious business," Gavin agreed.

"I've been in politics for twenty years now. I've seen other politicians come and go. Some voted out. Some sent to jail. Over the years, I've even seen one or two die under less than clear circumstances. Yet I remain. Do you know how I've managed to do that?"

"I wouldn't presume to guess."

"I stay *out* of serious business. I see serious business coming, and I step aside, and I let it pass. Live to fight another day."

"Yet here you are," Gavin said. "Out here fishing."

"Against my own better judgment, yes. And against all counsel. Here

I am on this fine, clear day, drowning worms off this pier." He swung his arm back and threw a long cast out into the choppy water. The lure made a splash and then disappeared. He reeled it in slow and steady, the line carving a slight ripple on the water. "The thing about fishing, though. If I hit a snag, I can cut bait anytime."

Gavin considered this. "Fair enough," he said.

"So I hear you have information for me."

"We do. We think you'll find it interesting."

"I'm interested in a lot of things. And while I'm always keen to keep my ears open, there is an important distinction between information that is interesting and information that is useful. I trust you understand this distinction."

"Information is information. What you do with it is up to you."

"Spoken like a man who knows that his information is useful. Convince me."

"Martial is a thorn in your side."

"True." The congressman took a breath and released it slowly, the long sigh of resignation—like a middle school teacher about to discuss his most difficult student. "Martial is a difficult man. A driven man."

"And you want him neutralized."

"I stay out of his way."

"That's not what I understand."

"When I *can,* I stay out of his way. Lord knows he doesn't make it easy. Our constituencies are at odds, it seems. I have friends who would like nothing more than to see Martial taken down."

"Martial is behind a series of murders and cover-ups that stretch back over a period of years."

"I'm afraid that if Martial could be neutralized for something as simple as a few murders, it would have happened a long time ago."

"The cover-ups are scientific in nature. He's covering up the discoveries of new bones. Suppressing the release of new research."

The congressman frowned. "You tell me things I already know. So this is what you come to me with? Rumors?"

"And there are things going on at the compound. Experiments that would never be sanctioned—"

"Speculation. Sensationalism."

"Facts."

"Facts." The congressman spit the word with contempt. "I'm a lawyer by training; perhaps you weren't aware."

Gavin shook his head.

"Before politics I spent ten years as a trial lawyer, and even I can't tell you what a fact is, exactly. The more time I spent in law, the more malleable that term became. Facts change with the telling. Squeeze a fact hard enough, and it'll change shape in your hand. Facts don't mean anything."

"Proof, then."

The congressman raised an eyebrow. "Proof," he said, "is an altogether different animal."

Gavin cast his line out on the water. In the distance, a powerboat rumbled a slow arc across the water. It was the second time the boat had made that exact pass, a half mile out from the pier. Paul could see two men on board. It occurred to Paul that this boat, too, might belong to the congressman. He wondered how many eyes were trained on them right now.

"Proof of what, exactly?" the congressman said.

"Of the conspiracy. Of the suppression."

"I'm listening."

"We have a piece of bone."

"The bone of what, exactly?"

"The bone of a tool-using hominid that isn't human. A bone that Martial has conspired to keep hidden. A bone that he's killed people to keep hidden."

"Why?"

"Because his congressional benefactors wish it to remain so."

"The churches, you mean?" The congressman looked at Gavin. He stopped cranking on his fishing pole. His lure sank deeper in the water until the ripple disappeared altogether.

Gavin didn't answer.

"Where is it?"

"Not with us. Not here. But we have it."

"A piece of bone," the congressman whispered to himself, and then cast his line out into the water again.

"Yes."

"It corroborates your story?"

"Yes. We also have a DNA sample and a flash drive with genetic results."

"That might be something."

Paul reeled his lure in.

The congressman's face was unreadable now. Gone was the irritation, replaced by a blankness that seemed carefully cultivated. "I'll need to make some calls."

"Sir, you understand . . . we can't—"

The congressman stopped Gavin with a raised hand. He reached into his back pocket and pulled out a phone.

"Disposable. Untraceable. Just answer it tomorrow morning when it rings. Wherever you are staying now, you need to move. Use a different hotel. Hell, leave town if you want. I don't need to know where you are, but I need to know you'll answer that phone when it rings. Can you do that?"

Gavin stared at him. "We can do that."

"I was pretty sure you'd be full of shit," the congressman said. "But I brought the phone just in case. It pays to be prepared."

Gavin slid the phone into his front shirt pocket. They laid their fishing poles on the wet cement.

"Have a good afternoon, gentlemen," the congressman said and cast his line into the water again.

"Good afternoon, sir."

They walked the beach back toward the car. The fisherman stayed behind, as did the conspicuous men.

"A series of murders?"

Gavin nodded.

"You worked with him at this time?" Paul asked.

"Never directly. I was in the field. A lecturer at the university. I supplied bones, and he supplied money."

"And my father?"

"He was there for a while, in the lab. And then he wasn't. He left. Or tried to leave."

"Tried to leave?"

They stepped off the sandy beach, up onto the hot concrete parking slab.

"He left," Gavin said. "He got out. He did. When it got to be too much."

Paul stopped. "He died of a heart attack."

Gavin turned. "They all do," he said. "All the ones who leave. The old man makes sure it looks like that."

Paul and Lilli spent the night in a hotel overlooking the water. From their seventh-floor balcony they could see for miles. It was a better hotel than they'd grown accustomed to over the previous weeks. It would have been an unimaginable indulgence just a few days earlier, but now the cost of the room hardly mattered. The next couple of days would decide things one way or the other. Either way, their running had come to an end.

Gavin had chosen a different hotel, somewhere in the city.

"Best if you don't know which one, exactly," he'd said as he'd dropped them off at the entrance of their chosen lodging. "I'll meet you back here in the morning." Then he'd pulled away and was gone.

Paul and Lilli ate dinner at a nearby restaurant called the Crabble. They could pretend it was a date. It felt normal, and normal felt good.

Paul ate chicken wings.

"What do you think is going to happen tomorrow?" Lilli asked, swirling her drink. There was no reason not to get drunk, one last time.

"I don't know."

That night they slept in the same bed again, and in the morning Paul watched the sun rise.

He glanced over at Lilli's still-sleeping form. The dress she'd bought now lay strewn near the foot of the bed. Her hair spiraled across the pillows, black as deepest space. Her eyes were open just a slit—a gap that never quite closed, even in sleep. He remembered it from college, those eyes that didn't close, as if some part of her were ever watchful. He shook his head. Her watchfulness hadn't been enough. Now she was in danger. And it was his fault.

He pulled his pants on and decided to go for a jog to release the tension. He left Lilli a short note on the back of hotel stationery, then took the elevator down to the first floor. The oppressive southern heat had yet to kick in. He got only about a half mile before he had to stop. He leaned against a light pole, catching his breath. He wasn't a runner. Not by a long shot. He walked back, staying to the side of the road while cars passed him and the sun rose higher in the sky.

Back at the hotel, he found Lilli still sleeping, wrapped up in his rumpled white T-shirt.

When he got out of the shower, she had fewer clothes on.

They met Gavin downstairs around ten. He was eating the continental breakfast. Paul and Lilli each grabbed coffees, and they all headed out to the car. It was as gloomy today as it had been sunny the day before. Dark clouds threatened rain, but the pavement was still dry. They got to the car but didn't climb inside, instead leaning against the trunk. The car sat near a ridge of trees at the edge of the parking lot. A breeze was blowing. They waited.

It was ten-thirty when the phone rang.

Gavin answered.

"Hello," he said. "This is Gavin."

There was a pause.

Gavin nodded—a reflexive movement wasted on the person on the other end of the line, but informative nonetheless to Paul. "Yeah," Gavin said after a moment. "I can find it." There was another long pause. "When?"

He nodded again and then looked over to Paul and made a scribbling motion with his hand. Paul found a notepad in the glove compartment, ripped off a piece of paper, and handed it to Gavin. He also dug a pen from the hotel out from his pocket and handed that over as well.

"Uh-huh," Gavin said. "The congressman will be there?" He wrote something down on the paper. He stood up straighter.

"We have it," he said. "We'll bring it." Another subtle nod. "I'll hand it to him personally."

He hung up.

"Well?" Paul asked.

Gavin looked at Lilli. "You have the bone sample with you?"

Lilli patted her purse.

"A place called Josami Park," Gavin said. "Thirty minutes."

Lilli MapQuested the location on her phone.

On the little screen, it appeared as an oval of green attached on one side to the sprawl of the city, 9.2 miles from their current location.

They climbed into the car and backed out of the parking spot. Ten minutes later, they left the main road, turning onto a side road that hugged a railroad track for a mile before crossing through an ungated entrance. JOSAMI PARK, the sign declared through an obstruction of overgrown weeds.

They took a winding drive past rusting swing sets, following the curve of the asphalt as it wound its way through a copse of dense trees. It was a quiet place. Out of the way. Deserted.

"I don't like the look of this," Paul said. He scanned the woods just beyond the roadway. It was too carefully isolated. Too private. The park's name had the *sound* of a public place, but it wasn't public. Not when you came down to it.

The road terminated in a narrow turnaround next to a small wooden pavilion that had seen better days. It had ostensibly been intended as a picnic area, though now it looked more like the kind of place where drug deals went down.

Gavin eased the car to a stop with a squeak of brakes.

"Well?" he said.

Paul studied the surroundings. The clouds that had threatened all morning finally let loose with a gentle drizzle, dotting the windshield with drops of moisture. "I think we're here," he said simply.

Gavin shifted into park and turned the engine off. They climbed out. The sprinkles felt good on Paul's face.

"Are we early?" Lilli asked.

Gavin checked his watch. "We're right on time." He gestured toward the pavilion. "Let's get out of the weather."

They walked to the musty pavilion and Paul took a seat on one of the warped wooden picnic tables. It shifted dangerously under his weight, so he stood again. Behind him, a steel drum overflowed with garbage, the refuse of picnics past.

"So this is a pickup?" Lilli asked.

"Yeah," Gavin said. "Protection in exchange for the sample. That's what he said."

The sound of an engine turned Paul's head. In the distance, coming around the curve in the road, was a van. A moment later, a second van came into view. Both identical. Dark blue. The vans followed the road to the back of the turnaround and pulled to a stop a dozen yards from their parked car.

The vans idled there. Paul shot Gavin a nervous look. Then, the vehicles cut their engines.

The passenger door of the lead van opened and out stepped a man Paul had never seen before. A moment later the driver stepped out, and the two men approached.

The first man was tall and brown-haired, in his mid-thirties. He wore a button-down shirt and looked like an accountant, if your accountant happened to be six-five. The second man was shorter with darker hair, the thinner of the two.

When they finally crossed the empty lot, it was the taller man who spoke. "I'm glad to see you found the place," he said.

"It's a bit out of the way," Gavin said.

"Our mutual acquaintance thought it would give us a chance to discuss things." The man looked at each of them in turn, pointing a finger: "Paul Carlsson, Gavin McMaster, and you must be Lillivati." His smile widened. "So we're all here then, present and accounted for."

Paul felt Lilli's hand go into his. A nervous hole opened in Paul's stomach. As far as he knew, Lillivati's presence should have been a surprise.

"Where's Congressman Lacefield?" Gavin asked.

"Oh, you didn't think he'd be here personally, did you?"

"That's what he said. Very specifically."

"Plans have changed. Did you bring the bone sample?"

The nervous hole in Paul's stomach grew larger.

"I don't like plans changing," Gavin said.

"Well," the man said. "Nonetheless." He turned and looked directly at Lilli.

"The sample, miss, did you bring it?"

Lilli's eyes went to Gavin for a moment. Then she looked back at the man who'd addressed her. "Yeah," she said. "I have it."

"Excellent. Then we're all set." The man gestured toward the vans. "If you'll come with us, we'll be on our way."

Gavin didn't move. The pit in the base of Paul's stomach had blossomed into something different. No longer a hole but a familiar coldness that was spreading out from the center of him.

"Who's in the other van?" Gavin asked.

"Nobody to worry about," the man said.

"I worry."

"Well, you needn't. We're all friends here, are we not?"

"How do we know you're with the congressman?"

The tall man smiled again, a broad, white-toothed grin. "Well, how would we have known where to find you if we *weren't* with the congressman? Do you think we stumbled upon you by accident and happened to know your names?"

"Why isn't the congressman here?"

"He's indisposed at the moment. Pressing business. So he sent us to come pick you up."

Gavin nodded, but he didn't look convinced. "That's all fine and good. But I think we'll need to get the congressman on the phone before we go any further." He pulled out his phone and prepared to dial.

"You're wasting your time," the man said.

Gavin looked him in the face, then echoed his own word back at him: "Nonetheless."

The man straightened. "As I said, the congressman is indisposed. You need to come with us now."

"And what will happen if we *don't*?"

The smile on the man's face slid away. He looked suddenly resigned. "Then you get to see what's in the second van after all."

For a long time nobody said anything. The stranger's words hung in the air as both sides took time to arrive at an accommodation with how things had shifted and continued to shift—the subtle balance of their interaction tilting more with each passing second, until all pretense had come crashing down. The man sighed.

He flicked his hand, a subtle gesture. The tiniest gesture. Toward the second van.

A moment later there was the sound of metal on metal as the van door slid open. The door faced away from them, hidden on the side of the van next to the woods.

There was only silence.

Then a footfall. The van rocked slightly as weight shifted—the barest suggestion of movement from beneath its undercarriage, a shuffle of shadows, then gone. Slowly Paul bent to get a lower perspective, tilting his head to see beneath the van.

He saw the dark feet, bare and strange. The chill in the base of his stomach filled his entire body, surging up and out his throat to take the form of a wordless shout—

—and in the next instant Gavin screamed, "Get back!" and shoved Paul hard. Lilli whirled around, eyes wide, and Gavin grabbed the edge of the picnic table and flipped it on its side, and then his gun was out and firing.

The men were almost as fast. The sound of gunfire was deafening. Shots rang out as Gavin dropped to a crouch behind the overturned picnic table. "Get down!" he shouted.

Lilli screamed and clawed her way across the cement patio, keeping low to the ground as Paul dove behind a metal drum. Bullets zinged through the drum as the men returned fire.

Gavin stuck his hand around the side of the table and fired blindly. *Pop, pop, pop, pop, pop.*

Splinters of wood flew from the edge of the table before the men seemed to reconsider their exposed position. They bolted for cover, sprinting behind the protection of their vans.

The gunfire subsided.

"Is anyone hurt?" Gavin growled.

Lilli only shook her head, eyes still wide with terror. She was huddled behind a square wooden support pillar, her narrow body almost the exact dimensions of the post.

Gavin looked to Paul. "No," Paul answered. "I'm good."

Shots rang out again, chipping the picnic table into puffs of splinters. Some of the rounds passed straight through the wood to make *thwick* noises in the trees behind the pavilion. Gavin stuck his hand around the side of the table and fired again, but this time, from their protected position, the men didn't stop shooting. More bullets whizzed through the table. Wood chips exploded near Gavin's face. "Shit!" he hissed. He scrambled backward, away from the table, keeping low.

Gavin fired as he retreated. Paul eased his good eye around the side of the metal barrel just enough to sneak a look. Dark shapes spread out from the van, moving through the shrubs at the edge of the parking lot. The men fired from around the front of the van but didn't advance.

Paul ducked back behind the barrel as another barrage of bullets plinked through the pavilion.

After a moment, the shots went quiet.

Paul made eye contact with Gavin. Gavin pulled a clip from inside the breast pocket of his suit jacket. He'd come prepared. *Who the fuck are you*, Paul wondered. Gavin ejected the clip from his gun and slammed the new clip home.

A voice called out from behind the vans: "Let's take a moment here, shall we? A cease-fire." There were a few seconds of silence. "Are we agreed?"

Paul slid his eye around the steel drum again. He could see the vans. One had a shattered side window, bullet holes perforating the side.

"Well, isn't this an unexpected turn of events?" the voice continued. "So it appears the good professor not only has a gun but also knows how to shoot it."

Gavin called out a response: "You'd do well to remember that."

"Oh, we'll remember. You seem to have shot my partner."

Gavin gave Paul a questioning look. Paul shrugged. He couldn't see anything.

Gavin called out, "Sorry to hear that. In that case, we accept your unconditional retreat."

There was movement, then a muzzle flash from around the side of the bumper, and then *thwack!* Wood chips sprang from the table a couple of inches from Gavin's head.

"You sonofabitch!" came a shout from a different voice.

A heated conversation followed from the other side of the vans. It was unintelligible for the most part, though Paul was able to discern the word "prick" spoken loudly in a strained voice, then, "Calm the fuck down."

A moment later, in a casual tone, the first voice spoke again: "My apologies for that errant shot. It seems my wounded comrade here didn't particularly like the sarcastic tenor of your last statement and he chose to express himself through less than friendly means. And that is unfortunate, because the fact of the matter is that we've got instructions to bring you in alive."

Paul met Gavin's eyes again, another questioning look.

"So you see the predicament we're in," the voice continued. "If we kill you, well, that's less than ideal. On the other hand, you must know that we can't let you drive out of here."

"Looks like we're at an impasse then."

"Oh, I think that's the wrong way to look at it. You see, if it's an impasse, then we really are stuck. If it's an impasse, then we've got no choice but to go to Plan B."

"What's Plan B?"

"You're not gonna like it."

"Try us," Gavin called out.

"No, really now, I'm telling you. Plan B is a surprise. And you'll just have to take my word for it—it's not a *good* surprise."

Paul scanned the woods behind the pavilion, wondering if the thick underbrush would work for or against them in a foot chase.

The voice continued: "So we need to reach an accommodation here. What do you say you come out with your hands up? No more gunfire. Nobody else gets hurt. We bring you in, no muss, no fuss."

"Bring us in where?" Gavin called.

"You haven't figured that out yet?" It was a new voice. A third man stepped into view from behind the van. He had blond hair and a short, red beard.

"Shit," Gavin hissed under his breath.

"What?" Paul whispered to Gavin. "Where do they want to take us?"

"This is as good an offer as you're going to get," the red-bearded man said. "I suggest you take it, Gavin."

Somewhere in the distance a bird chirped. Wind sighed through the trees. Beyond that, there was no sound. No answer. Gavin kept his head down, silent.

After thirty seconds had passed, the red-bearded man spoke again: "Gavin, there's one more thing I feel compelled to mention, since you're taking time to think things over. It was really only Paul that was mentioned in regard to being brought back alive. Seems the old man wants to meet him. We were willing to include you under that general umbrella, though. As a courtesy. But the orders regarding the rest of you really didn't specify."

Gavin made a hand gesture that caught Paul's attention. When Paul looked, Gavin motioned toward the woods just beyond the pavilion. "Run," Gavin whispered.

Paul shook his head. "We're not leaving you."

"You go first, and I'll cover you. I'll be right behind you."

"No. All together or not at all."

"Paul, that's just not gonna work."

"I'm not leaving you," Paul repeated. "We stand a better chance together."

"No, we don't. We stand no chance, just sitting here. I can cover your retreat, and with any luck, I'll pick another one or two of them off. You make it to a road, flag somebody down, and then get the hell out of here. Get to a police station. That's our only hope now."

Paul said nothing. Just stared at Gavin.

"Do it for her." Gavin cocked his head toward Lilli.

Lilli still sat with her back to the wooden support beam. She was hunched as low to the ground as she could go, legs extended out in front of her in a straight line. Her dark hair clung wetly to her face.

"What do you think?" Paul asked Lilli.

"I think I want a gun," she said.

"Sorry, lass," Gavin said. "I've just got the one."

"Then that reduces me to target practice."

"So we run?" Paul said.

She nodded. "I'm game if you are."

"Shit," Paul mouthed softly to himself. "Okay, on the count of three."

Paul took a deep breath and shifted his feet, ready to spring. "One. Two . . ." He chanced a look around the steel drum and didn't see any guns pointed at them. "Three!"

He and Lilli bolted for the woods. Gavin stood and aimed.

Pop, pop, pop, pop, pop, pop, pop, pop.

Gunshots rang out as Gavin covered their escape. The men fired back, the sound of shots blurring together as both sides exchanged fire.

Paul and Lilli sprinted into the woods, knocking aside branches and shouldering their way through the underbrush.

From behind them, the sound of shots changed, the closer shots going quiet. Paul knew that either Gavin's gun had run out of bullets or he was dead.

He let Lilli pull ahead, and he slowed to look behind. He heard the sound of branches breaking, then Gavin's voice say, "Shit!"

"This way!" Paul urged as Gavin came into view through the underbrush. Gavin was barely visible, fifty yards behind them, his legs pumping.

"For fuck's sake, run!" Gavin shouted.

Paul turned and ran full out. He leapt over a fallen log and dodged a bramble prickly with thorns. Low branches scratched at his cheek. He'd gained on Lilli a little when he heard a different sound from behind him. The sound of crashing limbs suddenly louder, as if something enormous was barreling its way through the woods.

Paul turned back, and what he saw changed everything.

Two things.

Demon things.

Different from what he'd seen before.

Different from anything he'd ever imagined. Faces like something older. Things that were not human.

For a moment Paul faltered. He missed a step, and his foot came down on something soft, and suddenly he was rolling. He sprang to his feet, turning again to look behind him, and the things were closing in on Gavin. Gavin's face was white; he'd seen what was chasing him.

The things closed in.

"Run!" Paul shouted helplessly. But Gavin was already running, still thirty yards back. He was too slow.

The creatures converged on Gavin and dragged him to the ground. The screaming started—screeching—as heavy clublike arms rose and fell. Paul froze, his gaze wide with horror. The things lunged in on Gavin, mouths gaping, teeth bared. Blood sprayed. It happened in an instant. Paul started to move toward Gavin, an instinct to help his friend, but a hand grabbed at his arm.

"No! Too late," she said. She was right. In that moment, the screaming stopped.

The creatures pulled and ripped at Gavin's flesh. Blood covered their inhuman faces. They were like the thing on the bridge, but they were different, too. Smaller, darker. More animal. One of them lifted its face and glared at Paul. It rose up, baring huge teeth, and screeched—an alien, almost-human sound. A gravelly howl of rage.

Behind the creatures, the men from the vans broke through the underbrush.

"Come on," Lilli told Paul.

She pulled at him, breaking his paralysis. They bolted through the trees.

"You really don't want to do that!" the red-bearded man yelled after them.

Paul jumped a log and knocked aside tree branches as he broke his way through the woods.

"You can't outrun them," the voice called after them. "But you might outrun us. You don't want *that* to happen!"

Paul jumped another fallen log.

The voice continued: "Because when they catch you, we're the only ones who can make them stop."

They burst onto a trail. Sudden openness. Without thinking, Paul reacted, following the trail to the right.

A moment later, the things burst out of the woods behind them.

There is a clarity that comes to you when you're running for your life. Everything is condensed into a simple formula: How fast can you make your legs move?

Paul didn't turn back. Wouldn't turn back. Lilli was a few yards ahead of him again; that was all he cared about. His legs were on fire. He heard ragged breathing behind him, but none of that mattered. The only thing that mattered was making his legs work, one in front of the other, as fast as he could.

But it wasn't enough.

Paul was knocked off his feet by the force of the blow. He rolled, caught up in a gripping, thrashing tornado. He struck out with his hands and feet, but the thing was faster than him, stronger than him. A blow caught him across the side of his head—quick deafness, then a sound like a feedback whine. He swung wildly as his hearing returned. His fist connected, but the thing turned, grabbed his arm, and flung him—it felt like his arm was nearly torn off. He landed and rolled, and the thing was on him again.

For two semesters in high school he'd wrestled. He knew how to throw a man. Knew how to grapple. But he'd never felt strength approaching this. Nor speed. A thing smaller than him but multiple times stronger, faster. Paul swung again, and the thing bared its teeth and ducked away. The return blow sent stars spilling through his head.

Just up the trail, Lilli screamed. The other thing had run past Paul to grab her, flinging her to the ground. Her dress ripped. Paul struggled with the beast in front of him, trying to pull free. He fought with every ounce of strength in his body, but it was too strong. Too fast. Lilli screamed again.

The creature moved in, landing another sidelong blow to Paul's head, and he lost time for a moment—one second standing, the next with leaves in his mouth, face in the soil. Lilli was screaming again, louder. He turned his head. She was trying to get away, but the thing was on her. She'd been pulled almost completely out of her dress now. Exposed bra and panties—screaming and kicking. The thing screeched in maniacal frenzy.

Paul staggered to his feet and saw the men coming up the trail. He turned toward where Lilli fought with the creature. He ran full out and landed a vicious kick to the thing's side, knocking Lilli free.

The other creature launched itself at Paul, knocking him off his feet. It loped away on strange legs, circling around. Paul spun in the dirt so he wouldn't expose his back to the thing.

"Jesus, you really just need to stop," the red-bearded man said. "You're not going to win."

Lilli screamed, and the second creature grabbed her leg and pulled her along the ground.

"Stop struggling," the man said. He was standing only a dozen feet away now, observing the fight with detached interest. "Seriously, for your own good, stay down."

Paul dragged himself to his feet. The thing moved in again, knocking him down again, raining punches on him. Paul did his best to cover up, to protect his vital organs, but the blows kept coming, and then he felt a bite on his arm, and the thing was away.

"See now, look," the man said to one of his comrades. The tone was conversational, as if they were discussing a child who needed punishment. "I told them not to run."

Lilli screamed again. Paul spit dirt from his mouth and turned his head. She was nearly naked now, bra pulled loose in the struggle. She was kicking and thrashing, still trying to get away, but the thing still had her by the leg. It flung her over. Her panties came apart in its grip.

The two beasts were distracted by her struggle. Paul rose to his knees, looking for some weapon. Any weapon. A few feet away, a thick tree branch angled from the detritus at the edge of the trail. It showed the mark of a chain saw, part of a limb fall that had been cleared away by park workers. Paul's hand curled around the branch. He stood, bringing the branch with him. It was five feet long, heavy in his hand. Solid. Nearly as thick as his forearm.

As Paul stood, the creature in front of him reacted. It bared its teeth and spun itself just out of reach, finding new reserves of rage. It knew what a stick was. But it wasn't Paul's target. Paul made momentary eye contact with the red-bearded man. The man only stared at him, making no move to stop him.

The second beast grabbed Lilli's legs and forced them apart. She shrieked, "No!"

Paul turned and launched himself toward Lilli's attacker. The thing behind him followed but would be a second too slow. Swinging the branch high as he ran, Paul brought the wood down on the creature's skull with every ounce of strength in his body. The skull made a sickening sound as it caved in on itself. Paul let go of the branch, and it hung suspended for a moment, buried in the thing's skull. The creature toppled next to Lilli.

A moment later, the other creature struck him like a train, sending him flying, and the world went away.

He heard gunshots then. Two gunshots in quick succession.

Then: "That's about enough of that."

Paul opened his eye and saw the red-bearded man pointing his gun at the creature that stood over him. Puffs of dirt were still settling around its feet where the shots had churned the soil.

"I said, enough. The boss wants him alive." The man was talking to the beast.

The thing turned its head away from the man and looked down at Paul. Its eyes burned into him with an insanity that Paul had never experienced in life. Flecks of foam shot from its mouth with each exhalation.

"Alive," the man stressed, a scar twisting his upper lip. "So stop."

The beast's eyes never moved, never lost their laserlike focus. A few feet away, Lilli curled into a ball to cover her nakedness, crying softly into the dirt. The beast's lips peeled back from its teeth. Its hands curled into fists as it stared down at Paul.

The man took a step forward. "I will fucking shoot you."

The thing's head snapped around. It stared up at the man—murder in its eyes.

It looked at Paul again, muscles still twitching. On the edge of decision.

The man fired his weapon a third time, and dirt exploded in front of the thing's feet.

"Next one is in your skull."

The creature backed away, one slow step at a time. When it was half a dozen feet off, it screamed in frustration and slammed its fists into the dirt with enough force that Paul felt the blows through the ground. It shrieked up at the sky in rage. Then it stood, chest heaving, eyes lowered—lost in an inhuman rage controlled by the barest of margins.

It slunk over to its fallen companion. It touched the thing's lopsided skull, then looked toward Paul again.

"Fuck you," Paul said.

The thing froze. Its black eyes went wide, its lips curling back from its teeth as it started to shake.

"Shut the fuck up!" the man yelled at Paul. He raised his gun again and said to the creature, "He's trying to get you killed."

The thing's eyes narrowed. It turned and bounded off down the trail, tearing at the branches.

The red-bearded man walked over to Paul. He sank down on one knee. "They take direction sometimes. Unless they get angry. When they're *really* angry, all bets are off."

Paul looked in the direction where the thing had disappeared.

"And one more thing," the man said. "They don't forget."

The man leaned forward. "Wanna hear something else?" He placed his mouth close to Paul's ear. "I'm not really allowed to kill them. These things. I hate them. Vile creatures. But I'm not allowed to shoot them, no matter what." The man straightened, speaking now in his normal voice. "One day, they're going to figure that out. But that day wasn't today. Lucky for you."

Paul turned his head and looked over at the thing he'd killed. Its misshapen head was now further misshapen. It lay facedown in the dirt a few feet away. Coarse black hair, a wide torso. Paul stared at its feet. If you could call them that. In truth, they were something between hands and feet. Something that was neither. It might have weighed two hundred pounds, all muscle. Broad as doorwary.

The bearded man motioned for the other two men to pick Paul up. They grabbed him under the armpits and hauled him to a standing position. Everything hurt. His head swam. Blood ran into his eye. "But you," the man continued. "Bravo. That's quite a swing you have. I've wanted to do that for a long time." The other men started to half-pull, half-carry Paul toward the van. Paul jerked his arm away.

"Come on, don't be like that," the man said. "Tell you what. Would you rather I let your new friend there help your girlfriend?"

Paul let his arms be gripped. Lilli was still crying, putting her ripped dress back on. Its gossamer fabric had simply dissolved in the creature's grip. Her black hair stood wild atop her head. Tear marks made tracks in her dirty cheeks. They made the long walk back to the van.

Paul kept losing time. His head wasn't right. His ears still rang.

They backtracked through the woods the way they had come. Suddenly he was at Gavin's body. The face smashed. Unrecognizable.

"Gavin," Paul said, unsure why he was saying it. The word just spilled out. And then he lost time again, and they were passing through the pavilion. Paul slumped to the pavement, cool concrete on his face.

Lilli's face looked down at him. She was kneeling, trying to help him up. "You have a concussion."

"How many fingers am I holding up?" she asked.

"I'm fine," Paul said.

Somewhere, a man laughed. "Not like he can have double vision, now, is it?"

Paul pulled himself upright and kept walking but stumbled again as they approached the vans. The two men yanked him back to his feet this time. The world swam.

"Where is the sample?" one of them asked.

"Sample?" Lilli asked.

"Don't play dumb," the man said. "We don't have the time."

"Just check her purse," one of them snapped.

"She's not carrying a purse."

They pushed Paul against the front of the first van, his legs spread, hands held in a firm grip behind his back like they were cops. He felt the windshield on his left ear.

"The car." The red-bearded man sighed with irritation. "Check their fucking car."

The man did as he was told. A moment later he shouted, "Found it." He dumped the contents of Lilli's purse on the hood of Gavin's rental. *Gavin's rental.* It seemed ludicrous that Gavin was dead. Impossible. He had a rental car to return. "Got it," the man called out, holding up a plastic baggie wrapped in tape.

The other men brought Paul around to the side of the van. That was when Paul saw the man Gavin had shot. The wounded man was lying in the back of the van. His eyes were gummy. His shirt bloody. The bullet had taken him high on the shoulder.

"He doesn't look good," Paul offered.

"You're no fashion model yourself," a man said from behind him. "Get in."

Paul allowed himself to be pushed toward the open van doors until he saw Lilli being pulled in another direction. The man holding Lilli's arm tugged her toward the second van. Paul jerked his shoulder back.

"I'm riding with her," he said.

"You're going separate," the bearded man snapped.

"The fuck I am." Paul pushed back with his 235 pounds. Another man stepped into position to help manhandle him.

Lilli starting screaming. Paul looked over, and she'd dropped to the ground, kicking at the man trying to get her in the vehicle.

The man grabbed her arm and twisted. Lilli screamed in pain. "Let go of me!"

Paul braced his leg against the side of the van and pushed off. The two men behind him grunted as they tried to force him inside. "Get. In. The fucking. Van."

"No! I ride with her."

"Motherfucker, I will shoot you."

"Then do it, because that's the only way she and I don't end up in the same van."

The creature moved into view, coming slowly out of the woods, observing the scuffle from a distance. It crouched low to the ground as it moved, tension building in its haunches. That same barely controlled anger on its face.

The red-bearded man saw it too.

"All right, all right, for fuck's sake," he said, letting go of Paul's arm. "Jesus. Get in the fucking same van, the both of you, or you'll both be fucking dead, and I'll have to explain. Jesus."

The men behind Paul relaxed their grip, and Paul stood straighter. He adjusted his shirt, which had twisted around his body, and he walked to the second van and helped Lilli climb inside.

"Your face," she said, and touched him.

A moment later, the door slid shut.

The darkness like a gift.

Outside the van, voices argued, getting farther away. Paul crept toward the front of the van and looked out the windshield. He could see one of the men standing a few yards away, keeping an eye on the vehicle. His gun was in its holster at his side. Paul slunk back to where Lilli was sitting. He held her hand. Neither of them spoke. A few minutes later, the voices returned.

There was unintelligible conversation. The other van door slid open. There was a thud. More time went by, and Paul knew they were loading the bodies. Gavin. The creature. The van door slid shut.

There was more talking outside the vans. Voices pitched low so Paul couldn't hear.

Suddenly the driver's door opened, and one of the men climbed behind the wheel. He started the engine. A moment later, the red-bearded man opened the front passenger door and climbed in.

He turned to apprise them. "You've no idea how fucking close." He held his hand up, thumb and forefinger positioned a centimeter apart. "This close, and things would have gotten out of control, and I'd have some explaining to do about how our target got his arms ripped off. It might have been worth it."

He tossed two pairs of handcuffs back to them. "Now lock yourselves. Hands in front of you. Both of you."

Paul picked up one of the handcuffs. He clicked his left wrist. Instead of handcuffing his right, he clicked Lilli's right. He stared into Redbeard's face the whole time.

The man just shook his head. "Oh, the old man is gonna love you."

The van pulled away.

They drove throughout the night. Paul slept with his back wedged against the hard metal side of the van. In the morning he woke and could barely move, and his eye was nearly swollen shut. This was not good. If the swelling got any worse, he'd be blind.

"I've got to piss," he said.

There was a shuffle of movement from the front seat, and an empty two-liter cola bottle was tossed back to him.

"Fucking watch your aim when you go," Redbeard said. "Don't be pissing all over the back of the van."

Paul knelt and fumbled with his pants.

Lilli looked up at him. "Do you want me to . . ."

"What?"

"Hold the bottle?"

"Jesus, no. Just . . . I got it."

The van took a curve in the road, and Paul swayed. After a moment of fumbling, he said, "Okay, yeah."

It went easier than he expected. One hand on the side of the van for balance, the other on himself.

The distinct sound of urination filled the van. He heard laughter from up front.

"You watching your aim, right?" the driver called back.

"You'll see my aim when I throw this on you."

"Do that and I'll shoot you. For real. I will pull this van over and shoot you."

"If you could shoot me, you would have."

"Then I'll shoot her. Or let her ride in the other van."

Paul was silent. He finished pissing and zipped up.

"It's like dealing with fucking children," the red-bearded man said to himself.

Paul buckled his belt. "What do you want me to do with it?"

There was more fumbling from the front seat. A moment later, the lid was tossed back. Paul screwed the top on and tossed the bottle to the far back of the van.

They drove for another hour. Finally, Lilli asked, "And what about me?"

"What about you?"

"I have to go."

"Je-zus," the driver said, and made no other comment.

Lilli laid her head on Paul's shoulder and asked, "Where are they taking us?"

"I don't know," Paul said.

"We're not getting out of this, are we?"

Paul didn't answer.

He held her against his chest. He felt her trembling. After a while, the trembling stopped.

A few minutes later, they pulled to the side of the road. At first Paul thought they'd arrived at whatever destination they'd been traveling to, but then the men stepped out to urinate in the weeds. After a minute the van door slid open.

"Get out."

Paul and Lilli exited. Blinking up at the bright sun. "Your turn," the driver said to Lilli. She held up her shackled wrist.

The man turned to look at the second van, which had pulled to a stop just behind theirs. It sat idling a dozen yards back. In it, Paul figured, was Gavin's body. Also, the creature. He wondered if they kept it caged or if it only sat in the back of the van. He wondered if it was watching them through the glass.

The driver pointed to the van. "If you run, we let it out again."

"I won't run."

The man unlocked Lilli's handcuff. She rubbed her wrist. She stepped forward and squatted in the shallow ditch along the road.

Even with the driver's warning still in his ears, Paul considered their odds. His head was a bit better now. The effects of the concussion had faded over the hours. He counted the men. Two in the van. And two more in the van behind them—one of those, shot. But there was the thing, too, in the van. The thing he didn't have a name for. They wouldn't have a chance if they ran. Even without the men and the guns, they wouldn't have a chance.

Lilli stood and straightened her tattered dress.

"Now back in the van," the driver said.

They climbed in and the man slammed the door.

"Throw these back on," he said and tossed the handcuffs back.

Paul handcuffed them together like before. Using opposite arms this time, though.

The driver from the other van walked up to the window and dropped a bag from Burger King into the front seat.

"Did you get no pickles?"

"Yeah, no pickles."

"No tomato?"

"No pickles, no fucking tomatoes, just like you like. Eat."

The man fished two wrappers out of the bag. He tossed them back to Paul, along with a two-liter of Coke. "For both of you."

He started the engine and pulled away from the curb, heading back to the highway.

Paul lay back as the van picked up speed. Lilli lay on his chest. At some point, he slept.

40

Paul woke to the sound of tires on gravel. He didn't sit up to look.

When he was a small child, his family had sometimes gone on short road trips into the city. They'd visit the university where his father gave talks. They'd visit zoos and parks, because that's what normal, happy families did, and it was important to his parents that they seem, and be, normal and happy. Inevitably, after a day of sightseeing, Paul would fall asleep on the way home. The sound of gravel always woke him when they pulled into the drive. That sudden transition from pavement to the noisy crunching of the long, stony driveway of their first house. It was a distinct sound that he came to associate with home.

But now the gravel kept coming. Minute after minute, so that Paul realized this wasn't a driveway entrance but a rural road.

"Where are we?" Paul asked.

The man in the passenger seat said nothing. Only looked back at him.

But the driver spoke—one word, slow and heavy with meaning: *"Everglades."*

The man in the passenger seat flashed the driver a look of irritation.

"What?" the driver asked. "It's not like he's gonna tell anyone, now, is it."

What the hell were they doing in Florida? They'd been driving south forever, it seemed, but he'd had no idea they'd traveled so far.

The gravel road got rougher.

Eventually, he felt Lilli stir. He envied her the last moments of her slumber. Asleep, she was free of this place. These men. This nightmare.

Her eyes opened, dark and confused. He watched the understanding coalesce in them—saw the exact moment when she realized where she was, when it all came back.

Paul looked away.

After an hour of gravel, the road smoothed out again. Paul sat up straighter, looking out through the front windshield. Around them was swamp—low and flat and overgrown.

The van took a right, leaving the main road and bumping its way down to a kind of access road. Mostly one lane, with occasional turnouts. A beaten mud track. The van slowed to twenty miles per hour.

Thirty minutes later, the van crossed through an open, swinging gate. "Rise and shine," Redbeard said. "We're here."

Lilli and Paul craned their necks for a better look. The view out the front windshield wasn't particularly clear, but from what he could see, they'd arrived at some kind of military outpost. No, not military. Not quite. It had the wrong feel. A string of buildings spread out before them—low block buildings set at some distance from the road. Then the road curved and the whole of the complex suddenly loomed up into view, anchored by a huge gray building, as sprawling as an outlet mall. But set here in the middle of the Everglades, like a cult compound in the swamp.

The van came to a stop. The two men climbed out. A moment later the van door slid open. The sudden light was blinding. Heat and muggy air poured in.

"Get out."

Paul stepped to the ground, shielding his eye.

Lilli followed.

As Paul's eye adjusted, he saw an old man standing off to the side, surrounded by a phalanx of guards. He wore a white coat, but also a hat to keep the sun off his head. His face was buried in shadow.

The two men from the van stepped aside as the old man hobbled forward.

"Do you have the samples?" the old man asked. The question was pointed at Redbeard.

Redbeard pulled the baggie from the armrest of the van. The old man smiled and gestured to one of his guards. Redbeard handed the baggie to the man.

"See that Lee, in the cytology lab, gets that," the old man said. The guard turned and headed into the building.

"Paul Carlsson," the old man said, finally turning his attention to his new visitors. He extended a hand.

Paul didn't shake it.

"I haven't seen you since you were a baby."

Paul blinked. He had no response to that. Lilli looked at him, confusion showing in her eyes.

"I'm assuming our friend Gavin has informed you of the peculiar situation we now find ourselves in?"

"Friend? You have an interesting way of dealing with friends."

"Oh, but he *was* a friend," the old man said. "Though that must seem strange to you now. But he made his own choices. I understand he used a gun to exercise his choice. I don't see how there was ever another option for us. I also understand he fired first?"

"It wasn't like that."

"Our friend didn't flip the table over and draw his gun? Because that's how it was described to me. Are my men lying to me?"

Paul was silent.

"No? And then there was Margaret. I assume Gavin had some hand in that as well. Now, you never answered my question. Did our mutual friend inform you of the facts regarding the current situation? In short, do you know who I am?"

"Yeah, he told me about you."

"Good," the old man said. "Then this will go faster."

The old man turned to the guards. "Put him in the guest quarters."

"And her?" Redbeard said, gesturing to Lilli.

The old man waved his hand absently. "Same," he said. And with that, he turned and walked away. But before he'd gotten very far, he glanced at Paul from over his shoulder. "We'll talk later tonight."

The guest quarters had bars on the windows.

Lilli sat on the bed while Paul moved through the room, opening every drawer in the dresser and both nightstands. The room was small and appointed very much like a hotel room, right down to the sturdy furniture.

"What are you doing?"

"Looking for a weapon of opportunity."

"What kind of weapon do you expect to find here?"

"That's why it's called 'of opportunity.' You know it when you see it."

He opened the bottom drawer of the little desk that sat near the wall. He slammed it shut again. His gaze cast about the room. He bent low and looked under the bed.

Eventually, he sat next to Lilli on the bed.

"Nothing," he said.

She touched his hand.

"You didn't think they'd be dumb enough to leave anything danger-ous in here, did you?"

"I had to check."

Her hand slipped into his, and she squeezed.

Later, just as the light was leaving the window, a knock came on the door. A moment later, the door opened, and a guard stepped in.

"Paul, Mr. Johansson would like to see you."

The guard was six-four, all shoulders—a linebacker in a suit.

"I'm not leaving without her," Paul said.

"She's staying here," the linebacker responded.

"No."

Another guard appeared in the doorway, even bigger, if possible, than the first one. Paul assumed the choice of guards was intentional. A way of saying something without saying it. A way of discouraging an independent opinion about whether he'd be leaving the room or not. Paul made the decision not to give in.

"If I'm leaving this room, she's coming with me."

"You're making this more difficult than it has to be, Mr. Carlsson," the second guard said. He spoke over the shoulder of the man in front of him. His tone exuded reasonableness.

Paul shook his head. "I'm not leaving her."

The first guard's tone wasn't as patient as the second's. "You *are* leaving her," he snapped. He obviously wasn't used to this kind of open defiance. "Now."

Lilli touched Paul's arm. "Paul, go."

"Lilli—"

The reasonable guard broke in: "He says he wants to see you, and that means we're going to bring you. The condition you arrive in is the only matter up for debate here."

"I'll be fine," Lilli soothed. "I'll be here when you get back."

Reluctantly, Paul allowed himself to be convinced. He followed the men out of the room, and the first guard locked the door behind him.

They made their way down a long hall, then climbed a winding stair to another level. The stairs, Paul noticed, were designed to look like a DNA double helix.

"After you," the guard said when they came to an enormous door at the end of the hall.

Paul pushed through the door, into a library.

The old man was standing before the stacks, looking up at the wall of books. Big, hardbound tomes filled shelves from floor to ceiling, extending the full length of the chamber. Here the lighting wasn't fluorescent; instead, the warm, full glow of incandescence exuded from a series of panels along the back wall, and ceiling, and floor. An enormous wooden table dominated the room, while the table itself was dominated by yet more books, piled like an uneven cityscape—leather-bound skyscrapers stacked in mimicry of some blocky 1950s metropolis. Altogether there must have been thousands of books. It was as impressive a private library as Paul had ever seen.

"Have you heard of *The Modern Synthesis*?" The old man's voice seemed to filter through the piles of books. It was the opposite of an empty church, where your voice might echo hollowly off the walls. Here your voice was eaten by the room.

"Yeah."

"Have you read it?"

"It's one of the banned books."

"Have you read it?" the old man repeated.

"I have."

"And what about this?" he asked, pulling a large dark book free from the shelves. The old man held the book out for Paul to see.

"The Bible?"

"Also a banned book, in some parts of the world."

The old man placed the book down on the table and gestured for Paul to come closer.

Paul stood next to the old man, his leg brushing the table. The old man was tall but frail. Paul thought about killing him. The image flashed through his mind. His hands around the old man's neck. The way his throat would feel when he crushed it. What his eyes would look like when the life had gone out of them.

"Turn to Genesis chapter three, verse twenty," the old man said.

Paul turned the pages.

"Now read it."

"'And Adam called his wife's name Eve; because she was the mother of all living.'"

"'Mother of all living.' What do you think of that?"

"I don't think anything."

"They were cast out from the garden for their sins," the old man said. "God was angry, because they'd eaten the fruit of knowledge. His punishment was swift." The old man closed his eyes and quoted from memory: "'I will greatly multiply thy sorrow and thy conception; in sorrow thou shalt bring forth children.'"

The old man opened his eyes and looked at Paul. "Thus were Cain and Abel begotton. And then Cain slew Abel. There is another verse I'd like you to read. Genesis four, lines sixteen and seventeen."

Paul flipped through the Bible until he found the verse. He read aloud, "'And Cain went out from the presence of the Lord, and dwelt in the land of Nod, on the east of Eden. And Cain knew his wife; and she conceived, and bare Enoch.'"

The old man smiled. "You see, Paul, that was what got me. That was what started all this." He gestured around himself, but Paul had the sense that he meant something larger. The entire compound. Everything. "That is what sent me down this path. Reading Genesis, when I was a young boy in school."

The old man held out his hand, and Paul gave him back the Bible. The old man looked down at the pages, creased and yellowed with age.

"Because even as a boy I wondered . . ." The old man closed the Bible. "This boy Cain, cast out from paradise, who did he marry?"

Paul stared at the old man. "It's an origin story."

"Is it now? Come, sit," the old man said. He gestured to a high-backed chair near the table. Paul sat, while the old man continued looking through his books. He took a pair of bifocals from the front pocket of his suit jacket and studied the spines, searching for titles he had in his head. One by one, he pulled down other books. Books on paleontology. Books on bones. And these books, too, like the Bible, were banned in various parts of the world, Paul knew. Or some of them, anyway.

"Tell me, Paul, did you find your room to be comfortable?"

"I'm not particularly interested in the accommodations."

"I see; nor would I expect you to be. But still, so long as you aren't uncomfortable, I suppose that's fine. Aha!" The old man slid a book from its place on the shelf. "This is what I was looking for. Very rare, this one."

He placed it on the table with the others and sank down into a nearby chair. They were sitting side by side, like dear friends. Paul imagined that a security camera recorded their every interaction. He pictured men in riot gear just outside the door, waiting to step in if he made the wrong move. But he could do it quick, he knew. But maybe not quick enough. Could he kill the old man before anyone had time to reach him? And then there was Lilli. Of course. And what would happen to her? The old man was no fool. For all Paul knew, there might be a gun trained on him right now, unseen.

"I knew your father for many years," he said. "He was a talented scientist."

"So I am told."

"I see him in you."

"Few people do."

"Ah, but they're not looking at the important things, are they?" The old man flipped through the pages of the book before him. He continued: "Aristotle wrote that, at his best, man is the noblest of all animals; also he is the worst. Your father and I had a parting of the ways. It pained me bitterly at the time, but I understood the reasons. Your father . . . was a difficult man, in many ways. Perhaps you knew this?"

"It escaped my attention."

"Oh, I doubt that." The old man smiled. "And your mother. She, too, was a brilliant worker, though perhaps not as gifted. Nor as afflicted. It is a trade-off, no? Do you understand about trade-offs?"

Paul understood.

"Let Lilli go," he said.

The old man looked surprised. "So now it's you who speak of trade-offs. Tell me, what do you have to trade, I wonder."

"She has nothing to do with this."

"Oh, but she does. Now." The old man paused. "Paul, you must understand the position I'm in. This is a very delicate time—thanks in no small part to your own activities. The political situation is fragile at the moment, a circumstance you attempted to exploit to your advantage. Fortunately, Congressman Lacefield was amenable to negotiation."

"He sold us out?"

"Traded you, more like."

"For what?"

"Senate votes, of course. Politicians all have their constituencies to keep happy. And to be clear, the information you want to divulge would be uncomfortable to a large number of people on *both* sides of the aisle. The status quo is hardly ever served by rocking the boat."

The old man opened the book lying before him. In it were large full-color prints of bones. It was a specialist's book.

The old man's eyes lingered on a glossy image of a skull. He touched the photo. "The magic is in the minutiae, isn't it?" he said. "The careful measurement. The interpretations come and go like the tides, argued over like fashion, but the measurements themselves stay. Unassailable. I'm told that you're a man who appreciates this also."

"She won't say anything, if you let her go."

"In Java, *Homo erectus*. In Europe, Neanderthals. In Siberia, the newest DNA evidence points to something else entirely. As distinct as Neanderthals, but different. Bones found in a cave just outside Denisova." The old man flipped through several more pages, his rheumy old eyes moving from photograph to photograph.

"*Homo erectus. Homo heidelbergensis, Australopithecus, Ramapithecus,* all these different things. These, Paul, are what we bred with when we left our garden."

"You're mad," Paul said.

The old man smiled. "You've seen so little. You can't possibly understand it all. You're like a fish calling a turtle mad for telling of dry land. Do you think this is just a theory of mine?"

The old man stood. He closed the book, hiding its photographs.

"Here, Paul, let me show you."

They took the hall to a stairwell and then descended to a deeper level of the building. Two guards fell into step behind them. They'd been standing just outside the door of the library.

The old man pushed through a set of security doors and led Paul into a laboratory. "This is the anthropogeny lab," he said.

The lab was white and sterile. Jars and microscopes graced shelves that lined one wall. Banks of computers occupied the other side of the room.

"It took us years to perfect the procedure," the old man continued. "This is where we made them."

"Made what, exactly?" Paul asked.

The old man ignored him, moving ahead with the guided tour. "The jars are the miscarriages. Chromosomal abnormalities, mostly."

Paul saw then that the jars contained fetuses. A moment earlier, the jars had seemed to hold formless brown shapes that could have been anything. But now he recognized them for what they were, all at once, the whole wall of monsters. Arms and legs and twisted hands. Misshapen skulls. Faces like blooming flowers. Things with tails.

"The difference in chromosome count is small," the old man continued. "But it does complicate things. Less in the first generation, though. Backcrosses are the real problem."

"I still don't understand."

"You will. Follow me."

Paul followed him through the lab to a set of double doors that led to a long hallway. He had a sense that they were leaving the main building and entering one of the wings.

The old man carded them through a security door, and they stepped into a dark room. A moment later, the lights clicked on with an audible click. They were standing in an enormous atrium. It took Paul a moment to recognize it for what it was. An ape house.

As if in response to the light, the apes moved to the front of their cages and began to call out. Soft hoots at first, but growing louder and more intense as the moments passed.

"This is where we house the juveniles," the old man said.

Floor to ceiling, twenty-five feet high, cages were stacked one atop another like children's building blocks. Each cage five feet cubed. Each housing a young chimp. The noise was deafening.

Paul lifted his hands to cover his ears.

The old man smiled. "Of course, the staff came up with their own name for this room."

He spread his arms wide while the chimps shrieked all around them. The cages shook, the dark shapes inside spitting in rage.

"They call it hell."

Lowering his arms, the old man continued walking. Paul stayed close, his hands still over his ears. Behind them, the two guards followed at a distance.

The old man led them through another set of doors and into an outdoor area. High cement walls closed them in. It was obviously an animal run of some kind.

"For the very young chimps," the old man offered. "Before they get too dangerous." At the far end of the run was a narrow steel door. He opened it with a key that hung around his neck.

"A bit old-fashioned," he said. "But then, I'm an old man, and old-fashioned security gives me comfort at times."

He led them into another building.

"And here," he said, stepping aside so that Paul could enter, "here is the final destination for your bone sequences. This is where the data goes. This is what it is all for."

Paul looked around, trying to take it all in. They stood just outside a vast nursery.

Paul moved forward. His mouth hung agape. It was impossible to process what he was seeing.

In this room, a dozen toddlers played behind glass.

Things almost human. They wore diapers and nothing else.

"What . . ." he began, but he could not finish. Could not formulate a coherent sentence.

"In Aristotle's time, chimps were unknown to civilization—did you know that?"

"No."

"It's true. Aristotle was preoccupied with nature, and with man's position within it. And all the time that he was writing, and theorizing, and formulating his understanding of what it meant to be human, there were these beasts living in the jungles of darkest Africa—beasts with ten fingers and ten toes, small primates who are so like us, and not. And what would Aristotle have thought, I wonder? If he'd seen one. If he'd known that they existed and walked the same world as us."

"These aren't chimps."

"No."

"What are they?"

"Clones," the old man said. "*Australopithecus. Homo erectus. Homo habilis.* Our newest creations."

Paul moved closer to the glass. He touched it with his hand, feeling the cool, smooth surface. On the other side, small miracles played. Rangy-limbed. The inhuman side by side with the almost human.

"And others, too," the old man continued. "The Denisovans. KNM-ER fourteen-seventy. *All* the archaeological finds. Here they are, Paul. The bones you've been studying your entire life. Here they are."

The old man put a hand on Paul's shoulder. "That's what I offer."

Paul looked at him. Speechless.

"And next will be Flores," the old man said softly.

Paul stood, entranced, and watched the toddlers play for nearly an hour. Beyond the glass, activity in the nursery continued without noticing him. A man and woman in white lab coats took turns caring for the children. *Children.* The word snagged in his mind. Not quite right. But close. Closer than any other word that might be applied. For what else could they be called? Yet they were most decidedly not like any children he'd ever seen before—strange little child-things that scrambled around the room.

"Do you want to go inside?"

Paul could only nod. Martial took him to the door and let him into the glass room. The children backed away at first, fearful of the large stranger. Paul took a knee, and one of the little ones moved across the padded floor. Crawling. This one was bare-skinned, but with a face like no toddler he'd ever seen. The skin a medium brown, the hair a shade lighter than the skin. An unusual combination, but not unique.

"Hold your hand out," the old man said.

Things that aren't man. But almost man. It crawled around in a diaper.

The child was a boy, Paul decided. Something masculine in the face, even at so young an age. The hair was tawny-colored, like wet beach sand. Straight and coarse. Paul held out his hand, and the child moved closer and wrapped its fist around his finger. Muscles bunched in its shoulder, and Paul marveled at its strength.

"One of our most vigorous specimens." The old man had come up behind him without Paul noticing.

"What is he?"

"We call him Samson."

"No, I mean . . . what is he? Which one? Which kind?"

The old man looked down at Paul appraisingly. "Which one do you think? I'm curious to hear your guess."

Paul looked at the child. It looked very human, but it was hard to say how it might develop. The infants of many animals looked very much alike—more alike than the adult forms. It was one of the mysteries of biology. The babies of many species were indistinguishable, while the adult forms varied wildly. A baby puma and a baby house cat looked very much alike.

"One of the Java specimens," Paul said.

The old man smiled. "A reasonable guess."

"Am I correct?"

"It's possible."

"Aren't you going to tell me?"

"No, I only said I was curious to hear your guess, not that I'd give you an answer. But there's still more to see. Would you like to see more?"

"More than this?"

"So much more."

Martial led him out of the nursery and down a long hall to still another room. Martial handed him a mask. "Until the children are vaccinated, we can't have you breathing on them without a mask. We have to vaccinate them for *everything*. What is a minor sickness in us tends to kill them. It's like the early colonial die-offs, but worse."

Paul donned the mask and stepped through the door.

"I'll leave you to it," the old man said. "But before I do, I have something for you." He motioned to one of his guards. The guard handed Paul a folder.

"The report from your computer technician," the old man explained. "It was saved on the flash drive. We took the liberty of printing it out for you."

Paul opened the folder. Inside were a dozen pages of type.

"Interesting reading," Martial offered. "Feel free to peruse it at your leisure. But for now . . ." He gestured to the door.

Paul stepped inside. The old man didn't follow.

Paul wasn't alone in the room. Lillivati was sitting in a rocker, holding a bottle in an infant's mouth.

The infant was tiny, little more than a newborn. Its bare limbs were covered with a fine, downy coat of hair a few centimeters long. Its feet were square and blocky—the toes slightly long, but aligned in the familiar configuration. Only the slightest gap between the first and second toes gave any hint that the feet were anything but human. The face, though, could scarcely be confused. Broad and projecting, with a low, bony brow and a sloped forehead. The top of the skull seemed small in comparison to the size of the face. The mouth simian, lipless. The eyes were large and dark and lacked any whites at all. The sclera of its eyes as black as any ape's. The ears were the ears of any hominoid, delicate and curled and perfect. The nose was broad, cartilaginous, projecting—a nose truly, and not the nasal depression found in apes.

Although the infant was small enough to be a newborn, it looked up when Paul entered the room and watched him alertly with its dark eyes. It reached up and held the bottle in its hands. The thumbs were prehensile, grasping the bottle.

Lilli rocked the child as she fed it.

When Paul finally tore his gaze away from the infant to look at her, he saw that there were tears in her eyes.

"It's impossible," she said.

The guards took them back to their room an hour later. The door latch made a loud click behind them.

A moment later, Paul tried the doorknob. "Locked," he said.

They both sat on the bed. They sat for a long time without speaking.

Finally, Paul opened the folder and began reading the report. He thought of Alan on the bridge. His black eyes, his broken nose. The results in the report were clear. When Paul finished reading, he closed the folder.

"What is that?"

"It's a phylogenetic analysis of the Flores sequence."

"What does it say?"

"Other," he said softly.

"What?"

"They're divergent," Paul said. "The bones from the Flores dig are from a population divergent from humans."

"How divergent?"

"More divergent than the age of the earth." They were an other who used stone tools. Who hunted as humans hunted and lived as humans lived. Beings who weren't human. And whose existence no religion on earth had ever mentioned.

There was too much to take in. Most of all, the question. And finally she voiced it.

"Why show us all this?" she asked. "The lab, the report, the babies."

Paul didn't answer at first. "To brag," he said. "For men like him, without somebody to show it to, it makes it matter less."

"But he has colleagues. He has the politicians to show. So why us?"

Paul shook his head. "I suspect not many people have seen what we've seen—and I bet most of them work here. He can only show people he trusts, or people he can control. Which is the same thing. But politicians . . ." Paul let the word linger. "They wouldn't want to see this. They'd make a point of it. Even if they saw it, they wouldn't see it. Plausible deniability. They'd *have* to not see it."

"Maybe," Lilli said, but she looked doubtful. "But there's got to be more than just ego behind it."

"Never underestimate ego."

Lilli's face went slack. She lay down on the bed, resting her head on the pillow. Paul knew that she'd come to the same conclusion he had regarding another matter. "Regardless of whatever else it might mean," she said, "it most surely and definitely means one thing in particular."

Paul nodded but didn't speak.

"It means he's never going to let us leave."

41

Paul walked the river ice. An endless ribbon of white. He saw tree branches scrawled black against a chalky winter sky. The girl was up ahead somewhere, he knew, though he couldn't see her. Around the bend. Just out of sight. He followed her footsteps in the snow. Though he shouldn't, he ran. The ice cracked like gunshots, but that meant it was safe. Then the sound changed, dying out, becoming another kind of sound. A sound like old leather. Paul rounded the bend in the river, the girl's name on his lips . . . but when he looked, there was no girl. Only a hole in the ice where she'd fallen through.

Paul opened his eye and turned his head toward the doorway. He nudged Lilli awake, and she startled. He realized she'd been lost in her own dream.

Paul swung his feet to the floor and walked to the door. "Yes?" He spoke through the thick wood.

There came the sound of a key in the lock, and a moment later the door swung open.

It was the guard. The same big one who'd first come for them. He stuck his face into the room. "Breakfast is in ten minutes," he said. He shut the door behind him. The key jangled in the lock.

"Breakfast?" Lilli said, dumbfounded.

They showered and dressed quickly.

Ten minutes later, the guard was back. He led them along the corridor, then down a flight of stairs that opened to an outdoor veranda. The old man was already there, sitting at a vast table spread with a white tablecloth and bearing several bowls of fruit.

"Coffee?" he asked.

Paul nodded as he sat. "I'll take some."

A server materialized out of nowhere and poured coffee for the three of them. Then the server just as quickly disappeared again, sliding behind the hedge that divided the veranda from the rest of the exterior space.

"Lillivati Gajjar," the old man said. "A beautiful name for a beautiful woman. Bilingual. You attended college with Paul. Trained in primatology. Until recently, employed as a museum researcher."

"*Still* employed," she said.

"You've lived in the U.S., Sri Lanka, and India. Divorced. You tried teaching, but your contract wasn't renewed."

"It wasn't renewed because I wasn't interested."

"Really? You weren't interested, or they weren't interested?"

She remained silent.

"And now he brings you in on this," the old man continued. "Some girls have quite the luck. Tell me, what do you think of all this?"

"I suppose you'll tell me that next."

The old man laughed. "You're quite the surprise, I must admit. Sometimes I'm not sure what to think myself, but there is one thing I'm sure of. We do great things here. Things that can't be done out there, where prying eyes can see and judge."

"Because the world would shut you down," Paul said, speaking for the first time.

"Sometimes things go wrong," Martial said. "True. And there are those who would use that as an excuse to stop our work."

"What do you intend with us?" Lilli asked.

"Intend with you?" The old man leaned forward, a serious expression on his face. "I intended to kill you, let me be blunt about it. But we don't get many visitors here, as you may imagine."

The old man leaned back in his chair. He seemed to consider his breakfast companions. "But Paul here, I have some qualms about. You

see, I knew his father. So I am somewhat conflicted. I'm not a bad man—
not really. I'm just efficient, and sometimes it looks like the same thing."

"Sometimes it is the same thing," Lilli said.

"I've a story for you. A hundred years ago in Australia, there was a
man of Dutch descent, demented and deranged by all accounts, who took
for a wife a young aboriginal woman. They lived out in the bush somewhere, a hermetic existence, rarely in contact with civilization. And during the course of their marriage they had several half-caste daughters—if
I can make use of the term commonly used there at the time—who they
raised in the bush. And the daughters grew, and it came to pass that the
mother died. The father took his own daughter as his wife, in violation
of nature, and she, in turn, bore him several children, who were themselves only a quarter aboriginal. Such unnatural pairings have happened
from time to time, no doubt, throughout history. But what makes this
case so remarkable is that this next generation, too, produced a child who
grew to marry that same man, who was in his sixties by this time, and
she, too, produced several children in what can only be described as the
most intensive form of human line breeding ever documented by science. When this small clan was discovered in the bush, they numbered
more than a dozen, some of them lame, some of them touched, and it
was the strange brightening of each successive generation that first got
the investigator's attention. He found it odd that the youngest child—a
poor mentally handicapped boy—looked nearly white, while each older
generation seemed darker and darker."

"Do you have a point?"

"The point, my dear, is that any privileging of humanity above other
forms of life would be a fallacy. It's a waste of time to assign external
causes to internal drives. We fight because it is in us to do so. That's also,
incidentally, why we fuck. One doesn't need an excuse to do so, but instead
must be given a reason not to do so."

"You make us sound like animals."

"We are precisely animals. No different from cows or pigs or wolves.
I have been looking for what makes us different, and I cannot find it.
You are the monkey woman, no?" There was sudden rage in the old man's
face now. An unexplained anger.

"What do—"

"Primatology, this was not your specialty? You graduated with a degree in primatology, a three-point-seven grade point average, attended a graduate program at Washington University. This is you, correct?"

"Yes."

"What makes us different from apes?"

"There are numerous things."

"But what, specifically, makes us different?"

"Genetically there are a lot—"

"Ninety-seven percent identical, yes," the old man snapped. "We've all heard that figure, but *where* are those differences?"

"They're spread over the entire—"

The old man slammed his hand down on the table. The silverware jumped.

"Humans have twenty-three pairs of chromosomes. Chimps, twenty-four. This is the obvious difference, easily visible on a simple karyotype. A basic difference in chromosome structure."

The old man reached for his silverware. He unrolled the napkin and spilled the silverware across the table. He grabbed a second and third napkin and did the same. Then a fourth. He laid the silverware out in a pattern: two forks, two tablespoons, two teaspoons, two knives, side by side. He laid out a second group of silverware in an identical pattern. "You see, they are the same," he said. "These are our chromosomes. Forks are chromosome one. Tablespoons are chromosome two. Teaspoons, chromosome three. Knives, chromosome four, and so on. Us and them." He gestured to the two matching sets of silverware.

He continued: "Our chromosome number one looks like their chromosome number one. Our chromosome three looks like their chromosome three. Do you see?" He slid the fork from one group and he set it next to the first fork from the other, putting them side by side. "They line up just right. If you butt them up against each other in a petri dish, you'll get linkage, chiasma, meiosis, all the old black magic."

The old man glared at them from across the stretch of silverware.

"But then what of the chimp's extra chromosome, you ask?" Martial took a sip of his water. "Chimps have an extra pair, after all."

The old man looked at Lilli. She stared back at him without flinching.

"Did it come from thin air?" the old man asked. "What is this strange piece of DNA that makes a chimp a chimp?"

The old man was giving a class, Paul realized. They were his students.

The old man took one little teaspoon from the second grouping and bent it at the thin point of its neck. He bent it again, back and forth at the same spot until the spoon snapped in two. He laid both halves back on the table. "This is the chimp," he said. "Not an extra chromosome, not really. Simply a broken one. Consider it for a moment. Maybe in this way, God created the animals. Taking a piece of this and a piece of that, moving the DNA around like a composer might shift the register of a sonata."

The old man smiled and leaned forward again, staring at them now.

"And now I confess my greatest sin. It occurred to me to wonder how He might have done it." His smile widened, showing worn and ancient teeth. "Poof!" he said. "Like magic? Or with a methodology behind it? Was there a lab, I wonder? Different tries? Failed experiments?"

"You're crazy," Lilli said.

The old man's smile flitted away, and he slammed his hand down on the table again. The silverware jumped, scrambling the carefully assembled order, shifting the pattern into a new configuration. Mutation before their eyes.

"There are those who would look away from uncomfortable truths. I have never been one of those men. What about you, Paul? How uncomfortable are you willing to be?"

The old man took a bite of pineapple and stood. He wiped the corner of his mouth with a napkin.

"What were those things that attacked us?" Paul asked.

"Perhaps you'd like to see." The old man turned and walked outside.

Paul and Lilli looked at each other for a moment, then followed Martial out of the veranda and along a trail leading to another part of the facility. The facility was like a web with many parts. Martial was the spider.

The old man hobbled his way up the trail. He moved slowly, his breath coming in a sickly whistle. Though his words were still sharp, his body was failing him. He would not be long for this world. A few years more, maybe. Following the old man up the trail, Paul wondered what would happen if they tried to escape. How far would they get? He had no doubt they were being monitored. He saw men just at the edge of his vision. Standing alert. Watching as they passed. As if the old man's casual-seeming walk had been scripted at a security meeting that morning, gone over in intricate detail. Paul wondered how much of today had been planned in advance.

The old man came to a huge white building. He opened the door and they entered a large room, much like the ape house from the previous night. Huge, domed ceiling. White walls. Cages nearly to the ceiling. Light streamed through skylights overhead. The place had the smell of newness to it, like it had never been used. It had the look of something that was about to be, rather than something that was.

"This is where we will house them," the old man said.

"Them?"

"The specimens, when they are born."

They walked through the booming expanse, Martial's leather dress shoes clicking on the hard cement floor.

They came to the other end of the room and exited to the outside. An identical building stood across from them, connected by a short cement sidewalk. From inside the building came a strange screeching sound. Whatever would someday fill the empty cages now lived in there.

The old man stopped and considered the building.

"Are we going in?" Paul said.

The old man turned, the fibrous tendons in his neck seeming to creak. "After you," he said.

Paul opened the door and stepped inside.

They passed into another nightmare room. A lower ring of hell.

Sunlight streamed through the skylights, but the place was a screech-ing madhouse. Alive with hoots and calls, maddening shrieks. Paul brought his fingers up to cover his ears as the screaming grew louder—a chorus of dozens, a hundred.

Cages lined the walls. On one side chimps, on the other gorillas.

"We crossed them," the old man said. "The success rate was lower than I'd expected, but viable offspring were produced. Several dozen survived to adulthood, as you can see." He gestured.

Paul saw then that, farther into the room, most of the cages held not chimps or gorillas but something intermediate.

"As with all hybrids, it depended on the nature of the cross. Chimp-gorilla produced a different phenotypic expression than gorilla-chimp."

They continued walking. The faces in the cage leered out at them. Lilli stayed close to Paul.

Halfway across the room was a small control room. Thick glass and bars on the windows, and inside, against the wall, a small bank of switches set in a gray panel. "The cage doors are all controlled from here," Martial said, gesturing at the room. "State-of-the-art." He kept walking, leading them farther in. "Handling apes successfully requires a high degree of specialized care. Apes are hierarchical by nature—driven not just for resources but to be at the top of the social order. This does not change in captivity. Even in the absence of a food shortage, they will still sometimes kill each other if we let them. In this way they are very like humans."

The old man slowed and turned toward Paul. "Primates come programmed to compete. It is our specialty. Some would say that it is the runaway amplification of this trait that has led to everything you see—cities, technology, civilization itself."

Finally the old man stopped. He stood before a cage at the end of the tier. "This," he said, "was our first chimp-gorilla hybrid. Chimp father, gorilla mother."

The creature was strange—huge, almost like a gorilla, but lean and long. Its face was narrow. Its shoulders wider than a chimp's. Neither chimp nor gorilla but something of both.

"Like the chimp, the gorilla has forty-eight chromosomes, but genetically, chimps are more closely related to humans than they are to gorillas."

"How can that be if the chromosome count is different?" Lilli asked.

"It is simple. When God made humans, he fused two chimp chromosomes together. We know exactly which ones."

The old man scraped a line in the sawdust with the tip of his shoe. The line was a yard long. He drew another line that intersected it, forming a V. He drew a third line that intersected the first.

He said, "Before the late 1980s, we assumed the association between the species was this. Us, gorilla, chimp."

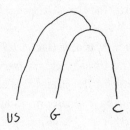

US   G   C

"But testing proved how wrong we were. The eighties showed us it wasn't so simple as that. In actuality, it is this." He scraped a new diagram out on the floor.

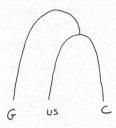

G   US   C

"Gorilla, us, chimp," he said. "So, armed with this knowledge, we did the responsible thing first. We crossed the two more distantly related clades as a proof of principle, before ever involving humans. Chimps and gorillas, after all, are more different from each other than are humans and chimps. So if crossing chimps and gorillas worked, then crossing humans and chimps, well"—he spread his arms—"that would be easy."

Paul looked into the cage. The creature crouched at the back of its enclosure. Black and massive. A dumb animal. But the things he'd seen at the park hadn't been dumb. And the thing on the bridge certainly hadn't been.

"Where are the other crosses?"

"Which ones?"

"The human crosses."

"You've met them," the old man said. "You've met them all."

"Only three in total?"

"Two now," said a strange, raspy voice. "Thanks to you." The creature stepped from around the side of the cages, materializing from the shadows. It walked over to stand near Martial, its huge bulk hunched beneath a hooded sweatshirt. The beast from the bridge. It smiled its impossible teeth. Black eyes hidden beneath its heavy brow.

"Where is the soul in all this?" the old man asked Paul. He gestured to the creature, looking truly confused by the hulking thing that stood before him.

The hooded figure ignored the old man's question. It shuffled around behind Paul and Lillie, seeming to sniff the air.

"You've met Trieste, I believe," the old man said.

Paul only nodded.

The old man continued: "I look for that place where the line isn't blurry between our species, and I can't find it. Are these things bound for heaven, I wonder? Are they beasts with human hands?" He moved to the cage and stuck his hand inside his pocket. He pulled out an apple and tossed it inside the cage where the chimp-gorilla hybrid crouched. The hybrid picked it up and ate it in three huge bites. "Or humans with the hearts of beasts? Or something in between."

The old man turned to look at them. "These are the questions we strive to answer."

hy us?" Paul asked.

The old man sighed. "Gavin is dead. People with your level of training aren't easy to come by. They're out there, of course, but to bring them in . . ." He shrugged. "It is a risk. How do you show them, and then if they say no . . ." The old man shook his head. "It's messy. But with you, it's already messy. But it is more than that, I admit. Come."

The old man led them past the cages and out the door. Trieste followed close behind. There was a short sidewalk leading to another, smaller building. A guard in a black suit stood just outside. They entered the building, crossing an empty expanse to a room tucked into the back of the structure. At first Paul thought it might have been an office of some kind, or a storage room, but then he noticed the stainless steel table. A dissection room. Silver walls. A rack of equipment lined the back wall. A small hoist hung suspended from the ceiling. Near the door frame, a long steel handle leaned against the wall—a part of the hoist that had been disengaged.

On the table was a single folder.

The old man gestured for them to come closer. The creature Trieste stayed watchful at the door. Martial opened the folder and pulled out a photograph, which he held out to Paul.

"That was your father when I first met him."

Paul took the photo. It looked to have been taken somewhere in China. His father, tall and brooding, standing in a lecture hall.

"You look like him," the old man said.

"I look like my mother."

"You're big like your father. Your father's size. Tell me: your father's temper, too?"

"No."

"Your father's cold-bloodedness."

Paul was silent.

"Oh, yes." The old man smiled. "Some of that, I suspect."

The old man took the photo back and closed the folder.

"Your father worked here, and now here we are with the son. It feels fitting somehow, don't you think? It feels like fate. So I have shown you all the wonders, and now I have this question: Will you finish what your father started?"

Paul considered the old man. He wondered how Martial would kill him. He wondered how long ago this had all become inevitable. Was it when he broke into the lab? Was it when he first told Charles about what he'd found? Or was it earlier, even. When he'd first gotten on the plane to Flores? Or was it way back in childhood somewhere? Had it all been set in motion on that day when he'd started building the cages? At that moment, a small brown mouse skittered across the floor. Only Paul saw it. A flash of brown fur, then gone. Or maybe it hadn't happened at all. Maybe he only thought he saw it.

"You're considering my offer, I can see. I respect that. If you'd said yes too quickly, I would have known you were lying. There is great work we can do here, Paul. Without the government to get in the way. Without the churches and the oversight. We exist in a bubble. Nothing is off-limits. We have nearly endless funding and no oversight. Imagine what is possible. Other scientists work at the edges of things, but we can tackle the large questions themselves."

The old man moved back to the doorway. He gestured out at the cage that held the chimp-gorilla hybrid. "You see, Paul, why I did not wish to be rash in my decision on how to deal with you. Though there are many qualified scientists who work in this branch of cytology, it is a rare man with the vision to look past ethical vagaries to what is really important.

But this is a special kind of work—a calling. When you need a specialist, you can't just interview several candidates for the job. You can't invite someone to do this and then take no for an answer."

Paul and Lilli stared at the man and said nothing. Behind him, the hooded creature swayed slightly, rocking on its feet. Paul eyed the hoist handle that leaned against the door frame. Three feet of steel.

"Gavin said you killed him."

"Who?"

"My father."

The old man froze. The smile left his face.

"Gavin said that?"

Paul nodded.

"Then Gavin was a bigger betrayer than I'd suspected. It was you he betrayed as well."

"How is the truth ever a betrayal?"

"Because it means you'll never forgive. It means you'll say no. Your friend Gavin killed you when he told you that."

The old man lowered his head for a moment. When he raised it, he looked at Paul. "The beast you killed was born of woman," the old man said after a long silence. "Artificial insemination, of course."

Paul took Lilli's hand in his.

"A volunteer," he added, his voice trailing off, "of sorts." The old man seemed lost in his memories. "A woman named Sacha Etting."

"How did she live with it?" Lilli asked.

"Not well. Not for long. She died some years ago. Cancer, unrelated to the procedure."

Paul stared out through the doorway, at the cages against the far wall. His eye found the steel handle again, leaning against the door frame. "Human mother, chimp father."

The old man nodded. "And Trieste here was the opposite cross."

Paul didn't turn to look.

"Chimp mother, human father," the old man said. "And there are differences between the two crosses, it would seem. Just as a liger is different from a tigon and a hinny is different from a mule. This cross is better."

"Your son?" Paul spit the words out. He thought of the beast pulling him up on the bridge.

"My son?" At that, the old man started laughing. He laughed long and hard, until the laugh turned into a coughing fit, and the chimps joined their voices in screeching. "You haven't figured it out yet, my boy? You haven't guessed?"

"Guessed what?"

"I have cystic fibrosis, which impacts the motility of cilia in my cells. This causes my lungs not to function correctly. I would have been dead decades ago if not for lung transplants. But the disease has many pleiotropic effects. It also affects the motility of sperm cells and the development of vas deferens—all men with cystic fibrosis are sterile."

Paul's brow furrowed.

"The sperm, Paul, was provided by your father." The old man gestured to the hooded shape that stood off to the side. "Trieste is your half brother."

"No." Paul jerked his gaze toward the creature. A few inches shorter than him, but massively muscular. Black hair. Prognathic face. Wide, powerful shoulders.

"Is he not?" the old man asked. "Look at him."

"No!" Paul screamed. He lunged for the hoist handle, curling his hand around the cool steel. He swung it with all his strength, catching Trieste in the face, smashing the creature in the eye. Trieste went down hard—the thud of meat on cement.

Paul grabbed Lilli's hand and ran.

They were at the other end of the building when Paul heard it. A roar of anger and pain. He chanced a look back. Trieste was rising, rage twisting its strange features into a demon mask, teeth bared. It shrieked again.

"Kill them!" the old man shouted. "Kill them both!"

Trieste surged forward.

Paul and Lilli ran for their lives.

They made it to the far door, bursting through to bright sunlight, stumbling into the guard posted just outside. Paul saw the confused expression on the guard's face as he ran past. The guard hesitated for a moment. He had no orders. Then Paul and Lilli were past him, still running as the guard called out, "Hey! Stop!"

Paul ignored the guard and pushed open the door to the next building. The guard followed but was too slow. Paul and Lilli darted inside, swinging the door closed before he got there. The guard hit the door hard, but Paul kept his shoulder against it. He realized that he still carried the steel bar in his hand, and he wedged it between the door and an I-beam, preventing the door from opening.

"Open the door!" the guard shouted. "Open it ri—" The guard paused, as if startled, his voice leaving the doorway, and a moment later the entire steel door shuddered in its frame as something huge smashed against it. The beast roared again, a sound beyond insanity. The fists came again, and the steel bar shuddered and flexed.

Paul and Lilli backed away. The door wouldn't hold for long.

They were back in the ape house. Inside the room, the noise had risen to a sickening level. The gorilla-chimp hybrids pulsed in hysteria.

The door frame shook again, as Trieste's fists struck twin dents in the metal door.

Paul's gaze darted around. In the center of the room was the control booth. A room with steel bars. "Come on," he shouted. They ran for it. From behind them came the sound of twisting metal as the door broke inward off its hinges.

Trieste screamed in wordless rage. Paul looked back. The creature's left eye was swollen nearly shut, its massive brow split and bleeding. It charged, dropping to an inhuman lope, lunging across the room on four limbs.

Paul looked back toward the control booth and knew they wouldn't make it.

"In there!" Paul screamed at Lilli and shoved her toward it. Then he turned to face the charge, to buy her time. Trieste might have been a locomotive. Paul was knocked off his feet. He skidded across the room, sliding close to the cages as a huge thigh-sized arm reached out from between the bars but missed. Paul rolled away from the steel bars.

Trieste came for him, lost in rage, charging in too close to the cages, and the dark arms clutched through the bars for him, just out of reach. Just brushing Trieste's shoulder. Trieste raised its arms in a killing attack, but Paul rolled away just in time. The huge fists came down on concrete. Paul rose to his feet. Trieste picked Paul up and threw him at the control booth. Paul struck the safety glass and collapsed. From inside, Lilli screamed.

The creature came for Paul.

Paul raised one arm in defense. The blow would have killed him otherwise. The fist came down like a hammer, battering his arm away.

It was like the creature he'd fought in the woods. Only worse. Bigger. Stronger. Paul realized then that he was going to die.

Trieste grabbed him by one leg and flung him again, knocking him back against the wall near the broken door.

Inside the gated room, Lilli screamed again: "Paul, run!"

But Paul was beyond running now.

The creature approached slowly, taking its time. It seemed to notice something on the floor near the twisted door.

The creature stepped over Paul. Then it did something very human. It picked up a weapon. The same steel bar that had been used to wedge the door closed, the one Paul had used against it. It walked back to where Paul lay, and it stood over him. It raised the bar high in both hands.

"Die, brother," it hissed in a sandpaper voice.

At that moment, there was a loud clang, metal on metal. Propagating forward, so that Paul heard it next to him and up ahead at that same time.

Trieste froze for a second, confused. Paul turned his head and saw Lilli behind the safety glass, her face pale and bloodless. She mouthed a word to him. His foggy head took a moment to process it, and then he understood. *Run.*

At that instant, one of the cage doors swung open. No longer locked. Then another. And another. The first gorilla hybrid stepped out of its cage, and then others followed, exploding outward in a snarling burst of black fur, and suddenly the room was filled with beasts.

Trieste turned, eyes wide. The first beast charged. Trieste swung the bar, and the gorilla hybrid batted it away. The two creatures struggled, and then another hybrid, and another, joined the fight. Screaming, thrashing violence. Hair flying, the thud of breaking bones. Paul dragged himself along the floor, trying to attract as little attention as possible. Trieste screamed in rage and pain as it was slammed to the ground. Paul heard bones break, and then fists came down. Inside the control booth, Lilli ducked under the table, staying out of sight.

Paul crawled.

He made it to the far door. He slid across the portal and pulled

himself to his feet. As best he could, he walked. Those things wouldn't
be distracted for long. Paul crossed the narrow cement walkway between
buildings and made it to the next door. He pushed inside, crossing the
room. The room under construction. He hobbled to the far door and
opened it. He looked out and saw a gorilla hybrid charging across the
open space between the buildings, chasing down a man in a white lab
coat. The man didn't have a chance. It was over quickly. A shot rang out,
and the hybrid turned. More shots. The guards were defending themselves. It was a war zone out there. A noise from behind him turned him
around. He saw nothing but he knew he wasn't safe. There was a loud
thud as something huge struck the other door.

He looked around for a place to hide but there was none. The room
was mostly empty, except for the cages piled up to the ceiling. Paul went
to the cages. He looked up, reaching out to touch the cool bars. He
started climbing. He climbed all the way to the top. The unstable structure shifted under his weight, swaying slightly. Because the room was
still under construction, the cages hadn't been secured to the wall yet.
When he got to the top, he climbed up and over and plastered his body
down against the roof the cage.

The thud came again, louder this time. Then again. And again, and
the door twisted inward.

Paul looked out over the side of the cage, and he saw a pair of hybrids
enter the room. They passed through, barely slowing. One of them was
covered in blood. Trieste's blood.

Outside, the gunshots grew nearer.

A moment later, another hybrid charged into the room. Agitated, it
shuffled across the cement floor on all fours. It turned.

Paul prayed that Lilli was still okay. Still locked in her cage.

There was a sound by the door. Then a gunshot, loud in the echoing
expanse of the room. The hybrid screeched, and two more shots put it
down. The other hybrids bolted through the far door.

Martial walked into the room.

Beside him was the red-bearded man, gun in hand. Redbeard was
limping and his suit was torn. He'd crossed paths with one of the hybrids
and come out the worse for the wear.

The old man walked to the far end of the room, then stopped at the door, just as Paul had. He looked out the door, just as Paul had. He closed the door.

He turned and considered the room. "It's suicide out there for a man without a gun," he called out. "Which means you're still in here. You set us back many months today, Paul. It's my own fault, really. I should have known you'd be a problem. But I am too kind. It is my fatal flaw."

Paul slunk backward across the top of the cage so that only an eye peeked over the edge.

The old man watched as the red-bearded man stalked through the room, gun held at the ready, looking behind tables and around construction equipment.

Paul changed positions slightly, and he felt the cages shift under him. He dared not move. At the top of the cages, up near the ceiling, he waited.

The old man spoke aloud to the room: "We both know you're in here, so why don't you just come out? We saw your girlfriend in the other room. Locked behind bars, which she refused to open for us. Understandable, considering the circumstances. Safe behind high-impact glass, which has proved remarkably bulletproof, I might add. Lucky for her. But we've got a man positioned there now, and when this is all over, we'll just cut her out, if we have to. But first we need to find you." The old man started walking, moving along the wall to get a better look through the room. "We saw what you did to Trieste, Paul. That was unnecessary. Trieste was unique. One of a kind. But in many ways, too smart. Too independent.

"The other hybrids were more utile in many ways. But there's the bottleneck in producing them, of course. Because not many women are up for the task. Though we've gotten around that. A recent development. Ovarian transplants from human to a chimp, a regimen of anti-rejection meds, and then the rest of the reproductive cycle works nicely. Of course, ovary donors are in short supply. But now we have your friend Lillivati."

Heat surged through Paul's body.

Open rage like an open sweat—a flower opening its petals into something beautiful, a simple, ancient sort of purity. It is not confusing. It has no subtext, no nuance, no alternate interpretation—just the winnowing down of want to a pinpoint laser of need.

He pushed off the wall with all his strength, and the cages shifted.

They were right beneath him now.

The old man looked up, startled. The red-bearded man raised his gun, but too late—it was done. Their mouths dropped open in wordless horror as the great wall of cages began to tip. Slowly at first, then faster, tipping farther and farther out. Paul clutched at an I-beam on the ceiling as the cages slid away from the wall. It was happening in slow motion—the steel dropping away beneath him—and then the cages came crashing down. A cataclysm. *This is how it happens.*

Paul got a grip on the central I-beam at the last possible moment, feeling the cages fall away, and he was left hanging. The sound was deafening, and when he looked down, twisted metal covered the floor in a shattered regolith. Nothing moved. The old man and his guard lay crushed under thousands of pounds of steel.

Paul hung from the beam on the ceiling. Twenty-five feet up, dangling by his hands. A two-story drop, if he fell. He moved hand over hand, heading toward the wall.

His fingers screamed in pain.

He kept going. His arms shook.

He had ten more feet. Then five. Then three. His fingers cramped in agony. He tried to pull himself farther, but the muscles in his forearms locked. Just a few more feet and he'd be at the wall. *And then what?* He could see a handhold where the beam met the cinder block. But he'd be in the same predicament. Hanging by his fingers.

His fingers convulsed into claws. He felt his left hand start to slip, slow movement under his fingers. He willed himself to grip.

He let his biceps relax, dropping down so his arms were straight. At furthest extension. He couldn't keep going. He hung. The last moments of his life.

His fingers white on the beam, sliding—losing friction. His left hand fell away, and he dangled for a split second by his right, and time seemed to slow, and his fingers snapped free, and he fell.

43

He woke in pain. Lilli was cradling his head in her arms.

"Shhh, it's okay." She was crying.

"What—"

"I thought I'd lost you."

"Where . . ." His head felt wooden. He couldn't think.

"It's fine. It's fine. We've got to get out of here."

Paul tried to stand, but his left leg wasn't working.

"I think it's broken," he said.

He leaned on Lilli as the two of them climbed across the twisted remains of the cages. Paul had landed on the sprawling wreckage and somehow survived the fall. They trudged forward and collapsed near the wall.

"It's death out there," she said. "Those things we let free . . . they're still running. Guards killed about half of them. But they've killed all the guards now, I think. The guard outside the control booth tried to leave and they ripped him apart. I waited for hours before I unlocked the door. I thought you were dead. I thought everyone was dead. The shooting stopped a long time ago."

"We've got to get out."

Paul let himself be pulled to his feet again. He leaned heavily on Lilli, putting most of his weight on his right foot.

They limped their way to the door. She helped him sit with his back to the wall. He opened the door and peered out. It was night. The trail leading back to the main structure looked empty, but it was hard to tell. No movement. It was a short walk back. Maybe a hundred meters, but it might have been a hundred miles.

"Do you think we can make it?" she asked.

"We don't have much of a choice."

They crossed the gap as quickly as they could, trying to keep quiet. When they entered the building, it looked like a tornado had moved through the area. Everything they'd seen the day before was overturned. Knocked asunder. Destroyed. The creatures had torn through the place.

In the lobby, they found two bodies. They recognized them as two of the guards who'd kidnapped them. One's face was crushed. The other's neck was twisted at an odd angle.

"Look," Lilli said. She stepped across the room and bent to pick something up. She returned with a gun. Paul checked the ammunition.

"Four in the clip."

She nodded.

Paul bent and checked the other body.

"No gun," he said. "But . . ." He fished in the man's front pant pockets and pulled something free. "Keys."

They moved deeper into the building. Moving through the nursery now. A distant mewling could be heard, right on the edge of perception.

"Wait. Wait here," Lilli said. "I have to check something."

She disappeared into the darkness. It was the longest four minutes of Paul's life.

Then she was back—with a small form swaddled in her arms. She was crying.

"It would die if we left it," she said.

"What about the others?"

"There are no others."

Paul felt sick to his stomach.

The creature waved its strange hands up at her. A cute hairless face.

Dark eyes. Staring up and out. Eyes that hadn't seen the sun in five thousand years.

"Come on."

Lilli followed Paul through the facility, down a familiar hall. Paul got to their room and pushed the door open. He grabbed the report off the bed; he'd left it there earlier that morning. Alan's report of divergence. They headed toward the front doors.

They waited in a corner of the front entrance lobby, huddled against the wall.

A few hours later, dawn came.

Out the window, in the world materializing in the growing light outside the building, Paul saw the vans, parked in a line by the curb. There were three of them now. A third van parked behind the others. He scanned the grassy front lawn and the trees beyond the driveway. Just past the flagpole, several massive shapes lounged in the morning sun.

He nudged Lilli, waking her.

"It's time."

Beside her, the bundle moved. A soft sound. Then quiet again.

They stood.

"Are you ready for this?"

"No."

Paul pointed the keys at the vans. "It's now or never," he said and hit the unlock button.

There was a chirp, and the middle van's hazards flashed briefly. "The middle one," Paul said. "It had to be the middle one."

"What's wrong?"

"The other vans are parked close. It's going to be hard to pull out." He gestured to the swaddled form she cradled in her arms. "Do you want me to carry it?"

"No, I can manage."

Paul pushed the door open slowly, watching the dark shapes beyond the flagpole. He exchanged a look with Lilli, a slight nod.

They slipped through the doors. Paul covered ground as quickly as his mangled leg would allow.

They crossed the dozen yards to the vehicles, kicking up gravel as they moved. Paul flung open the driver's door and hopped into the seat. Lilli climbed into the passenger side—the bundle crying now, jolted awake by the run.

Their movement had attracted attention. Paul put the key in the ignition. Across the lawn, two big males swiveled their heads toward them, not bothering to rise. But the third big male stood. Blood caked its bare chest.

"Come on," Lilli said.

Paul turned the key and the van rumbled to life. The baby's gentle cry changed into a scream.

The first gorilla hybrid charged.

Paul put the transmission into reverse and hit the accelerator. Their vehicle smashed into the van behind it. A moment later, the hybrid slammed into the side of the van. The whole vehicle shook. Paul's side window collapsed inward in a cascade of glass.

"Jesus!"

Paul pulled his gun.

The hybrid lunged at the door.

He fired two shots through the window, center of mass, and the hybrid juddered forward. Paul fired again, twice, this time at its head, and the thing went down, rolling as it crashed. Paul squeezed the trigger again, and again, and nothing happened. The gun was empty.

Near the flagpole, the others took notice. The largest of them rose up and charged.

Paul put the transmission in drive and hit the gas, slamming the van into the vehicle in front, pushing it forward a few feet. He hit reverse and floored it, smashing into the van behind, making room. The gorilla-thing hesitated, confused by the movement. Paul put the vehicle in drive again and slammed into the forward van, pushing it farther this time.

The beast hit the van like a car crash. It hammered its arms down on the front, crinkling the hood.

Paul shifted into reverse again, turned the wheel, and floored it. The van sideswiped the van behind it but pulled free, ripping off the mirror on Lilli's side. Paul kept his foot on the accelerator, pulling away in reverse. The gorilla paused for a moment, confused, and then it gave chase, gaining on them. Paul spun the wheel so he could back out and turn around, and the gorilla caught up and smashed a huge shoulder into the side of the vehicle, rocking it on its suspension. Then its arm came down on the windshield.

Lilli screamed as the glass spidered but did not break. The baby screamed louder. Paul shifted into drive.

Another blow from the gorilla rocked the van, and now the glass from the side window exploded inward, showering Lilli. Paul punched the gas and the van lurched ahead, sliding past the beast. He glanced in the rear-view mirror as the gorilla-thing stood in the road behind them and beat its chest in frustration.

The baby shrieked on, while Lilli tried to soothe it.

The van bumped along down the empty roadway, heading for the highway, leaving the facility behind.

44

They pulled into a town called Immokola with a quarter tank of gas. The battered van rolled past the small police station without stopping, continuing on past restaurants and stores to the town's main drag, where it finally came to a stop in front of a small storefront with the name IMMO-KOLA TRIBUNE stenciled across the plate glass.

Paul shifted into park and turned the van off. The engine ticked.

He and Lilli stepped out. Lilli held the baby close to her, covered in a blanket, as they walked to the front door. A small group of onlookers had already begun to assemble from random passersby on the sidewalk, their attention caught by the wreckage of the van, and now the two strangers with ripped and bloody clothes.

Paul and Lilli stepped into the cool air-conditioning of the office and walked up to the receptionist.

"Can I help you?" she asked.

"My name is Paul Carlsson, and I have numerous deaths to report."

The woman behind the desk stared at him. Lilli stood beside him, rocking the baby softly, which was still swaddled in a blanket.

"If you'll excuse me," the woman said, and stepped into the other room.

The receptionist returned with her boss and Paul repeated himself.

"How numerous we talking?" the boss asked. He was a heavyset man in his fifties with a sun-creased face.

"Hard to say."

"That so?" The boss's expression was unreadable.

The boss got on the phone and made a call. The conversation was short, and Paul couldn't hear what transpired. "If you'll take a seat," the boss said.

Paul and Lilli sat and waited until a police car arrived, its lights spinning.

It was a county officer who arrived first.

The officer stepped through the door, and the boss gestured to Paul and Lilli, and Paul repeated himself a third time.

"Who died?"

"A lot of people. The workers at a laboratory. The whole lab. Everyone."

The officer looked at Paul, sizing him up, then got on his radio, requesting backup.

The baby started to cry.

"Does the child need assistance?" the policeman asked.

"Milk," Lilli said. "If you can get it, baby formula."

The man looked at the infant, then at Lilli, his confusion growing. For a moment he seemed on the edge of asking something, a question about the child that was not a child, but then he kept it to himself.

Two more police cars pulled up outside. More policemen. More questions. Paul tried to tell them about James. "He was the first to die. His throat was cut."

"Where did this happen?"

"An island called Flores."

"Do you have a last name for James?"

Paul glanced out the front window, saying softly, "Herpetology, mate."

An older cop with a thick gray mustache seemed to be in charge.

"We're going to need you to come back to the station."

Paul and Lilli stood and followed the officers outside. More people had gathered on the sidewalk now, staring at the clump of police cars.

"We'd like to get a complete statement from you," the officer said. "For the record."

"I'll tell you everything," Paul answered. It's what prophets did.

They ushered Lilli to one squad car, Paul to another.

Lilli started to pull back, but Paul told her, "Just go with them. It's okay. Just tell them what you know."

She nodded and let herself be steered away gently by the arm.

Paul's officer opened the back door of his squad car, and Paul ducked his head and sat. He pulled the report out and set it on the car seat next to him. The papers were crinkled but still legible. A dozen pages that might or might not matter. The car idled while the officer talked to the newspaper boss for a moment, and then the two shook hands and the officer headed for the car.

Paul watched the newspaper boss head back inside his building to write the next day's headline. He wondered what it would look like. He wondered if there would be future headlines, in other cities, as the scope of what had happened was finally revealed.

The officer climbed into the car and shut the door. The back of his head was slick with sweat. "It's gonna be a hot one today," Paul said.

"Yeah," the cop said. "Feels like."

The cop started the car and eased past the throng of onlookers crowding the sidewalks. They stood staring from both sides of the wide city street, watching the police lights. Paul took off his eye patch and looked out the window at the curious faces, with both his good eye and the ghost eye, and then he closed his eyes in silent prayer as the cop car pulled down the road, leaving the faces behind.

SOURCES

Arka, I. W., and J. Kosmas. "Passive without passive morphology? Evidence from Manggarai." Australian National University conference paper (2002), available online at http://hdl.handle.net/1885/41059.

Behar, D. M., M. F. Hammer, D. Garrigan, R. Villems, B. Bonne-Tamir, M. Richards, D. Gurwitz, D. Rosengarten, M. Kaplan, S. Della Pergola, L. Quintana-Murci, and K. Skorecki. "MtDNA evidence for a genetic bottleneck in the early history of the Ashkenazi Jewish population." *European Journal of Human Genetics* 12, no. 5 (May 2004): 355–64.

Bertranpetit, J., and F. Calafell. "Genetic and geographical variability in cystic fibrosis: evolutionary considerations." *Ciba Foundation Symposium* 197 (1996): 97–114.

Biello, D. "Searching for God in the brain." *Scientific American Mind* 18, no. 5 (October/November 2007): 38–45.

Clan Donald USA website. Online at http://clan-donald-usa.org/CDCMS/index.html.

Clarey, M. G., J. P. Erzberger, P. Grob, A. E. Leschziner, J. M. Berger, E. Nogales, and M. Botchan. "Nucleotide-dependent conformational changes in the DnaA-like core of the origin recognition complex." *Nature Structural and Molecular Biology* 13, no. 8 (August 2006): 684–90.

Currie, L. A. "The remarkable metrological history of radiocarbon dating [II]." *Journal of Research of the National Institute of Standards and Technology* 109, no. 2 (March/April 2004): 185–217.

Cuthbert, A. W., J. Halstead, R. Ratcliff, W. H. Colledge, and M. J. Evans. "The genetic advantage hypothesis in cystic fibrosis heterozygotes: a murine study." *Journal of Physiology* 482, pt. 2 (January 15, 1995): 449–54.

Derenko, M. V., B. A. Maliarchuk, M. Wozniak, G. A. Denisova, I. K. Dambueva, C. M. Dorzhu, T. Grzybowski, and I. A. Zakharov. "Distribution of the male lineages of Genghis Khan's descendants in northern Eurasian populations" [article in Russian]. *Genetika* 43, no. 3 (March 2007): 422–26.

Deshpande, O., S. Batzoglou, M. W. Feldman, and L. L. Cavalli-Sforza. "A serial founder effect model for human settlement out of Africa." *Proceedings of the Royal Society B* 276, no. 1655 (January 2009): 291–300.

Dienekes' Anthropology Blog. "Forbidden DNA sequences." Available online at http://dienekes.blogspot.com/2007/01/forbidden-dna-sequences.html.

Doughty, B. R. "The changes in ABO blood group frequency within a mediaeval English population." *Medical Laboratory Sciences* 34, no. 4 (October 1977): 351–54.

Electric Scotland, "MacDonald Genetic Project." Available online at http://www.electricscotland.com/webclans/m/macdonald_genetic.htm.

Electric Scotland, "The Norse Code." Available online at http://www.electricscotland.com/history/articles/norse.htm.

Fehér, O., H. Wang, S. Saar, P. P. Mitra, and O. Tchernichovski. "De novo establishment of wild-type song culture in zebra finch." *Nature* 459, no. 7264 (May 28, 2009): 564–68.

Founder Scots DNA website. Online at http://www.ourfamilyorigins.com/scotland/founderscots.htm.

Gabriel, S. E., K. N. Brigman, B. H. Koller, R. C. Boucher, and M. J. Stutts. "Cystic fibrosis heterozygote resistance to cholera toxin in the cystic fibrosis mouse model." *Science* 266, no. 5182 (October 1994): 107–9.

Hammer, M. F., A. J. Redd, E. T. Wood, M. R. Bonner, H. Jarjanazi, T. Karafet, S. Santachiara-Benerecetti, A. Oppenheim, M. A. Jobling, T. Jenkins, H. Ostrer, and B. Bonné-Tamir. "Jewish and Middle Eastern non-Jewish populations share a common pool of Y-chromosome biallelic haplotypes." *Proceedings of the National Academy of Sciences of the United States of America* 97, no. 12 (June 2000): 6769–74.

Hampikian, G., and T. Andersen. "Absent sequences: nullomers and primes." *Pacific Symposium on Biocomputing* 12 (2007): 355–66.

Kirsch, J. "Moses Unmasked." *U.S. News & World Report* special issue, *Mysteries of Faith: The Prophets* (2006).

Kwiatkowski, D. P. "How malaria has affected the human genome and what genetics teaches us about malaria." *American Journal of Human Genetics* 77, no. 2 (August 2005): 171–92.

Morwood, M., and P. van Oosterzee. *A New Human: The Startling Discovery and Strange Story of the "Hobbits" of Flores, Indonesia.* Washington, D.C.: Smithsonian, 2007.

Nebel, A., D. Filon, B. Brinkmann, P. P. Majmuder, M. Faerman, and A. Oppenheim. "The Y chromosome pool of Jews as part of the genetic landscape of the Middle East." *American Journal of Human Genetics* 69, no. 5 (November 2001): 1095–1112.

Nebel, A., D. Filon, M. Faerman, H. Soodyall, and A. Oppenheim. "Y chromosome evidence for a founder effect in Ashkenazi Jews." *European Journal of Human Genetics* 13, no. 3 (March 2005): 388–91.

Oriá, R. B., P. D. Patrick, H. Zhang, B. Lorntz, C. M. de Castro Costa, G. A. Brito, L. J. Barrett, A. A. Lima, and R. L. Guerrant. "APOE4 protects the cognitive development in children with heavy diarrhea burdens in Northeast Brazil." *Pediatric Research* 57, no. 2 (February 2005): 310–16.

Page, M. Book review of C. M. Woolgar, D. Serjeantson, and T. Waldron, *Food in Medieval England: Diet and Nutrition. English Historical Review* 123, issue 501 (2008): 419–21.

Pestana de Castro, A. F., P. Perreau, A. C. Rodriques, and M. Simoes. "Haemagglutinating properties of Pasteurella multocida type A strains isolated from rabbits and poultry." *Annals of Microbiology* (Paris) 131, no. 3 (May/June 1980): 255–63.

Peters, F. E. "Abraham's Miraculous Journey." *U.S. News & World Report* special issue, *Mysteries of Faith: The Prophets* (2006).

Sheler, J. L. "The Lure of the Prophetic Word." *U.S. News & World Report* special issue, *Mysteries of Faith: The Prophets* (2006).

Sykes, B. *Adam's Curse: A Future Without Men.* New York: W. W. Norton, 2004.

———. *Blood of the Isles: Exploring the Genetic Roots of Our Tribal History.* London: Bantam, 2006.

by the water where I could finish the book. I'll be back. I'd like to thank the entire Seattle-area writer community for being so open and supportive toward a new member of the kindred.

I'd also like to thank Aaron Schlechter, my editor, who believed in this novel and took a risk on it. And, of course, my agent Seth Fishman, and the Gernert Company, who got the book into the right hands and made the sale possible. I'd like to thank my parents again, in this book, too, because you can never thank your parents enough. I'd like to thank Jonathan Long for the great discussions on science and religion back when we were lab partners. I'd like to thank St. Patrick's Elementary School and the old church where I was an altar boy. I have fond memories of those days. And Bob I'd like to thank for walking the ice all those years ago. You did fall through. And you pulled yourself out.

ACKNOWLEDGMENTS

No book is an island. This one in particular owes an immense debt of gratitude to a great many people. I'd like to thank the many biologists, archaeologists, geneticists, and anthropologists throughout the years whose combined body of knowledge I have been the fortunate recipient of. Without their scientific efforts, this novel could never have been written. I'd like to thank the scientific thinkers John Hawks, Razib Khan, Carl Zimmer, Dienekes Pontikos, and Blaine T. Bettinger, whose blogs are amazing repositories for cutting-edge thought in the fields of genetics and anthropology. This book would have looked very different without their influence. I'd like to especially thank the archaeological dig team who did the *real* work on the Flores fossils. I've never met you—and nothing about this book was meant to intersect in any way with *anyone* associated with the real find—but without the discoveries made in Flores this work of fiction would have lacked a factual foundation to build upon. You have my respect and gratitude. If at any point in the novel I got the science wrong, it is nobody's fault but my own.

I'd like to thank my writer friends Jack Skillingstead, Michael Poore, Nancy Kress, and Marc Laidlaw for hanging out with me and talking shop during the time I was writing the novel. I'd like to thank Patrick Swenson and the Rainforest Writers' Village for giving me a quiet place

ABOUT THE AUTHOR

Ted Kosmatka was born and raised in northwest Indiana and spent more than a decade working in various laboratories before moving to the Pacific Northwest. His short fiction has been nominated for both the Nebula Award and the Theodore Sturgeon Memorial Award and has appeared in numerous year's best collections. He now works in the video-game industry, where he's a full-time writer at Valve, home of *Half-Life, Portal,* and *Dota 2.*

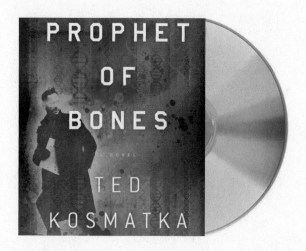